Daisy was in a deep, blank sleep when she startled awake to a man's hand clamped over her mouth.

Her muffled scream quickly fell silent when Harry's face hovered into focus above hers. He pressed a finger to his lips in the universal sign of shushing and didn't remove his hand until she nodded her understanding to remain quiet.

Something was wrong. Even in her nearsighted haze, she could see Harry was strapping on his gun again. She pulled the sheet around her and sat up as he handed her the brown glasses they'd left in the living room.

She slipped them on, hoping that bringing clarity to his grim expression would give her understanding. "What is it?" she whispered softly. She heard one of the dogs growling from the foot of the bed, and all the beautiful aftermath of making love and sleeping contentedly in his arms vanished in a clutch of fear. "Harry?"

He pushed her phone into her hands. "Call 9-1-1. There's someone outside."

That was when Daisy jumped at the *pop, pop, pop* of tiny explosions and shatter~~ing~~ ~~~~ back deck.

MILITARY GRADE MISTLETOE

BY
JULIE MILLER

MORAY COUNCIL
LIBRARIES &
INFO.SERVICES

20 43 55 91

Askews & Holts

RF

First Published in Great Britain 2017
By Mills & Boon, an imprint of HarperCollins*Publishers*
1 London Bridge Street, London, SE1 9GF

© 2017 Julie Miller

ISBN: 978-0-263-92939-3

46-1217

MIX
Paper from
responsible sources
FSC™ C007454

This book is produced from independently certified FSC™ paper to ensure
responsible forest management.

For more information visit: www.harpercollins.co.uk/green

Printed and bound in Spain
by CPI, Barcelona

Julie Miller is an award-winning *USA TODAY* best-selling author of breathtaking romantic suspense—with a National Readers' Choice Award and a Daphne du Maurier Award, among other prizes. She has also earned an *RT Book Reviews* Career Achievement Award. For a complete list of her books, monthly newsletter and more, go to www.juliemiller.org.

In honor of the seventy-fifth anniversary of Camp Pendleton, home of the 1st Marine Battalion.

My dad and brother were both once stationed there.

For the real Muffy. Yes, that dog is a he. And yes, he's in charge. Just ask him.

Prologue

"You're not the first marine this has happened to."

But it was the first time it had happened to *him*. Master Sergeant Harry Lockhart didn't fail. When he was given a mission, he got the job done. No matter what it cost him. But this? All the doctors, all the physical training and rehab, all the therapy—hell, he'd talked about things nobody knew about him, and it had gutted him worse than that last firefight that had sent him stateside in the first place—and they were still going to give him the boot?

Harry didn't know who he was going to be if he couldn't be part of the Corps, anymore.

His given name was Henry Lockhart Jr., but nobody called him by his daddy's name unless he or she outranked him or wanted a fist in his face. Henry Sr. was serving time in a prison in Jefferson City, Missouri for a variety of crimes, the worst of which was being a lousy excuse for a father. Between Henry's drinking, neglect and natural affinity for violence, it was a miracle Harry and his older sister, Hope, had survived to adulthood. Hope wouldn't have done that, even, if at the ripe old age of nine, Harry hadn't picked up his daddy's gun and shot one of the dogs that had attacked her when she tried to leave the house to get him food so he wouldn't starve.

A muscle ticked beside his right eye as a different memory tried to assert itself. But, with a mental fist, he shoved that particular nightmare into the tar pit of buried images from all the wars he'd fought, determined to keep it there.

"How many years have you been in the Corps?" The doctor was talking again.

If Dr. Biro hadn't also been a lieutenant colonel, Harry might have blown him off. But Biro was not only in charge of his fitness assessments, he was a decent guy who didn't deserve his disrespect. Harry met his superior's gaze across the office desk. "Seventeen, sir."

Biro nodded. "A career man."

"Yes, sir."

Hope was the only family he'd ever had, the only person he'd ever trusted, until he'd enlisted in the United States Marine Corps the day after he'd graduated from high school. The Corps had whipped his rebellious butt into shape, given him a home with regular meals on most days, introduced him to the best friends he had in the world and given him a reason to wake up every day and live his life.

Now his sister was married and had her own family. So he'd really, really like to keep the one he'd found. His physical wounds from that last deployment had left their mark on his stiff, misshapen face, but the scars were a sign that those had healed. He knew it was the mental wounds the lieutenant colonel was worried about.

Not for the first time in his life, Harry was going to have to prove himself worthy. He was going to have to earn someone else's unshakable trust in him again.

He was going to have to relearn how to trust himself.

Do this. That was Harry's motto. He couldn't lose the only home he had left. He scrubbed his fingers over the bristly cut of his regulation short hair. "You said I was improving."

"You are."

The medical brass seemed to like it when he talked, so he tried again. "I've done everything you asked of me these past four months."

Biro grinned. "I wish all my patients were as dedicated to following my orders as you. Physically, you could handle light duty, maybe even a training assignment."

"But…? Tell me the truth, Doc." Was he washed out of the Corps or not?

The lieutenant colonel leaned back in his chair. He wasn't smiling now. "You need to get your head on straight or we can't use you."

"You're not comfortable sending me out in the field?"

"I'd be doing you a disservice if I did." Biro leaned forward again, propping the elbows of his crisply pressed lab coat on the desktop. "At the risk of oversimplifying everything you've gone through—something broke inside you. I believe it's healing, but the scar is still new and I don't want you to rip it open again."

"I appreciate the honest answer." Harry did some mental calculations on how long he'd have to play this game before he could come in for his next assessment and change the doctor's prognosis. "So, peace and quiet, huh? Normalcy?"

The lieutenant colonel didn't understand how far away from *normal* civilian life was for Harry. The jarheads he served with didn't care where he'd come from or how rough his altered face looked, as long as he did his job. But on the outside, expectations were different, and he was ill-equipped to handle them.

"That's my prescription."

"And I don't need pills on the outside? I just need a shrink?"

Lt. Col. Biro opened a folder and pulled a pen from his chest pocket. "That's my recommendation. If you can't sleep, or the mood swings become unbearable, call me. Otherwise, take the time off. Relax. Give yourself a few weeks to reconnect with civilian life. Enjoy the holidays. Get yourself a Christmas tree and eat too many sweets. Kiss a pretty girl and watch football all New Year's Day. Whatever you like to do to celebrate." *Relax* and *celebrate* sounded like daunting tasks for a man who didn't have much experience with the examples on the good doctor's list. "If you still want to after that, make an appointment with my office in January and we'll reevaluate your fitness to serve. Or, if you decide the clean break is what you need, I'll have your honorable medical discharge waiting for you. It's not like you haven't earned it."

Harry stood, clasping his utility cover, the Corps' term for a canvas uniform hat, between his hands. "I'll be back, sir."

The lieutenant colonel nodded before signing off on his medical leave papers and dismissing him. "You're from Kansas City, Missouri, right?" Harry nodded. "You might have snow there this time of year."

What was Biro going to prescribe now? Building a snowman to get in touch with the inner child Harry had never had the chance to be? "Sir?"

"My best buddy from basic training was from KC. I've always enjoyed my visits. I'll have my aide give you some recommendations for therapists you can see there."

"Thank you, sir."

Harry's cover fit snugly over his head as he pulled the bill down and hiked outside into the sunny Southern California weather. He drove to the base housing he shared with two other Non-commissioned Officers, or NCOs, slammed the door on his truck and hurried inside before he cussed up a blue streak that would have all of Camp Pendleton talking by sundown.

Thankfully, his bunk mates were both on duty so he had the house to himself. But that empty echo of the door closing behind him was a curse as much as it was a blessing. Damn, he missed the way his best friend used to greet him.

The remembered thunder of deadly fireworks and images of blood and destruction seared him from the inside out, leaving him with beads of sweat on his forehead and his hands clutched into fists.

Hell. The doc was right. His head wasn't on straight.

Using some of the calming techniques Lt. Col. Biro had taught him, Harry breathed in deeply through his nose and out through his mouth. Then he grabbed the pull-up bar hanging in his bedroom doorway and did ten quick reps until he felt the burn in his biceps, triceps and shoulders, and the anger that had flared behind his eyes receded.

He took the pull-up bar off the door frame and tossed it onto the bed beside the duffel bag he'd already packed that morning, having known he was either shipping out or going home by the time the medical team was done with him today.

You need to get your head on straight or we can't use you.

The lieutenant colonel's blunt words made the tiny, impersonal bedroom swim around him. Squeezing his eyes shut against the dizzying, unsettled feeling he hadn't felt since he was a little boy wondering if he was going to eat that day, Harry sank onto the edge of the mattress. He needed to find that happy place inside him. He needed to feel the holidays and the hope they inspired. He needed to find a way to push aside the nightmares and the anger and learn how to cope again. Or else the brass wouldn't let him be a marine anymore.

On instinct, he opened his duffel bag and pulled out a bulky, crumpled manila envelope that held the lifeline to sanity that had gotten him through that last hellish deployment and the long days in the hospital and physical therapy which had followed. He brushed his fingers over the torn envelope flap before sliding his thumb underneath and peeking inside. Now here was a little bit of sunshine. He pulled out a homemade angel ornament that had been a gift to him last Christmas. Then he studied the stack of cards and letters that were battered and smudged from travel and rereading. Words from a compassionate oracle who understood him better than he knew himself. His stiff jaw relaxed with the tremor of a smile that couldn't quite form on his lips.

Harry hadn't been this uncertain since he was that starving little boy with a black eye and clothes that didn't fit. He didn't need a shrink. He needed the Corps. But he'd need a miracle to make that happen. He needed the angel from all these cards and letters to work her magic on him again.

None of them were recent, but that didn't matter. The effect on him was always the same. He opened the very first letter and started to read.

Dear MSgt. Lockhart...

Chapter One

Dear Daisy,
Merry Christmas from your Secret Santa.

Daisy Gunderson stared at the gift tag, dotted with sparkles of glitzy snow, in the top right drawer of her desk and wondered who hated her enough to wage this terror campaign against her. This should be the happiest time of year for her, with the holidays and her winter break from school coming soon. Either somebody thought this sick parade of presents left on her desk or in her mailbox in the faculty work room was a clever idea for a joke, or that person intentionally wanted to ruin Christmas for her.

Typically, she made a big deal of the holidays, as evidenced by the greenery and ornaments decorating her classroom, and the hand-carved menorah and colorful Kwanzaa mat she had on display that had been gifts from former students. But the red glass candy dish filled with rat poison, the decapitated elf ornament and the X-rated card that had nothing to do with holiday greetings hidden away in her drawer were disturbing signs that not everyone shared the same reverence for celebrating this time of year.

The gifts were an eerie reminder of the tragic mistake she'd made three years ago that had cost her so dearly. But Brock was locked up in a prison cell, and would be until her roots turned gray. Daisy had already called the prison to confirm Brock Jantzen hadn't escaped or been accidentally released. These gifts couldn't be his handiwork. Men in prison who'd tried to kill their ex-girlfriends didn't get to send them cards and presents, right?

Daisy inhaled and let the long exhale flutter her lips. Of course not. These gifts had nothing to do with Brock. Or losing her father. Or even losing her mother, in a way. They had nothing to do with the scars on her chest and belly or her missing spleen.

Deciding that her thinking made it so, Daisy adjusted her purple-framed eyeglasses at her temples, spared a glance for the lone student muttering at the laptop on his desk, then looked up at the clock on the wall to wonder how much longer it was going to take Angelo to finish his essay before they could both go home for the day. Since she'd promised to give the teenager all the time he needed to complete his work, Daisy closed the drawer, picked up her pen and went back to grading papers.

But her thoughts drifted to the small stack of letters she'd locked away in a keepsake box under her bed at home. Letters from a marine overseas. Short, stilted and impersonal at first. Then longer, angrier, sadder. Master Sergeant Harry Lockhart yearned for quiet and routine just as much as he longed to complete the job he'd been sent to the Middle East to accomplish. She could tell he loved serving his country. That he loved the military dog he worked with, Tango. That he grieved the young men and native soldiers he'd trained and lost. She'd grieved right along with him when he'd written to say that Tango had been killed. Those letters had been part of a class writing project she'd initiated last year, with help from a friend at church, Hope Taylor, who had connected Daisy to her brother and his unit. She'd give anything to hear from

Harry Lockhart again, even one of his short missives about the heat or the sand in his bunk. But sadly, those letters had stopped coming months ago. She hoped the unthinkable hadn't happened to her marine. More likely, he'd simply tired of the friendship after the class had ended and those students had stopped writing the servicemen and women with whom they'd been pen pals.

Now the only notes she received depicted graphic sexual acts and violence. All under the guise of a friendly game of Secret Santa.

She'd reported the gifts to her principal, and he'd made a general announcement about the appropriateness of everyone's anonymous gifts at the last staff meeting. And, she'd alerted the building police officer, who promised to keep an eye on her room and try to figure out when the gifts were being left for her. But, short of canceling the faculty party and gift exchange, and ruining everyone else's Christmas fun, there was little more she could do besides staying alert, and doing a little sleuthing of her own to try and figure out who was sending them. Daisy wondered if the wretched gifts might even be coming from someone who hadn't drawn her name in the annual gift swap—a disgruntled student, perhaps. Or maybe there was someone else in her life who thought this terror campaign was a cute way to squash her determination to make the most of every holiday celebration.

If that was the case, she refused to give in and take down one tiny piece of tinsel or play her Mannheim Steamroller music any less often. She already had enough reasons to mourn and resent the holidays. The Scrooges didn't get to win. If grief, abandonment and solitude couldn't keep her from saying *Merry Christmas* every chance she got, then a few morbid trinkets from a disturbed mind weren't going to make her say, *Bah, Humbug*, either.

"Finished. Five hundred and two words." A small laptop plunked down in front of her on her desk. "Before the deadline."

Daisy smiled up at Angelo Logan, a favorite student with as much talent as he had excuses for not doing his work. She knew no one in his immediate family had gone to college. And since that was a goal of his, she didn't mind putting in some extra time and pushing him a little harder than some of her other students. She skimmed the screen from the title, *The Angel and the Devil*, down to the word count at the bottom of the page. "Wow. Two words over the minimum required. Did you break a sweat?"

"You said to be concise." A grin appeared on his dark face.

"Did you map out why you're deserving of the scholarship?"

"Yeah. I talked about my home life, about being a twin and about what I can do for my community if I get a journalism degree."

Daisy arched a skeptical eyebrow. "In five hundred and two words?"

Angelo tucked the tails of his white shirt back beneath his navy blue sweater and returned to his desk to pull on his blue school jacket. "Can I have my phone back now, Ms. G?"

"May I?" she corrected automatically, and looked up to see him roll his deep brown eyes. The standard rule in her class was "No cell phones allowed," and anytime a student entered her room, he or she had to deposit their phones in the shoe bag hanging beside the door. Getting a phone back meant the student was free to go. Daisy smiled at the seventeen-year-old who looked so put upon by grinchy teachers who held him accountable for procrastinated essays and college application deadlines, when he probably just wanted to take off with his buddies for some Thursday night R & R. "You're too good a writer to miss this opportunity." She turned the laptop around. "Email me this draft and I'll get it edited tonight. I can go over any changes that need to be made with you tomorrow. Then we can send the whole thing off before Monday's deadline."

Angelo zipped back to her desk and attached the file to an email. "I've got basketball after school tomorrow. I won't be able to come in. Coach will bench me if I miss practice two days in a row."

Ah, yes. Coach Riley and the pressure he put on his players, despite the academic focus of Central Prep. "Can you do lunch?"

"Yes, ma'am."

She pointed to the shoe storage bag hanging by the door. "Grab your phone. Have a good night and I'll see you tomorrow."

But he didn't immediately leave. He exhaled a sigh before setting his backpack on the corner of her desk and digging inside. He pulled out a squished plastic bag with a red ribbon tied around the top and shyly dropped a gift of candy on her desk. "Thank you, Ms. G."

An instinctive alarm sent a shock of electricity through her veins. But then she saw the blush darkening Angelo's cheeks and realized she couldn't be paranoid about everything with a gift tag this time of year. Plus, the smushed present didn't look anything like the carefully prepared gifts she'd received from her Secret Santa. She feigned a smile before genuinely feeling it, and picked up the gift. "Are these your grandmother's homemade caramels?"

"Yeah. She wanted to thank you for the extra hours you're putting in on me."

Daisy untied the bow and pulled open the bag to sniff the creamy brown-sugary goodies. This present was safe.

She'd seen it delivered, and there was nothing hinky about the candies wrapped in this modest bag. She could let herself enjoy it. "I love her caramels. She made a special batch without nuts for me?"

The blush faded as the grin returned. "I don't know why you want to eat them without the pecans, but she remembered that was the way you like them."

Daisy pulled out one of the individually wrapped caramels and untwisted the waxed paper. "Hey, between her and me, we're going to get you into college."

"Yes, ma'am. Um… I wanted to…"

Wondering how long Angelo was going to stand there before he said whatever was making him shift back and forth so nervously, Daisy popped the caramel in her mouth and started to fill the awkward silence. "These are the yummiest—"

She almost choked on the chewy treat when a sharp knock rapped on her door. "'Lo. You coming or what?" Although the baggy jeans and sideways ball cap were a vastly different look than the school uniform Angelo still wore, Albert Logan shared his twin brother's face. "Just because you got in trouble with the teacher doesn't mean I have to be late."

"I'm not in trouble," Angelo insisted.

"I don't care. I just know I have to drive your sorry ass home before I meet the guys."

"Granny's going to kill you if you skip dinner again."

"She ain't killed me yet." Albert jerked his head down the hallway toward the exit. "Move it."

"Hey, Albert." Daisy stood and offered a friendly greeting.

"Hey, Ms. G."

Despite looking alike, the two brothers couldn't be more different. "You know, my offer to stay after school and work with students who need extra help extends to you, too."

"I ain't in your class no more."

"You aren't anymore," she corrected. "I'm here with Angelo. I could easily tutor you, too. Get your grades back up so you can be on the basketball team again."

"Whatever." He turned down her repeated offer to help him raise his D's and F's into acceptable grades and pointed to his brother. "My car leaves in five. Be in it or walk home."

Although she was already plotting different arguments to convince Albert to get the help he needed, Daisy trained her smile on Angelo while he zipped his backpack and hurried to grab his phone. "Be sure to thank your grandmother for the caramels."

"Bye."

Once the teens had left her room, the silence of an empty school long after classes had ended closed in on her. Shaking off the instant sensation of loneliness before it could take hold of her, Daisy packed up her pink leather shoulder bag. She jotted a note to Bernie Riley, the boys' basketball coach, asking him to have a chat with his former player to encourage Albert to take her, or someone else, up on the tutoring offer. Without sports to keep him interested in school, she feared he'd wind up dropping out without a diploma. Then she grabbed her scarf and wrapped it around the neckline of her tunic sweater and pulled her coat from the closet before shutting off the lights and locking the door.

She'd make one quick stop at the faculty lounge to drop off the note, then head out. Besides hurrying home to let out her three dogs to do their business, she needed to get the place tidied up before showing the upstairs suite to the potential renter who'd answered her ad in the paper. Her friend Hope's husband was a KCPD cop, and he'd done a routine search on the guy and a couple of other tenant prospects to ensure they didn't have a criminal record or pose any obvious threat to her.

Having the dogs with her eased her concerns about living alone. But with the advent of the creepy cards and gifts, she'd decided that having a man on the premises, preferably an older one who reminded her of the security her father had once provided, would scare away whoever was threatening her. Besides, one of the hazards of living alone in the two-story 1920s Colonial her parents and grandparents had once lived in was that she was spending a small fortune renovating it. With taxes due at the end of the year and her savings already tapped out, thanks to the new HVAC system and roof she'd been forced to install, she could use the extra income of a tenant to get through the expense of the holidays.

Her steps slowed on the hallway tiles as her imagination surged ahead of her logic. Of course, the idea that her tenant might wind up being a serial killer, or even the sicko who was sending her that crap, was more than a little unsettling.

But no, Officer Pike Taylor had vetted this guy, so he couldn't be a danger to her. She sifted her fingers into the wavy layers of her hair and shook it off her shoulders. "Stop imagining the worst, Daisy Lou, and go home."

Her stop in the faculty lounge and work room revealed that she wasn't the only staff member working late this evening. "Hey, Eddie."

Daisy dropped her bag onto the chair beside one of the school's science teachers. It hit the seat with a thunk and Eddie Bosch laughed. "Taking a little work home tonight?"

"Just some papers to grade. And my laptop." Plus all the items a woman would keep in her purse, along with a few emergency snacks, a stash of dog treats and an extra pair of shoes in case the knee-high boots she wore got too wet with the snow outside and she needed to change before her feet froze. Daisy shook her head as her friend in the loose tie and pullover sweater grinned. "I guess I carry my life in there, don't I?"

"Well, you won't have to go to the gym and work out if you keep lifting that thing." He closed the laptop he'd been working on and pointed a warning finger at her. "Now about that chiropractor bill you'll be getting…"

"Ha, ha." Squeezing his shoulder at the teasing remark, she circled around him and went to the wall of cubbies that served as the staff's mailboxes and searched the alphabetized labels for Bernie Riley's name.

She was glad Eddie had gotten to the point where he could joke with her. When they'd first started at Central Prep together, he'd had a sadness about him he wore like a shroud. He'd been new to Kansas City, had moved there for a fresh start after losing his fiancée to a long illness. Daisy had made it her personal mission to cheer him up and make him feel welcome. Now, he often made it feel like she was working with the teasing big brother she, as an only child, had never had.

But the comfortable camaraderie quickly ebbed as her gaze landed on her mailbox. She backed away when she saw the corner of a red envelope lying there.

Daisy startled at the hand that settled between her shoulder blades. "Don't worry." Eddie reached around her to pull the red envelope from her box and hold it out to her. "It's the teacher appreciation gift from the school board. A gift card to your favorite coffee shop. We all got one."

Taking the envelope, she clutched it to her chest, nodding her thanks. Eddie and a few other teachers were close enough friends that she'd shared some of the weird messages she'd been receiving. They'd all agreed that none of the staff could be responsible, and were now on the lookout for any signs of a disturbed student who might be sending the gifts. She appreciated that Eddie and the others were protective of her.

He pointed to other red envelopes still sitting in the mailboxes of teachers who'd already gone home, to confirm his explanation. "It's nice that they remember us each year. Although I'd trade gourmet coffee for a bump in salary if it'd do us any good."

Daisy agreed. "I hear ya."

He nodded toward the paper in her hand. "Is Riley giving you grief about keeping Angelo out of practice again?"

During basketball season, Bernie Riley gave everyone grief. "I think we've reached a mutual understanding."

"You mean, you've agreed to do things his way."

"Bernie and I both have the students' best interests at heart. He let Angelo stay with me today, and I'll adjust my schedule tomorrow." She held up her message about Angelo's brother. "Actually, I'm hoping he'll help me with Albert."

"Albert doesn't have half the brains Angelo does."

She was surprised to hear the insult. "Maybe we just haven't found the right way to motivate him yet."

"Uh-huh." Eddie pulled away and opened his satchel to stow his laptop. "Deliver your note and I'll walk you out." He nodded to the window overlooking the parking lot and the orange glow of the street lamps creating pockets of light in the murky evening air. "I hate how early the sun goes down this time of year."

Smile, Daisy Lou. Don't let anyone bring you down.

"Me, too." Daisy stuffed the note into Coach Riley's cubby and put on her insulated coat and gloves while Eddie pulled on a stocking cap and long wool coat. "Although, I do love it when the sky is clear at night, and the moon reflects off all the snow." She pulled the hood with its faux fur trim over her head. "In the daylight, the city snow looks dirty, but at night it's beautiful."

"You're a regular Pollyanna, aren't you," he accused with a smile, holding the door open for her. "It's twenty degrees, it's dark and I'm tired of shoveling my driveway."

"Scrooge."

"Nanook." He followed her out the door and walked her across the nearly empty lot to her car. "Are you expecting a blizzard I don't know about?"

She fished her keys out of her bag and unlocked the doors. "Fourteen degrees? That's plenty cold enough for me."

Eddie swiped his gloved hand across her windshield, clearing a swath through the blowing snow that had gathered there. "Want me to scrape this off for you?"

"You're a scholar and a gent, Mr. Bosch." Daisy thanked him for his gallant offer, but shooed him back to his own car. "The windshield wipers will take care of it. Go get warm. I'll see you in the morning."

"See ya. And hey, I didn't mean to sound flippant earlier. If there's anything I can do to help you with Albert, let me know."

"I will. Thanks." With a smile that no longer felt forced, Daisy climbed inside. Once she had her car started, he waved and trudged away to his own vehicle.

Daisy locked her doors and shivered behind the wheel, waiting for the wipers and defroster to clear her windows. Allowing the engine time to warm up, she crossed her arms and leaned back against the headrest, closing her eyes. She took on a lot this time of year, and she was tired. The stress of dealing with her Secret Santa, and the mental battle not to compare his gifts to the terror campaign

Brock had waged against her three years ago, were taking their toll, as well. It was a challenge to get eight hours of uninterrupted sleep when every sound in the old house woke her. She made up for the fatigue by stealing short naps when she could. Like right now. Just a few minutes to rest before…

Daisy's eyes popped open as a sixth sense nudged her fully awake.

Someone was watching her.

She wiped the condensation off the inside of her window and peered out. Her gaze first went to Eddie's car. But he was busy brushing the thin layer of snow off the windows and top. His back was to her until he tossed the scraper into the back and climbed in behind the wheel. Then he was on his cell phone, chattering away in an animated conversation as he backed out of his parking space.

She pulled her glasses away from her nose to let the foggy lenses clear before sliding them back into place and scanning the rest of the staff parking lot. There were only four vehicles left. Coach Riley and the girls' basketball coach had both parked near the gym entrance while they finished with practice. She recognized the truck and van driven by the school custodians, as well.

The uneasy sensation of being watched crept beneath the layers she wore, making her shiver as if a cold finger was running along her spine. But a check of her rearview mirror revealed no one. Not one visible soul. Certainly no one spying on her.

Unless that person was hidden.

Behind one of the Dumpsters. Or around the corner of the building. Or peering out from the shadows of a dark room in the nearly empty school.

"Really?" Daisy smacked the steering wheel and pulled on her seat belt, irritated with the way her tired mind could play tricks on her. Those stupid gifts had spooked her more than she'd realized. "You are perfectly safe," she reminded herself, shifting the car into gear. Turning on her lights, she drove out of the parking lot. "The bad guys don't get to win." If she lived her life like a paranoid mouse, they *would* win. And she wasn't about to let that happen. She turned on a radio station playing Christmas music 24/7 and belted out rock anthems and traditional carols all the way home.

Daisy was a little hoarse from the songfest by the time she pulled into the detached garage behind her home. She pushed the remote button, closing the door behind her before unlocking her car and climbing out. Night had fallen, so she flipped the switch to turn on the Christmas lights lining the garage roof and fence, knowing they'd cast enough light to illuminate her path across the sidewalk to the deck and backyard entrance to her home. She smiled when she opened the door and looked out into the fenced-in yard. Beyond the edges of the walkway and deck she'd cleared, the red, green, orange, blue and white lights reflected off the snow like the warm glow of a sunset.

After pulling her hood up over her ears, she shut the door behind her and locked it. The damp bite of wintry air chapped her cheeks and hurried her steps past the gate and up onto the deck where the motion sensor light over the back door popped on, turning a small circle of night into day.

"Daisy? Is that you?"

Startled by the voice in the night, Daisy spun around. Once she'd identified the disembodied voice, she drifted beyond the edge of the light to bring her neighbor to the north into focus. "Good evening, Jeremiah." Although Jeremiah Finch's balding head was little more than a balloon-shaped shadow above the hedge on his side of the fence, she recognized his little Chihuahua in a pink and black sweater underneath the hedge where the snow wasn't as deep. As much as her neighbor loved his little princess, he liked to keep his yard in pristine condition, and would either immediately clean up after the dog, or hook her onto a leash and lead her to the bushes as he had tonight. "I see Suzy is bundled up against the cold. New sweater?"

"Knitted it myself. Are you coming down with a cold?" he asked, no doubt hearing the rasp in her voice.

"I'm fine. Just a little too much singing. And you?"

"I'm well. Suzy and I will be going in now. Good night."

"Good night." As formal and shallow as their conversations might be, Mr. Finch had proved himself to be a good neighbor. Besides maintaining a beautiful home, he didn't mind picking up her mail and watching over her house when she had to leave town. And she often returned the favor.

After he and Suzy had gone inside, Daisy slipped her key into the dead bolt lock.

One sharp, deep bark and the excited sound of yapping dogs told Daisy her furry family already knew she was home. She peeked through the sheers in the window beside the door and saw her beloved trio gathering in the mud room with tails wagging to welcome her before pushing open the door. "Yoo-hoo! Mama's home."

Muffy, her little tiger of a Shih Tzu led the charge out the door. A silver-and-white-haired boy cursed with a girl's name by the elderly owner who had to surrender him when she moved into a nursing facility, Muffy often made up for the insult by being the toughest and loudest guard dog he could be, if not the most ferocious-looking. Patch, her deaf Jack Russell terrier mix, took his cues from the other dogs, and followed right behind the smaller dog, no doubt barking because Muffy was. Both stopped for a friendly greeting and some petting before dashing out into the snowy yard. Patch, especially, loved being outside, leaping from snow bank to snow bank and snuzzling through the drifts as though feeling the cold against his skin made him giddy.

Her senior dog, Caliban, hobbled out the door on three legs. Daisy got the feeling that when her biggest dog stopped for a scratch around the ears, the Belgian Malinois was humoring her rather than seeking her affection. Poor guy. He'd spent a career at KCPD before the cancerous tumor that had led to the amputation of his left front leg forced him into retirement, and then he hadn't been able to live at his handler's home because the K-9 officer's child was allergic. Daisy reached inside the door to grab one of the rope toys that seemed to be the tan-and-black dog's only joy and tossed it out into the snow. As she watched him trot down the two steps into the yard, Daisy's heart squeezed in her chest. The experts who claimed that dogs didn't feel emotions didn't know Caliban. That dog was sad. He'd lost his job, lost his favorite person, lost his home and routine. When Pike Taylor had asked if she could take the dog for the last year or so he had left, Daisy had willingly opened up her home and her heart. Muffy and Patch had welcomed the older dog, although the two little spitfires made him cranky at times. Caliban had a good home here, but Daisy was still looking for the key to breaking through that reserve of his.

Smiling at the distinct personalities of each of her *children*, Daisy crossed to the railing to watch her three charges. Muffy was all business, inspecting the perimeter of the yard and trees along the back fence. Caliban was nosing around the gate and garage, avoiding the snow as much as possible. And Patch...

"Patch?" Daisy hiked her purse behind her hip and leaned over the railing. Where had he snuck off to? He wouldn't answer her summons unless he was looking right at her or following one of the other dogs. "Where did you go?"

Daisy looked down to see the clear impression of man-sized boot prints in the snow. The security light created shadows through the deck railings that had obscured them earlier. But there they were, a messy set of prints circling around the deck to the gas and water meters on the back of the house. She spotted Patch, his muzzle and jowls white with a snowy beard, following the tracks past the meters to the dormant lilac bushes at the corner of the house.

That wasn't right. Goose bumps pricked across Daisy's skin. She crossed to the side railing and squinted into the darkness beyond her porch light. Between the blowing snow and the shadows, she couldn't make out whether the tracks ended at the side of the house or if they continued into Mr. Finch's yard next door. Or maybe they'd originated from there? Maybe Jeremiah had spotted something that concerned him in the backyard. Still, she couldn't see the fastidious gentleman climbing over the chain-link fence when there was a perfectly good gate between the house and garage that granted easy access to the yard. It would be hard to tell exactly where the footprints led unless she went out in the knee-deep drifts to look with a flashlight. And as much as Daisy wanted answers, she wasn't keen on being anywhere alone in the dark.

She swallowed hard, trying to come up with a logical explanation as to why someone would be wandering around her backyard. She'd had the same utility worker from the city for years. He knew his way around her backyard, and didn't mind the dogs when they were out. Maybe he had a substitute walking his route, someone who didn't know there was only one gate. Patch spent a lot of time snuffling around in each footprint until he lifted his leg and peed in one. Why were there so many tracks? Had more than one person been in the backyard?

"Muffy? Caliban?" She put her chilled lips together and tried to whistle, but she doubted even a dog could hear the wimpy sound that came out.

Then she spotted Caliban's white muzzle as he carried his toy back up the steps to dutifully sit beside her. "Good boy." Had he sensed her fear? Did he just have impeccable timing? "Good, good boy." Daisy scratched around his ears and rewarded him by pulling on one end of the rope and letting him enjoy a gentle game of tug of war. But the game ended quickly when Caliban released the toy and spun toward the back door. A split second later, Muffy zipped past her, barking like mad. That response could mean only one thing. They'd heard the doorbell at the front of the house. She had a visitor.

Although she was hardly prepped for company, she was more than ready to go inside. She caught Patch's attention and gave the signal for him to come. He dashed through the doorway in front of her.

The doorbell chimed again while she bolted the back door. The dogs raced ahead of her, yapping and tracking snow across the long, narrow rug and refinished oak of her hallway floor. Patch leaped over the two plastic tubs of Christmas ornaments she'd stacked beside the stairs, waiting for the tree she planned to get this weekend. Daisy hurried after them, dumping her purse on the bottom step of the staircase leading up to the second floor, pulling off her hood and stuffing her gloves into her pockets.

She pushed her way through the semi-circle of barking dogs, put Caliban and Patch into a sit and picked up Muffy, her brave boy who had the most trouble following orders and greeting an unfamiliar visitor. If this was the potential tenant Pike Taylor had okayed for her, she wanted time to explain that her pack of dogs were looking for treats and tummy rubs, not the opportunity to take a bite out of a stranger. Daisy flipped on the Christmas lights over the front porch and made sure the dead bolt was engaged before peering through the window beside the door.

"Wow." She mouthed the word, fogging up the glass.

The man standing on her front porch was hot, in a rugged sort of way. He stood six feet tall, give or take an inch. He wore a black stocking cap fitted tightly to his head and a beige coat that pulled at his broad shoulders and thick arms. With his hands down at the sides of his jeans and his legs braced apart, he stood there, unmoving. If it wasn't for the puffs of his warm breath clouding around his gray eyes, she'd have thought him a statue, impervious to the cold. Daisy's throat went dry at the inverse response of heat that could be nerves, or something decidedly more… aware…that he triggered inside her.

Not the fatherly figure she'd been hoping for. His face was a little too craggy to be handsome. The scars that peeked above the collar of his sweater and crept up his neck to the edge of his mouth and cheek to circle around most of his left eye, coupled with the stern set of his square jaw, added to his harsh look. She was certain Pike wouldn't send her anyone she wouldn't be safe with. Still, *safe* was a relative term. This guy didn't project calm reassurance so much as he looked as though he could scare off anyone who glanced crosswise at him. Although he would fulfill the purpose of having a tenant, she wasn't sure she'd be comfortable having a man like him in the house.

Still, if Pike said he was okay, she'd at least interview him.

She startled when his head suddenly tilted and his gaze shifted to her silhouette in the window. He'd caught her staring at him. He didn't smile, didn't wave an acknowledgement, didn't react, period. He simply locked his gaze onto hers until she muttered, "My bad," and hurried to atone for her rudeness. Muffy whined in her arms, and Daisy unbolted the door and opened it, leaving the steel-framed storm door secured between them.

The rush of heat she'd felt dissipated with the chill that seeped through the glass. "Hi. Are you here about the room to rent? I thought we weren't meeting until after dinner."

"Master Sergeant Harry Lockhart, ma'am," he announced in a deep, clipped voice. "Are you Daisy Gunderson?"

Recognition and relief chased away her trepidation and she smiled. "Master Serg...? Harry? Pen pal Harry?" She plopped Muffy down between the other dogs, then unlatched the storm door and pushed it wide open. "Harry Lockhart! I'm so excited to finally meet you." The dogs followed her out onto the brick porch and danced around their legs. Daisy threw her arms around Harry's neck, pressed her body against his rock-hard chest and hugged him tight. "Welcome home!"

Chapter Two

Welcome home?

Harry's vision blurred as something gray and furry darted between his legs. A mix of squeals and barks blended with the deafening boom and shouting voices inside his head, and his nose was suddenly filled with the stench of burnt earth and raw skin.

One moment, the memories were there, but in the next, he blanked them out and focused on the here and now. His body was hyper-aware of the softness wrapped around him like a blanket, and the creamy chill of the woman's cheek pressed against the side of his neck.

Daisy Gunderson was on her tiptoes hugging him. Bear-hugging him. Giving him a squeeze-the-stuffing-out-of-him kind of hug. What happened to polite introductions and handshakes? This wasn't the greeting he'd expected. She wasn't the woman he'd expected.

But when a woman hugged a man like that, it was his natural instinct to wrap his arms around her and…pat her back. He could hear his men ribbing him now, giving him grief over his lousy moves with the ladies the same way he gave them grief about staying sharp and keeping their heads down. He'd been short on this kind of contact for a long time. Months. Years, maybe. The instinctive part of him wanted to tighten his grip around her. A baser part of him wanted to reach down and see if the curves on the bottom half matched the ones flattened against him up top—or whether all that luscious body he felt was just the pillows of her coat squished between them. A different part of him, the part that was still fractured and healing, wanted to bury his nose in the sugar-cookies-and-vanilla scents radiating off her clothes and hair and skin, and let it fill up his head and drive out the nightmares.

Harry did none of those things. Although her scent was as sweet as he'd imagined, nothing else about this meeting was going according to plan. Dogs were barking. She was plastered against him. He patted her back again because he wasn't sure how he was supposed to react to this welcome. After all, he'd never met Daisy in person before.

She started talking before pulling away. "This feels like a reunion between old friends. I just got home myself. A few minutes earlier and you would have missed me. What are you doing here?" She shooed the dogs into the house and grabbed his wrist, pulling him in, as well. "Sorry. I'll stop talking. Come in out of the cold."

He watched the little gray-and-white fuzz mop dart back and forth across the area rug in the foyer while the white terrier jumped over him with a yip of excitement when he got too close. Those dogs were wired. They needed a good bit of exercise to take some of that energy out of them.

After locking the thick mahogany door behind her, Daisy pointed to the little one. "Muffy, down." Muffy? The long-haired one was clearly a dude, but he had to give the little guy credit for flopping down on his belly to pant until he got permission to go nuts again. "I can put them in their kennels if you want, but they'll mind if you tell them to stay down. Make sure Patch is making eye contact with you and use your hand. He's deaf. But smart as a whip. Jack Russells usually are. He knows several commands. Patch?"

She demonstrated a universal hand signal. The terrier sat, all right, but so did the Belgian Malinois. Who looked a lot like… That muscle ticked beneath Harry's right eye as he slammed the door on that memory and focused on the dog with the graying muzzle. Poor old guy had lost a leg. But those deep brown eyes were sharp and focused squarely on him, as if awaiting a command. Maybe the dog recognized another wounded warrior. "Is he a working dog?"

"KCPD-retired," she answered. "That's Caliban. He lost his leg to cancer. I inherited him when his handler couldn't keep him. Sorry about the mess. I'm in the middle of decorating for the holidays." Daisy was moving down the hallway beside the stairs, which were draped with fake greenery and red bows tied along the railing. She swerved around a couple of plastic tubs and kicked aside little bits of melting snow with her low-heeled boots. "Stick to the runner and it won't be slippery," she advised. "Could I get you something hot to drink? Coffee? Cocoa? Are you hungry? I baked a ton of cookies last weekend."

Did the woman never stop talking? He couldn't even say hello, much less ask a question or explain the reason he was here. "That's not necessary."

"Don't be ridiculous. It's cold. I'm cold. I'd be fixing it, anyway."

Clearly, she expected him to follow her through the house, so Harry pulled the watch cap off his head and stepped out. A parade of curious dogs followed him into a cozy kitchen that opened up to a dining room that appeared to be a storage area for unwanted furniture, more plastic tubs and paint cans.

"Ignore that room. My goal is to clear that out this

weekend and finish decorating. I'm hosting my school's staff Christmas party next weekend." She shed her coat and scarf and tossed them over a ladder-back chair at an antique cherrywood table. "Have a seat."

"I wanted to talk about the letters."

"Sit." She pulled out a stool at the peninsula counter and patted the seat. "I'd love to talk about the letters you sent. Wish you'd kept writing after the school year ended." He'd stopped in June because that's when he… He hadn't written any letters from the hospital. "You're the first one of our pen pals I've met in person."

"That was nice of you to keep writing, even after I dropped the ball." Harry put his leather gloves on the counter, unzipped his coat and settled onto the stool. He didn't have the heart to tell her that some of those pen pals were never coming home. "I want you to know how much my unit appreciated all the letters you and your class sent them. Even if we, if I, didn't always respond."

She was running water now, measuring coffee. "That was one of my more inspired projects. I started it with last year's composition class. Anything to get them to write. Plus, at Central Prep—the school where I teach—we encourage our students to be involved in the community, to be citizens of the world and aware of others. It seemed like a win-win for both of us, supporting the troops while improving their communication skills. When your sister mentioned your Marine Corps unit at church, looking for Christmas cards to send them last year, I jumped right on it." She tugged at the hem of her long purple tweed sweater after reaching into the refrigerator for some flavored creamer. As she moved about, Harry noticed that her glasses were purple, too, and so were the streaks of color in her chocolate brown hair. "I always model what I ask my students to do, so I adopted you. I don't mean adopt you like that—no one would adopt…you're a grown man. We drew names out of a hat. You were the one that was left, so you lucked out and became my pen pal. It's nice—no, amazing—to finally meet you in person." She stopped to take a breath and push a plate of sugar cookies decorated like Christmas trees and reindeer in front of him. "And now I'm rambling. Thank you for your service."

Now she was rambling? Harry was still replaying all the dialogue in his head to catch everything she'd said. "You're welcome. I was just doing my job. Thank you for your letters. They meant a lot to me."

"*You're* welcome. And I was just doing *my* job." She pulled two turquoise mugs from an upper cabinet while the earthy smell of coffee brewing filled the room. "You're home on leave for the holidays, I imagine. Are you visiting Hope?"

"I'm staying with my sister and her husband for a few days."

"How's their little boy? He's about two, right?"

"Gideon is…" A little afraid of the growly uncle who was rooming with him for the time being. Or maybe the fact that Harry was a little afraid of holding his energetic nephew without breaking him was what created the awkward tension between them. Who was he kidding? Pretty much every relationship was awkward for him right now. "Yeah, he's two in a couple of months."

"And Hope is pregnant with baby number two? That's good news. Although that apartment over her bridal shop only has two bedrooms, doesn't it? She and Pike will have to be looking for a bigger place soon." Daisy filled two mugs and carried them to the counter across from him. Although that bulky knit sweater covered the interesting bits between her neck and thighs, her leggings and boots hinted at earth-mother curves. He was busy filling in with his imagination the shape he couldn't see, enjoying the mental exercise a little more than he should when she set a fragrant, steaming mug in front of him, and cradled the other between her hands, warming her fingers. "What can I do for you, Master Sergeant?"

Harry dutifully pulled his gaze up to the blue eyes behind her glasses. "Top. You don't have to call me Master Sergeant every time. Top is the nickname for an NCO of my rank."

"All right, Top. What can I do for you?"

"I wanted to meet you in person and thank you for your letters."

"You said that already." She picked up a red-nosed reindeer cookie and dipped it into her coffee before taking a bite, waiting for him to continue.

Exactly how did a guy broach a subject like *I need the woman from those letters to help me regain my sanity? The golden, ethereal one with the soft voice, gentle touch and quiet mien I imagined in my dreams? I need that angel's healing touch.* He definitely didn't need a woman who talked nonstop, owned a pack of dogs and triggered a lustful curiosity he hadn't acknowledged for longer than he cared to admit. Harry picked up his mug by the handle, then turned it in his hands, staring down into the dark brew that reminded him of one of the colors of her hair. "Writing your students gave my unit something to do during the slow times. Getting those letters could really… You know, some days were harder than others, and, um…" This wasn't right. *She* wasn't right. Time to abort this crazy ass mission and call one of the shrinks Lt. Col. Biro had recommended for him. Harry set his mug down on the counter with enough force to slosh the coffee over the edge. "Sorry." He shook the hot liquid off his skin and shot abruptly to his feet. "Now's not a good time, is it?" While she retrieved a dish cloth to clean up his mess, he grabbed his gloves and headed toward the front door. "Sorry to show up on your doorstep unannounced."

"You haven't even touched your coffee." Harry strode past the trio of dogs who hopped to their feet to follow him. He heard Daisy's boots on the floor boards behind him. "You must have stopped by for some reason. We have lots to talk about, don't we? Your dog, Tango? Your friends who were wounded in that IED explosion? Are they okay? Were you hurt? I mean, I can see the scars, so clearly you were, but—"

"That was a different skirmish."

"You were hurt more than once?" Harry had his cap on, his coat zipped and the front door open when Daisy grabbed his arm with both hands and tugged him to a halt. "Wait."

Her fingers curled into the sleeve of his coat, tightening their hold on him. Harry glanced down at her white-knuckled grip, frowning at the unexpected urgency in her touch before angling around to face her.

"Please don't leave." Her face was tipped up, her eyes searching his as if she was struggling to come up with the right words to say. Odd. Words didn't seem to be a problem for her. "If you really have to go, I understand. And if you don't want to talk, that's okay. But..." She looked back over her shoulder, past the dogs and holiday decorations before she finally let go of his sleeve and shrugged. "Totally unrelated thing, but, before you go, would you do me a favor? I'm not saying you owe me anything. I mean, you barely know me—"

"I know you better than most people." Correction. He knew the person who'd been his lifeline to normalcy and home and hope. This chatterbox with the wild hair and effusive personality felt like someone different. "After reading your letters, that is. You shared a lot. About your ex, your parents, this house…" He glanced around at the refinished wood and fresh paint of the drafty old Colonial that was far too big for one person—even if she did live with a pack of dogs. "Some of your school stories made me laugh or made me want to wring someone's neck."

She took half a step back. "You remember all that?"

He'd memorized nearly every sentence. *Laughter. Concerns. Wisdom. Compassion.* The Daisy Gunderson he knew had shared her heart.

"I know the men and women I work with," he clarified. "My sister and her husband… I mean, you're not the only person I know."

He couldn't tell if the pinch at the corners of her mouth and eyes meant she was touched by his confession, or if she felt a little sad to learn how few connections he had outside the Marine Corps. "Thank you. I feel like I know you better than someone I just met a few minutes ago, too. You wrote some touching things that, well, some of them made me cry."

He made her cry? Harry shifted uncomfortably inside his coat. "Sorry about that."

"Don't be. You shared the truth about what was on your mind, what you were feeling. I was honored." She hugged her arms around her middle. "You made me smile sometimes, too."

So why wasn't he seeing that smile? The Daisy in his dreams always smiled. This was not going well. Daisy Gunderson was supposed to have a serene smile and a calm demeanor that made all the crap he had to deal with go away. But just because the real Daisy didn't fit the ethereal angel he'd imagined, it didn't mean he should blow her off. "You were going to ask me something?"

"Right." She shrugged one shoulder. Then she pointed

at him, at herself, then back at him. "I'm here by myself and I wondered… Would you…?"

Now she couldn't come up with words? "Ma'am, I really should be going."

Her manic energy returned in a burst that faded into breathless hesitation. "One. Don't call me ma'am. My students call me ma'am, and it's after hours and I'm off duty. Besides, it makes me feel like I'm old enough to be your mother. And two… I could use a man right now." Now wasn't that a suggestive request. The parts of him south of his belt buckle stirred with interest, even as his chest squeezed with anxiety at the possibility she wanted something more than a pen pal, too. "But I don't have a big brother or a boyfriend or a dad to call and…" She gestured down the hallway toward the back of the house. "Would you check something out for me?"

His disappointment surprised him more than the relief he felt. "You've got a problem?"

"Maybe. I don't know." She tucked a stray lock of hair back into the purple and brown waves behind her ear. "I hope not, but…"

He could change a flat tire for her, or do some heavy lifting or pull something down off a high shelf. He owed the fantasy Daisy from his letters at least that much. But as Harry waited for the details, he read something more troubling than the awkwardness of this conversation in the blue eyes behind her glasses. She was scared.

Seventeen years of military training put him on instant alert.

"Show me."

Stopping only to put on her coat and order the dogs to stay inside the mudroom, Daisy walked out onto the back deck, and Harry followed. She went to the railing and pointed down into the snow. "Those footprints. Something seems off to me."

This was about something more than tracks through her backyard. Her cheeks should be turning pink with the dampness chilling the air. Unless the colored lights were playing tricks on him, her skin had gone pale. The buoyant energy that had overwhelmed him earlier had all but disappeared. Seemed he wasn't the only one keeping secrets.

With a nod, he accepted the simple mission she charged him with and went down into the yard. Stepping farther out into the snow so as not to disturb the suspicious tracks, Harry switched his phone into flashlight mode and made a quick reconnaissance. This was an awful lot of traffic through the yard of a woman who lived alone. And all of these tracks were too big to be Daisy's. His boots were digging into snow instead of sand, but the hackles at the back of Harry's neck went up just as they had overseas when he sensed an enemy lurking somewhere beyond his line of sight.

Trusting suspicions he wasn't sure he was equipped to deal with yet, he retraced his own path a second time, kneeling to inspect some of the deeper tracks. They'd frozen up inside after a bit of melting, meaning they'd been there long before the afternoon sun had reached them. He pushed to his feet and moved closer to the house to confirm that the deepest boot prints were facing the house, a good five feet beyond the gas and water meters. Harry looked up to a window with a shade drawn halfway down and curtains parted a slit to reveal the blackness of the room inside.

Harry glanced up at Daisy, who was watching his every move from the edge of the deck. She was hugging her arms around herself again. Something definitely had her spooked. "That's not just a case of a new meter reader guy thinking he could get out on that side of the yard, is it?"

"I don't think so. He'd only have to see that part of the fence once to know there's no gate over there." And yet her visitor had walked back and forth multiple times, then stopped here to look inside that window. "What room is this?"

She paused long enough that he looked up at her again. "My bedroom."

Harry walked straight to the deck, braced one foot on the bottom planks and vaulted over the railing. The snow flinging off his boots hadn't settled before he'd turned her toward the door to walk her back inside. "You need to call the police. You've got a Peeping Tom."

Chapter Three

Harry sat in the darkness of his truck watching Daisy's light blue Colonial with the dark blue shutters and dozens of Christmas lights, wondering if she was going to give the balding guy at her front door the same kind of hug she'd given him when he'd left a half hour earlier. He already wasn't a fan of the older gentleman who'd insisted she leave the barking dogs on the other side of the glass storm door and finish their conversation on the brick porch where Daisy was shivering without her coat. If she hugged the guy, then Baldy was definitely going on Harry's do-not-like list.

Not that he'd handled either her enthusiastic greeting or grateful goodbye terribly well. But something simmered low inside him at the idea that Daisy's stuffing-squishing hugs were available to anyone who came to her front door.

Finally. The would-be renter handed Daisy a business card and shuffled down the steps. Harry exhaled a deep breath that fogged his window, relieved to see the thoughtless twit depart without a hug. He approved when Daisy crumpled the card in her fist, clearly dismissing the inconsiderate anti-dog man. She huddled against one of the big white pillars at either corner of her porch to watch the rejected tenant drive away.

"Go back inside," Harry whispered, urging the woman

to show a little common sense and get out of the cold night air. But she was scanning up and down the street, searching for something or someone. Was she still worried about those snowy footprints in her backyard?

Harry hunkered down behind the wheel as her gaze swept past his truck. The brief glimpse of fear stamped in the big blue eyes behind those purple glasses when she'd asked for his help had been imprinted on his brain. And since the gray matter upstairs was already a bit of a jigsaw puzzle, he wasn't quite ready to have any worries about her safety lingering on his conscience. So he'd decided to hang out at least until Baldy left. But Daisy already had one pervert who thought looking through her bedroom window was a fun idea. She probably wouldn't be assured to know that he was still out here in the darkness, spying on her, too.

After one more scan, she went back into the house, petting the dogs and talking to them before closing the door. The colored Christmas lights winding around the pillars went out, followed by the bright light of the foyer. She must be moving toward the back of the house because a few seconds later, the lights decorating the garage went out, too. From this vantage point, Harry wouldn't know if she was fixing dinner or changing her clothes or making a path through the mess of projects in her dining room.

Not that it was any of his business how she spent her evenings. Baldy had left her house and it was time for him to go.

Harry started his truck and cranked up the heat, obliquely wondering why he'd felt compelled to sit there in silence, putting up with the cold in lieu of drawing any attention to his presence there. Probably a throwback to night patrols overseas, where stealth often meant the difference between avoiding detection and engaging in a fire fight with the enemy.

But he shouldn't be thinking like that. Not here in Kansas City. He watched Daisy's neighbor to the north open his garage and stroll out with a broom to sweep away the snow that had blown onto his front sidewalk. That was a little obsessive, considering the wind would probably blow the dusting of snow back across the walkways by morning. The neighbor waited for a moment at the end of his driveway, turning toward the same revving engine noise that drew Harry's attention. They both watched from their different vantage points as a car pulled away from the curb and made a skidding U-turn before zipping down the street. Probably a teenager with driving like that. The neighbor shook his head and started back to the garage, but paused as a couple walking in front of his house waved and they all stopped to chat. Yeah, Christmastime in suburbia was a real hotbed for terrorists.

Muttering a curse at his inability to acclimatize to civilian life, Harry pulled out, following the probable teen driver to the stop sign at the corner before they turned in opposite directions. Although this was an older neighborhood, the homes had been well maintained. The sidewalks and driveways had been cleared. Traffic and pedestrians were the norm, not suspicious activity he needed to guard against.

Bouncing over the compacted ruts of snow in the side streets, Harry made his way toward his sister's loft apartment in downtown Kansas City, avoiding the dregs of rush hour traffic as much as possible. This evening's visit to Daisy's house needed to go on his list of dumb ideas he should have reconsidered before taking action. What had he thought was going to happen when he showed up on her doorstep? That the woman who'd sent him all those letters while he'd been overseas and in the hospital, would recognize him? They'd never exchanged pictures. He'd thought that trading news and revealing souls and making him laugh meant that they knew each other. That the same feeling he got when he saw her name at mail call would happen to him again when they met in person. If he was brutally honest, he'd half expected a golden halo to be glowing around her head.

Golden-halo Daisy was supposed to be his link to reality. Seeing her was supposed to ground him. The plan had been to let go of the nightmares he held in check, and suddenly all the scars inside him would heal. He could report back to Lt. Col. Biro and never look back after a dose of Daisy.

So much for foolish miracles.

Daisy Gunderson wasn't fragile. She wasn't golden-haired. And she certainly hadn't been glowing. She was a brunette—a curvy one, if his body's humming reaction to those impromptu bear hugs were any indication. A brunette with purple streaks in her hair and matching glasses on her nose and a need to chatter that just wouldn't quit.

And the dogs. He hadn't expected the dogs. Or the mess. Everything was loud and chaotic, not at all the peaceful sort of mecca he'd envisioned.

The fact that some pervert had been peeking in her bedroom window bothered him, too. He'd foolishly gone to a woman he only knew on paper—a stranger, despite the letters they'd shared—for help. Instead, it looked as if she was the hot mess who needed help.

Harry needed the woman in the letters to help him clear his head and lose the darkness that haunted him.

He didn't need Daisy Gunderson and her troubles.

He'd done his good deed for her. He'd assuaged his conscience. It was time to move on.

To what? What was a jarhead like him supposed to do for six weeks away from the Corps?

If he was overseas, he'd be doing a perimeter walk of the camp at this time of the evening, making sure his buddies were secure. Even if he was back at Camp Pendleton in Southern California, he'd be doing PT or reading up on the latest equipment regs or putting together a training exercise for the enlisted men he intended to work with again. He was used to having a routine. A sense of purpose. What was he supposed to do here in Kansas City besides twiddle his thumbs, visit a shrink and reassure his sister that she didn't need to walk on eggshells around him?

He supposed he could find the nearest mall and do some Christmas shopping for Hope, his brother-in-law, Pike, and nephew, Gideon. But even in the late evening there'd be crowds there. Too many people. Too much noise. Too many corners where the imagined enemy inside his head could hide.

Pausing at a stop light, Harry opened the glove compartment where he'd put the list of local therapists Lt. Col. Biro had recommended and read the names and phone numbers. Even before he'd finished reading, he was folding the paper back up and stuffing it inside beside the M9 Beretta service weapon he stored there. He closed the glove compartment with a resolute click and moved on with the flow of traffic.

He'd already made an appointment for tomorrow afternoon. He wasn't ready for an emergency call to one of them yet. Maybe he should ask his brother-in-law where he could find a local gym that wouldn't require a long-term commitment. He could lift some weights, run a few miles on a treadmill. That was all he needed, a physical outlet of some kind. A way to burn himself out until he was too tired to have any more thoughts inside his head.

It was almost eight o'clock when Harry pulled into the driveway beside Fairy Tale Bridal, the wedding planner business his sister owned. He pressed the buzzer and announced himself over the intercom before Hope released the lock and he jogged up the stairs to the apartment over the shop where she and Pike lived. He heard her warning Pike's K-9 partner, Hans, to stay before opening the condominium door. His sister had a quiet beauty that seemed to have blossomed with the confidence she'd found in marriage and motherhood. He was happy to see her soft smile when she welcomed him home.

But that smile disappeared beneath a frown of concern before she shooed the German shepherd into the living area of the open layout and locked the door behind her. "That coat is too small for you. You need to get a new one that fits."

"Guess I've filled out a bit since the last time I needed my winter coat. There's not much call for them in Southern California or the Middle East."

Although he'd fully intended to put his own things away, Hope took his coat from him as soon as he'd unzipped it. "You're later than I thought. Did you get any dinner? I can heat up some meatloaf and potatoes in the microwave." Seven months pregnant and wearing fuzzy house slippers with the dress she'd worn to work, she shuffled into the kitchen, hanging his coat over the back of one of the kitchen chairs. "Would you rather have a sandwich?"

Harry followed her, feeling guilty that, even after all these years, she felt so compelled to take care of him. "I'm good."

"Did you eat?" she stopped in front of the open refrigerator and turned to face him.

Hope was only a year older than Harry, and he topped her in height, and had outweighed and outmuscled her for years. But she could still peer up at him over the rims of her glasses with those dove-gray eyes and see right into the heart of him, as though the tragic childhood they'd shared had linked them in some all-knowing, twin-like bond. Lying to Hope wasn't an option.

"No."

"I wish you'd take better care of yourself. It wasn't that long ago you were in a hospital fighting for your life. Besides getting winter clothes that fit, you need sleep and good food inside you." She nudged him into a chair, kissed his cheek and went to work putting together a meatloaf sandwich for him. "You found Daisy's house okay? What did you think of her?"

Harry pictured a set of deep blue eyes staring up at him above purple glasses, in an expression similar to the pointed look Hope had just given him. Only, he'd had a very different reaction to Daisy's silent request. Yes, he'd reacted to the fear he'd seen there and taken action like the marine he was trained to be, but there was something else, equally disconcerting, about the way Daisy had studied him in her near-sighted squint that he couldn't quite shake.

"She's a hugger." Surprised that those were the first words that came out of his mouth, Harry scrubbed his palm across the stubble itching the undamaged skin of his jaw.

But the faint air of dismay in his tone didn't faze Hope. In fact, something about his comment seemed to amuse her. "I told you she was friendly and outgoing. She approached me that first morning in our adult Sunday School class. I'd still be sitting in the corner, just listening to the discussion if she hadn't sat down beside me and started a conversation."

Yep. The woman certainly had a talent for talking.

"There's Uncle Harry." Pike Taylor strolled into the living area, carrying their squirmy, wheaten-haired son,

Gideon, who was decked out in a fuzzy blue outfit for bed-time. Even out of uniform, dressed in jeans and a flannel shirt, Pike carried himself with the wary alertness of the Kansas City cop he was. But the tall, lanky man who'd been there to protect his sister from both their abusive father and a serial rapist while Harry had been stationed over in the Heat Locker reminded Harry of an overgrown kid when he set his son down and chased him over to his play area in the living room. Even the dog got into the game, joining in with a loud bark and circling around the toddler, which only made the little boy chortle with glee. That muscle ticked in Harry's cheek as the urge to smile warred with the images of something darker trying to surface. Gideon lost his balance and plopped onto the extra padding of his diaper before using the German shep-herd's fur to pull himself back onto his pudgy little feet and change directions. "Look out," Pike warned from his wrestling position on the floor. "He's been asking for his roommate all evening."

Gideon toddled over to Harry's knee, joyfully repeat-ing a phrase that sounded a lot like "Yucky Hair," which was apparently going to be his nickname for the duration of this visit. Gideon's little fingers tugged at Harry's jeans and reached for him, demanding to be picked up. Although Harry was half afraid to hold the stout little tyke, he could feel the expectation radiating off Hope not to deny her son the innocent request. Unwilling to refuse his sister any-thing that would put a smile on her face, Harry picked up his nephew and set him on his lap. He pushed aside the salt and pepper shakers that Gideon immediately reached for, and let him tug at the buttons of his Henley sweater, instead. Hans lay down close by Harry's feet, keeping an eye on the little boy as if he didn't trust Harry with the toddler, either. Harry shifted in his seat, uncomfortable being the center of all this attention. Gideon batted at Harry's face and he lifted his chin, pulling away from the discomfiting contact. Hell, the dog was better with the child than he was. He needed to distract himself fast, or he was going to end up in a dark place that no one in this room wanted him to visit.

Turning his chair away from the watchful German shepherd, Harry latched onto the first thought that came to mind. "Daisy's a little scattered, isn't she?"

Pike tossed a couple of toys into Gideon's playpen before rising to his feet and crossing to the table. "Scattered? You mean her house? She's been working on it for three years. I can't imagine what it's costing her to redo it from top to bottom like that. Plus, she's doing a lot of the cosmetic work herself."

"I meant she rambled from one topic to the next. I had a hard time keeping up."

"She does live alone," Pike suggested. "Maybe she was lonesome and wanted to talk to somebody."

Hope snickered at her husband's idea. "She's been at school all day, with hundreds of students. She's had plenty of people to talk to."

"Teenagers," Pike countered. "It's not the same as talking to an adult."

Dismissing the explanation with a shake of her head, Hope opened a cabinet to pull out a bag of potato chips. "It's not exactly like you're Mr. Conversation, Harry. You're quiet like I am with new people. Maybe you made her nervous and she was chatting to fill the silence. I do that when my shy genes kick in."

Not in any universe would he describe Daisy Mega-Hugger as a shy woman. But maybe something about him *had* made her nervous. The scars that turned his ugly mug into an acquired taste? Not announcing his visit before showing up on her doorstep? Was there something more to those footprints in the snow than she'd let on? The idea of a Peeping Tom had upset her, yes, but now that he considered her reaction, she hadn't seemed surprised to discover signs of an intruder.

Hope ripped open the bag of chips and crunched one in her mouth before dumping some onto the plate beside his sandwich. "She is one of those women who seems to have a lot of irons in the fire. She's always volunteering for one thing or another. Daisy has the biggest heart in the world."

Harry pulled a toddler fist away from the tip of his nose. Was that big heart why she'd even considered giving Mr. Rude a place to live as her tenant? "I actually waited there a little while after I left. She had a guy coming in to talk about renting her upstairs."

Pike came up behind Hope and reached around her to snatch a chip and pop it into his mouth. "Mr. Friesen is the uncle of one of our receptionists at the precinct. I ran a background check on him for her."

"He showed up before I got out of there. I waited outside for half an hour to make sure he left without incident."

Hope's eyes were wide as she set the plate in front of Harry. "Without incident? That sounds ominous."

Harry ate a bite before breaking off a morsel of the soft bread for Gideon to chew on, in an effort to distract the toddler from grabbing the whole sandwich. "While I was there, she had me check out some suspicious tracks in her backyard. Looked to me like someone had been casing her house."

Pike pulled out the chair at the head of the table and sat. "Did you report it to KCPD?"

So, he thought the situation seemed troublesome, too. "I advised her to."

Hope moved a subtly protective hand to her swollen

belly. "You checked out the house for her, didn't you? Her locks and everything are secure?

"She's got new windows on the ground floor. Dead bolts on the doors." But he hadn't checked any of them to see if they were locked. Surely, the woman had sense enough to... The second bite of his sandwich went stale in his mouth. He should have done that for her, at least.

Pike pulled Hope onto his lap, soothing her concern for their friend. "We've had a rash of burglaries across the city. Pretty standard for this time of year. Thieves looking for money or credit cards, or even wrapped presents they can pawn."

Either coveting his meal or sensing Harry's increasingly testy mood, Gideon squealed and stabbed at the plate, scattering the pile of chips across the table top. Harry shoved the plate aside and pulled the boy back, scooting the chair across the tile floor. His boot knocked against Hans, sending the dog to his feet with a startled woof.

All at once, the dark place inside his mind erupted with a fiery explosion. He felt the pain tearing through his flesh. He heard the shouts for help, the whimpers of pain.

Harry staggered to his feet. "*Platz*, Tango," he ordered, mixing the past and the present inside his head. "Hans, I mean. *Platz*." Pike's well-trained dog instantly obeyed the German command to lie down. Slamming the door on the flashback, Harry thrust Gideon into his frightened sister's arms and grabbed his coat. "I'm sorry. I need to walk around the block a couple of times. Clear my head."

"Harry?"

"Let him go, honey."

An hour later, Harry had come in from the cold, apologized to his sister, finished off the meal she'd saved for him and shut himself inside the bedroom he shared with Gideon.

The flashback had receded to the wasteland of buried images inside his head, although he was still having a hard time settling his thoughts enough to sleep. With Gideon snoring softly from his crib across the darkened room, Harry lay back on the double bed, using the flashlight from his duffel bag to read through the stack of cards and letters that normally soothed him on nights like this.

He grinned through Daisy's account of catching one of her students licking a potted plant in her classroom because the girl had been curious to find out what the sap oozing from the stalk tasted like. The girl had been perfectly fine, but the spate of dumb jokes that had followed would have given a stand-up comic plenty of material. The story had made his unit laugh to the extent that when any one of them made a boneheaded move, they'd teased the marine by calling him or her a plant-licker.

Gideon gurgled in his sleep, reminding Harry that he was the interloper here. In another couple of months, Hope and Pike would need this space for Gideon's new little brother or sister. Although he had every intention of returning to his duties with the Corps by that time, Harry acknowledged another stab of guilt. Maybe Hope wanted to redecorate this room. She had talked about expanding their loft into the shop's second-floor storage area, but a renovation of that scale wouldn't happen until after the baby's birth. Maybe he was in the way here, and Hope was too kind-hearted to say anything. Maybe he could camp out in their condo for just a few days longer, then find himself a quiet place to rent until his penance was over and he could report back to Lt. Col. Biro.

Daisy was looking for a tenant.

Harry returned the letter to the thick manila envelope. Nah. He couldn't. He needed a quiet place to heal for a month or so. He didn't want to get locked into a long-term lease, and he didn't want the place to be chaos central, either.

Dismissing the idea, he pulled another letter out of the envelope and turned his flashlight on it.

Dear MSgt. Lockhart,
I'm so sorry to hear about your friend. I know your work is important to you, but it sounds as though you need more time to grieve. Can you take leave for a couple of days? Please talk to someone there if you need to. A chaplain? Another friend? You're probably not comfortable dropping your guard like that.

When my father died so suddenly, I was in shock. It just didn't seem right that one tragedy should lead so soon to another one. That hurt me worse than Brock's assault because it felt so random. I could fight Brock, but I couldn't fight my dad's heart attack. Fortunately, I had a counselor who reminded me of the different stages of grief. That we all grieve differently, and that there's no timeline for when you stop being angry about your loss, or you get over feeling so heartsick. I sense that you're toughing this out. Be kind to yourself. I'm thinking kind thoughts for you.

Rainbows and unicorns and apple pie. Or chocolate cake? Steak dinner? What's your favorite food to eat or thing to do when you want to have fun and spoil yourself? Let me know, and that's what I'll imagine for you.

Despite her attempt at humor, Harry's thoughts darkened as he thought about Daisy's old boyfriend breaking into her apartment and attacking her with a knife. No wonder she was leery of someone scoping out her house. Harry swung his legs off the side of the bed and sat up. A few letters earlier, Daisy had said her ex had been sent to jail. How long would a guy be locked up for a crime like that? Was she worried about him returning? Sleep was feeling more elusive than ever as Harry made a mental note to ask Pike to check into her ex's status.

His breath stuttered through his chest as he forced his concerns for her aside. There were cops for worries like that. He wasn't in a good place to take on somebody else's trouble right now.

Harry turned his gaze and the beam of his flashlight down to the rest of Daisy's letter, needing to recapture the peace and comfort of her words.

If I was there right now, I'd listen to whatever you wanted to say. For however long it takes to get it all out. If the feelings are too private for you to share with me, maybe you could write them down just for yourself. Get them out of your head so there's not so much you're holding inside that you have to deal with. You don't have to send the words to me, but I find journaling like that helpful.

Believe it or not, I'm a good listener. And a good hugger, or so I'm told. If you're ever in Kansas City, I'll have a hug waiting for you.

Take care,
Daisy

The hint of a smile eased the tension in him at the hugging part. She hadn't been kidding. But the smile never fully formed. Because Harry had taken her up on that offer to write down all his anger and grief. He'd sent her a vitriolic letter—three and a half pages of crap that no one should have to know about. And she'd still answered with another note saying that she had cried on his behalf because she understood that he'd never been able to, that marines didn't cry.

She'd helped him through that nightmare when all had seemed lost. Forget about his own present needs for a second. He owed Daisy a lot more than a brusque brush-off and the silent blame he'd heaped upon her for not living up to the image of the all-knowing angel of his fantasies.

Steeling himself for a half-formed mission, Harry folded up the letter and returned it to the others before shutting off the flashlight and tying his boots back onto his feet.

Hope was right. He was a man of duty. His brain might have a missing chunk filled with anger and darkness, but he was trained to protect and serve.

Maybe all Daisy needed was a man on the premises to scare off lusty lookie-loos or potential burglars or a crazy ex-boyfriend. She'd be safe. He wouldn't feel this added guilt. Hope wouldn't look at him with those big worried eyes and he'd have a roof over his head for the next six weeks.

Hard to argue with logic like that.

Peace of mind and sleep weren't happening tonight until he dealt with at least one of the problems bugging him.

He picked up his phone, but realized he didn't have a number for Daisy. Just the Gunderson address.

Harry grabbed his keys and his coat and quietly shut the bedroom door behind him. Pike and Hope were in the living room, snuggling on the couch as he suited up and walked to the front door. "I'm heading out for a bit."

Hope set aside the book she'd been reading. "It's late."

Harry pulled on his watch cap. "It's not that late."

She shifted her awkward weight and turned to face him. "Are you okay? Did I say something that upset you earlier?"

Pike had muted the news show he'd been watching and risen to his feet. The taller man was watching Harry very carefully, probably to make sure he didn't say or do anything to hurt her. Good. Harry was glad that Hope had someone in her life who loved her enough to take care of her like that.

Did Daisy?

I don't have a big brother or a boyfriend or a dad to call.

Harry leaned over the back of the couch to kiss Hope's cheek. "I'm fine. I just need to run an errand."

"Take the spare keys," Pike advised. He strode into the kitchen and pulled a ring of keys from the nearest drawer before tossing them across the room to Harry. "In case you're out after we've turned in. I'll put Hans in his kennel, Remember, the down command is—"

"*Platz*. Yeah, I know." He knew a lot about working with trained dogs like his brother-in-law's K-9 partner. That had been his job overseas. Him and Tango and… *Nah. Don't go there.* Shutting down the memory he couldn't yet face, Harry stuffed the keys into his pocket. "Hans won't be a problem."

"Let us know how Daisy is doing," Hope prompted.

No sense lying about where he was headed. His sister knew him better than he knew himself. Harry paused in the open doorway before letting himself out. "I will."

Chapter Four

Sleep wasn't happening tonight.

Although the logical part of Daisy's brain told her that the scratching noise at her bedroom window was the wind blowing bits of wintry debris against the panes, she sat up for the third time, clutching her spare pillow against her chest. She stared at the gingham drapes, her vision blurred by nearsightedness and shadows, half expecting them to fly open and reveal a man standing on the other side. Fighting to form a coherent thought over the pulse thundering in her ears at that unsettling idea, she picked up her old tortoise-shell framed glasses from the bedside table and blinked the glowing red numbers of her clock into focus.

2:49 a.m.

Her breath seeped out on a weary sigh. Her six o'clock alarm was going to beep mighty early if she couldn't shut down her fearful imagination and get some sleep.

She flipped on the lamp beside her, flooding the room with a gentle light. Muffy stretched his short legs on top of the quilt, scooting closer to reclaim the warmth from the crook of her knees where he'd been sleeping. Patch sat up behind her on the far side of the bed, his posture indicating he was alert and ready to start his day.

"Not yet, you silly boy," she chided. But her smile was the only invitation Patch needed to climb into her lap to lick her chin in exchange for some petting. Daisy indulged in a few seconds of warmth and affection before looking past him to see Caliban curled into a ball at the foot of the bed. The older dog seemed annoyed to be disturbed from his slumber yet again and tucked his nose under his front leg and tried to go back to sleep.

The furnace kicked on and Daisy startled again, rattling the headboard against the wall. Damn. Who needed some creeper sending her unwanted gifts when she could spook herself with her own imagination? By the time she reminded herself that the drapes were swaying because the vent beneath the window stirred the air and not because a Peeping Tom had moved them, all three dogs were sitting up, looking at her intently, no doubt wondering if they were going to be taking another jaunt with her around the house in search of an intruder they knew wasn't there.

A floorboard creaked overhead and Daisy tilted her gaze up to the ceiling. Again, logic said the noise was the old wood of the house shifting with the changing temperature of heat ducts running through the walls and beneath the floors. But the board above her creaked a second time, and a third, and logic became a voice her fears wouldn't let her hear anymore.

That sounded like footsteps. It shouldn't be possible. The dogs would be barking. The police had taken her statement about the tracks in the snow. She'd locked all her doors and windows.

Downstairs.

She hadn't been upstairs since she'd hung the lights and greenery on the bannister earlier in the week. Not that there were any outside doors or even fire escapes on the second floor where someone could…

Something banged against an upstairs wall and she jumped inside her skin. Brock had shattered the lock on her apartment door the night he'd broken in to assault her. The locks on this house were doubled, heavier.

Didn't make any difference.

She heard another bang. Then another that was slightly muffled.

"Sorry, guys." Daisy couldn't stay there a moment longer, fighting her imagination. Pushing the dogs aside, she tugged on her sticky-bottomed slipper socks and tied her chenille robe over her flannel pajamas. "If I don't double-check what that noise is, none of us will be getting any sleep."

While the dogs jumped down from the bed and stretched, Daisy crossed to the window. She pulled aside the edge of the drape and window shade underneath, bracing for a gruesome face staring at her from the other side. Relieved to see nothing but the dim glow of moonlight reflecting off the snow in her backyard, she exhaled the breath she'd been holding. Quickly tucking the window coverings back into place, she pulled her cell phone and keychain with its pepper spray from her purse and opened the bedroom door.

Daisy had no qualms about running up her utility bill if it meant feeling safe. She flipped on the hall light and the mudroom light, along with lights in the kitchen, dining room and living room. After a quick check of her office, she flipped the switch to illuminate the second-floor landing and climbed the stairs. Muffy followed at her heels, with Patch darting up ahead of them.

"Please be a tree branch caught in the wind and knocking against the side of the house. Or snow." Snow was good. Normal. Maybe a clump had melted off the eaves and landed on a window sill. Ignoring the logic against anything melting in this single digit weather, Daisy nodded, liking that explanation for the discomforting noises. "Please be snow."

A sweep of the empty landing allowed her a moment's reprieve to look back down to the foyer. Her heart squeezed in her chest when she saw Caliban standing with his one front paw on the bottom step, anxiously looking up at them. He bravely hopped up two more steps, but his paw slipped from underneath him on the polished wood and he reversed course, returning to the area rug at the foot of the stairs and sitting at attention. "It's okay, boy. You keep an eye on things down there."

Although she suspected he'd push through his phobia and obey the command to join them if she called to him, Daisy turned her back on Caliban's big brown eyes and flipped on the switch in the first bedroom. This was the room she planned to rent out, along with the bathroom across the hall. This was where she'd heard the floorboards creak, and the thump against the side of the house. Her eyes had barely adjusted to the bright light when Caliban let out a deep warning bark. Daisy answered with a startled yelp. A split second later, someone banged loudly at her front door and she clutched her chest at the double shock to her heart. "Brock is in prison," she reminded herself out loud. "He can't hurt you."

But Secret Santa could.

All three dogs ran to the door, sounding a ferocious alarm. Her thumb hovered over the numbers on her phone. 9… 1…

"Daisy! Daisy, open up!" Did she know that voice? A man's voice. Loud enough to be heard above the barking dogs. Brock had a scary, loud voice, usually slurred by alcohol. But this voice was sharp, succinct. "It's Harry Lockhart. Open up!"

"Harry? What…?" The relief surging through her veins made her light-headed as she raced down the stairs. She pocketed her phone and pepper spray before attacking the locks.

He was a broad, imposing silhouette outside her storm

door until she thought to turn on the porch lights. Adding the glow of Christmas colors to his stern features did nothing to ease the frantic mix of urgency, confusion and relief that made her hands tremble on the latch. Her fingers lost their grip on the storm door as he pulled it right out of her hand.

"Caliban, *sitz*!" Harry ordered the dog to be quiet and sit while he clamped his hands around her shoulders and pushed her inside.

"Is that German? What are you doing here?" she asked, obliquely marveling that her Belgian Malinois obeyed commands in two languages, while Muffy managed to ignore orders in any language. "Is that a gun?"

She barely had time to recoil from the holster cinched around his thigh with a web belt before he trapped her between the thick wood door and his equally solid body and locked the dead bolt. The holster and webbing were military khaki in color, a sharp contrast against the dark denim of his jeans. The wood was cold against her back as he flattened her there, folding his shoulders around her as his chin swiveled from side to side, his gaze inspecting the crossroads of archways that met in the foyer.

"You turned on all the lights. What's wrong?" he demanded in the same clipped tone he'd used with the dogs. Without surrendering the shielding posture of what she could only describe as warrior mode, he pulled back just enough to look down into her eyes.

"What's *wrong*?" she echoed. Daisy curled her fingers into the nubby weave of his charcoal sweater exposed by the unzipped front of his coat, feeling so off-balance by his surprise visit she needed something to cling to. She wanted to push some space between them. The heat of his body was too close, his gun too hardpressed against her hip, his masculine scent too distracting for her to think straight. But all she could do right now was hold on. "Have you been watching my house?"

His gray eyes narrowed on her face. "Your glasses are different."

"What?" Oh, right. She was wearing the brown frames. That observation was as random as her own thoughts right now. Damn, the man had muscles. With his coat hanging open she could see that the burn and shrapnel scars on his face and neck ran down beneath the collar of his sweater. He had been so terribly hurt. An explosion? A fire? He'd nearly lost his eye. And that would be a shame because they were such a beautiful, deep color, like an endless, storm-tossed ocean. *Focus!* Daisy shook her head, still not comprehending why he was here. But she could answer his question. "I have different frames for different outfits. These are my knock-around-the-house pair."

He pulled away as suddenly as he'd pinned her there, and her knees nearly buckled as chilled air rushed between them. He peeled off his gloves and stuffed them into his pockets. "Caliban, *fuss.*"

Foos? Apparently, that meant *heel*, at least to Caliban. Harry spun away to inspect her living room, with the three dogs trotting behind him. Once she thought she could walk again, Daisy tightened her robe around her waist and followed them in a circle through the house, watching Harry stop at every window and door.

When they ended up back at the front door, Daisy caught the sleeve of his coat and halted his search. She could think now, at least clearly enough to know that she still didn't understand why Harry Lockhart was prowling through her house at three in the morning. "What are you doing here?"

"I didn't check your locks before I left earlier."

Was that supposed to make sense to her?

"Why did you turn on all the lights?" he went on. "Something's happened. I thought someone might have broken in."

He *was* spying on her. Daisy tucked her hair behind her ears, unsure whether to be flattered or creeped out. He couldn't know about those disturbing gifts she'd been receiving, could he? Why was this man who'd been so anxious to leave her the last time they'd met so eager to protect her now?

"Daisy?" he prompted. "Why did you turn on the lights?"

She responded to that succinct tone as readily as the dogs had. "I heard noises upstairs. Something hit the side of the house. We went to check."

And then he was off again, taking the stairs two at a time with Muffy and Patch right on his heels.

Daisy knelt on the rug beside Caliban, hugging her arm around his shoulders to stroke his chest, soothing the thrumming energy quaking through the muscular dog's body. Either she was absorbing his edgy alertness or she was just as anxious as Caliban to know what Harry was seeing up there before muttering the word "Clear" as he left each of the three bedrooms and bathroom.

She pushed to her feet as he turned off the second-floor lights and came back down the stairs. Patch's entire butt was wagging with excitement at the late-night adventure as he propped his front paws against Harry's thigh. But Harry pushed him away and signaled for the Jack Russell mix to sit. With Muffy dancing around his legs, paying no heed to either voice commands or hand signals, Harry muttered something under his breath and bent down, picking up the dog.

"Har…" For a split second, Daisy reached for the Shih Tzu, worried that Harry's limited patience couldn't tolerate another yap. Instead, he set Muffy down between Caliban and Patch, pushed the dog's rear end to the rug and ordered him to sit. He repeated the process twice more before Muffy got bored enough with the exercise that he stretched out on his tummy and batted at Harry's boot.

She arched an eyebrow in apology. "He's a hard-headed one to train."

"Yep. He needs an exercise program like fly-ball or agility training to get rid of some of that energy." Harry straightened, propping his hands at his waist, reminding her of the military issue gun strapped to his side before his chest expanded with a heavy sigh. "You got any irate neighbors?"

"What?"

"Kids who'd be out roamin' the neighborhood on a school night?"

"No." Not the questions she'd expect from a man who hadn't found anything to worry about. Daisy was suddenly aware of the icy remnants of slush left from Harry's boots on the foyer rug soaking through her socks and chilling her from the toes up. "What did you see?"

He pulled back the edges of his coat to splay his fingers at his waist. "The house is secure. No signs of forced entry."

"But?"

"It's hard to tell from inside, but it looks as though someone used the side of your house for target practice." He inclined his head toward the stairs. "You've got a snow-ball stuck in the screen of that bedroom window. I opened it up to knock it clear, but it looked like a couple more splats of snow just beside the window, too."

A few minutes ago, she'd been hoping that snow was the culprit. Not so much now. "Someone was throwing snow-balls at my house at three in the morning?"

"Whoever threw them isn't there anymore."

"Or never was." She thought of the sick gifts hidden inside her desk at school and wondered if she was just being paranoid to think that that terror campaign had somehow followed her home. "Maybe the snow fell from the roof or blew off the branches of Mr. Finch's sweet gum tree."

"Don't discount your instincts. Being aware of danger is half the battle of protecting yourself from it."

But Daisy wasn't any kind of marine. "Sometimes my imagination gets the better of me. I remember that night Brock broke into my old place… I told you about him, didn't I?" She interpreted his unblinking glower as a yes. "I know he's locked up in Jefferson City…" She put up her hands, blocking the mental images of her ex's bared teeth and wild eyes, and that bloody knife poised above her. "Bad guys don't get to win." Brock didn't even deserve the time and space inside her head to sour her thoughts. "A few snowballs aren't any kind of threat. I let the noises of the old house get to me."

"The ghosts caught in our heads can be—"

"Relentless." His gray eyes locked on to hers, wide with surprise before narrowing to question her response. That look was too intense for her to hold, so she shrugged, nervously catching her hair behind her ears before looking directly at him again. "You said that in one of your letters."

"I remember. Didn't think you would." Harry shifted on his feet and glanced at the front door, as though an alarm had just gone off inside him, warning him it was time to end the conversation and leave. But then that piercing gaze was on her again. "One of the parts that made you cry?"

"I suppose I wear my emotions pretty close to the surface." While he barely showed his at all, other than this urgent need to escape her company. Again. "Crying isn't a bad thing." When he nudged aside the dogs and turned toward the door, Daisy followed, stopping him before he could leave. "Do I make you nervous, Harry? Is it the dogs? Do they remind you of Tango?"

"Tango?" He glanced over the jut of his shoulder at her.

"Your K-9 partner."

"I know who Tango is." A muscle ticked across his taut cheekbone and he reached for the doorknob. "Was."

"I'm so sorry you lost him. I can't imagine what that must feel—"

"Like I said, everything looks secure. I'll walk around the house to see if I can find signs of where the snowballs came from before I leave."

"You're leaving?"

Of course he was. Only the crazies wanted anything to do with her. Harry just had an overdeveloped sense of responsibility, the kind of alertness and protective instincts she'd expect from any career marine. He might be her friend on paper. She might have fancied herself half in love with the uniformed hero from their letters. But that was her fantasy, not his.

That still didn't stop her from moving between him and the door and sliding her arms beneath his coat, hugging him around the waist. With his coat unzipped, she could get closer than she had yesterday evening. Turning her cheek against the thick wool of his sweater, she felt his body warming hers. She breathed in the rugged smells of soap and Harry. "Thank you for looking out for me."

A fraction of a second longer and she would have pulled away. But his thick arms folded around her, his hands settling between her shoulder blades to gently pat her, almost as if he was trying to burp a baby. Not the most romantic embrace. But this was just a friendly hug, right? At least he wasn't holding himself completely stiff or pulling away. Maybe the taciturn tough guy with the scarred-up face was shy? Smiling against the beat of his heart at that tender notion, Daisy snuggled beneath his chin. She knew he wasn't married, and he'd never mentioned a girlfriend—past or present—in his letters. His sister, Hope, seemed to be the only woman in his life. Could his reticence to carry on a social conversation extend to the physical expression of emotion, as well? But if he was willing to hold on right now, she was more than willing to surround herself in his strength and heat.

"It's not like I could sleep, anyway." Harry's hands stopped their awkward petting and settled against the ribs of her chenille robe long enough for her to feel their warmth seeping through the layers of cotton and flannel. His voice was a growly whisper at the crown of her head. "Thought I'd put my time to good use. Those boot tracks worried me enough that I wished I'd run a security check like this before I left. Felt guilty that I hadn't. It was so late I didn't want to wake you. I thought it'd be enough to watch from outside the house."

"So I'm not the only one with insomnia. We're a pair. I toss and turn in bed out of worry, and you sit out in the cold out of guilt."

His nose rubbed against her temple as he breathed in deeply. Was he sniffing her hair? Why not? Standing here, she'd been memorizing the scent of his clothes and skin. His fingers curled into the back of her robe, pulling it tight across her back for a moment, as if he wanted to hold on tighter but didn't dare, before he released her and backed away. Filled with static electricity, a few wisps of her hair clung to his sweater like tiny, grasping fingers. Before she could smooth them back into place, his hand was there, tucking the wayward strands behind her ear. "Will you be okay now?" he asked.

She reached up to cup the side of his face. When he tipped his head away from her touch, Daisy suspected it was vitally important that she not retreat. Maybe it wasn't just shyness, but a self-consciousness about the wounds he couldn't hide that made him so awkward around her. She brushed her fingertips along his cheek and jaw, noting the rough textures, marveling that she could still feel the warmth and rugged bone structure beneath the stiff ridges of scar tissue there. She imagined Harry had a lot of reasons why socializing and human contact might not come easily for him. "I know you went through something horrible when you were deployed. I'm sorry if bringing up Tango upset you. I know that dog meant a lot to you. You mentioned him in nearly every letter."

Harry turned away and opened the door. "I'll wait on the porch until I hear the dead bolt engage."

Clearly, they hadn't gotten off on the right foot in person. But if he wouldn't talk to her, she didn't know how to fix whatever the problem was between them. "I'm sorry if I've done anything to—"

He spun around, leaning toward her with such a hard expression that she backed away a step. "Don't apologize to me. Ever. If anything, I owe you." Owe her what? But he wasn't going to explain that cryptic remark, either. He was already on his way out the door. "Good night, Daisy."

"Good night, Harry."

She locked both doors and moved to the side window to watch him stride through the snow around the side of the house. A few minutes later, apparently satisfied with his reconnaissance mission, he returned to his truck and climbed inside. She was glad to see he had a cup of coffee waiting for him, and wondered if it was still hot. She wondered if he'd appreciate her brewing up a fresh pot and offering to refill his disposable cup. If sleep was an issue, though, he wouldn't want more caffeine. And if being with her made him so edgy, he'd probably appreciate her turning off the lights and going back to bed so he could relax his vigil. If she could do that much to thank him for both his service to their country and standing watch here on the home front, she would.

"Good night, Top," she murmured before shutting off the Christmas lights. "Come on, boys."

Daisy turned off the rest of the lights except for the lamp beside her bed. After she gave each of the dogs a crunchy treat to chew on, they settled into their respective spots on top of her quilt. She draped her robe over a chair, along with her damp slipper socks, and set her glasses aside. Sensing that sleep would remain elusive, either out of fear of the unknown crazy stalking her or curiosity about the US marine who'd made it his mission to make her feel safe tonight, Daisy dropped to her knees and lifted the eyelet dust ruffle to pull her father's old metal tackle box from beneath the bed. She sat on the bed, pulling the quilts over her lap and tucking Muffy against her side before opening the box.

She pushed aside the keepsakes she stored there and pulled out the small stack of letters she'd tied together with a ribbon. Then she propped up the pillows behind her and leaned back to read through Harry's letters again. She held one close to her face to bring the tight, angular handwriting into focus.

Dear Daisy,
Thank you for your letter from 2 May. I hope you are well.

Not that you asked for my opinion, but one of my jobs here is to correct disruptive behaviors. I wouldn't let a man I outranked talk back to me, and you shouldn't let that student talk to you with that kind of language, either. My first instinct would be to shove the jackass *young man up against the wall and wash his mouth out with soap. But I suppose your principal and his parents would frown upon that. Are there parents? I had a potty mouth until I got placed with my second set of foster parents. Used to shock the hell out of Hope. (Clearly, I've gotten a little lax. If my pen wasn't about to run out of ink, I'd rewrite this thing so I wasn't swearing in front of you, either.) But if he's not learning it at home, he needs to learn it from you. That student needs to respect your command. Take charge.*

I recommend avoiding direct eye contact, not speaking to him unless absolutely necessary, not giving him the attention he's looking for. That works on the dogs I train when we need them to be quiet. I'm not telling you to treat your students like dogs, but I can see that regular, consistent training in expected behaviors would be beneficial to managing a classroom.

We've had a slow week here. It makes me nervous when things get too quiet. Your letter offered a nice reprieve from the tension. Tango appreciated the dog treats, and I enjoyed the cookies. And no, I didn't get the two packages mixed up. (Although Tango did actually have some of both. I think he liked the cookies better.)

Yours truly,
MSgt. H. Lockhart

Daisy was in the middle of her third letter when she drifted off to sleep, surrounded by her dogs and watched over by the mysterious marine who had touched her heart.

Chapter Five

It was a good day to be a teacher. But then, Fridays usually were.

Daisy deposited the holiday-scented hand soap on Mary Gamblin's desk, straightening the gift bag and Secret Santa card before peeking into the hallway to ensure the coast was clear before dashing across to her own classroom to grab her bag and coat. With the gift delivered, her to-do list at school was done. She locked up her room and hurried down to the teachers' lounge. She needed to zip in, grab her mail and get out of here for a couple of hours.

She'd had a busy day, working through lunch with Angelo Logan, dressing up in toga-draped sheets with her sophomore literature class to reenact scenes from *Julius Caesar* and celebrating a stack of vocabulary quizzes that everyone in her composition class had passed. Despite having such a short night's sleep, she'd enjoyed a couple of hours of the deepest slumber she'd had in a long time. When she awakened, she'd rolled over onto a pile of letters strewn around her in the bed and on the floor. Remembering the closeness she'd felt reading Harry's letters, remembering he'd been worried enough about her to keep watch over her house all night, remembering the abundant strength of his arms folding around her, all made her smile. She woke up feeling hopeful, renewed and unafraid to face the day.

With the light of day, Harry's truck was gone. But the feelings remained. While coffee brewed and the dogs ran around the backyard, Daisy had unpacked a few more Christmas decorations and hung them around the house. She wouldn't be putting up a tree until this weekend, but little by little she was getting the rest of the house ready to go for the faculty holiday party. Although she still had no explanation for the snowballs tossed against the side of her house, there had been no more boot prints in her yard beyond Harry's that she needed to worry about, and Daisy was feeling Christmasy again. For a little while last night, she hadn't felt as horribly alone as she usually did in that old house. Harry had offered her enough of a reprieve that she could put her imagination to rest and find her fighting spirit again.

Daisy zipped up her coat and looped her bag over her shoulder, heading down the hallway with a purpose to her step, humming a holiday tune. She was going all out this Christmas, partly because of the party, but mostly because she hated that fear, paranoia and even a little depression were such easy moods to succumb to this time of year. Especially this year, when her mom was celebrating Christmas with her stepfather's family and her creepy Secret Santa gifts were making December feel like a scary Halloween movie.

She exchanged a wave with her principal, Ryan Hague, as he locked up his office and headed out. He was probably heading home for a quick bite of dinner before coming back to supervise tonight's basketball game with a cross-city rival. Daisy smiled, glad she'd taken the time to hang up the white silk ball decorated with plastic mistletoe in the archway leading into her living room. She wasn't expecting any kissing action herself over the holidays, but Mr. Hague was a newlywed who'd married his second wife over the summer. It would be a fun way to start the Christmas party when he and other staff members arrived with their spouses or dates and she ushered them inside.

The clicking of her boots on the marble floor slowed as she tried to remember the last time she'd been kissed. The memory of Brock's dark head bending toward hers while she pushed his sour breath out of her space gave way to an illusory image of Harry Lockhart's damaged face with all its interesting angles and soulful gray eyes. She didn't suppose he was a mistletoe kind of man, indulging in silly holiday traditions, but that didn't stop her from picturing his mouth sliding over hers and those massive arms gathering her up against his chest again. Daisy's breath caught in her throat and she was suddenly uncomfortably warm inside her coat.

When had her patriotic pen pal become the stuff of her fantasies? She had a feeling she hadn't made a terribly good impression on Harry. He seemed to have a hard time relaxing around her. Although he'd been kind enough to check out her backyard, and set up a guard around her house last night, she didn't have to be psychic to sense the antsy energy coming off him. Without any kind of explanation beyond his obvious injuries or perhaps being an introvert, it was far too easy to suspect that *she* was what made him so uncomfortable.

Other footsteps, heavier and moving faster than her own in the hallway behind her, dragged Daisy out of her thoughts. She peeked over her shoulder and saw Bernie Riley's familiar blue and gold jacket and light brown hair. She nodded a greeting to the tall, lanky man. "Coach."

"Gunderson." He jogged a few steps to catch up and

walk beside her. Apparently, he was en route to the teacher's lounge, too. "You coming to the game tonight?"

"I'm working the front gate." Selling tickets, checking passes from the other school's staff. "But I'll try to get into the gym to watch some of it. Are you starting Angelo?"

"That kid's my star point guard. Not as tall as his brother. But faster. Smarter on the court, too."

Speaking of brothers… She knew Bernie was focused on tonight's game, but she had to ask, "Did you get my note about Albert?"

"I did." He stuffed his hands into the pockets of his slacks and chuckled. "So he's your new pet project, huh? Always trying to rescue somebody, aren't you."

Daisy bristled at the condescension hidden behind his teasing tone. "We need to do the best we can for all our students, not just the star athletes."

His long fingers clamped around her upper arm, stopping her. "You're not implying that I only care about the students who play for me, are you?"

She had to tilt her head back, way back, for him to see the glare in her eyes as she tugged her arm from his grip. "We're an academic prep school. We shouldn't have students who are failing English. We're going to lose Albert if we don't do something." She wasn't fond of being grabbed like that, but for a man with Coach Riley's ego, perhaps she'd be smarter to make this request about him. "You know how much Albert loves basketball. He respects you. If you encouraged him to—"

"Did you ever stop to think that maybe *you* were the problem?"

"Me?" Daisy rocked back on her heels, as surprised by the accusation as she'd been to feel his hand on her arm. "What do you mean?"

Bernie shrugged, his gaze checking up and down the

hallway before landing on her. "Some of those boys—they're young men, really—aren't comfortable being in your class or working one-on-one with you because, well, they have a crush on you."

"Impossible." How could they? She was more than a decade older than the teenagers. She made them write nearly every day, and most of the novels she taught weren't on any high schooler's must-read list. "Did one of them tell you that? Miss Wadsworth is younger than I am. Prettier, too."

"Yeah, but you're friendlier, funnier. You've got that cool hair vibe going." He flicked at a strand of her hair. "Wasn't this red last year? And you were a blonde when I met you. Like my Stella. The kids like that kind of stuff."

"I have never encouraged any one of them on a personal level. When it comes to teaching I have never been anything but professional with my students." She was appalled to hear that she was any part of the school's gossip mill. "There has never been one complaint filed against me."

Bernie's hands were up in surrender and he was grinning again. "Hey, I'm not accusing you of anything. But when you're a walking hormone, it doesn't take much for a kid to think he's in love with somebody who smiles at him or gives him a good grade. You should hear some of the questions I get in health class."

"About me?"

"About women." He arched his brows in a wry expression. "And sex."

No. *Sex* and Ms. G should not be anywhere together in a sentence where students were concerned.

"You think Albert has a crush on me?" Was that why he'd dropped her class? Or was that the explanation for those sick gifts she'd been receiving? Could the beheaded elf and other disturbing mementos be Albert Logan's idea of expressing his feelings for her? Or expressing his frustration that she didn't return his feelings?

"I don't know. The boys don't usually talk about specifics."

If there were some misplaced emotions going on, she shouldn't try to help Albert personally. But that didn't mean she was giving up on helping the young man succeed. "Encourage him to talk to another teacher, then. You could help him."

Bernie took a step back, shaking his head. "Whoa. I'm not an English teacher."

"Even if he starts turning in his assignments, it'll raise his grades. You can teach him responsibility, can't you?"

Bernie considered her request for a few moments, scratching at the back of his head before replying. "I could use his height back on the team. But I'm so busy this time of year."

Daisy took half a step toward him, encouraged that he would consider her request. "Would you at least promise to talk to him?" When he nodded and turned toward the faculty lounge again, Daisy fell into step beside him. "And if you do find out that he's got the hots for me, will you please remind him that I will never be available to a student in that way. It's not just school policy, it's *my* policy."

Bernie reached over her head to open the door. "I'll sit him down and we'll have a chat."

"Thank you." She had to raise her voice to be heard over the animated conversation inside. Eddie Bosch was regaling a couple of their coworkers with a story while Mary Gamblin ran off copies of worksheets and Carol Musil sorted through the catalogues in her mailbox. They were laughing at the light-up tie Eddie had gotten from his Secret Santa, and lamenting other unfortunate fashion choices they had made over the years.

So much for making a quick exit. While Bernie joined the conversation, Daisy moved toward the bank of mailboxes, already spying the stack of reworked papers from a student who'd been serving an in-school suspension. She'd tuck those into her bag and go, knowing she couldn't linger if she wanted enough time to get home to let the dogs out, change into a pair of jeans and get back to school for tonight's game. Dinner would have to be a hot dog from the concession stand.

She was sorting through the papers, making sure they were all there, when Eddie came up beside her. "How did that interview go last night? You got a new tenant?"

Hardly. When the guy had said he'd only move in if she kenneled her dogs or left them outside 24/7, she'd been only too happy to show him the door. "No. But I'm meeting with two more prospects tomorrow."

Bernie pulled down a six-pack of sports drinks with his name and a big bow on it from on top of the mailboxes. "Nice."

Clearly, he was faring better with the gifts he'd been receiving from his Secret Santa. Daisy braced herself and stuck her hand inside her own mailbox, dreading what she might find today. She breathed an audible sigh of relief when she found no surprise packages, which made her feel good enough to elaborate on her answer to Eddie's question. "Mr. Friesen liked everything about the place except for me and my dogs. Didn't think we'd be a good fit."

Eddie laughed. "Probably not. But I think you're on to something, leasing part of that big house. Income property. That's what they call it on TV. I'm thinking about finishing my basement and renting it out. How much are you asking for rent? I'm curious to know if it'd be worth the investment."

But Daisy didn't hear the question. She couldn't hear

much of anything over the pulse thundering in her ears. She'd been a fool to think her tormentor would have forgotten her for even one day. There it was, clipped to the bottom of the stack of papers—a plain white envelope with just her name and the usual message, typed onto a Christmas label.

Dear Daisy,
Merry Christmas from your Secret Santa.

"Daisy?"

She ignored both Eddie's prompt and Bernie's effort to join the conversation. "You didn't fill the vacancy at your house? Are you still lookin' for someone to rent that room? I might know a guy. Strictly short term."

She hated that her fingers were shaking as she peeled open the back flap of the envelope. She hated that Eddie, Mary and Carol knew enough about the gifts she'd been receiving that Eddie placed a steadying hand on her shoulder, and the two women stopped their work to watch as she pulled out the enclosed card and opened it.

Suddenly, it hurt to breathe. If she'd been alone, she would have screamed.

The graphic sexual act, although drawn in stick figures, left nothing to the imagination. Neither did the caption beneath the picture. *You and me, bitch. When you least expect it. Merry Christmas to me.*

"You okay?" Eddie asked.

No. She wasn't. But the words wouldn't form.

"Is that from your Secret Santa?" Bernie's height made it far too easy to peer over her shoulder to inspect the defiled holiday card. Daisy crushed it in her fist and stuffed it into the pocket of her coat before he could see the disturbing missive. She didn't need anyone else knowing her fear and shame. "You don't like your gift?"

Daisy tilted her face to Bernie's, thinking for one brief second that his friendly smile was a cruel joke. It took a few seconds longer to realize he hadn't seen the sick drawing and remember that he wasn't one of those close friends who knew about the other gifts.

"What's wrong with it?" Bernie asked. "There's not a gift card in there? Is it empty?"

"I have to get out of here." Daisy shrugged off Eddie's hand and hurried to the door while she wasn't too blind with terror to see it.

Coach Riley cursed behind her. "I need to call my wife. If that bitch is playin' another game—"

"Put a sock in it," Eddie warned before hurrying after her. "Give me ten minutes, Dais. I need to finish entering these grades and then I'll walk you out."

"I don't have ten minutes." She glanced in Eddie's direction without really seeing him. "I need to go home and take care of the dogs before I come back for the game."

"Bernie." Eddie snapped at the tall man and gestured for him to follow her.

Bernie glanced up from the cell phone at his ear. "It's still daylight. But if you want me to walk you out, I guess I can."

"No." Daisy needed to get out to her car so she could scream, and maybe get a hold of her thoughts again. No one had hurt her. This was just about getting under her skin and scaring her. She needed to get away from this place and these people and remember she was strong enough to deal with the fear again. "I'm fine," she lied. "Make your call. I'll see you tonight."

HARRY WAS BEGINNING to wonder if anyone in this neighborhood spent much time looking out their windows and butting into other people's business. Although he knew a lot about staying off the radar when he needed to, he wasn't about to assume that he didn't look like some kind of suspicious figure. He glanced into the rearview mirror to study his reflection. Black cap, scarred face, perpetual scowl? Not suspicious—make that threatening. Unless you got to know him. And maybe even then, that was the impression he made on the civilian world.

But clearly, there was no neighborhood watch on this block because he'd been sitting across from Daisy's house or walking the area for most of the past twenty hours without anyone approaching his truck or calling the police to come check him out. That didn't bode well for anyone else keeping an eye out for the well-being of the purple-tinted hug-meister who lived alone in that big blue house.

He spotted her in his side-view mirror, turning the corner in a mini-SUV. Lime green. Obviously, the woman loved color and couldn't get enough of it in her life. Black and khaki suited him just fine. Maybe that opposing difference in their tastes explained a lot about why he was having such a hard time connecting with her. More than the fact she didn't look like the woman he'd imagined in those letters, her cheerful, touchy-feely, ninety-mile-a-minute personality didn't match the reserved, ladylike angel he'd hoped was going to save him from himself.

But those differences hadn't stopped him from looking out for her. He was certain the shrink he'd talked to earlier this afternoon would say he identified with her isolation. Those early years when it had just been him and Hope in a remote cabin in the Ozarks, when they'd had no idea whether their father was going to come home drunk and angry, or not come home at all, had certainly taught him to be self-sufficient. Had taught him to appreciate the comradeship he'd found in the Corps. But what that little boy wouldn't have given to have a real daddy he could truly depend on, someone who would have looked out for him and Hope. Daisy needed someone reliable in her life. For right now, at least, he was it.

Harry raised his hand to wave as she drove past him. But she didn't see him and he curled his fingers into a fist and drew it back into his lap. Like everyone else in this neighborhood, Daisy was unaware of his presence. She was singing along with the radio or talking to someone on a hands-free phone, as she turned into her driveway and shut down the engine. Why didn't she pull into the garage? Was she waiting for the song or phone call to finish? Was this just a quick stop before she went somewhere else? Should he follow her if she left again? Just how far was he going to take this new let's-spy-on-Daisy hobby of his?

After checking his watch, Harry huddled down inside his coat and waited to get a better idea of her immediate plans before he made that decision.

Maybe this need to keep an eye on her had something to do with the unexpected curiosity that made him want to understand her better. Or maybe his fractured brain needed to resign itself to the differences between imagination and reality so that he could put that ideal Daisy to rest and get on with a new plan for getting himself fit to return to active duty.

Ten minutes later, he sat up straight behind the wheel, wondering how long she was going to sit inside her car.

At fifteen minutes, he got out of his truck and jogged across the street.

Harry walked up her driveway, assuming she'd see him approaching in one of her mirrors. But when he reached the driver's side window, he saw her clutching the steering wheel, resting her head against it. There was no music playing. No phone that he could see. She was unaware of his presence. And he could see her lips moving, muttering something over and over. Was she praying? Angry? Crazy?

Already uneasy with her just sitting in the parked car, Harry rapped his knuckles against the window. "Daisy?"

She screamed in response, sliding toward the center console. Harry stepped back, but pointed to the lock on the door, asking her to open it. He retreated another step into the snow as she shoved the door open and climbed out.

"Damn it, Harry, you need to announce yourself." She slammed the door and swatted his shoulder. Now that she was standing and facing him, he could see she'd been crying. Even her glasses—blue this time, a shade lighter than her eyes—couldn't hide the puffy redness behind the lenses. With a noisy harrumph, she grabbed the front of his coat and pulled him out of the snow bank before venting her emotions with another painless swat. "This is the second time your surprise visits have nearly given me a heart attack. Why don't you call first?"

"I was worried." The suspicion that had brought him out of his truck twisted in his gut at the sight of those crystallized tears drying on her cheeks. "People don't sit in their car for fifteen minutes without going someplace unless something is wrong. Besides, I couldn't call. I don't have your number."

He wasn't going to get it, either. Her little fit of temper vanished with an unladylike curse. "Fifteen minutes? It's been that long?" She opened the door again and reached inside to drag her heavy pink bag over the console. "I have to let the dogs out and then be back at school in an hour. I'd like to eat something and change out of these clothes."

She looped the bag over her shoulder and hiked it onto her hip so she could reach back inside to pull her keys from the ignition. But the bag slipped and the door tried to close, and when she jostled between them a wadded-up card fell out of her pocket and bounced across the concrete to land beside his boot. Harry bent down to pick it up, catching a glimpse of green sparkles in the shape of a Christmas tree and… "What the hell?" He smoothed the wrinkled card stock in his palm, ignoring the pornographic artwork to read the threat typed underneath it. "First you've got some guy peeking in your bedroom window and now this crap? Is it the same guy? Have you gotten other garbage like this from him?"

Dots of pink colored her cheeks and she snatched it away. He'd take that as a yes. She stuffed the card into her pocket and hurried through the back gate.

Harry followed right behind her, demanding answers. "Daisy, where did that come from? Who sent it to you? An angry student?"

"I don't know."

"You don't know who sent you that filth?"

She spun around to face him when she reached the deck. "If I did, don't you think I'd put a stop to it?" She looked down on him from the top step. "What are you doing here, anyway? Don't you have a life?"

He didn't, actually. A wry sigh clouded the air around him. "I'm home on leave for six weeks. I don't have anything to do except hang around Hope's apartment and make her worry. The Corps gives me a job to do every day. Here in Kansas City I'm going nuts. Nothing to do but think and walk and think some more."

"I'm a project for you? A hobby to keep you busy?"

He wondered if that hurtful note of sarcasm in her tone was aimed at him or herself. "You're a friend." The women in those letters was even more important to him. "Something's going on and I can help by keeping an eye on things."

"You've been watching my house all day?"

Except for that hour he'd met with Dr. Polk. "Pretty much. I walked around the neighborhood a little bit. In the daylight, I found where the guy was standing when he used your house for target practice last night." He moved past her up the steps and pointed over to the neighbor's house. "That guy's backyard. I missed the tracks last night because of the shrubs, but once I got over the fence—"

"You trespassed in Mr. Finch's yard?" She joined him at the railing.

Could the threat be that close to home? "You got issues with your neighbor?"

"No. It's just—he's so compulsive about his yard and taking care of things. You didn't knock any leaves off his boxwood bushes, did you? Or dent the top of the fence? Patch dug under the fence last summer, tore up some of the roots—"

"You've got somebody stalking you, Daisy." He pounded his fist against the top of the railing. "I wouldn't worry about the damn shrubbery!"

His outburst shocked her. Hell, he hadn't raised his voice like that for weeks now. Watching her clutch the strap of her bag over her chest and retreat from him, he wished he'd been able to control his frustrated concerns. The dogs were barking inside the mudroom and her back was pressed against the door. Her eyes never left his. "I'm sorry. The last thing I want to do is be the person who scares you." That muscle ticked beneath his eye as he buried the useless rage inside him where it belonged. He put his hands up and stepped back, suspecting where her mind had gone and hating himself for taking her there. "I remember you said your ex was violent. I swear I would never hurt you." He shook his head as he heard the words leave his mouth. "That's probably what your ex said, too."

"Actually…" He held himself still as he waited for her

to finish that sentence, praying she didn't believe he was as messed up as the man who'd stabbed her. He prayed even harder that she'd be right. "Brock promised that he *would* hurt me if I left him." She pushed her glasses up at her temple, the action making him think she wanted to make sure she was seeing Harry clearly, evaluating him. "He was too controlling. Obsessive. I had to break it off so I could have a life. Rescue dogs. Stay after school with students. Visit my parents and friends. He was drunk that night he broke into my apartment." She dropped her hand to clutch the strap of her bag again. "He kept his promise."

Harry's hands curled into fists again. With the violence he'd seen, it was far too easy to picture how she'd been hurt. But knowing his response should be his issue, not hers, he blanked the images—both real and imagined—and drew in several breaths of the cold winter air to chill the anger simmering through his veins. "Could he have anything to do with those messages?"

"Brock is in prison."

"You know that for a fact? He doesn't have friends on the outside who might be willing to do some dirty work for him?" Daisy was wilting, like a colorful flower that he'd just sprayed with pesticide. He stuffed his hands into his coat pockets and leaned his hip against the railing, hoping the relaxed posture made him look a little less intimidating, a little more like the friend he meant to be. "Look, I know I'm short on tact and charm, and I've got issues with PTSD that I can't always control. But I protect people for a living. I know how to get a job done. I'm trained to assess the enemy. I know how to scout a perimeter and keep the people I'm guarding safe." He looked away, needing a break from those searching blue eyes. "Right now, I'm trying to protect you. I'm not bothering anybody by keeping an eye on your place. And clearly, somebody's trying to bother *you*. Let me do this." When she didn't answer, he faced her again. "You said you didn't have anybody."

"You feel you owe me this protection because of those letters?" He wouldn't deny it. But he was here for other reasons, too, ones that were too difficult to put into words right now. "I can't have somebody around me whom I can't trust."

"I'm the man in those letters, Daisy. I promise. You can trust me with your life." Maybe he couldn't promise her anything else, but that much he would guarantee. If she'd let him. "I'm here now. Use me."

She considered his vow for several moments before she nodded. She turned away to unlock the door. "It's been a long day and I'm tired, and I have no time to rest. I'm probably extra sensitive to probing questions and hot tempers." Not to mention receiving that message, which had clearly unnerved her. The dogs darted out, circling around her with wagging tails for a warm greeting. Once they'd been sufficiently petted by their mistress, they trotted over to greet him. Seeing Patch prop his front paws against his thigh and Caliban push his head into Harry's hand while Muffy tried to squeeze between the other two dogs seemed to reassure Daisy more than any words he could utter. "I'd be lying if I said I didn't appreciate you keeping an eye on things. I felt safer last night after you left."

Instincts took over the dogs' need for affection and they trotted down the steps to explore the yard. Harry followed Daisy inside the mudroom and stomped the snow off his boots while she hung her coat and bag on a hook.

But when he pulled off his gloves and watch cap and followed her into the hallway, she stopped him with a hand at the middle of his chest, straightening her arm to keep him from coming any farther into the house. He wasn't used to Daisy needing space. In the twenty-four hours since they'd met face to face, she hadn't once been this eager to put some distance between them. He should relish her backing off from all the touchy-feely stuff that bamboozled him.

But now, it only made him worry. "I thought you were okay with me being here."

She pulled her hand away. "Would you make sure the dogs do their business and get some exercise while I change my clothes?"

Harry hesitated a moment, both in leaving her and in being alone with the dogs. But he'd made a career out of doing what needed to be done. "I can do that."

"Thanks." She reached for his hand and gave it a friendly squeeze. Why hadn't he noticed sooner that she had a beautiful smile?

He reversed the grip to hold on to her when she would have pulled away. "And then you're going to tell me what's going on. I want to know how many other threats you've received and when they started. I need to know your schedule, where you'll be and when, and I need to know if there's anyone you suspect."

Smile killer.

Seemed he had a habit of doing that with this woman.

"Daisy, I…" Another verbal apology didn't seem sufficient. And he couldn't just tell her things would be okay because he knew far too well how *not* okay the world could be. Obeying an impulse that felt as right as it was unexpected, Harry tugged on Daisy's hand, pulling her up against his chest and wrapping his arms around her in one of those hugs she seemed to like so well. He turned his nose against the clinging static of her hair and breathed in that sweet scent that was hers alone.

He patted her back a few times, until he thought he heard a soft giggle. Daisy relaxed against him, slipping her arms beneath his coat and flattening them against his back.

She rubbed her palms up and down his spine in strokes that warmed his skin through his sweater and soothed the guilt and concern tensing every muscle. Harry stopped patting and started mimicking the caressing motion up and down her back. He felt pretty lame for not having much experience with comforting embraces, but he felt pretty lucky, too, that Daisy was making the effort to help him improve his skills. And he was a quick study, down to the curve of her hip, up beneath the silken weight of her brown and purple hair.

Idly, Harry wondered how the sensations of curves and gentle heat would change without the ribs of her sweater and wrinkled blouse between his hands and her skin. An interested party stirred behind the zipper of his jeans at the idea of touching Daisy's warm skin. He'd like to kiss her, too, to see if those lips were as soft and luscious as they looked—to find out if they'd respond with the same bold enthusiasm of her hugs or be more like the gentle tutelage of her hands. His whole body thrummed with anticipation as he rubbed his lips against her temple, kissing the earpiece of her glasses before adjusting his aim to press his lips against the warm beat of her pulse there. Daisy's arms tightened around him, aligning her body more perfectly against his. Her breasts pillowed against his chest and the tips beaded into pearls that poked through the layers of clothing separating them, making his palms itch to touch those, too.

"Why do I get the feeling you haven't had much of this kind of contact, Top?" she murmured against his neck. "Which is a shame because you're good at it." She added the undeserved compliment, reminding him that while he'd had sex, he'd never once been in a relationship with a woman. Not long distance and certainly not up close and personal like this.

But this was Daisy, his pen pal angel and long-distance friend, and she was scared. He might even be a big part of what scared her. This wasn't the time to give in to curiosity and crude impulses. Right now, all he needed was for her to be safe.

Reluctantly, he loosened his grip on her, turning his head to kiss the same spot on her hair. But never one to be demure or predictable, Daisy lifted her chin and caught his lips with hers. The kiss was surprising, but not so brief that he didn't have a moment to press his mouth over hers, confirming at least one of his speculations. Her lips were as soft and succulent as he'd imagined. And he wanted to kiss her again.

Daisy dropped back onto her heels and pulled away before he fully acknowledged that impulse. "You gonna be okay?" he asked.

She was smiling again when she nodded, and his chest swelled. Yeah. There was a lot to be said for trading hugs and comfort. He didn't feel quite so guilty about stealing that smile away in the first place.

He tugged his hat back over his short hair and pulled on his gloves. "I'll go take care of the dogs."

Chapter Six

"One hot dog with ketchup and extra relish."

Daisy closed the money box and stamped the hands of the three students who'd paid their fee at her table outside the Central Prep gym, encouraging them to enjoy the games before accepting the dinner Harry offered. "I'm starving. Thank you." She took a big bite, savoring the tangy flavors before nodding toward the bottles of soda in Harry's hands. "You're not hungry?"

"Already finished mine." He set one of the sodas on the table and pulled a paper napkin from the pocket of his jeans. He reached over and wiped a dribble of ketchup and pickle juice from the side of her mouth, showing her the stain on the napkin before she snatched it from his fingers. "Why doesn't it surprise me to discover you have a healthy appetite?"

Daisy turned away, feeling the heat of embarrassment creeping into her cheeks. She wiped her mouth a second time before facing him again. "I haven't eaten since lunch, and that was seven hours ago."

"I'm not criticizing." His bottle hissed as he twisted the cap and released the carbonation pressure. "Just observing. You don't do anything halfway. Decorating for Christmas. Hugs. Eating hot dogs."

"Are you sure you're not making fun of me?" Daisy took a daintier bite this time.

"No, ma'am."

She arched an eyebrow. "We talked about that, Master Sergeant."

"Ouch." For a split second, his stiff mouth crooked into a smile. But then there was a big roar from the crowd in the gym as someone on the junior varsity team made an exciting play. Harry's alert gaze darted through the doorway toward the bleachers. A muscle tightened across his angular cheekbone before he swallowed a drink of soda and brought his gaze back to hers. "No more fancy titles for you and me. In my defense, though, we are back at school. Technically, you're on duty."

Daisy wadded up her napkin and tossed it at him. He deftly caught it and tossed it into the trash can beside the table. Although this familiar camaraderie had settled between them, not unlike the conversation they'd shared in their long-distance letters, Daisy felt raw inside. Harry had insisted he drive her to school, and for a man so averse to long conversations, he'd had plenty of questions to ask about her Secret Santa. At his insistence, she'd unlocked her classroom to show him the gifts hidden inside her desk, as well as her mailbox in the teachers' lounge where most of the messages and gifts had been delivered. Seemingly immune to the curious stares at his scarred face, he'd asked her to introduce him to several coworkers, glossing over thank-yous for his service to the country and turning the conversations around to learn a little more about Principal Hague, Eddie Bosch and Mary Gamblin.

Despite security protocols that were in place to protect the school from outside threats, access to her inside the school was too easy, he'd complained. And she was too isolated at home for him to deem either place safe. Although she'd teased him about his natural talent for bringing down the mood of a room, the underlying truth to his words had left her feeling unsettled. His advice that she be hypervigilant to her surroundings, avoid being alone or even one-on-one with any of the male students or faculty in the building, and report anyone lurking near her classroom or faculty workroom to the principal made her that much more edgy and distrustful of the people she interacted with nearly every day of her life.

Two weeks ago, before the first message had been delivered, she'd been content to surround herself with students and work. She was a social creature by nature. She was proud of her school, liked her students and coworkers, reveled in the holiday season, loved being busy and doing for others.

But tonight, despite her spirited blue and gold facade, all she wanted was to go home to her dogs and lock her doors. She couldn't say whether it was Harry's reserved, imposing presence, casting suspicion in a wide net around her, or the fact this damaged yet fit, virile man was enduring his aversion to the crowd to not only protect her, but to also be kind to her, that left her feeling so off-kilter this evening.

"Daisy."

She hadn't realized how far into her troubling thoughts she'd sunk until Harry spoke her name and nodded toward the group jostling for position on the opposite side of the table.

Complete with two sets of grandparents, two elementary-aged children and a curly-haired toddler who was fussing to climb down from her mother's arms and explore, the family's arrival required Daisy to focus on her job. After calculating the discounts, she gave them the price for their tickets, even splitting the cost in half for them when both grandfathers insisted on paying.

By the time she finished counting back their change and stamping hands, Daisy realized the little girl had stopped squirming and was staring at Harry. Harry was staring right back. In that grim, clenched-jaw look that made the muscle beneath his right eye spasm. The little girl smiled and pointed at Harry. "Bomba No-man."

"Abominable Snowman?" The mother saw where her daughter was pointing, and pulled her hand away. "I'm sorry. You must remind her of a character in one of those animated Christmas shows she watches."

"Not a problem, ma'am," Harry reassured her. "I've been called worse."

But it *was* a problem. Even as the family moved into the gym to find seats on the bleachers, Harry was retreating against the cinder block wall behind him. She heard the plastic of his soda bottle cracking as he squeezed it in his hand.

However, pointing out the disfiguring scars didn't seem to bother him as much as the noise. The referees blew their whistles and the timeout buzzer sounded. The pep band struck up an enthusiastic rendition of the school fight song. That muscle ticked across Harry's cheek and he turned his head as if the cacophony hurt his ears.

"Are you okay?" She took a drink, trying to hide how much his charged, yet overtly still, posture worried her. She gestured to the metal chair beside hers. "You can sit if you want."

"I'm better standing." So he could make a quicker getaway if he had to, no doubt.

With no one waiting in line for tickets, Daisy sat on the edge of the table, facing him. "You said you suffer from PTSD. Do the loud noises bother you?

Harry's dark gray eyes scanned the lobby, from the glimpse inside the gym to the line waiting at the concession stand. "A basketball game is not going to make me freak out."

"But other things will?"

His gaze landed on her. He hesitated a moment before dropping his volume and answering. "Sometimes a loud bang will trigger memories. Your dogs charging at me last night kind of…" He twirled his fingers beside his head, indicating some kind of flashback, she supposed. "Usually it's the smells that are the worst."

"Like what?" More than once, she'd caught him sniffing her hair. And she'd already memorized his unique scent, undoctored by any aftershave or cologne. He must be particularly sensitive to certain odors. "Do you smell anything here?"

He rolled his shoulders as if his sweater was suddenly uncomfortably tight. "This isn't the place for that kind of conversation."

"Maybe when we get home. You could stay for a while." Daisy pushed to her feet, needing to touch him to comfort him somehow. She reached for his free hand and squeezed his fingers. "Do you need to talk about it? I could make us some hot chocolate and stay up as late as you need to. You mentioned things in your letters—like you needed to get them off your chest. I don't claim to understand everything you've been through, but I do know a little about how horrible the world can be."

He stared at her hard for a moment, muttering something about an angel that she couldn't quite make out over the squeaks of rubber-soled shoes on the polished gymnasium floor.

"I've got a therapist for those kinds of talks." Harry's

grip pulsed around her hand. "I'm not interested in making you cry anymore."

Daisy leaned in, matching his hushed tone. "Even if I did, it would be all right. If I can help... I want to."

"Are you asking this guy for a favor, too?"

Recognizing the smug woman's voice behind her, Daisy plopped her forehead against Harry's chest for a moment and audibly groaned. Then she released his hand and turned to the statuesque blonde in a coat most likely from a pricey boutique. "Excuse me?"

Stella Riley, resident trophy wife and all-around ego buster as far as Daisy was concerned. Stella grinned, waving off what had sounded like an accusation. "I'm just teasing. Bernie said you'd asked for his help."

"With a student."

"Is this your new gentleman friend? Bernie thought you might have met someone, but that you were keeping him a secret." The woman extended her hand across the table. "Hi. I'm Stella, Coach Riley's wife."

"Basketball coach," Daisy whispered, explaining the pronouncement. While part of her wanted to correct the assumption that Harry was her boyfriend, she also knew this conversation would end sooner if she just let Stella say what she wanted to and move on.

Daisy startled at the brush of Harry's fingers against the small of her back. Was he reassuring her? Or grounding himself? He tossed his empty bottle into the trash before shaking Stella's hand. "Harry Lockhart."

"Military, right?"

"Yes, ma'am. Marine Corps."

"I could tell by the haircut." She winked before releasing him. "It suits you. We're proud of you boys. And we're all glad that Daisy has found someone again." Stella pulled her ID card out of her wallet and flashed it at Daisy. "Not that you need this to know who I am. But I want to follow the rules."

"You're good to go, Stella." Daisy had a hard time zeroing in on Stella's name on the list of faculty and spouses who got in free because Harry's palm had slipped beneath the hem of her gold cardigan and flattened against her back. Daisy felt the brand of his touch through her blouse as surely as the stamp she inked onto Stella's hand.

Stella tipped her blond curls toward the gym. "How's it going?"

"I haven't been able to check the score yet, but there's lots of cheering, so I'm guessing pretty well."

"Great. Bernie will be in a good mood, then." Stella's wave included both Harry and Daisy. "Nice to meet you, soldier boy. Don't be a stranger. I'll see you next week, Daisy. If you need any help with the party, let me know."

"That was like a tornado blowing through," Harry muttered, absentmindedly rubbing his hand in small circles against her spine. "Is she a friend of yours?"

Whether soothing her taut nerves or assuaging his own, Daisy had to step away from his distracting touch so she could think of words to speak. "She *is* first lady of the basketball court. When the team has a winning season, I guess she deserves some of the credit, too."

"You didn't answer my question."

"I work with her husband."

"Still not an answer." Daisy busied herself straightening the items on the table. "You know, other people say bad things about people. You're too big-hearted to do that, aren't you? The fact that you won't makes me think there's some friction between you and the first lady."

Daisy stopped her busy work. "I never have understood people who think they're all that. It feels like I'm back in high school whenever I'm around her. Of course, maybe if I'd been one of the popular kids back then instead of an artsy geek, I might feel differently."

"Still avoiding the question, Ms. Geek."

"I liked you better when you wouldn't talk to me."

Harry laughed. Although far too brief, his laugh was a rich, chest-deep sound that made her smile. She adjusted her glasses to see the pliant side of his mouth smiling, too.

A hundred little wishes locked up inside her heart unfurled at the knowledge she'd put that smile there. "Maybe her snootiness stems from insecurity. I imagine she's alone a lot during basketball season with all the games and practices. Sometimes, I think she's jealous that other people get to spend more time with her husband than she does."

Harry's smile vanished as quickly as it had appeared. "How jealous?"

"Jealous enough to send me those threats?" Daisy shook her head. While she'd never felt especially comfortable around Stella Riley, she couldn't see any reason for the woman to have a personal grudge against her. "Those have to be from a guy. Right?"

Harry wasn't probing for answers anymore. He was moving to intercept the tall young black man who circled around the table.

"Now you got Coach Riley callin' my granny on me?" Albert Logan's Central Prep ball cap was cocked off to the side, giving him a deceptively juvenile look. But there was nothing childlike about the anger in his expression. "Ain't 'Lo man enough for you? You want to give me some private tutoring, too? Let's do it, Ms. G."

Daisy planted her feet, cringing at his grammar and hating the innuendo in his tone. "Not if you're going to talk to me like that. I'll report you to Mr. Hague. This isn't a punishment. We're concerned about you, Albert."

"You stay out of my business, or I'm gonna get all up in yours."

The moment Albert's pointing finger got too close, Harry palmed the teenager's shoulder and pushed him away, sliding between her and Albert.

Albert knocked the restraining hand away. "Get your hands off me, old man."

Harry squared off against the bigger, younger man. Although she couldn't see Harry's face, she could read every wary line of tension in his muscular stance. There were rules against touching students. Harry wasn't staff, but this standoff could escalate in a heartbeat if he thought he had to protect her.

"It's okay, Harry." She closed her hand over his rock-hard bicep, knowing she had to reach him with words and touch because there'd be no way she could physically restrain him. She splayed her other hand against his back, remembering how distracting his touch had been to her just a few minutes earlier. "This is Albert Logan, a former student of mine." With Harry's hands fisting at his sides, she appealed to Albert, as well. "Master Sergeant Lockhart is my pen pal from last year's writing project. He's home on leave."

"Take a step back," Harry warned. His muscles vibrated with tension beneath her fingers.

"Albert, please. I don't want to call the principal."

Albert glanced back and forth between the two of them, considering how a confrontation with Harry would play out, then wisely decided to retreat a step. Curiosity replaced the wounded pride and anger that had puffed up his posture, reminding Daisy that in many ways, these nearly grown students were still just big kids. Albert rubbed his knuckles across his cheek. "Dude, did that happen to you over there?"

The poised wariness didn't waver. "Yes."

"Was it a car bomb?"

"Albert…"

Picking up on subtle clues had never been Albert's strong suit. "You know Corporal Benny Garcia?" he asked. "That's the guy I wrote to. When I still had Ms. G for class. He drove one of those armored cars."

"I knew Garcia." *Knew?* Harry's shoulders lifted with a deep breath. "He drove an LAV—Light Armored Vehicle."

Compassion squeezed Daisy's heart. Was Albert hearing any of those past-tense references? She curled her fingers into the back of Harry's sweater, wishing they were in a less public place so she could wind her arms around his waist.

"Yeah. He used a bunch of initials I didn't understand. But it was cool when he talked about the motor and stuff." Albert's dark gaze suddenly shifted to her. "Angelo know you got a boyfriend, Ms. G?"

Why was everyone assuming that she and Harry were an item? Then she saw the way she had latched on to Harry, and the way he'd blocked her into a corner between the table and wall, defending her. Was there some unacknowledged longing she was projecting out into the universe that everyone but her could see?

"Who is Angelo?"

Albert dragged his focus back to Harry. "'Lo's my brother. He's playing tonight. He and Ms. G… He…" He glanced to her, looking for what? He knew exactly what kind of relationship she had with his brother. Was he hinting at something else? "Uh…"

"I'm helping Angelo with his scholarship applications. He's one of my best students. I think Albert could be, too."

Apparently satisfied with Albert's family history, Harry gave a curt nod and switched topics. "Where I come from, a man doesn't wear his cover inside. His hat," he explained, when Albert frowned. "And he speaks to a woman with respect. I suggest you do the same."

Albert shrugged. "Okay."

"Okay, what?"

"Okay, sir?"

Harry eyed the sideways hat until Albert pulled it off and stuffed the brim in the back pocket of his jeans. "Now we understand each other."

Instead of acting chastised, Albert grinned. "Benny said you were a tough son-of-a…" He glanced at Daisy, watched Harry's stance change, and thought better of finishing that phrase. "Benny respects you, sir."

"It was mutual."

Albert looked at Daisy and shrugged. "Sorry, Ms. G. Granny said I had to check in with you Monday before I go to work. Just don't call her no more."

"Anymore," Daisy automatically corrected.

"Yeah. She's scarier than both of you put together." The whole confrontation forgotten, Albert whistled to a couple of friends and joined them in line at the concession stand.

Harry dropped his gaze where her hand still clung to his arm. "Afraid I was going to take him out?"

She released her grip. "Were you?"

"I know I'm not surrounded by insurgents." His breathing seemed a little labored, though, when he faced her. "But you don't let them get close like that unless you know them. I didn't know that kid. The way he was coming at you…"

She wanted to ask about Corporal Garcia, find out if he'd lost his friend in an enemy attack. She desperately wanted to wind her arms around him and hold on until that tightly leashed tension quaking through his body eased.

But the buzzer sounded, marking the end of the first

basketball game. Fans cheered. The band played again, loud even to her own ears. A swarm of students and families spilled through the archway, flooding the lobby between the JV and varsity games. Harry muttered the very curse he'd kept Albert from saying and grabbed his coat from beneath the table.

"Are you okay?" Daisy moved to keep his face in sight, worried he was having some kind of meltdown. "This is too much for you, isn't it."

"I need some fresh air." He was struggling. His eyes were clear, but they locked on to hers while he zipped up, as if focusing on her, and not the people gathering in the space around them, centered him. Fine. She'd be still and let him focus. "I better call Hope and let her know where I am. She worries more than she needs to, and that's not good for the baby. Besides, I'd like to familiarize myself with the layout of the school grounds. I want to know every way somebody could get in or out."

Daisy understood his sister's need to worry. She sensed it was taking every bit of strength he had not to explode. "Will you be coming back?"

"I'm your ride home, aren't I? I just need to move. I'll probably run a couple laps around the building."

"Through the snow?"

"I like the cold." His fingers were unsteady when he threaded them into the hair at her temple and smoothed the waves down behind her ear. He cupped the side of her neck and jaw, and the trembling stilled. Daisy turned into his touch. With his heat warming her skin, her concerns ebbed to a less frantic pitch, and she hoped he was taking at least the same from her. "When you're ready to leave, go to the front door. I'll watch for you. You don't step foot outside until I'm here to walk you out, okay?"

"Okay."

His fingertips tightened against her skin. "I mean it, Dais."

She smiled. "Okay, *sir.*"

His eyes widened for a split second at her sass. And then he was leaning in, kissing her. The press of his lips was firm, their movement stilted, but urgent enough to demand her response. The tip of his tongue moistened the point of contact between them with a raspy caress, but retreated before she could catch it. Harry's kiss was not quite chaste and over far too quick. Slightly breathless, she was still clinging to his bottom lip when he pulled away. His eyes had darkened like charcoal, and she wondered which of them was swaying on their feet.

Without a word, Harry released his grip and turned away. He darted through the crowd and disappeared out the double front doors into the night.

PDA might be frowned upon on school property, but Daisy wasn't complaining. The warmth of that surprising kiss stayed with her the rest of the evening. And though she kept one eye on the door, even when she stood in the archway to watch the last few minutes of the second game, Harry never came back. She hoped he'd snuck in to get some hot coffee instead of waiting for her out in the cold for an hour. But she was half afraid that the run-in with Albert, the noise and energy of the crowd, or even the kiss itself had frightened him off.

She had no doubts that he was still out there, waiting to drive her home, making sure she was safe. But she was sad for him that it was so hard to relax and enjoy himself for very long. And she was antsy to get back to him to see if they could recreate a little of that one-on-one magic where they joked with each other, and touched and cared and kissed.

That was why Daisy had the money counted down and locked up inside the office before the final buzzer sounded.

While the building cleared, she did a quick walk-through of the gymnasium bleachers with Eddie and Mary, picking up trash while the custodian swept the floor. She kept her distance from the heated conversation between Bernie and Stella Riley outside the boys' locker room, quickly diverting her attention when both their gazes landed on her. "What did I do?" she whispered to Eddie before dumping the stack of paper cups she'd collected into the trash bag he carried.

"Who knows?" Eddie shrugged. "Sometimes I think that woman's even jealous of me. And Bernie's certainly not *my* type."

Daisy wanted to laugh, but couldn't. "That's sad that she's so insecure. I know Bernie's got an ego the size of Arrowhead Stadium, but has he ever really cheated on her?"

Mary climbed down the bleachers to add her trash to the bag. "I heard that she's the one who cheated on him, in college, before they got married."

Daisy tuned out the bickering couple and headed toward the lobby. "Whatever their issues are, I wish they'd leave me out of it."

The band parents who'd been working the concession stand for their booster club fundraiser had cleaned up their area and locked the serving window partition by the time she said goodbye to Eddie and Mary. Eddie made sure Harry was still there to drive her home before escorting Mary out to her car. Mr. Hague was doing a walk-around to make sure all the doors were locked. The players and the opposing team members would leave by the locker room entrance. Daisy was alone in the lobby when she realized the chairs and table from gate duty had been left out.

It wouldn't take her five minutes to fold up the chairs and take them down to the basement storage room. The table would be a two-person project to carry down the steps, but by the time she put away the folding chairs, either the custodian would be finished or Mr. Hague would be back, and they could help. Then she'd be done with her assignment and she could get to Harry and that private conversation and maybe even another kiss.

She stuck her keys into the pocket of her jeans, then pulled out her phone. She had a split-second idea to call Harry in to have him help her, but just as quickly she realized she didn't have his number. Was it too late to call Hope and ask for it? That seemed silly when it'd be quicker to run outside and ask Harry herself. But he'd insisted that she not leave the building without him. He said he'd be watching the front doors. She could step outside and wave…

"Stop overthinking this, Daisy Lou." She stuffed her phone into another pocket. "Just finish up and go."

Tossing her coat over her bag, she picked up the chairs. Using one of her school keys, she unlocked the metal gate blocking off the stairs from the public and pushed it open. She carried the folding chairs down the concrete steps and descended half a century into the past. The long gray hallway was broken up by four heavy steel doors. Hung on runners like an old barn door, these doors simply unlatched and slid open. After the boiler room, the rest of the doors led to old classrooms from the original building before state regulations and a school improvement bond had required a new facility be built around the old one. With the original windows enclosed by new construction, the storage rooms doubled as tornado shelters now.

She pulled on the latch of the second metal door and shoved it off to the right, cringing at the grinding whine of metal on metal. The keyless latches were a throwback to the original building, too, before terrorists and school shootings made it vital that every school could be locked down to keep intruders out. After flipping on the light switch, she carried the chairs over to the closest of several racks lined up against the far wall. After setting the chairs into place, Daisy glanced around her. Metal racks with metal chairs. Gray concrete walls. In a basement. With no windows.

She shivered. This level was uninviting enough in the daytime. No natural light. No color. No warmth. At night, it felt even colder, despite the boiler room cranking out heat next door. If she ever had to teach a full day down here in this tomb, the powers that be would be carrying her out in a straitjacket. She was more than happy to pay a few extra cents on her taxes to have two whole floors of bright, well-lit rooms above her.

Metal grated against metal behind her. Daisy turned to see the last few inches of hallway disappear as the door slammed with an ominous clank. "Hey! I'm in here."

She heard a second clank as she dashed across the room.

What was going on? Daisy pushed on the latch and stumbled into the door when nothing happened. "No," she whispered, pumping the latch a half dozen times with the same result. Nothing was catching inside the locking mechanism to release the door. She pulled on the latch even though the metal clearly said *Push*. She tried sliding the door along its runner, in case the latch was the only problem. But the heavy steel wasn't budging. "This isn't funny," she yelled, slapping the flat of her hand against the door.

She was locked in.

Had the custodian or Mr. Hague not seen the light and carelessly closed the door? Was this a practical joke? Not funny. She pounded on the door, pushed the broken latch. "Let me out of here!"

Daisy drifted back a step, feeling suddenly light-headed. Could someone have locked her in on purpose?

Then she heard noises that locked her breath up in her chest and turned her blood to ice.

Scratching against the metal. Something heavy being dragged across the floor. Someone breathing harder with the exertion. Whoever had locked her in was still there.

Her Secret Santa.

"Who are you?" she demanded. A pungent odor stung her nose. "Why are you doing this to me?"

She backed away even farther when the person on the other side refused to respond. Tamping down the fear that scattered her thoughts, she remembered her cell and pulled it from her pocket. "I'm calling the police," she warned.

As soon as the screen lit up, she said a prayer of thanks for good cell service and punched in 9-1-1.

Everything went quiet on the other side of the door as the call connected. "That's right. *You* be afraid this time."

But her bravado was short-lived.

The silent person on the other side nudged a familiar piece of cardstock beneath the door at her feet. White, with a sparkly green Christmas tree, and three words staring up at her.

Ho. Ho. Ho.

The 9-1-1 dispatcher answered the call, but Daisy couldn't speak.

The sick torment of another message wasn't the only thing coming from beneath the door.

Daisy blinked away the tears burning her eyes.

Smoke.

Chapter Seven

Harry rubbed his gloved hands together, keeping them warm as the visiting team's bus left the parking lot. He was more of a football guy than a basketball fan, but he knew enough about high-school sports to know the players and their coaches were generally the last people to leave the building. He bounced on the balls of his feet as two more cars followed the bus onto the main road. That left just his truck, a van and two other vehicles in the nearly empty parking lot.

"Come on, Daisy."

The images of how some sicko wanted to hurt her made his skin crawl. The bad joke gifts, graphic pictures and Peeping Tom all said coward to him. Daisy's stalker wasn't brave enough to confront her face-to-face. But he sure seemed to be getting off on scaring her, on watching her from afar and savoring how his psychological terror campaign controlled her life. He didn't understand enough about profiling to know whether her stalker had some skewed idea of love for her, or if this obsession was some kind of punishment.

But a coward like that could become unpredictable in a heartbeat if he thought his control over her was slipping—just like Daisy's ex. She'd been brutally honest in one of her letters about the night her ex had come after her with a knife. She'd wanted Harry to know that she could deal with the things he'd shared with her, that she was a survivor and that she was stronger for it. But a woman like Daisy, with such zest for people and life, should never be punished or controlled like that. Acid churned in the pit of his stomach at the thought of someone hurting her like that again.

He'd never thought he'd be stepping up for guard duty for a chatty, compassionate free spirit. For months now, he'd focused solely on fixing himself—and that project wasn't complete yet. Did he really think he had what it took to keep Daisy safe?

Like right now, Harry had a bad feeling about the number of vehicles left in the parking lot.

But then he was the one whose head wasn't on straight. He had a bad feeling about almost everything these days, seeing an enemy where there was none. He knew the van belonged to the custodian on duty tonight because the guy had come out for a cigarette during the second game. The well-appointed Cadillac must belong to the principal. Harry had seen him at more than one door, locking up. The other car could be abandoned for all he knew. It had a yellow sticker on the windshield, so it belonged to someone who worked at or went to the school.

He stopped at the front of his truck again. Although he couldn't see any movement through the bank of glass doors at the front of the building, the lights were still on inside the lobby and gymnasium, so chances were that Daisy was just fine.

He probably shouldn't have left her alone for this long. But the crowd and cheers and drums had been too much for him. That kid, Albert, had been ticked off with Daisy. Wounded pride over some school problem. Harry's instinct was to intervene—to keep the danger at bay before he had to become a part of it. But then Albert had mentioned

Benny Garcia, and that had taken him right back to the middle of that last firefight, and he knew he was losing it.

Lt. Col. Biro was right. He wasn't much use to anybody in this condition. A wounded warrior. Damaged goods. He had a Purple Heart and a Silver Star, but he couldn't handle teenage smart-assery and a noisy basketball game.

If he was at Hope's apartment with his duffel bag, he'd be pulling out one of Daisy's letters right about now. He'd read her words and feel her caring. He'd cool his jets and come back to the normal land of the living. At least, as normal as he could get.

This time, instead of reading the words and letting his angel lift him out of his mental hellhole, Harry's thoughts drifted back to myopic blue eyes and a beautiful smile. The real Daisy Gunderson was a far cry from the woman he'd imagined. But different meant just that—not any better or worse. And *different* hadn't stopped him when the noise and the stress had gotten to be too much, and he'd anchored his senses on her luscious, irresistible mouth. He'd kissed her. Not a peck on the lips like the thank-you she'd given him at her house that afternoon. A real kiss. He hadn't been sure he could still kiss a woman. But the need had been too powerful to resist.

He hoped his damaged nerves and scar tissue hadn't completely grossed her out because Daisy had been wonderful. He'd felt her mouth soften under his. He'd tasted her. He'd felt her response through every surviving nerve ending and deeper inside in places that had nothing to do with nerves.

Selfishly saving himself by coming to Kansas City and meeting her in person had become doing a favor for a friend. And now looking out for Daisy was becoming something…selfish again. So much for putting his ideal Ms. G. up on a pedestal. For a few blissful seconds, he'd forgotten everything except his desire to kiss that beautiful mouth.

A smoother operator in a less public place would have deepened that kiss. A man who was a little less *abominable* and little more sure this unplanned attraction he felt was mutual would have pulled Daisy into his arms and pushed her up against that wall to feel every inch of those curves and grasping hands while he plundered her heavenly soft mouth. Those unexpectedly heated thoughts about all the ways he wanted to kiss Daisy had required a third hike through the snow to ease the ill-timed fantasies about the earthy, purple-haired temptress and the embarrassing hard-on they'd aroused.

He hadn't felt like that much of a man in months. He hadn't felt that kind of normal. He hadn't felt such a deep connection to another human being since opening that first letter overseas all those months ago.

And already he felt like that connection was fading.

"Come to the damn door, woman." The wintry night air was moving past being a healing remedy and was becoming a nose-numbing reminder that he'd been out here far too long without having any contact with her.

Harry pulled out his phone to call her and swore. He'd known Daisy for almost a year and a half and had been with her most of the past twenty-four hours—and he'd never once remembered to get her phone number. Not very slick. Or practical.

He was scrolling through information on his phone, looking for the Central Prep Academy number when he heard the first siren in the distance.

If an empty parking lot had given him a bad feeling, the sinuous noise of two more sirens cutting through the crisp night air was telling him to trust that feeling. "Daisy?"

A shrill, uninterrupted ringing from a much closer source jerked him around. Fire alarm. "Daisy!"

He needed her with him. Now.

Harry pulled a crowbar from the toolbox behind the seat of his truck. He ran to the front doors, tried two of them, but they were both locked. He didn't bother with the third or fourth door. He jammed the crowbar between the door and frame and forced it open. He'd probably just triggered another alarm in the office or at a nearby police station. But he knew he could use the backup the moment the door swung open and he dashed through the vestibule. A thin, gray haze hung in the air, stinging his sinuses with the distinctive smell of smoke. The memory of an explosion went off inside his head, but he clenched his jaw, forbidding the nightmare to seize hold of his thoughts. No Tango. No bomb. He was home in Kansas City. The damn school was on fire and Daisy was in it.

Harry surveyed the lobby and saw no one, just a folded-up table with Daisy's pink purse hidden behind it. He found the custodian inside the gym on his cell phone, talking to a dispatcher. Harry waved him toward the front doors, ordering him to report that there were at least two other people inside the building.

Then he followed the hazy wisps of toxic fumes to the top of a stairwell where a darker cloud of smoke was gathering beneath his feet. He inspected the open padlock and gate, heard the distinctive whoosh and pops of live flames. The smoke swirled around his ankles as he went partway down the steps. "Daisy? Daisy Gunderson, are you down here?"

His answer was a couple of loud bangs, a muffled curse and then a croaky, "Harry? I'm trapped. There's smoke. I called 9-1-1. I pulled the fire alarm in here."

Smart woman. Harry took the stairs two at a time, running straight at the sound of her voice. "I heard the sirens. The fire department is on its way." The smoke was denser down here, the breathable air more pungent. There was nothing accidental about this blaze. The fire itself was a small pyre in the middle of the hallway, piled with rags, a bag of trash and what looked like a woman's coat, all shriveling into ash and goo as they burned and melted. The concrete and metal down here would be hard to burn, but he smelled enough acetone, probably varnish or paint solvent, to make his eyes water. He shoved open the first door and discovered the boiler room. "Daisy?"

He heard her coughing again and kept moving. Metal banged against metal. "In here."

The next door. Right beside the blaze. With more accelerant splashed on the door itself so that rivulets of fire ran down the heavy steel.

"Hang on, honey, I'm coming." Harry edged around the puddle of flames dripping on the floor to get his hand on the door, but he quickly snatched it away. Even through the leather and lining of his glove, the rising temperature scorched him. "Don't touch the door," he warned. "It's hot."

"That's why I've been hitting it with this metal chair." Her brave voice stuttered with another fit of coughing. "I can't get it open."

He couldn't, either, unless he could put out some of those flames and get closer. He swung his gaze around. Through the chimeras of heat rising toward the ceiling, Harry caught a glimpse of a ghostly figure climbing the stairs at the far end of the long corridor. Was that a trick of the smoke? A flashback to tracking insurgents in that village outside Fallujah? The instinct to give chase to the potential enemy tensed through every muscle. "Hey!" he shouted. "Stop!"

"What is it?" Daisy gasped.

The apparition was gone. The reality was here. "Nothing. Never mind."

"He's jammed the door or broken the lock." Daisy's

coughing reminded Harry that his priority was to keep her safe. That meant finding a way to get her out of there.

He spotted the fire extinguisher cabinet anchored to the wall. On the other side of the fire. "Are you hurt?" Harry asked, using the crowbar to shove the center point of that fire, a heavy bucket that was melting with the heat, off to one side. The bucket tipped, and more flames shot out across the floor. But in that split second the fire was moving away from him and the door, Harry darted past.

"I burned my hand on the door, but it's not serious. It's getting harder to breathe."

He couldn't breathe. The old memories snuck around his defenses, blending with reality. *Tango had hit on something. He knew that dog's reactions the way he knew his own thoughts. Harry raised his fist, warning his patrol to stop their advance. "What is it, boy? Show me." He heard the thwap of the bullet and watched Tango fall. "Tango!" Harry's world exploded around him. IED. The dog had known. He ran toward the heat. He couldn't leave his partner behind. "Top, you got to leave him! We have to retreat!" He jerked his arm away and raised his rifle, charging toward his downed partner when the second blast hit.*

"Harry?" It was a woman's voice calling his name. Daisy's voice. "Harry, are you still there?"

Do this, Marine!

Harry swore, forcing himself into the present. He ducked his head and swung the crowbar, shattering the glass in front of the fire extinguisher.

"I'm here, honey." Harry pulled the pin and fired a stream of foam into the flames, dousing a path before aiming the extinguisher at the door itself. "I'm going to get you out."

The sting of the burning chemical was in his eyes now. The toxic air tickled his throat and filtered into his lungs.

The heat from the flames themselves had puckered every pore in his skin, making him feel like his boots and clothes were melting. The foam trickled down the door, taking the flames with it. Every new inch revealed burnt streaks and blistered paint and a single word etched into the metal itself. *Mine.*

A rage as hot as the fire itself seared through Harry's brain. How could one person be so sick in the head that he would want to hurt a woman with a heart as big as Daisy's? He turned down the smoke-filled hallway. He should have run down that SOB. He didn't need to be armed to take a man down. He could have put a stop to this insane terror campaign once and for all.

"Harry, please." She was coughing again.

Stay focused on the mission, Top. Harry tossed the extinguisher aside and picked up the crowbar. "Stand back. When I open this, it may suction the flames into the room."

"I'm ready."

The latch was busted, useless. This was going to take brute force. Finally. Something he could manage without thinking twice. Harry wedged the crowbar between the door and wall and pushed against it, then pulled back, roaring with the strain through his arms and shoulders before the warping metal finally gave way. Once he'd moved the door a couple of inches, he dropped the crowbar and muscled the hanging door across its track. He was coughing now, too. "Daisy?"

"Harry!" She launched herself against his chest, heedless of the flames licking into the room she'd just vacated. He cinched an arm around her waist and turned her away from the conflagration, carrying her several feet beyond the worst of the fire. He felt her lips press against his damaged cheek and jaw again and again. "Thank you. Thank... Oh, my God."

Harry turned her away from the hateful epithet and tried to keep moving. But she squiggled in his grasp, wanting to see. "Did you see him? Was that who you were yelling at? Who was it? Is that my coat? Why would he—?"

"I didn't get a good look." Her body shook with another fit of coughing and he tried to pick her up. "Keep your head down. The smoke is getting thick."

"He slipped a card under the door. We need it for evidence."

She batted his hands away, turning sideways against him, although he wasn't letting her get any closer to the blaze. "No you don't. The cops will know this was intentional."

"There may be fingerprints."

"No."

"I heard the scratching. He was carving…" Her toes touched the floor, tangling with his feet. He lost his grip as they stumbled into the wall. She fought with him, struggling to get a better view of the destruction. "…that. *Mine?* I belong to him? He owns something I need to stay away from?"

He grasped her shoulders. "We have to move."

"He must have been watching, waiting until I was—"

"Stop talking and get your butt moving!" Daisy flinched away from him, her red-rimmed eyes wide behind her glasses as she clutched at the wall instead of him. Harry heard his voice echoing through the hallway and truly understood why Lt. Col. Biro had been so worried about his ability to serve. "I'm sorry." He backed away to the opposite wall, his hands raised in apology. He'd just yelled in her face as if she was a raw recruit. As if he wasn't any better than that bastard who'd hurt her. The fumes rubbed like grit in his eyes. "My head's not right. I didn't mean that. Don't… Don't ever stop talking to me. Please."

And then that woman did the most remarkable thing. She pushed away from the wall, grabbed the front of his coat and dragged him toward the stairs. "Get me out of here, Top," she ordered. "We both need fresh air."

When she doubled over in another coughing jag, Harry's training took over. He swung her up into his arms and carried her up the stairs and out the front door. By the time he reached the median in front of the school, his lungs were screaming for oxygen and he collapsed to his knees in the snow. Daisy tumbled from his arms. He bent over, coughing again. But suddenly, she was on her knees in front of him, rubbing a palmful of snow across his face and another along the nape of his neck, coughing right along with him as she shocked his senses. "Are you with me? Harry, are you okay?"

He raised his head to meet her worried gaze. He hoped her eyes were irritated and watering, and that she wasn't wasting any tears on him. Still, he pulled off his heat-damaged glove and reached out with the pad of his thumb to wipe away the lines of moisture cutting tracks over her soot-stained cheek. "I'm okay."

"Don't lie to me." Even red-rimmed and weepy, that look over the top of her glasses wasn't one he could ignore.

"I'm okay *now*," he amended. Her skin was cool to the touch and she was shivering. "You're freezing." From the snow soaking through her jeans or the adrenaline leaving her system, it didn't matter. Harry pushed to his feet and peeled off his coat to wrap it around her shoulders. He hugged her to his chest and guided her to the cleared asphalt of the circular drive as a third fire engine pulled up.

A team of firefighters was already grabbing gear and fanning out around the building. A tall man in a white helmet was on his radio as he stepped down from the last truck. His slight limp didn't detract from the square set of his shoulders and air of authority. He was clearly the man in charge. After a brief chat with the principal and custodian, he sent one of his men off to cut the power to the building. Daisy huddled even closer against Harry when the chief approached them. "You're the teacher who called this in?"

"Yes. Daisy Gunderson."

Harry relished the cold night air seeping through his sweater and T-shirt because it kept his head clear, but he wished he had a little more body heat to share with Daisy. If she wasn't coughing, she was shaking, but he held her upright in one of those bear hugs she was so fond of. While she detailed the events and the chief deployed his crew into the building, Harry surveyed the parking lot through the swirl of emergency vehicle lights and first responders. The car with the yellow sticker was gone. Why hadn't he written down the license plate number? He hadn't even thought to look. Of course, the arsonist could have walked out the back door or had a car waiting for him someplace else. He was still no closer to identifying the creep terrorizing Daisy than he'd been when he'd first set up camp outside her home.

Harry snapped to when the crew chief addressed him. "She said you saw someone?"

Had he? "He was running up the east stairs, away from the fire. I didn't get a good look at him. That was five minutes before we got out of there."

"So, chances are he's clear of the scene and there's no one else inside. Can you describe him in case we run into him in there?"

Harry closed his eyes and replayed that brief impression distorted by heat and smoke. "Taller than me. Slender build." Shrugging, he opened his eyes. That was almost less than nothing to go on. "I can't even give you a hair color. I saw him from behind and he was wearing a blue coat and yellow hat."

Daisy lifted her chin. "Blue and gold? Like school colors?"

"Maybe. It was a blur."

"That narrows it down to about three-hundred people," she grumbled in a wheezing voice.

But the description seemed to be enough for the fire chief. "I'll go ahead and send a team in to sweep the building. Once we have the fire contained, we'll check the basement, too."

"He'll be long gone," Daisy added. "He thrives on me not knowing who he is."

"We'll check, all the same." He nodded toward the uniformed police officer waiting a few yards away. "The police will want to ask you the same questions."

Daisy nodded, but Harry felt her fingers curling into the front of his sweater. Her spirit might be willing, but her strength was flagging. "She needs a medic first. Probable smoke inhalation and shock."

"The ambulance is pulling up now." Harry and the chief walked her over to the ambulance where two EMTs sat Daisy in the back of the truck and immediately gave her oxygen and a blanket, and started taking her vitals. Before they made room for Harry to climb up, the tall firefighter tapped him on the shoulder. "Marine?" Harry nodded. The crew chief extended his hand. "John Murdock, USMC Retired. Did a couple of tours in Afghanistan."

Harry shook his hand, appreciating the bond that was always there between marines of any generation. "Master Sergeant Harry Lockhart. First Marine Expeditionary Force out of Pendleton. How did you know?"

"Not many men run *into* a fire except for firefighters and Devil Dogs." And maybe a crazy guy who thought he was about to lose someone he was learning to care about more and more with each passing minute. Before Harry could process exactly what that revelation meant, Murdock continued the conversation. "Lockhart. You any relation to Hope Lockhart Taylor?"

Harry nodded. "My sister."

Murdock nodded. "I thought something about you looked familiar. My boss, Meghan Taylor, is Hope's mother-in-law. I went to Hope and Pike's wedding a few years back." That had been the last time Harry had come home to Kansas City. He'd never realized how many people he was connected to beyond his sister here. "Small world, isn't it?"

"Bigger than I thought, actually."

Chief Murdock inclined his head toward the ambulance's interior. "Your friend hasn't taken her eyes off you. You'd better get in there and get checked out, too, so she stops worrying."

"Yes, sir."

Harry realized he shared another connection with John Murdock. As the older man limped away, he saw the distinctive void space of his pants catching around a steel rod above his boot. The KCFD crew chief had an artificial leg. They'd both sacrificed for their country. And apparently, John Murdock had adapted to civilian life just fine, even though all of him hadn't come home from the war, either.

Harry had never considered civilian life as an option for him. But if he did ever move on to life outside the Corps, he wanted it to be his choice—not because he was so broken that the Corps didn't want him. If he wasn't good enough for the USMC, how could he be good enough for anything, or anybody, else?

How could he be good enough for Daisy?

Forty minutes later, the fire was out and the building had been cleared. There was no sign of the man who'd set the blaze, unless his footprints were one of the hundreds tramped through the snow in the parking lot left by students and fans attending tonight's games or by the firefighters and police ensuring the entire school was secure. Harry sat on a gurney across from Daisy in the back of the ambulance as she sorted through her bag, making sure all her belongings—beyond the coat that obsessive creep had burned—were there. They reeked of smoke, and he couldn't detect that homey sweet scent that was uniquely hers anymore. He'd given his statement to the uniformed officer and a pair of detectives. He'd had his eyes rinsed, his vitals checked, and he'd held an oxygen mask over his nose and mouth for longer than he wanted, simply because Daisy took her mask down and asked him if he was all right every time he stopped the flow of purified air he wanted her to keep breathing. They were both wrapped in blankets, waiting to be cleared by the EMTs.

If he wasn't scaring her, then she was worried about him. He was raw with guilt. Hard to feel like much of a marine—like much of a man—when the only two emotions he could evoke from a pretty woman were fear and concern. He should reassess this unofficial mission. While he wasn't about to leave her alone against the jerk who wanted to hurt her, maybe he needed to rethink his whole plan to have Angel Daisy help him heal. She didn't need his kind of mess in her life.

"Harry?" He must have been quiet for too long because Daisy was sliding across the ambulance to sit on the gurney beside him. She tucked her hands beneath his arm and leaned her head against his shoulder. "Talk to me. We've been long-distance friends for a long time, and I know I don't have any real claim on you. Still, it's crazy how fast I've gotten used to having you around. But for a few seconds down there in the basement, I thought you'd left me."

He adjusted his blanket around both of them and rested his cheek against the crown of her head. Dr. Polk had advised him that the first step in dealing with his problem was admitting the extent of it.

"For a few seconds there, I did."

Chapter Eight

Harry got up to pace the house again.

The first two times he'd come downstairs from the guest room, the dogs had trotted out from Daisy's bedroom to inspect the noise and identify his presence. The two little dogs had trotted back into her room to go back to sleep. Caliban limped around the house with him, reminding Harry of the hundreds of night patrols he and Tango had gone on together. It was a bittersweet treat to work with a well-trained dog again. Caliban was willing to answer his commands to go out ahead of him and come back, to seek, to sit and to play a game of tug-of-war with his rope toy before the older dog, too, tired and went back to his comfy spot in Daisy's bedroom.

Losing a leg hadn't stopped the retired K-9 officer from belonging somewhere and having a purpose. Just because Caliban wasn't serving KCPD anymore didn't mean he didn't have a home and companions and a reason to get up in the morning—or the middle of the night when restless house guests roamed the halls and raided the cookie supply in the kitchen.

There was a lesson to be learned there. But the hour was late and a lot of the things Harry was feeling since first ringing Daisy's doorbell were new and alien to him.

The dogs must be getting used to the sound of his tread

on the floors because none of them came out to greet him this time. Good. He hoped they stayed close to their mistress and that all of them were getting a good night's sleep. Daisy had stayed up far too late, running their clothes through the laundry twice, to rid them of the smells of smoke and acetone. Pike had brought over Harry's duffel bag with all his belongings and stayed to keep watch on the house while Harry showered the grime and nightmares off his skin. Then Daisy had soaked in the tub for nearly an hour before declaring she finally felt tired enough to sleep and had gone to bed.

Harry came down the stairs in his jeans and bare feet, with his M9 strapped to his hip. The enemy was different and the temps were colder, but this detail wasn't different from any other watch he'd served over the years. There was somebody out there who wanted to hurt the thing he'd sworn to protect. He stopped at the window beside the front door, folded his arms over his bare chest and stared out into the moonless night. Although the snow on the ground reflected the glow of the street lights, there were plenty of shadows, plus darkened vehicles and shaded windows in other homes where someone could hide. Still, the neighborhood looked secure for the moment. Unlike all the activity at Daisy's school earlier that night, this part of Kansas City seemed quiet.

Didn't make it any easier for him to fall asleep.

But he'd be damned if he'd get hooked on those sleeping pills Lt. Col. Biro said he would prescribe for him.

Harry could get by with an occasional nap and dozing on and off through the night. Maybe staring at something besides the tin-tiled ceiling in the upstairs guest room would be enough of a change of pace for him to grab some much needed rest. He'd give one of the recliners in Daisy's living room a try. At least on the ground floor, he'd be closer to any ingresses an intruder might use to break in. Surely, that was enough of an advantage to drop the alert buzzing through his veins to a level that would allow him thirty winks.

After checking the mudroom door and backyard, Harry wandered into the kitchen. He poured himself a glass of milk and downed half of it before eyeing the cookie jar again. One more reindeer cookie would take the edge off his growly stomach and give his taste buds something to savor instead of focusing every brain cell on replaying nightmares and envisioning the stalker he wanted to take down with his bare hands. He hoped the cookies weren't all for that party Daisy kept talking about, because he'd made a serious dent in her supply. He'd have to buy her some groceries or run to the bakery for her, although he had a feeling store-bought cookies wouldn't taste as good.

He was licking the icing off his fingertips when he strolled into the living room and found Daisy standing there in front of the empty fireplace, staring at him. His hands went instinctively to his shoulder and chest to cover himself, not out of modesty, but out of horror that she was getting a full-on view of the scarring he hid from the rest of the world. He couldn't hide his face, but why the hell hadn't he taken two seconds to put on a T-shirt?

He was glad that the only light in the room seeped in from the night-light in the kitchen and the glow from a street lamp filtering through the sheer curtains at the front door. "Have a nightmare?"

"I was worried about you, beating yourself up because you don't think you did a good enough job protecting me. The way I see it, the alternative is that I would have suffocated from the smoke and fumes if you hadn't been there."

Daisy crossed the room and reached for his hands, lacing their fingers together and holding on as she pulled them away from his disfigurement. He held himself still as she studied the hard ridges, stitch marks and skin grafts that were pinker and lighter than the rest of his chest, wishing he could spare her the horrific events that she must be imagining. She tilted her gaze above the brown glasses—that were far too plain for her colorful style—up to his for a moment before she released his hands and walked straight into his chest. She wound her arms around his waist and turned her cheek against the very scars he thought would repulse her. Her breasts pillowed against him, and the undamaged half of him was awkwardly aware of the tender nipples pearling against him. When her damp hair caught beneath his chin and her lips grazed across his collarbone, Harry surrendered to their mutual need to be held, and wound his arms around her back.

Daisy squeezed him in a hug, and Harry automatically tightened his hold on her, pulling her onto her toes. "Yes, I had a nightmare. About what happened tonight, and I was wondering if we could talk?"

Her voice trailed away, allowing him a glimpse of the vulnerability she worked far too hard to hide. He nuzzled the crown of her head, unsure that comfort was the best thing he could give her. From this angle, he could see the damp tendrils of purple and brown clinging to the collar of her flannel pajamas. And heaven help him, he could see and feel the siren silhouette of her hourglass figure cinched in at the waist by her robe. As much as he wanted to hide his own body, he wanted to see more of hers. He imagined everything about her was soft and touchable—from that shampooed hair to those sweet lips and delectable curves, right on down to the fuzzy green socks that covered her toes.

An answering male heat licked through his veins, reminding Harry that at least one part of him hadn't been affected by nightmares or injury. Everything about Daisy being here, standing close enough for him to breathe her scent, reminded him of how much time had passed since he'd been with a woman, how badly he needed a woman's gentle touch. But he reined in that feverish blast of longing that was stirring where her thighs pressed against his—this woman only wanted to talk.

"What's up?" he asked, mentally beating back his hormones and focusing on her needs, not his. He moved his grip to her shoulders and urged her warm body away from him.

Her gaze had landed on the gun he wore. "Do you sleep with that?" Before he could answer, her gaze bopped up to his. "Or don't you sleep at all?"

"I don't wear it *in* bed if that's what you mean. But I keep it close." Harry released her to unhook his belt and remove the Beretta and its holster. He set the weapon up on the mantel. "I don't want to be too far from our best protection. But I don't want to scare you more than I already do." He gestured toward the pair of recliners facing the fireplace. Separate seats would be best, considering the ill-timed lust simmering in his veins. "Shall we?"

"You don't scare me, Harry. I'm not afraid for me, at any rate." Once she settled in the first recliner, Harry sat in the other. But before he could raise the footrest, Daisy surprised him by moving over to his chair and sitting in his lap. "Is this okay? I want you to be comfortable. I have a feeling you won't like what I need to talk about."

He had a feeling he wouldn't, either. She wanted to finish that conversation they'd started during the game. For some reason he couldn't yet comprehend, Daisy was feeling the same attraction he was, but she wanted to know just how screwed up he was before anything else happened between them.

And yet, she was sitting in his lap, her hand braced at the center of his chest. Her hip and bottom warmed his thighs and…other things. "After everything that happened, you want to be with me?"

Her fingertips clenched into his skin. "Do I scare *you*?"

"A little. But I'm not saying no." Harry raised the footrest and leaned back, pulling Daisy into his arms and letting her settle into the chair, half beside and half on top of him, giving his body a taste of her curves pressed against him. He curled his right arm around her back, his hand hovering above her before settling on the swell of her hip in a grip that felt more possessive than it should. Her body was as perfect a fit as he'd imagined it would be, and that desire he'd tried to check flared to life again. But she needed to talk, and maybe he did, too. With his left hand, he sifted his fingers into her hair, smoothing damp strands off her face, stirring her sweet scent around him. "I should have stuck closer to you tonight, and not let everything get to me."

When her glasses butted against his chest, and got pushed askew, he took them off and lay them on the table beside them. She snuggled into a more comfortable position, brushing her stockinged feet against his bare toes and tucking her forehead at the juncture of his neck and shoulder. He was okay with her not being able to see him clearly. Talking about his past was going to be hard enough without Daisy seeing how ill-equipped he was to handle this kind of emotional intimacy.

"I don't blame you for what happened, Harry."

"I blame myself."

"You have post-traumatic stress. I remember when I was in the hospital after Brock's attack, I was so afraid of men that I only wanted female doctors and nurses working on me. Then Mom told me my father had died. She blamed me for bringing Brock into our lives and causing Dad so much stress. I blamed myself." Where was she going with this? When he felt her tensing against him, Harry covered her hand where it rested against his chest, silently telling her it was okay to continue. "I curled up into a ball in that hospital bed and wanted to be left completely alone. I didn't want anyone touching me, talking to me. I holed up in this house once I was released. I didn't see anyone but my lawyer. I didn't do anything but help Mom go through Dad's things and sleep."

"You? You're the most social creature I've ever met."

She switched the position of their hands, lacing her fingers with his. "PTSD. I was depressed. I got counseling. I made it through Brock's trial and Mom remarrying and moving away. And then, finally, one day I was done with it. I didn't want to be sad and paranoid anymore. I didn't want the bad guys—the bad feelings—to control my life. I got busy living again. Got a new teaching position. Got Muffy from her elderly owner who was moving into a nursing home and rescued Patch from the shelter. I started fixing up this house. I wanted to do for others and make friends and have a meaningful life."

"You've succeeded."

"But I needed that time to heal. So do you. Losing Tango must have devastated you." He tightened his grip around hers, confirming her suspicion. "I know you've lost friends. You nearly lost your own life. Be kind to yourself. Be patient. I believe you'll eventually learn to cope, too."

"I don't know. I was almost out of control tonight."

"Almost. So you yelled. To my way of thinking, you were yelling for help." She tilted her face away from his neck and cupped his damaged jaw, asking him to meet her solemn gaze. "You didn't hurt me. Trust me, I know what it's like to be hurt."

Harry touched his lips to hers for a brief kiss, sitting up enough to slide his hand behind the crook of her knees, pulling her across his lap so he could hold more of her in his arms. "I hate that you know that."

"The smells of the fire were a powerful trigger for your flashback. I imagine someone coming at me with a knife would do the same for me. In the meantime, I do the best I can every day. I try to be honest about what I'm thinking and feeling, but I try to stay positive and keep moving forward." She wiggled in his grasp, innocently planting her hip against his groin and snuggling beneath his chin again. "And I give myself a break when I don't. You should try it."

The tension in him eased at the gentle reprimand. "How do I express what I'm thinking and feeling without completely losing it?"

She traced mindless circles across his chest and shoulder as she considered her answer. "What would you say if you were writing it to me in a letter?"

He was aware of each surviving nerve ending waiting in hopeful anticipation for her fingers to brush across it again. "Dr. Polk suggested something similar—that I start journaling. Write things down and get 'em out of my head so I'm not always fighting to control everything in there. But I wouldn't know where to start."

"Sure you do. Give me the rough draft. I'm an English teacher—I can make sense of just about anything. The beginning is usually the hardest part for my students. But you know how to start a letter."

"Dear Daisy?"

"So far, so good."

"I thought I was going to lose you tonight."

The circles stopped. "That's a dramatic opening."

"I'm not very good at jokes."

But she wasn't letting him off that easily. "The point is honesty, not humor. When you flashed back tonight, where did you go?"

His hand traveled up and down her back, squeezing her bottom and coming back to hug the nip of her waist before he mustered the courage to tell her about the insurgent sniper taking out Tango before the dog could pinpoint the two IEDs planted in an ambush. He told her about the two men he'd lost that day, including Albert Logan's pen pal, Benny Garcia. He glossed over the details of shrapnel shredding his body and fire searing his face and neck. His speech was halting, his sentences disjointed. But with his senses focused on the scent of her hair and the heat of her sensuous body warming his, other defenses inside his head crumbled. He'd gotten what was left of Tango and his men out of there before blacking out. Then he didn't remember anything until waking up in the hospital in Germany.

He'd been angry. All the time. Afraid he might lose his eye or the use of his arm. He'd been wild with guilt—about the dog who'd been with him since Day One of shipping into the hot zone, and about the men he was responsible for who weren't coming home. He'd endured numerous surgeries and painful rehab. He'd been taken off active duty, told he wasn't good enough to do the job he loved anymore. He'd talked to shrinks—reawakened memories of the violence from his childhood, felt that same violence seething inside him and had been afraid he couldn't control it. He'd read Daisy's letters, over and over, clinging to the hope in her words, internalizing the wisdom and compassion she'd shared.

When he made it back to the present, Harry realized his skin was wet and that Daisy was trembling against him. He cupped her chin and tipped her face up to his, inspecting the pain he'd inflicted there. "Damn it, I'm making you cry again."

"That means I'm not just hearing, I'm feeling what you're saying." Bracing her hands on his shoulders, she closed the few inches separating them to press a kiss to his lips. When he responded, she lingered, and the quiet kiss lasted for several endless moments. Her tongue reached out to his in a tentative mating dance and Harry caught it, caressed it, before thrusting his tongue into her mouth and continuing the dance there. Harry felt the tender solace all the way down to his toes before he tasted the salt of her tears on her lips and he pulled away.

"Daisy—"

"Stop it. If you can yell, I can cry." She slid a hand behind his neck, scraping her palm over the short cut of his hair. "It's an honest expression of emotion. You should try it sometime."

Harry anchored his hands at her waist, keeping her from moving close enough to resume the kiss. "You want honest? When I lost it tonight in that fire, you were afraid of me." She squinted, keeping him in focus, listening to his words as she always had. "I never want to see that look in your eyes again. What if something happens and I scare you?"

"What if it doesn't? What if I cry again? Are you going to stop caring?"

She knew he had feelings for her? "No."

"Then why do you think *I* would?" She stroked the back of his neck, sending soothing comfort and tremors of anticipation down his spine and out to every working nerve in his body. "Crap happens to people sometimes. You get help, you work through it—you do the best you can. Sometimes you falter, but you get up and try again—and with the important people in your life, that's all that really matters."

His arms shook, the whole chair vibrating with the tension and doubt working through him. "You've never been afraid of me, have you? Even beat up and scarred like I am, you hug like it's going out of style. You kiss, you grab, you talk—"

"Sounds a little annoying when you put it that way."

He shook his head, still wrapping his mind around the

idea that Daisy wanted to be with him. "I'm taking advantage of your kindness."

"You're giving me value by trusting me with your fears, by sharing your darkest feelings, by helping me understand you." She pushed a lock of hair out of her eyes and Harry's fingers were there to capture the silky wave and tuck it behind her ear. "I was with Brock for a year and a half. Believe me, I'll take trust and honesty with a fractured brain and sexy masculinity over control and isolation any day."

His fingers feathered into her hair. "Sexy?"

"Beautiful eyes, muscles for days." He held himself still as she crawled up his body. She gently kissed the lid above each eye, then kissed his cheek, the point of his chin, the hollow of his neck, gently, seductively working her way down to his chest where she kissed both the scarred surface and the healthy skin that leaped with eagerness at her touch. "Interesting that *sexy* is the word you keyed in on."

"After everything I've told you, you still want this— us—to happen?"

She harrumphed a dramatic sigh, folded her arms over his chest and rested her chin there. "I'm lying on top of you, I can feel your arousal pressing against my hip, which is really good for my ego because it means I'm halfway irresistible, and if you don't kiss me—I mean, really kiss me like I think you want to—soon, then I'm just going to keep right on talking. And you will never be able to shut me up."

"You aren't halfway anything." Harry didn't need much encouragement to give in to what his body had been craving.

He righted the chair, spilling Daisy into his lap. His hands were there to catch her bottom and pull her back against his chest. She slipped her arms around his neck, welcoming his kiss as he laid claim to her beautiful mouth. He wasn't smooth, but he was hungry for her. Her fingers teased the nape of his neck again, skidded over his prickly hair, then boldly framed his face to keep their lips aligned as her knees parted and dropped to either side of his thighs. Her warm soft heat cupped the aching desire growing stiff inside his jeans and he moaned. He needed more. He needed everything.

Harry moved his hands to the front of her robe to free the knot, knocking into her hands as they worked the top button of his jeans. She laughed and he pressed his lips to the sound in her throat. The angle was wrong, and he was a little too ready for her to work his zipper down, so he caught her wrists and moved her hands to his chest where they happily explored each spasm of muscle that yearned for her touch.

Harry pushed her robe open and tugged at the buttons of her pajama top. Flowered flannel shouldn't be so damn sexy, but it was as he dragged the soft cotton over her shoulders and down her arms, revealing her heavy breasts to his appreciative gaze. The tips were a pretty pink, and straining to attention in the chilly air.

Her arms were trapped in the ends of the sleeves, but he let her wiggle herself free. He was too busy sliding his hands around to the soft skin of her back while he dropped his lips to the generous swell of one breast, and then the other, catching a nipple in his mouth when it bounced too close. Harry closed his lips around the tip, laving the sweet bud with his tongue until he heard a whimper against his ear.

"I'm sorry." Harry withdrew immediately, drawing in deep breaths to reclaim his equilibrium. He clasped her face between his hands and sought out any sign of pain he might have caused in her darkened blue eyes. "I can't feel everything I do to you. There's nerve damage. If I'm doing something you don't like—"

"That, sir, was the brink of ecstasy. I'll let you know when I'm not enjoying myself." Daisy freed her arms from the sleeves that bound her, cupped either side of his jaw and guided his mouth to the other breast.

She didn't say another word.

Harry scooped Daisy up in his arms and carried her to her bedroom. After scooting the dogs out and closing the door, he pulled out his wallet and tossed it onto the bedside table before shucking his jeans and shorts and climbing onto the bed beside her.

Daisy had stripped off her pajama bottoms and was reaching for him. But he pushed her back into the pillows, wanting to feast his eyes first. In the soft glow of the bedside lamp, he took in every inch of her. She was too much, too beautiful…too vulnerable. His gaze stopped on the small pucker of scar tissue on the underside of her breast. He gently touched the tip of his finger to it. He wasn't the only wounded warrior here.

Harry leaned over to kiss the permanent evidence of the brutal attack she'd survived. She flinched and tried to roll away, but he wouldn't let her. "You've seen me."

After she lay back against the pillows, baring herself completely to him, he reverently touched each scar, first with his hand and then with his lips. He kissed her chest, her belly, her breasts, until her hands were on his hair again, holding his mouth to each mark as if his touch healed her the way she was healing him.

He lingered over one mark just below her belly button, his heated breath raising goose bumps over her quivering flesh. "Are you…okay…inside? Did he…?"

"The surgeon removed my spleen and one ovary and the Fallopian tube, and he sewed up a nick in one of my lungs and my stomach. Theoretically, I can still make babies, so we need to use protection." He lifted his head to meet her squinting gaze. "Otherwise, what you see is what you get."

"I want it." Harry climbed over her the way she had

climbed up his body in the chair, and claimed her mouth for a deep, drugging kiss. "I want you."

"Please tell me you have something in that wallet."

Harry rolled off her to retrieve the foil packet from the bedside table. "It's dusty, but it should be reliable."

He felt a kiss between his shoulder blades as he sat on the edge of the bed and sheathed himself. "Dust it off, Marine. You have a job to do."

Do this.

It was the most glorious order he'd ever obeyed.

Daisy climbed onto his lap before he'd even considered a position. But he was just fine with this one. Stars exploded behind his eyes as she sank, wet and hot and ready, over his shaft. Oh, yeah, he was more than fine with this position. Already matching her rhythm and rocking inside her, he kissed her breasts, nibbled her neck, claimed her lips until the need became too great. Harry squeezed her in a tight hug, clamping every curve of her body against his as he detonated inside her.

Daisy cried out with her release and Harry held her to him until the waves of her climax faded away and her head collapsed against his neck. They fell back onto the bed together, with Daisy resting on top of him for several long minutes until their breathing returned to normal and the perspiration on their bodies began to cool.

Then Harry tucked her under the covers and made a quick trip to the bathroom to dispose of the condom. Daisy was half asleep when he returned, but she was smiling as he crawled under the quilts with her and gathered her into his arms.

She wedged one soft thigh between his and wrapped her arm around his waist, clinging to him in a very sexy version of a hug. Harry stroked his fingers up and down her back, feeling a rare, satisfied fatigue creeping into his muscles.

He couldn't believe that any man would try to control this woman's brave spirit and generous heart. She was such a gift.

Such a completely unexpected gift. This Daisy wasn't anything like the woman in his letters.

Harry's fingers came to rest beneath her soft, damp hair. "For some reason, from your letters, I pictured you as a blonde."

"I was once." That made him laugh and he felt her smile against his skin. "You have a wonderful laugh. You should practice it more often."

He'd never had much reason to. "I will if you don't change your shampoo."

Don't change anything about you.

"Strange request." She yawned and burrowed in beside him.

Harry drifted off to sleep along with her, his nose buried in the sweet scent of her hair. No stranger than Harry Lockhart falling in love with her all over again.

This time, with the real Daisy Gunderson.

DAISY WAS IN a deep, blank sleep when she startled awake to a man's hand clamped over her mouth.

Her muffled scream quickly fell silent when Harry's face hovered into focus above hers. He pressed a finger to his lips and didn't remove his hand until she nodded her understanding to remain quiet. Her clock was a blur of red light from this distance, leaving her adrift with no idea of the time or situation. The sun wasn't even up yet. But sometime in the hours since that cathartic conversation and making love, while she was replete with satisfaction and feeling more cherished than she had with any man in her life, Harry had been getting dressed and sneaking around the house.

Well, half-dressed. As far as she was concerned, the man never needed to put on a shirt again. Not that that was terribly practical, but Harry's fit, supple body moving over to the window and back to the edge of her bed certainly improved the scenery.

"Dais?" he whispered. "Honey, are you awake?"

Honey? Focus!

Something was wrong. Even in her nearsighted haze, she could see Harry was strapping on his gun again. She pulled the sheet around her and sat up as he handed her the brown glasses they'd left in the living room.

She slipped them on, hoping that bringing clarity to his grim expression would give her understanding. "What is it?" She heard one of the dogs growling from the foot of the bed, and all the beautiful aftermath of making love vanished in a clutch of fear. "Harry?

He pushed her phone into her hands. "Call 9-1-1. There's someone outside."

That's when Daisy jumped at the pop, pop, pop of tiny explosions and shattering glass out on the back deck. Muffy leaped onto the corner of the bed and barked an alarm. Patch jumped up beside him, yapping with equal fury. Harry swore at the noisy outburst.

Those pops hadn't been gunshots. But they definitely weren't anything natural. Neither was the distinct sound of running footsteps.

Harry was already moving to her bedroom door, drawing his gun. The man wasn't prepped for battle. He didn't even have shoes on. "You can't—"

There was no pretense of hushed and discreet now.

"Get dressed. Stay in this room. I'm leaving the dogs in here with you. Caliban, *Pas Auf.*" Apparently, that meant he should guard the place because the Belgian Malinois never moved from his post, even after Harry pulled the door shut.

Daisy slipped out of bed, pulled on her jeans and the first top she could find and placed the call.

Chapter Nine

At the swirl of red and white lights pulling up in front of the house, Daisy zipped up Harry's coat and ran to the mudroom door, eager to see where Harry had gone when he'd run out the back. Had he found the man who'd been terrorizing her? Or—the frightening possibility entered her head before she could stop it—had the man found Harry?

She unlocked the door and dashed onto the deck. "Harry?"

Her boot crunched with the first step, then the second, and she stopped. She was walking on glass. The security light had been shattered and she was walking across dozens of broken Christmas light bulbs. The path of so much destruction littering her deck and the sidewalk down to the gate was disturbing enough.

The little dots of blood that grew into half a bloody footprint triggered a different kind of fear. "Harry!"

Without the lights, the air was dim, but with the sun cresting the horizon in the east, the trail of bloody prints through the snow was easy to follow. There were two sets of footprints now, far apart, left by one man running after the other. "Harry?"

Daisy broke into a run. Harry was hurt. Protecting her, he'd gotten hurt.

"Harr—" She spotted his back and the legs of his quarry

when she reached the front of the house…the same time she saw the two uniformed officers duck behind the open doors of their cruiser and pull their guns, ordering Harry to stand down. Daisy ran toward the cops, her hands raised in a plea. "Officers, wait! Don't shoot!"

"Damn it, Daisy, I told you to stay inside," Harry warned. He was facing the house, his broad body blocking the man he had pinned to the siding. The tension radiating off his body was thicker than the wintry dampness hanging in the air. Tiny shards of colored glass littered the snow out here, too, and she looked up to see dangling wires and empty sockets where her Christmas decorations used to hang. There were indentations in the snow beside the porch where a scuffle must have occurred, but apparently, Harry had put an end to it. Although she couldn't see the man, she could hear him panting, almost blubbering with fear after losing a fight to Harry. "This guy busted up every one of your decorations. He's angry with you."

"I know. I saw it. One of you is bleeding," she added, hoping he might reassure her that he was in one piece and the other guy wasn't mortally wounded.

"I'm not letting him go. If he'd done that to you instead of a bunch of—"

"Gun!" one of the officers shouted.

Daisy moved closer to the police car, placing herself in the potential line of fire. The two men immediately lowered their weapons if not their guard. "I'm Daisy Gunderson. I called this in. This man is with me. There haven't been any gunshots. He caught the intruder I reported. My house has been vandalized, and he caught this guy running away. Don't hurt him."

The shorter of the two officers holstered his weapon while the other came around the hood of the cruiser to back him up. "I'm Officer Cho, KCPD. I'd feel a lot better if that weapon he's wearing was secured."

"What if I hand it over to you?" Daisy suggested.

Cho nodded. "Slow and easy."

"Harry?" Daisy announced herself before creeping up behind him. His skin was wet and ice-cold as she touched his back. "I'm going to hand your gun over to the officer so they can put their weapons away. I don't want anyone here to get hurt."

The ramrod tension she felt beneath her hand didn't waver. "Do it."

She unhooked the snap on his holster and moved in beside him to pull out the gun. Once she had the weapon safely in hand she looked up and gasped in surprise.

"Angelo?"

Harry had her prize student flattened against the house. Stunned was an understatement for the shock chilling her from the inside out. The teenager was crying, but his eyes were clear as his gaze darted to hers.

"Ms. G.," he gasped. He pawed at Harry's forearm. Although his gold Central Prep ball cap had been knocked off his head and was crushed under his feet, he didn't appear to be harmed. Frightened, yes, but not hurt. "I wasn't thinking. Tell your boyfriend how sorry I am. I didn't mean it."

There was that boyfriend word again.

"Harry. Let him go. He's half your age. He doesn't know how to fight like you do." She handed the gun off to Officer Cho and came back to gently lay her hands on Harry's arm and shoulder. "He's just a kid."

"I've seen kids do worse. Decoys, suicide bombers."

"You're not in a war zone. You're in Kansas City. With me. And I'm safe. Look at me. I'm fine. KCPD is here now. Let them handle it. Angelo won't hurt me. Please let him go."

Harry shifted his gaze to hers. His eyes were shadowed, and that taut muscle ticked beneath his right eye. Then he nodded, stepped back and Angelo was free. "Sorry, kid."

"I did it," Angelo confessed, scurrying around Harry. The young man looked relieved to be dealing with the officer asking him about weapons, feeling his pockets and handcuffing him, rather than facing Harry Lockhart. "I broke all the lights. It was me."

Daisy's heart was crushed. She needed answers for any of this to make sense. Why would Angelo want to do this to her? Why hadn't she known he was sending her those gifts? Why? There were other questions that needed answers, too. She pointed to the trail of blood in the snow. "Whose blood is that?"

"Not his." Harry lifted each foot from the snow. Her heart stuttered again when she saw several small cuts oozing blood on the pale skin of his feet.

"Why don't you go inside and finish getting dressed. There's a first-aid kit in the downstairs bathroom. Unless you need my help?"

"I don't need anybody's help." He looked down at her concerned expression and relented the argument. He scooped up Angelo's cap and placed it back on the young man's head before the officer walked him to the cruiser. "Did I hurt you, kid?"

Angelo's head shook with a jerk. "No, sir."

"You scared of me?"

"Yes, sir."

"Good. Then you know not to do anything that'll upset Ms. G. again, right?"

Angelo nodded.

Harry shifted his gaze to the two police officers, glancing down at the gun tucked into the shorter man's belt. "I'm an NCO with the US Marines, home on leave. My

ID is inside the house, but I've got a permit to carry that thing. It hasn't been fired. I'll be back out in ten to give my statement and retrieve it."

Officer Cho identified himself in a way that Harry seemed to appreciate. "Captain. Missouri Army National Guard." The shorter man okayed Harry's departure with one condition. "Officer Bulkey here is going to accompany you."

"Yes, sir." Harry gave the officer a curt nod before the two men went inside the house.

Angelo took half a step toward Daisy before Cho tugged on his cuffs and warned him to keep his distance. "Sorry, Ms. G. I was just mad that you… That he…" He looked up at the house where Harry had disappeared before inhaling a deep breath and spewing out his confession. "You haven't had a boyfriend in all the time I've known you. And now GI Joe shows up for Christmas? In a month I'm going to be eighteen. Then those stupid rules at school don't apply. You and me, we've got a thing. I was going to ask you out."

"Angelo, I can't date you. Even if you are legal age. I wouldn't jeopardize my job or your school year. And we don't have a thing." Daisy sputtered, replaying the year and a half she'd had Angelo in junior and senior English, trying to think of what she might have said or done that would have given him the slightest hint of encouragement. "I've always enjoyed having you in class. Just because I believe in your talents and abilities doesn't mean I have those kinds of feelings for you."

"But I have those feelings for you." Angelo leaned toward her, his young face lined with hurt. "Then Albert said he saw you two making out."

That peck on the lips at the game? That was all Albert could have seen. Nothing else had happened between her and Harry until they'd gotten home. How could one tentative kiss in a public place equate to so much anger and violence?

"Angelo, I could have died in that fire last night."

"What fire?"

He didn't know? She couldn't help but notice he matched the vague description of the man Harry had seen running from the blaze—blue team coat, gold hat. "In the school basement, after the game."

The teenager's brown eyes widened with concern. "Are you okay? Is the school still there? We've got a home tournament next Saturday."

More than her suspicion that he wasn't a very good liar, Angelo's sudden shift in loyalty to his true love—basketball—eased her fear that her student could be Secret Santa. The broken decorations were a temper tantrum, a child not getting his way and lashing out. Hormones. Crazy teenage hormones and a misplaced crush. Not some sick obsession that promised to hurt her. That was all this was, right? All the same, she had to ask, "Have you been sending me gifts?"

He shrugged, confused by the question. "I gave you Granny's caramels."

"No anonymous cards? Presents?"

"No, ma'am." His concern had moved away from her. "Did the school burn down?"

She almost laughed. Almost. "No. You'll still have to show up for class on Monday."

Officer Cho interrupted the conversation. "Ms. Gunderson, I'm going to read Angelo his rights and put him in the back of the cruiser. No sense us all standing out in the cold. Since you seem to know him, do you want to handle this or would you like to press charges?"

"Press charges?" Angelo gasped. "Oh, hell no. I'll get benched."

He'd probably only get probation if this incident ever made it in front of a judge, but that could cost his chance at a good scholarship. The teacher in Daisy took over for the woman who'd been so worried and afraid. She squeezed Angelo's arm, giving him her sternest teacher look. "You wait in the car with Officer Cho for now. Let me make a couple of phone calls to see if we can get this straightened out. But there will be consequences."

Officer Cho nodded, turning Angelo toward the police car.

"Don't call Granny," Angelo begged. "Please, Ms. G. She will tan my hide and I'll be hauling groceries and taking out trash for every old lady in my building for a month."

Although she wasn't a proponent of hide-tanning, the rest sounded like a fair trade-off. Daisy pulled her phone from the pocket of Harry's coat. She had another idea, a consequence that would mean something to Angelo without jeopardizing his future. "I'll see what I can do."

An hour later, the sun was shining on her front porch. The daylight sparkled off the ice crystals in the snow and warmed the air to a tolerable twenty degrees. Officers Cho and Bulkey had left to file their reports, and Angelo was sitting in the passenger seat of Bernie Riley's car, waiting for the basketball coach to drive him home. Coach Riley promised to have a heart-to-heart talk with his starting point guard about inappropriate crushes on English teachers, and how it was a bad idea to trash her Christmas decorations because he was jealous of the grown man paying attention to her.

Hopefully, Bernie would get started on that heart-to-heart soon. For now, the tall man was standing on Daisy's porch, ignoring her surly house guest leaning against the white pillar behind him, thanking her for not pressing charges against his star player. "I'll have him running extra laps and coming in early to practice his free throws. And I'll make sure he's back here this afternoon to clean up the mess he made," Bernie affirmed, as if the idea had been his and not hers. "I'll clear things with his grandmother, too. We'll make sure he knows he's done something wrong without involving the police and endangering his standing at school."

"I appreciate you coming over, Bernie."

"Not a problem. Always happy to help you out, Gunderson."

He leaned in to give her a hug that felt awkward, not just because of the faintly pungent smell clinging to his clothes that stung Daisy's nose, or the fact that she'd hugged him maybe once, at last year's Christmas party—but because she was blatantly aware of Harry's gray eyes drilling holes in the other man's back. At least he made no effort to *take him down* as he'd reported to the police when Angelo had run from him earlier.

When Bernie pulled away and started down the steps, Daisy breathed a sigh of relief. But she regretted the momentary celebration when Bernie stopped on the bottom step and turned to face her. "Hey. I heard about those gifts you've been getting from your Secret Santa. The naughty ones."

Naughty was a politically correct way to describe them, she supposed. Daisy hugged her arms around the front of Harry's coat. "After the fire, I guess word has spread all over the school."

"Pretty much." Bernie reached up under his gold stocking cap and scratched his head, frowning before he smoothed it back into place. "I think you should know that I'm your Secret Santa."

"What?" She gasped, instantly recoiling. "You're Secret Santa?"

This time, Harry pushed away from the post. When he started down the steps after Bernie, she grabbed his arm. Although Harry halted at her touch, she slid her hand down to his and waited for him to lace his fingers with hers before she trusted that he was clearly in the moment with her.

"Let's hear him out," Daisy suggested.

Harry might be willing to listen, but he wasn't about to step down from protecting her from a possible threat. Standing with his shoulder between her and Bernie, he did as she asked. "So talk."

Bernie's green eyes looked serious for a change, and his tone was surprisingly genuine. "I'm not the one giving you those things. Someone must be replacing my gifts. I put the envelopes in your mailbox and the gifts on your desk—but I told Stella to get you the things on your list. Chocolate. Gift cards for coffee. Ornaments."

Daisy slipped her other hand down to hold on to Harry's unwavering strength. "Your wife is giving me those gifts?"

"I don't have time to shop." Bernie shrugged. "I don't like to shop. So she does all that for me. Wraps them up, sticks in the fancy cards. All I do is deliver."

"Why would your wife do that?"

"I'm not saying she's sending you those things. I mean, Stella gets crazy sometimes, but I don't think she even knows what some of that stuff in the pictures is. I mean, it's porn, right? She's uh, she's a lady."

Daisy had a feeling any woman of any background would know exactly the kind of violence the images in those drawings depicted.

"How do you know what's in the pictures?" Harry asked.

"Bosch and Gamblin were talking about it at the game last night."

"Eddie and Mary told you?" Her friends had betrayed her confidence?

"I could tell there was something funky going on with the present you got yesterday. I thought Stella might be trying to make me look bad by giving you a lump of coal." She should be so lucky. "I didn't know there was something wrong with the gifts until I saw what happened in the school basement. I was down there this morning after going over game tapes in my office. You must have been terrified. This morning I asked some people what was going on."

"Some people?"

"I called Principal Hague and he explained what was going on. Now that announcement he made at the faculty meeting about appropriate gifts makes sense." Bernie scratched under his cap again.

She felt the muscles in Harry's arm tense a split second before it snaked out and he snatched the gold stocking cap off Bernie's head.

"What the hell, dude?"

"You got a bad case of dandruff? Why do you keep scratching?" Harry put the cap up to his nose and instantly averted his face. "It smells like smoke and acetone."

Bernie snatched the cap back and pulled it over his head. "I told you I was down in the basement this morning. The place still reeks. Hague said they're airing out the whole school all weekend so we can get back in there on Monday."

Daisy supposed that was a perfectly logical explanation for a man with a blue jacket and yellow hat—like the man Harry had seen running from the fire—to have clothes that smelled like the crime scene. Although logic wasn't making it any easier to tamp down her suspicions about her colleague. "Where were you last night?"

"Coaching two ball games."

Harry took a step closer. "What about afterward? When did you leave? With the players? Later than that?"

Bernie puffed up to his six and a half feet of height. "Are you accusing me of something?" He sidled closer to Daisy, and Harry shifted, keeping his shoulder and dark-eyed glare between them. "Look, I came here to help you out, not to be given the third degree by your bully boy-friend here."

"Where were you?" Harry pressed. Had the smell of the cap triggered a bad memory? Was he getting angry again?

"None of your damn business." Bernie looked straight at Daisy, ignoring Harry. "I just wanted you to know that I drew your name for Secret Santa, and that Stella has been buying the gifts. She has high-class taste. I'm sure she's only getting you nice stuff. I don't know how they're getting swapped out for those other things or who's doing it. But I didn't want you to blame me. Or her." His forehead wrinkled with a rueful expression. "She and I—we've been having some troubles lately. Heck, I even thought about taking you up on renting that spare room of yours for a few weeks instead of staying in a hotel."

"A hotel?" Daisy knew she should feel sorry for Bernie instead of thinking that a struggling marriage could be a motive for either one of them to threaten her.

"Like I said, troubles. That room wouldn't still be available, would it? I've been keeping a change of clothes on me and showering at the school locker room in the morning. It'd be nice to be in a house again."

"She has a tenant," Harry announced. He draped his arm over her shoulders and squeezed her to his side, warning Bernie that no other man was going to get close to her while he was around.

A twinge of discomfort pinged in Daisy's memories

and she quietly extricated herself from Harry's grasp. Had being protective of her just taken a step over the line into Brock Jantzen land?

Bernie got the message loud and clear, instantly backing off from the possibility of moving in with her. "Yeah. Well, if I had known the kind of stuff you were getting, I'd have said something sooner."

Daisy nodded, putting another step between her and Harry. "Thanks for letting me know."

Perhaps Bernie still didn't realize the depth of terror she'd been living with the past two weeks. "Guess that's going to ruin the party for you next Saturday. It won't be a surprise for you when we reveal who had whose name."

She'd already had plenty of surprises this week. She glanced over at the back of Harry's dark, close-cropped hair that she'd had such fun tickling her palms against last night. Only one of those surprises had been good. Harry Lockhart. The surprise of this relationship—if that was what it even was—was awkward. Difficult and uncertain. But a good surprise, nonetheless.

Cognizant of their audience here and in the car, Daisy tabled her analysis over what, exactly, Harry meant to her, and whether the reality of a relationship with a man struggling with PTSD was something she wanted to take on. She waved to Angelo and offered Bernie a smile. "Thanks for helping with Angelo. And I'm sorry to hear about you and Stella."

"Thanks."

"Talk to her," Daisy suggested. "Listen, too. If you can communicate, you can solve just about anything." She wondered if Harry was hearing any of that advice. "And—maybe you shouldn't give me any more presents. Not even the big one for the party. Return it. Donate it to charity. Give it to someone else. If this guy doesn't have that anonymous way to send me gifts, maybe he'll stop."

"If you say so." Bernie strode around the clear path of the sidewalk and climbed into his car, doffing her a salute before driving away.

Harry watched the car all the way to the stop sign at the corner before looking up at her. "He won't stop."

Although she was the one wearing the coat, Daisy shivered and turned to the front door. "Thank you for those fine words of comfort."

He caught her hand and stopped her. "This isn't a joke. Perverts like that, they'll find a way to get to you if that's what they want. If you cut him off, if he thinks you're on to him, he might escalate."

"Someone locked me in a room and started a fire that could have killed me." So much for subtle hints. Daisy tugged her hand free, regretting that she'd forgotten the soldier sorely lacking verbal communication skills after being with the passionate, bravely vulnerable man last night. "Things have already escalated."

"Damn it, Daisy, I'm not making light of what happened." When she snatched her hand from his, he fell back to the top step. "Don't be a fool. What if Riley confessed to being your Secret Santa just to throw you off track so you wouldn't suspect him? Why do his clothes smell like that fire? What if Angelo isn't as innocent as you seem to think?"

"What if Stella Riley is so jealous of something she thinks I've done that she wants to torment me?" Daisy crossed the porch to look him straight in the eye. "I'm not stupid. You don't think I've thought of any of that? All I have are suspects and threats. What I don't have are answers. I don't know who to trust anymore. This isn't over.

Not until I know who is doing this to me, and that creep is in jail. But I am—"

"—going to stay positive?" That was sarcasm, deriding her for the very trait he'd praised the night before.

"I was going to say I'm keeping my guard up."

"You didn't with me." He threw his hands up. "You worry too much about everybody else. You're too forgiving. You're going to get hurt."

"You're being a jerk right now, you know that?" The differences between them had finally erupted into an argument that neither one of them could win. His heart might be in the right place, believing he was protecting her, but she couldn't live her life being judged and criticized and ordered around. "Where's my Harry? Where's the man from those letters?"

He jolted back, as if she'd slapped him across the face. When he spoke again, it was a quiet, unemotional tone. "I warned you I wasn't any good at this. I was a different man then."

Daisy touched his chest, splaying her fingers until she could feel the strong beat of his heart beneath her hand. Her tone was hushed, too. "No. You're the same man. That's the man who was with me last night. But you went through something awful, more than a good man should have to bear. You just have to find him again."

That muscle ticked beneath his eye again as he evaluated her words. "You don't have to welcome me into your bedroom anymore, but I'm not leaving you unprotected. My gear's already upstairs. I'll sleep up there and start paying you rent."

He was serious about becoming her tenant, about taking a relationship that had heated to incendiary in the span of forty-eight hours back to let's-just-be-friends. Her life was safer this way, right? Her heart most certainly was.

She should be glad that one of them could think sensibly here. Instead, she felt hollow inside, as though she'd lost something that was more important than she realized. "If that's how you want it."

"That's how it needs to be."

The man needed his distance. He didn't trust himself not to hurt her. But how was she ever going to accept that the man she'd fallen in love with didn't want to be in a relationship? He didn't believe he could be. "Harry—"

The dogs started barking inside the house, ending the conversation. All three of her fur-babies were at the storm door, telling her she had company. She recognized the bark. It was the I-spy-another-dog alert. Her neighbor, Jeremiah Finch, was strolling by with his Chihuahua, Suzy, on a long black leash. "Good morning, Daisy."

"Good morning, Mr. Finch." Harry didn't turn, didn't offer any polite greeting to the older man in his trim wool coat and neatly tied scarf. Harry snapped his fingers and used a hand signal to calm Caliban and Patch into a tail-wagging sit, leaving Muffy as the only noisemaker announcing their visitor. When Jeremiah stopped to let Suzy sniff out the new smells of all the visitors Daisy had had that morning, she moved off the porch to continue the conversation. "It's shaping up to be the nicest day we've had in weeks. I'm glad you and Suzy are getting out."

"I'm not sure I want to, even in the daylight."

"What do you mean?"

He clucked his tongue behind his teeth. "We have a crime wave in our neighborhood."

"A crime wave? You mean the police car that was here earlier?" She summoned a smile to reassure him that whatever was happening was only happening to her. "The situation has been taken care of."

"Has it?" He came halfway up her front walk, as if

she couldn't hear him tsk-tsking over the short distance already. "Some punk vandalized your house. I have trespassers in my backyard—one of my boxwood bushes was trampled on." He peeked around her, eyeing the gun strapped to Harry's thigh. "Men with guns are roaming at will—"

"Harry is not roaming the neighborhood."

Suddenly, Harry was interested in joining the conversation. He trotted down the steps to join her, holding up his phone. "Mr. Finch, do you mind if I take pictures of the footprints in your backyard?"

Jeremiah seemed taken aback to be addressed directly by the bigger man. "As long as that's all you do."

With a nod, Harry jogged through the snow and disappeared around the corner of the house.

Once Harry was gone, Jeremiah tugged on Suzy's leash so he could lean in toward Daisy. "Don't think I didn't see your thug sitting outside your house the night before last. He was probably casing the joint. He's casing mine now. But I could hardly stop him. And you've invited him into your home. After what happened with your last boyfriend, I would think you'd be more careful about who you associate with. I try to keep an eye on you and protect you—"

"First of all, Master Sergeant Harry Lockhart is no thug. He's a decorated marine. Second, my student may be a misguided young man, but he is not a punk and he is no threat to you. If he damaged one of your bushes, I'll make sure he pays to replace it. And third, what happened to me is my business, not yours. How I protect myself is none of your concern."

"I can see you're upset." Jeremiah's face had turned red all the way up to his hairline. "So, this person—is a bodyguard? What kind of threat are we talking about?" He clutched at his chest. "Am I in danger?"

"No." Daisy reached down to pet Suzy when the tiny dog put her paws on Daisy's knee. Dogs had always been a stress reducer for her. She couldn't imagine losing any one of hers the way Harry had lost Tango. "I'm sorry I lost my temper. I've been receiving threats. Harry is a…friend… who's helping me keep an eye on things."

"I see." Jeremiah tugged the Chihuahua back to his side. "I still don't like seeing guns in my neighborhood. And your friend is so…rough-looking. Are you certain you're safe with him?"

Wasn't that the question of the hour?

"I know you were friends with Mom and Dad, and you have been friends with me—but to come over to my home and lecture me about my choices…" Even if they were bad ones, he had no right to make her feel stupid for trusting her heart or wanting to help a good man. Mr. Finch didn't have that right. Harry didn't. No one did.

Jeremiah glanced over to the side yard where Harry had gone. "Well, if something happens and you do need me, you have my number. Come along, Suzy."

As Mr. Finch and Suzy moved on down the street to continue their walk, Daisy pressed her hands over her mouth, fighting back the urge to cry or cuss up a blue streak. She wouldn't apologize for defending the people she cared about, but there had to be a better way to cope with the fear and uncertainty and raging need to have control over her own life again. Maybe this was what Harry felt like when he lost it. But she was years past her trauma while his was still fresh. The stress was getting to be too much. She was tired of being afraid, of suspecting everyone she knew. She needed this to be done.

"Daisy?" She started at the clipped voice behind her, and quickly swiped at the tears in her eyes before they could fall. "Are you all right?"

She turned to face Harry, wishing she had the right to walk into his arms and be held. But there was a tension between them now that hadn't been there before, an underlying sizzle of attraction that was complicated in a big way by far too many issues that neither of them could control.

When she didn't answer, he pulled out his phone. "I found something important. Something that should exonerate Angelo."

"I never believed he was sending me those gifts."

"But would it make you feel better to know for sure? To have one less person around you who could be a suspect?"

He was trying to make her feel better? That earned him the shadow of a smile. He wasn't offering comforting words or a hug. But it would be nice to be able to look over her classroom on Monday and not have to be afraid of anyone there. "What did you find?"

"The footprints were made by two different kinds of shoes. Angelo's has a tread, like a running shoe. The prints in Finch's yard, like the ones by your window the other night, were made by boots."

She wasn't comforted yet. "Maybe Angelo wore boots the other night to peek my window. He's not so poor that he can't afford more than one pair of shoes."

"Only if he figured out a way to shrink his feet." Harry pulled up the pictures on his phone and showed her the images. "It's not scientific, but it's enough to make me suspicious." Harry had photographed all three sets of prints frozen in the snow, using his own boot as a marker beside each one to compare the size. Angelo's running shoes were a good two to three sizes bigger, while the others were smaller and skinnier than Harry's foot. "I'm going to send the pictures to Pike. He's not a detective, but he'll know who to show them to."

"Thank you." Daisy appreciated the effort he was making to ease some of her fear. Maybe it was the only way he thought he could help.

"I'm sorry I thought the worst of that kid. But it does prove that this guy isn't just targeting you at school. He knows where you live. He's been here. Watching you."

"And the gloom and doom is back." Daisy marched up the stairs into the house. She shooed the dogs ahead of her while Harry locked the door behind her. "You think I don't know that he's watching? That I don't feel him around me all the time?" Harry followed her into the kitchen where she poured herself a cup of coffee and held the steaming mug between her hands. "This is where you're supposed to say something to make me feel better."

When he didn't say anything, she shrugged out of his coat and tossed it at him. He dropped the coat onto a chair and followed her to the refrigerator. "I heard you defending me against Finch. You didn't have to do that. I was losing it with that kid. I got territorial with Coach Riley. I was making decisions without asking you. I'm fighting to keep you safe. But the way I talked to you—the words, the tone? I could tell I hurt you. Last night was…amazing. A perfect moment out of time between all the nightmares." Just as she closed her eyes to let the raw poetry of his words warm her battered heart, he added, "But I'm not good for you, Daisy. Maybe I am a thug."

She refused to believe that.

"Normal people have arguments just like we did. Normal people lose it every now and then. You're not going to be cured after one late-night conversation and…" *a perfect moment out of time.* Hugging the creamer to her chest, she closed the fridge and turned to find Harry standing right there. He was close enough to touch, close enough to stretch on tiptoe to kiss that handsome, awkward mouth that had loved her so thoroughly. But she did neither. The mixture of pain and longing stamped on his chiseled features tore at her heart. "You've taken a big first step toward healing. But there are bound to be relapses. Fight through them. Accept that sometimes you're going to fail, then move on. You don't think I get depressed sometimes? That I don't get angry? Look at me yelling at poor Mr. Finch. You have to give it time."

"Time is one thing I don't have. If I don't get my head on right before I return to the Corps in six weeks, they won't take me." He captured a strand of hair that had fallen over her cheek and rubbed it between his thumb and fingers before smoothing it behind her ear and backing away. "Maybe no one should." He grabbed his coat and headed to the front door. "Lock yourself in with the dogs. I need to clear my head."

Daisy hurried after him. "You can't go for a walk with your foot cut up like that."

"Then I'll drive." He opened the front door and pointed to the lock behind him. "I'll be back by lunch. Anything happens, you call me or the cops."

"What if something happens to *you*?" That stopped him.

Then he tunneled his fingers into the hair at her nape, cupped the back of her neck and pulled her onto her toes for a hard, potent kiss. He kissed her a second time. And a third. "I'll think about that. And how much I want…to be fixed. For you."

Chapter Ten

Harry returned two and a half hours later with several new strings of outdoor Christmas lights and an eight-foot Scotch pine tree for Daisy's living room. He'd also purchased a properly sized winter coat for himself in basic beige and a lavender parka with a bow on the belt he guessed would be about Daisy's size. The thank you hugs were a nice bonus, but he hadn't let her smile or welcoming arms sway him from his mission. He had something to prove, not only to Daisy, but to himself.

This time, he hadn't hiked through the snow or spent a couple of hours breathing fresh air. Sure, he'd driven around the neighborhood for about ten minutes, thinking he needed to clear his head. But then he realized he didn't need to clear anything—he needed to accept everything that was jumbled up inside him and attack it with a plan. He needed to think like a marine.

Protect the base. Get intel. Know your enemy. Trust your allies.

He'd called Pike to drive over and keep an eye on Daisy's house while he was gone. Then he'd asked his brother-in-law about the photos he'd taken, and ended up talking to one of his friends, a Detective Nick Fensom, who was familiar with Daisy's assault case. The detective confirmed to Harry's own peace of mind that Daisy's ex was still incarcerated, and that the people around her, Bernie and Stella Riley, Angelo and Albert Logan, didn't have criminal records. Nick reminded Harry that just because a person didn't have a record, it didn't mean he or she didn't have it in for Daisy. She might be the stalker's first target, or he simply hadn't been reported or caught for this kind of behavior previously.

Detective Fensom also wanted to know more about the threats she'd been receiving, and promised to contact both the Central Prep principal, Ryan Hague, and John Murdock at the KCFD to get details on the events that had happened at the school. Fensom also wanted to document the messages and gifts Daisy had received, along with a timeline so he could put together a case against her stalker once he was caught. And he would be caught, if Harry had anything to do with it.

When he got back to the house, Pike and his son, Gideon, were building a snowman in the front yard, away from where the shards of broken bulbs still littered the snow. Hope was in the kitchen helping Daisy fix them all some lunch. By the time Gideon and Hope lay down for afternoon naps, he and Pike had put up the Christmas tree, swept off the deck and put all the dogs through their paces in the backyard. Caliban was an old pro, slow but responsive to each command. Patch picked up on the training quickly, even learning a couple of new tricks. And Muffy was, well, what the dog lacked in attention span he made up for in personality. The misnamed Shih Tzu was never going to make it in the K-9 Corps, but he sure knew how to sound an alarm. Whether he was letting them know that Albert and Angelo had arrived to help clean up the yard, or he was chasing a bird off the fence, Muffy had something to say about it.

After they ordered pizza and finished dinner, Hope and

her family and the two teenagers left. Trying to remember that he was the tenant/bodyguard and not the crazy boyfriend who wanted to peel the bright red Chiefs sweatshirt and matching glasses off Daisy and see if the miracle of last night had been a fluke, he put the dogs out, checked the locks, then resolutely ignored Daisy's blue-eyed disappointment and went upstairs to shower and get whatever sleep he could.

After his shopping trip that morning, he'd also come back with personal supplies he needed to put away, and a wood train set for his nephew that he hid on the top shelf of his closet until he could get it wrapped. All in all, it was a productive day. A healthy, normal, "worn out by work instead of an ongoing mental battle" kind of day. He hadn't wigged out and he hadn't hurt anyone.

Now if he could do this again tomorrow. And the day after that.

Harry toweled off and pulled on a clean pair of shorts and the faded USMC sweatpants he slept in. The lights were off downstairs and Daisy and the dogs had gone to bed. Alone in the soothing quiet, he stowed his service Beretta in the nightstand and dumped out his recent purchases on the bed. He packed the fresh bar of soap, disposable razors and condoms in his toiletry bag, set the pack of gum on the dresser beside his wallet, and opened the box of bandages and antibiotic salve before sitting down to redress the cuts on his feet. None of them were bad enough to need stitches, but an infection was the last thing he needed right now. When he'd finished medic duty, he folded down the quilt, piled the pillows against the headboard and picked up the package of ink pens and the spiral notebook he'd bought.

This was going to be the hard part.

Harry flipped open the notebook and stared at the blank

piece of paper. He breathed deeply, steeling himself for the task at hand. He might not be a natural talent for this relationship stuff, or understand the intricate workings of the human brain, but he knew how to follow orders.

He started writing.

Day one. Mission accomplished.

A list was easier than coming up with sentences and paragraphs. He stated his objectives, and how well he'd met them.

Lt. Col. Biro had ordered him to get a Christmas tree and eat too many sweets. Check and check.

The lieutenant colonel had also ordered him to kiss a pretty girl. Definitely a check. Multiple checks. If he succeeded with this plan of action, he hoped to fill up this entire notebook with check marks on that assignment.

But for now, he'd sustain himself on the memory of Daisy's patience with him, her acceptance of his scars, her passionate abandon to touch and be touched that forced him to tip his head back and breathe deeply to cool his body's desire to march down those stairs to be with her again. She'd probably welcome him to her bed because she was Daisy—the woman who cared too much and forgave too easily. But Harry had every intention of proving he was worthy of that compassion and forgiveness before indulging his physical needs. He didn't want to be another rescue mission for her. He wanted to be a whole man—one who never left her second-guessing her willingness to trust him. He wanted to be a man she could love without any regrets.

The objective was clear. Follow orders. Complete the mission.

Back to the notebook.

Dr. Polk had advised him to get plenty of exercise, journal his thoughts and keep his appointments. Check. Check. Check.

Daisy said to write her letters.

Harry hesitated. What exactly was he supposed to say to her that wouldn't sound pitiful or controlling or downright scary?

He clipped the pen onto the paper and rolled out of bed to do twenty reps on the pull-up bar he'd hung over the door. When he focused on the burning muscles, the memories in his head sorted themselves.

Daisy liked to talk. And if he was a smart man, he would listen.

You're giving me value by trusting me with your fears, by sharing your darkest feelings, by helping me understand you.

He went back to the bed, turned to a new page in the notebook and started writing.

Dear Daisy...

HARRY LED A normal life for the next four days.

He drove Daisy to school and picked her up afterward. He restocked her groceries and took out her trash. He spent a long two hours babysitting Gideon so that Hope could take a break and have lunch with a friend. He and Daisy met with Nick Fensom in her classroom, handing over the evidence from her desk and briefing the detective on anyone she suspected.

Since his feet were too sore to do a daily run, Harry put the dogs in the truck and hauled them to a dog park for a good workout. He discovered Patch had an affinity for catching flying discs and Albert Logan had an interest in learning more about training dogs. He'd picked up Albert after a tutoring session with Daisy and brought him to the house to teach the young man some of the skills he'd learned as a handler. He took Daisy out to dinner one night on a real date, even kissing her good-night at the front door before heading upstairs to his room as if they were getting newly acquainted. Daisy was frustrated with the distance he was keeping. The frustrated desire was wearing on him, too. "I'm trying to get your Harry back," he promised her. Ultimately, she seemed to understand that he needed to do this and gave him the space he asked for.

There were no more messages from Secret Santa, no odious gifts delivered. Bernie Riley kept his promise and stopped leaving items for her at school. The quiet spell seemed to back up Riley's claim that someone had been swapping out the innocent gifts his wife had picked out with the cruel taunts and graphic images. Daisy wanted to believe that, with no outlet, the threats had stopped for good. But neither she nor Harry really did. This was simply the calm before the storm. Harry suspected that, like an enemy whose line of propaganda had been cut off, the pervert's frustration was building like a volcano about to erupt. Without a daily avenue to get his message across to Daisy, he was probably planning something even bigger and more terrifying to grab her attention. Harry intended to be ready to protect her from whatever that threat might be.

Harry might be broken inside, but he'd been trained to adapt and overcome to get the job done. If his job was proving to Daisy, and more importantly to himself, that he was healthy relationship material, then he was going to do whatever it took to make that happen.

Including writing in that spiral notebook every night.

Some of the entries were horrible, angry scratches that cut through five sheets of paper. Some were just a report of his day—his successes and his failures. The fresh batches of cookies he'd volunteered to sample. The training sessions with the dogs. Working with Angelo and Albert to move some furniture and crates into the garage and finish a couple of painting projects before the Christmas party, when the house would be invaded by thirty-seven teachers and staff, along with their significant others.

His chest got tight just thinking about a crowd of noisy revelers invading Daisy's home. If Secret Santa was one of her coworkers, would he try something that night? Or would he wait until he had a private time and place to finish whatever he had in mind for Daisy?

Tonight, those troubling thoughts about where all this was headed had morphed into a nightmare. Sitting bolt upright in a cold sweat, Harry kicked back the covers that had twisted around his legs and cursed the darkness. He flipped on the lamp beside him and focused on it, inhaling several cooling breaths. He didn't know how long he'd been thrashing in the bed, or if he'd been swearing out loud in his sleep, but he'd been caught up in a dream long enough to have knocked a pillow, his cell phone and the notebook to the floor. He straightened the mess and picked up his pen.

14 December 3:17 a.m.
Dear Daisy,
Thought I was having a good day today. But you were right. Relapses happen and suddenly I'm in the middle of a nightmare. I know it's just in my head. But the fear felt pretty damn real.

You were in that fire again. Only, I couldn't get to you. I don't know what's wrong with my brain that it can only picture the worst. Why aren't I dreaming about the way your blue eyes squint me into focus when you want something from me? Or the way they darkened like midnight when you flew apart all around me? Any other guy would be dreaming about the sex. And don't think I haven't imagined being with you again.

But no, my brain took you with me when I went back to that firefight with the IEDs going off. I had Tango in my arms that day, and I guess a lot of the blood I saw on him was my own. But it all got jumbled up and I was holding you and there was nothing but blood and fire. I couldn't see your smile. I couldn't hear your laugh. I couldn't stop screaming.

The smell of burning skin is an awful, awful...

A soft metallic clinking noise turned Harry's attention to the door. Any mild sense of alarm that he hadn't detected the noise sooner ebbed when he identified the familiar sound of jangling dog tags and the click, click, click of paws slowly coming up the stairs. Who was making the rounds tonight? "Patch? Fur ball?"

He slept with the door open so that he'd be able to hear anything happening on the ground floor he needed to investigate. But he was unprepared for the furry gray muzzle peeking around the door frame or the Belgian Malinois panting for breath as he stared at Harry from the doorway.

"Caliban?" The dog's dark ears pricked up with recognition. For a brief moment, Tango's dark muzzle superimposed itself over the old dog's face. Harry blinked and Caliban returned. But the same heart and spirit remained in those dark brown eyes. "You worried about me, buddy?" The dog cocked his head to one side as if they were having a conversation and Harry chuckled. "I would be, too." He tossed the notebook aside. "Come here, boy. *Hier.*" Caliban trotted over in his rolling gait and Harry patted the top of the mattress, inviting him up beside him. *"Hopp."*

When Caliban jumped up onto the quilt, Harry rewarded him with a little bit of wrestling that ended with a tummy rub and him smiling. "Good boy. I guess those sharp old ears heard me." Caliban thrust his front paw into the air so that Harry could scratch the leg pit there. "You're used to looking out for a partner. And now you're looking out for me."

The nightmare faded and some good memories of his time with Tango made his eyes gritty with tears. "Tango used to wake me up when I got to tossing and turning too much, too. You lost your partner and I lost mine. We'll look out for each other, okay?"

Caliban rolled onto his belly, sitting up like a Sphinx and eyeing the door.

Harry swung his legs off the edge of the bed. "I hear it, too."

A parade of dog paws rushing up the stairs, followed by the noise of creaking wood as someone slightly heavier hurried behind them. Muffy and Patch dashed in and jumped right up on the bed, jockeying for petting position beside him. "Hello, you two."

At the last second, he remembered to shove his notebook out of sight under his pillow before rising to meet Daisy when she appeared in the doorway.

"Hello." Her hair was tousled and sexy, she had a wrinkle on her cheek from her pillow, and she was wearing those shapeless flannel pajamas that were almost as soft as her skin. The hungry sweep of her gaze over his bare chest intensified the gut-kick of desire already rushing through his blood and threatened to undo every well-planned good intention of his recovery mission. He pushed the excited dogs away and took a step closer. "Did I wake you?" Dumb question. Clearly, she was worried about him.

"You mean the headboard banging against the wall up here?" She held up her thumb and forefinger pinched together. "Little bit."

"Sorry." He nodded over his shoulder. "Caliban came up to…"

"Are you all right?"

Her question topped his statement and they both fell silent.

Daisy hugged her arms beneath her breasts and nodded toward the three-legged dog. "When I woke up, I realized he was missing. This is the last place I would have looked if I hadn't heard you. He's never come up the stairs before. He must really like you."

"He probably recognizes a kindred spirit."

She wasn't wearing her robe or those fuzzy slipper socks. As she drew invisible circles on the hardwood with her big toe, he noticed something he hadn't before. She painted her toenails. Purple, like the highlights in her hair. It was hard to remember the way he'd first pictured Daisy—the golden angel dressed in white and bathed in sunshine. The real Daisy was meant for moonlight and bold color and ill-timed fantasies in the middle of the night.

"Do you need to talk about it? The nightmare?"

"I'm not dumping on you."

The circles stopped. "It's not dumping. It's one friend listening to another."

"No."

"What about your therapist? Or your sister?" Her shoulders puffed up with a sigh and she kept talking. "I know you're on some kind of healing journey. You're afraid that you're going to scare me or hurt me or make me worry too much. Well, I'm always going to worry about you. That's what people who care about each other do, so you're not doing me any favors by isolating yourself."

"I am not dumping on you." When her blue eyes peeked above the rims of her glasses, he put up his hands and tried to reassure her. "But I'm not bottling it all up inside, either. I'm following doctor's orders. And Lieutenant Colonel Biro's orders. And…your orders."

"Mine?"

"Something you said the other night. I've been writing letters."

"To me?"

"In a journal of sorts." Muffy knocked aside his pillow to claim a spot on the bed, and revealed his secret. "Thanks for ratting me out, fur ball." Harry picked up the pillow and set the spiral notebook on the bedside table. "I don't know if anyone is ever going to read it. But it helps to get it out."

"I'm proud of you, Harry. I know it can't be easy."

"It's important to me that I'm in control of myself—how I react to people, how I treat you—before I let you and me go any further." He'd already given her his heart—there wasn't much further he could go. But he didn't want to ruin the best thing that had ever happened to him before it had even gotten started. "The dream tonight kind of rattled me. Made me think that I wasn't the right man to protect you."

"Harry, I don't want—"

He pressed a finger against her lips to silence her argument. "I make no claims to be a hundred percent yet. But I'm not trusting anyone else with the job of keeping you safe."

"Okay," she murmured beneath his finger. "May I talk now?"

He lingered a little longer where he shouldn't before curling his fingers into his palm and pulling away. "I needed you to understand that."

"There's no one I trust more to protect me. I just wish you'd let me do something for you in return."

Maybe there was something. "Could I hold you for a while? After what I saw, I won't be able to sleep unless I know you're safe. And the only way I can know that when I'm dozing off is to—"

She walked straight into his chest and wrapped her arms around his waist. Her forehead found that familiar spot against his neck and she softened against him, fitting all her curves to his harder planes. "I can stay."

Feeling the tension of his nightmare leaving his body already, Harry wound his arms around her to complete the hug and nestled his nose against her hair. "Just to sleep, honey." He was reminding his own body's eager response to her touch, as much as clarifying the request for her. "You've got school tomorrow morning."

"I am happy to hold and be held by you anytime, Harry Lockhart." She pressed her lips to the scar beneath his collarbone. "Do you think I've been getting good sleep downstairs by myself? I need you close by so I know you're safe, too."

They stood like that until Harry's body began to respond in a way he hadn't intended. Forcing himself to pull away, he led her to the bed and tucked her under the covers. After setting her glasses aside, he claimed the spot Muffy wanted, lay down on top of the quilt and pulled Daisy into his arms. As the three dogs settled in behind her and at the foot of the bed, Harry reached over and turned off the lamp.

"This is better," she whispered, resting her head on his shoulder.

"Much better."

Daisy and the dogs were all asleep when Harry heard a car door slamming outside. He gently extricated himself from the arm around his waist and went to the front and side windows to peek through the curtains. He scanned up and down the block, looking for the exhaust from a running car or any signs of movement. But there was nothing suspicious—no one in her yard or walking the street. He went across the hall and looked out the bathroom window to see if the new motion detector light he'd installed over the deck had come on. But the back of the house was dark and still. No heartbroken teenager busting up the new lights, no one throwing snowballs at the house or standing outside her bedroom window.

By the time Harry returned, Caliban had raised his head in curiosity, but wasn't alerting to any signs of an intruder. Muffy would certainly be going off if someone was trying to break in. Harry petted the Malinois and climbed back into bed. The house was locked up tight. His gun was in arm's reach and Daisy was tucked safely in his arms.

If the dogs weren't worried about one lone sound in the night, he wouldn't be, either.

EVEN IF DAISY was willing to risk a little PDA in front of the students hurrying through the front doors for a morning practice or the breakfast program, the dogs wedged between her and Harry in the front seat of his truck would have prevented it.

"You're spoiling them," she teased, pulling Muffy back to her lap to avoid the Shih Tzu's marauding tongue. She was pleased to see that Caliban had claimed his spot beside Harry on the bench seat. The older dog had perked up in both energy and personality since Harry had moved into the house. Patch stood with his front paws on the dashboard, wagging his little bob of a tail and watching the students and staff walk past the truck in the circular driveway. He just wanted to be a part of what everyone else was doing. "You've been to the dog park every morning this week."

Harry rubbed his hand around Caliban's ears. "It gives

me a little exercise, too. Plus, there aren't a lot of people there this time of year."

"Do you think you'll ever be able to tolerate crowds again?"

"Who knows? I'm a work in progress." He shifted his petting hand to Patch, who instantly crawled over Caliban to sit in Harry's lap. His stiff half smile faded as he turned his attention to the people walking past. "Look at all the blue coats and yellow caps going into Central Prep. Maybe you should invite me to speak to your classes."

"About what?"

"PTSD? My career in the military? How letter writing is a lost art and they should be glad you're teaching it to them?"

She understood what Harry's sudden willingness to spend the day with a bunch of hormonal teenagers was really about. "So you can keep an eye on me?"

"Too controlling?"

She reached across the seat to pull his gloved hand off Patch and squeeze it. "You aren't Brock Jantzen."

He squeezed back. "I'm just trying to be a better Harry Lockhart."

"You know I'll be waiting for you whenever you're ready, right?"

"What if I'm never ready?"

Daisy wondered if never being Harry's woman would be worse than being the woman he had loved and left behind because he decided he couldn't do relationships, after all. But that was too heart-breaking a topic to discuss on this sunny winter morning when Harry was fighting like everything to find his new normal. She smiled, instead, pulling her hand away to adjust Muffy's red sweater. "Fridays I don't have to stay late, so be here at three-thirty."

"Yes, ma'am. On the dot."

Daisy dumped Muffy off her lap and looped her pink bag over her shoulder. "Have a good day, Top."

"Be safe, Ms. G." When she turned to assure him she would, he was already leaning in. "Come here," he growled.

His firm lips scudded across hers in a searing kiss. His touch warmed her all the way down to the toes of her boots. Not that she'd ever complained, but he was growing more confident, less self-conscious with every kiss. Daisy touched her fingers to his jaw and would have encouraged him to explore his craft to his heart's content, but there were suddenly cold noses and warm tongues trying to join in.

"Blecch." Daisy flattened her hand between them to ward off the licks on her neck and chin while Harry retreated to his side of the truck, his deep chest bouncing with laughter. Daisy joined him. A genuine laugh from Harry was worth a hundred kisses.

She opened the truck door and climbed out. "Bye."

Daisy walked through a gauntlet of "woo-hoos" and whistles, and a couple of thumbs-ups from students and staff as she headed inside and crossed through the lobby. "You people need to go study," she admonished, hoping they'd mistake the blush on her cheeks as a sign of the cold morning air and not her happy embarrassment.

She ran into Mary Gamblin in the teachers' lounge and poured herself a mug of coffee before walking down the hallway to their rooms together. "Are you still feeling up to that party tomorrow?" Mary asked. "With everything that's going on, isn't it stressing you out?"

"No," Daisy answered honestly. "It gives me something fun and positive to focus on. You better come and help me eat all the cookies I've baked this week. If everybody doesn't bring the potluck dishes they signed up for, we're all going to be on a massive sugar high by the end of the evening."

"It's good to see you in a happy mood again. Does it have anything to do with that marine you were kissing out front?"

There was no masking the blush on her cheeks this time. "Did everybody see that?"

"Enough people to start the rumor mill."

Daisy nudged her shoulder against her friend's, refusing to be the only fodder for gossip today. "What about you? Are you and Eddie coming to the party together?"

"I had to drop about every hint I could." Mary rolled her eyes and giggled. "But yeah. He asked me."

"Awesome." They reached their respective rooms across the hall from each other and inserted their keys into the locks. "Hey, I hung some mistletoe if you'd like to take advantage…"

"He's a slow mover."

"Maybe a Christmas kiss will help him move a little faster."

"Fingers crossed." They pushed open their doors. "Have a good day."

"You, too."

Once inside her room, Daisy turned on the lights and unhooked the lavender bow on her coat, unbuttoning the gift from Harry as she crossed to the front of the room to her desk. She set her coffee on the corner and pulled out her chair.

And froze.

No. Whatever she was feeling right now went beyond freezing. She couldn't think. Couldn't move. Couldn't feel.

Her bag dropped to the floor beside her. She stared at the neatly-wrapped oblong box lying on the seat of her chair. Decorated with an all too familiar card emblazoned with a sparkly green tree, the present taunted her with its ominous promise.

As the feeling returned to her limbs, she leaned over to read the words typed across the face of the card.

Get rid of him! Or I will.
You belong to me.
Merry Christmas from your Secret Santa.

"Oh, my God." A righteous anger suddenly flowed through her body, giving her the strength to move. Leaving her gloves on in case her tormentor had slipped up this time and left fingerprints, she picked up the box, finding it surprisingly heavy for its size. She dropped it onto the middle of her blotter and stooped down to dig her phone out of her purse.

Her first instinct was to call Harry. She needed him here with her. Now. Nobody else understood, nobody else cared as much, about how terrified she was of her stalker. She needed his arms. His growly comforts and complaints. His do-the-job-or-die attitude to make the terror go away.

Her hands were shaking as she pulled up the call screen. But it was pointless to pull up her list of contacts as she remembered they were more about touching and talking in person, and had been together so much of the past week that she hadn't needed to call him. Until she needed to call him. Like now. Daisy pushed to her feet. "Even if you can never say you love me, you are going to give me your phone number, damn it."

But the flare of anger, aimed mostly at herself, quickly abated. Red liquid was seeping through the wrapping paper from a corner of the box she must have bent when she'd dropped it. The liquid, viscous and thick, spread across the white blotter, creating a crimson puddle in the middle of her desk.

"Please don't be…" She untied the bow and lifted the lid. She squeezed her hand over her mouth, fighting back the urge to scream. The box held a soldier action figure, his face blacked out with ink. The whole thing was sitting in a pool of red liquid that could only be one thing. Blood.

Animal blood. Fake blood. A grotesque pint from her stalker, it didn't matter. Daisy turned away from the gruesome gift and swiped her hand across her phone, dialing 9-1-1. She needed to notify Mr. Hague, too. And more than anything, she needed to get a hold of Harry.

"9-1-1. What is the nature of your emergency?"

"My name is Daisy Gunderson. I'm a teacher at Central Prep Academy."

The bell rang and the hallway filled with noise as students came up the stairs and went to their lockers.

Daisy plugged her finger over her free ear and raised her voice. "Can you connect me directly to Detective Nick Fensom? Or take a report that will get to him? He's investigating a case for me and there's been another incident."

"It looks like Detective Fensom is attached to the Fourth Precinct. If this isn't an emergency, let me…."

Locker doors slammed and chatting students filtered into the classroom. "I'm sorry. Could you repeat that?"

"Yo, Ms. G."

"Do we have to take that test today?"

"How much of it is essay?"

She turned away from the friendly greetings and typical questions as the students came in, some automatically stuffing their phones into the shoe bag by the door, others gawking at the crude gift sitting in a puddle of blood on her desk.

"Ms. G., you can't have your cell phone in class."

"What is that?"

"Gross!"

She shushed the teasing and cringing so she could make her report.

And that's when the intercom over the door crackled to life and Mr. Hague made an announcement. "Attention, staff. Mr. Brown is in the building. I repeat, Mr. Brown is in the building. This is not a drill."

The students looked at each other. Some of the young faces were grave, others panicked a bit. A few were blessedly oblivious to the significance of the announcement.

"Everybody line up," Daisy ordered, pulling her phone from her ear. She picked up her attendance sheet, counted heads and quickly took roll. "Twenty. Twenty-one." All but one student accounted for. "Have any of you seen Angelo?"

There was a flurry of "nos" and "I-thought-I-saws" that were no help at all. "Somebody text him or call."

She opened her desk drawer to pull out her walkie-talkie for school emergencies, but it, too, was missing.

"He's not answering, Ms. G."

"He may not have his phone turned on. He knows you're not supposed to at school."

"Shouldn't we be going? Ms. Gamblin's class is leaving."

Daisy nodded. "If we pass your locker on the way out the door, you can grab your coat. Otherwise, keep moving." She searched two more drawers, knowing this was no drill, knowing they were all in serious trouble.

"Are you coming, Ms. G.?"

"I'm right behind you." She waved her class out the door. "Go."

She rummaged through the last two drawers. Secret Santa hadn't just left her the gift. He'd taken her walkie-talkie, isolating her from instant contact with the rest of the staff.

As per every evacuation, the fire alarm went off in a loud, continuous ringing, and Daisy's blood ran cold with fear. This was it. She felt it in her bones. Her fate was sealed.

"Ma'am, are you still there?" The dispatcher was prompting her to respond. She grabbed the clipboard with everyone's name and put the phone back to her ear. "My screen shows that we've already received a call from a Ryan Hague at that same location. Is this in relation to that call?"

Daisy mentally checked off the names on her list as each student filed past. But there was still one missing. It was too early in the day to have received the absentee list. She had to account for Angelo's location. "Down the stairs and out the door. Don't stop until you get to the church across the street."

"Ma'am? Are you there?"

Mr. Brown meant only one thing.

"Yes. There may be a bomb in the building."

Chapter Eleven

"Gunderson."

Daisy stopped her march toward the stairs and turned toward the summons. "Coach? What are you doing up here on the second floor?"

"Health class. Borrowing Musil's room since it's her free period. Showing a video—the kind you want a little more privacy for than in the gym." She scooted a group of students on past her and waited for Bernie to catch up before continuing toward the exit beside him. "Kind of sucky that I picked today of all days to borrow a room that's on the top floor." He snapped his fingers and pointed a young woman away from her locker. "Keep moving."

The frightened young woman linked arms with a friend and hurried to catch up with their classmates. "Slow down," Daisy reminded them, ducking away from the flashing light and deafening noise of the alarm as they walked past. "We want everyone to get there in one piece."

"Are we really taking all these kids outside in this weather?" Bernie asked.

"It's not a drill." Daisy lowered her voice so the students wouldn't overhear. "I just got off the phone with the 9-1-1 operator. Mr. Hague called them about a bomb threat."

Bernie let out a low whistle. "Somebody wanted Christmas vacation early, huh?"

More likely *somebody* didn't think she was frightened enough by threatening just her. Harry had been right about the violence escalating. Now her Secret Santa was threatening the people around her—the people she cared about—her students, friends and coworkers, Harry himself. And she had accused Harry of trying to control her. What an idiot. At least he had a legitimate reason for the pronouncements and territorial behavior—he was trying to protect her. Even Brock's obsession had never extended to hurting anyone beyond her.

Secret Santa had taken her life to a whole new level of scary this morning.

"My walkie-talkie is missing," she told Bernie. It was far easier to focus on her responsibilities as a teacher than to let one man's obsession get into her head and paralyze her with fear. "Will you call the office and find out if Angelo is absent today?"

"Don't have to. He's here."

"He wasn't in my first period class."

Bernie stopped in his tracks, muttering a curse that left a couple of students near the back of the line tittering at the grownup breaking a school rule. "They're cutting class now? That's the last thing Albert needs to do."

"But you saw them," Daisy clarified.

"Yeah. I had both brothers in my office before school to talk about putting Albert back on the team after the holidays. Part of Angelo's penance for the vandalism at your place will be helping his brother keep his grades up."

"Where is Albert now? Could they still be together? Maybe they've already exited the building with another group."

"I can find out."

"Mary? Ms. Gamblin?" Daisy dashed ahead to catch her friend at the top of the stairs and hand over her student roster. "Will you take my class with yours to the church? We have two missing students. The Logan twins."

"Of course." Mary herded both classes down the steps ahead of her. "Need any help?"

"We've got it covered. Just keep my kids safe." Daisy hurried back to Bernie, who was putting out an all call on the walkie-talkie on the missing student. "Who's got Albert Logan first hour?"

"I do," the answer crackled over the radio.

Recognizing the voice, Daisy pulled Bernie's device down to her level. "Eddie? Was Albert in class? Did you see Angelo with him?"

"No and no." Eddie Bosch sounded slightly breathless. "My chemistry class is already across the street. I'm running back in to look for him. I'll have to do a room-by-room search, including bathrooms and closets."

What were those boys up to? "I'm responsible for Angelo. I can help. What floor are you on?"

"I'll start in the basement and work my way up."

"I'll start on the second floor. I've got Bernie Riley with me."

The tall man nodded and put the radio back up to his mouth. "I'll check the first floor. Riley out."

"Bosch out."

Bernie caught Daisy by the shoulder and squeezed. "Will you be okay up here? You don't have a walkie-talkie."

She held up her phone. "I've got 9-1-1. As soon as you've cleared your floor, get out of here. I plan to do the same."

"All right." Bernie squeezed her arm again before releasing her. "Hague will be on the first floor, waiting for the first responders. I'll tell him that you, Bosch and I are still inside looking for the Logans. Meet me in the faculty parking lot when you're done so I know you're out of the building. Be careful."

"You, too."

He jogged down the stairs after the last of the students and disappeared around the corner of the landing.

Other than the jarring noise of the fire alarm, everything was a lot quieter now that the second floor had been evacuated and the main floor was emptying out. "Angelo? Albert?" Just like in their summer emergency training workshop, Daisy moved methodically down one side of the hallway, opening every door. "It's Ms. G. This isn't a drill. We need to evacuate the building."

When she reached the end of one row of classrooms, she crossed the hall and repeated the same search. "Is anyone up here?"

She reentered her own classroom, avoiding even an accidental glance at the bloody mess on her desk, and walked straight to her closet. Empty. There were only two classrooms left to search up here. There was probably a perfectly reasonable explanation for the missing twins. Maybe they'd never reached their first period classes and had been ushered outside by the first teacher who'd spotted them. But that teacher should have reported that they had them by now. Of course, without a radio, she wouldn't know if they'd been found. Best to keep moving, clear her floor and get outside.

She kept her focus out the bank of windows as she headed back toward the front of the room. From this vantage point, she could see the white steeple rising above the red brick church, and a sea of blue and gold Central Prep colors flowing slowly but steadily through the church's front doors. Maybe she'd be able to find the Logans once she was at the church with the rest of the evacuees, and they'd separated into their classes again in the various Sunday School rooms.

A latent image sharpened into focus and Daisy rushed back to the windows, wiping the condensation from the glass and peering closer. She recognized a loose-limbed stride and dark brown head. "Angelo? Albert?" She knocked against the window, knowing the church was too far away for anyone there to hear her. She could barely hear herself over the incessant ring of the fire alarm. Which one of the boys was that? With similar faces and matching uniforms, it was impossible to tell at this distance.

But she was certain she'd just spotted one of them. She pulled her cell phone from the pocket of her coat. Who should she call? She didn't keep student numbers in her phone. 9-1-1 would take too long. She needed an instant response. She could call one of the other teachers to track down the Logan she'd seen. But which one?

Daisy finally punched in her boss's number and hurried out the door. As the man coordinating the evacuation with KCFD and the police, he would definitely have his cell on him. When the principal answered, she quickly updated him. "I'm the last person on the second floor and I'm on my way down to the rear parking lot exit. I swear I just saw one of the Logan boys crossing the street to the church. Could you get someone down there to verify that for me?"

"Why aren't you on your radio?" Mr. Hague asked.

"*He* took it. I'm certain of it."

"He? The man sending you those messages?"

She entered the last room and checked the closet. "There was another gift on my desk this morning. Maybe the sickest one yet. I'm sorry, sir. I think this bomb threat is all about me. I never thought he'd endanger anyone else."

"I'll notify the police about your suspicions. Just get out

of the building. I'll call as soon as I hear anything about the Logan boys."

"Thank you, sir."

After disconnecting the call, Daisy hurried down the steps and walked as quickly as she dared without breaking into a run like the girls she'd chastised earlier.

But someone *was* running through the hallway.

"Daisy? Thank God, I caught you." She stopped and turned as Eddie Bosch jogged up to her. He grabbed her by both shoulders and gently shook her. "Why aren't you answering your radio? I thought something had happened to you."

Reaching up, she gave his wrist a squeeze of gratitude for his concern. "That sick Secret Santa of mine took it. He left me another present this morning."

"How bad?"

"Bad enough." She turned toward the exit, expecting him to walk with her. "Let's talk outside. I want to get to the church. I spotted one of the Logan boys there. Get on your radio and ask which Logan it is."

"It's Angelo."

She stopped again, frowning to see that he hadn't followed her. "How do you know?"

"Because I found Albert."

"That's wonderful news. Did you send him across the street?" When Eddie didn't immediately answer, she closed the distance between them. "What's wrong?"

"Albert is in the basement. He won't leave until he talks to you. Something about apologizing and doing right by you."

"That's ridiculous. Tell him to get his butt up here. I'll talk to him about anything—" she thumbed over her shoulder "—at the church."

"You don't understand."

"No, I don't." Why wasn't he moving?

"The bomb is real. I saw it with my own eyes."

Daisy shrank back at his grim declaration, hugging herself as an invisible chill washed over her. She'd known in her heart that this was no drill. But a real bomb? "I'd hoped it was just a threat."

Eddie shook his head. "I reported the location to Mr. Hague."

"Then we need to get Albert and go." She darted past him, moving toward the basement stairs.

But Eddie grabbed her arm and stopped her. "Maybe we should just let the police handle it."

Bernie Riley's voice cut through the static on Eddie's radio. "First floor is clear. If anyone has eyes on Ms. G., tell her I'm on my way out to meet her."

Eddie held up his radio. "Why are you meeting him?"

Daisy tugged her arm free. "He knows I don't have a walkie-talkie. We made a plan so that someone could confirm I was out of the building and the evacuation was complete."

"A plan? When did you talk to him? Where did you see him? His office and the gym are on the opposite side of the building from your classroom."

Daisy was backing away, needing to make sure one last student was safe. "A few minutes ago. Upstairs."

"You don't think that's suspicious? When did Coach Riley ever do something that benefitted anybody but himself?"

Bernie's explanation had been plausible. He'd had his class upstairs with him. But she supposed that could have been a cover. It would have certainly put him a lot closer to her room to leave that gift and steal her radio without being seen.

"You think Bernie is…" Daisy clenched her fists, shaking off the distracting thoughts. "Eddie, please. Either leave or come help me convince Albert to evacuate. This is my fault. That creeper who's after me—he's responsible. He can threaten me all he wants, but I am not going to let him hurt one of my students."

"Daisy." Eddie grabbed her by the wrist again, and she groaned with frustration. "The reason I couldn't get Albert to come with me…"

"What?"

"He's the one with the bomb."

HARRY PULLED OVER and slowed his truck as a third fire engine sped past in the oncoming lane. He didn't need Muffy sitting in his lap, barking at every flashing light, for the hackles on the back of his neck to go up.

Emergency vehicles didn't necessarily mean Daisy was in danger. There were other businesses and residential neighborhoods in that direction. There could have been an unfortunate vehicle accident.

Muffy spotted another speeding car and threw his paws against the window to bark at it. The fire chief this time. There were more sirens and flashing lights farther down the road, speeding toward them as if that part of Kansas City was under attack.

Speeding toward Central Prep Academy.

Toward Daisy.

Toward the woman he loved.

"Anybody else got a bad feeling about this?"

Muffy gave a sharp yelp as if the little dingbat understood the urgency firing through his blood. The rest of the troops were in agreement.

He could be wrong. The fractured bits of his brains had messed with his perception of the truth lately. But neither a dog, nor his gut, had ever once given him bad intel. And if Daisy was in trouble, he couldn't run away from the fight.

Harry made a U-turn at the next intersection, pulled his Beretta from the glove compartment, and raced back to the school.

DAISY KNEW IT was a trap the moment her foot touched the basement's concrete floor. The stairs had been cordoned off with yellow crime scene tape from the fire, but someone had torn through it and come down the steps.

"Hold up," Eddie warned her from the top of the stairs. He'd been trying to raise Bernie on his radio to tell him that she and Eddie were tracking down Albert. "Coach isn't answering. Daisy?"

"Tell whoever's listening that we need an ambulance."

The door to the storage room had been propped open with a concrete bucket, and the entire locking mechanism had been removed. The char marks had been painted over with more of that gloomy gray paint. But a fresh coat of paint couldn't hide the reminder of one man's obsession with her.

Mine.

She was frozen in place—her blood, her breathing, the sharpness of her senses locking up with fear. And while she desperately wanted to turn right around and run up those stairs and out the front door, she couldn't. She couldn't run away from the trap, because she was a teacher, a caring person, a human being—and one of her students was lying unconscious in the middle of the floor. A gash dented his curly dark hair, and his yellow ball cap lay on the floor, soaking up the blood dripping from his head wound.

"Albert?" She forced her feet to move forward, slowly approaching his unmoving body, scanning all around him for any sign of the bomb or Bernie Riley. Albert hadn't made that bomb. He was as much of a pawn in all this madness as she was. And no one wielded more control over this young man than the coach. She was vaguely aware of Eddie relaying the request for medical help. If Eddie had seen Albert with the bomb, it hadn't been by choice. No doubt the young man had been coerced into giving Eddie, and subsequently her, a message that would not only keep her in the building, but bring her down here. "It's Ms. G. I'm here."

Seeing nothing that looked like a pipe or briefcase, like the bombs she'd seen on television shows and movies, she knelt beside him. She pulled back the collar of his team jacket and pressed her fingers against his neck. Thank God. He had a strong pulse. But he certainly wasn't able to answer any questions for her.

"Albert?" She petted the back of the unconscious teen's head. "I'm so sorry you got hurt. I'm going to get you out of here, okay?"

The sirens of the vehicles she heard pulling up outside reminded her that she wasn't alone. The noises also reminded her that it was far too quiet down here.

"Eddie? I need your help to move..." There was no answer. No sound of footsteps following her down the stairs. Had her friend abandoned her? Oh, God. Had something happened to him, too? "Mr. Bosch, answer me!"

Silence.

Daisy got up. But when she turned toward the storage room, she instantly retreated. Now *that* looked like something she'd seen in a movie.

There it was, sitting in the middle of the floor beside one of the folding metal chairs. A bomb. It was wire-y and liquid-y in clear tubes bound together with duct tape attached to a doughy-looking brick and a cell phone. The screen was flashing a series of numbers—32:26, 32:25,

32:24. A countdown. She didn't need to know how the thing worked. She just believed that it would.

"Oh, my God." She needed to call Harry. She needed him here. To hold her. To take charge. To make the fear go away.

She imagined the words in his letters, offering solutions. Assuring her that her problems could be fixed. Telling her that she had the power to do anything.

32:13

The bad guys don't get to win.

"We have to get out of here." Daisy hurried back to the fallen student.

She knew that moving an injured person wasn't the recommended procedure, but with a bomb ticking down just a few feet away, she'd make an exception. She wrapped her hands around Albert's wrists and pulled. His head lolled between his arms and he groaned as she dragged him toward the stairs. Good grief, he was heavy. Not just tall, but solidly built. When the back of her boot hit the bottom step, she gently lowered him to the floor and rolled him onto his back.

"Come on, Albert, wake up." She slipped her hands beneath his arms. With a mighty push of her legs, she got his bottom onto the first step before she had to set him down and lean him against the wall. Unless he regained consciousness, there was no way she was going to get him up these stairs. "Eddie?" she shouted up the stairwell. "I need your help. Can anybody hear me?"

Maybe she shouldn't keep yelling. If something had happened to Eddie, then she was alone in the building with a man who equated rape and violence and fear with some sick kind of love. And she was only giving away her position to him.

"Ms. G.?" Albert slurred her name out on a moan of pain. "You gotta…"

"Albert?" She knelt beside him, capturing his face between her hands, willing his groggy brown eyes to stay open. "Can you stand if I help you?" His eyes drifted shut. "Albert!"

His eyes opened for one fierce warning. "Get out."

Something hard and unyielding whacked her in the back of the head. Fireworks exploded behind her eyes as she collapsed over Albert's body and everything went dark.

Chapter Twelve

Harry recognized a command center when he saw one. He could also identify the men in charge by the way everyone else scurried to do their bidding. He parked his truck behind the last police car in the circular driveway in front of Central Prep Academy and crossed the median to reach a group of men that included Daisy's principal, a black-haired cop in a SWAT uniform, John Murdock from the KCFD, Detective Nick Fensom and his brother-in-law, Pike.

SWAT? That explained the number of first responders.

His heart squeezed in his chest. Scenes like this were only supposed to happen in a war zone. He needed eyes on Daisy. Now.

Probably because he wore a gun like all the other cops here, and moved with an air of purpose and authority, no one stopped him until he reached the back of the SWAT van where the men in charge were going over building schematics and access points.

"Let him through." Nick Fensom waved him over. "He knows one of our hostages."

"Hostages?" He didn't bother asking if Daisy was safe. He knew she'd be in the thick of whatever was happening inside that building.

"We're not saying victims yet." John Murdock from

the fire department exchanged a nod of recognition with Harry. "But our guy won't talk to us. He's cut off all communication. We don't have many details other than most of the students and staff have been evacuated and are safe in the church on the other side of the school."

"All he wants is Daisy." Of that, Harry was certain. "If anyone else has been hurt, it's collateral damage."

"Agreed." Nick scrubbed his hand over the dark stubble on his jaw. "Our concern is that when a stalker reaches this level of violence, he's usually got an end game."

He'd seen friends brought down by sniper bullets and roadside bombs. He'd lost part of his face and half his soul over in Iraq. Whatever Nick was trying to find a delicate way to say wouldn't shock him. "Meaning?"

"Most of these situations end in a murder/suicide."

"Like a suicide bomber. Or an insurgent waiting to detonate an IED when it'll do the most damage." Harry weathered the emotional punch of knowing Daisy was in a similarly volatile situation right now. He waited for the flashback to take hold, but it never came. This was a mission briefing. All he needed were his orders, and he could take action. Daisy was too important for him to sit on the sidelines and nurse his mental wounds or second-guess himself. He was getting better. He needed to be a part of this. "You said hostages, plural. This guy's got someone else in there with him?"

"One of the students," Pike answered. "We believe our perp used him as a decoy to bring Daisy to him."

"You got an ID on this guy?"

Pike shook his head. "There are two faculty members besides Daisy who haven't checked in yet—Bernard Riley and Edward Bosch. The student is Albert Logan."

"Unless Logan's our bomber?" Nick suggested.

"He's a good kid." Harry had worked with the teen

enough this week to suspect Albert just needed the right thing to motivate him, and he'd turn his young life around. He'd had good instincts with the dogs, and had been interested enough to ask Harry where he'd gotten his training. "Rough around the edges. Makes some bad choices. But he wouldn't hurt Daisy. What about his brother?"

The principal piped in. "Angelo is fine. He and Albert were working with Coach Riley before school and were on their way to class when the bomb threat came in and I sounded the evacuation order. Angelo told one of the teachers at the church that Mr. Bosch asked Albert to help with a student who's wheelchair-bound. The handicapped student is accounted for. Angelo is pretty concerned that he hasn't seen his brother. I haven't told him about the hostage situation."

Harry had seen the pictures. He'd seen the fire. He'd seen the terror Daisy lived with every day because of that bastard. "You have to get her out of there. This guy's got a temper. He'll hurt her."

The nametag on the SWAT cop's uniform read *Delgado*. "We can't risk a full assault or he might blow everybody up."

Nick glanced around at all the swirling lights and imposing vehicles. "He already knows we're here. It's a little late for stealth mode."

"And, we don't know their exact location," John Murdock reminded them.

"They're in the basement," Harry said, knowing he was right on this. He was learning this enemy, and he wasn't all that unpredictable. "I don't know if the bomb is there, or if there's more than one. But that's where he'll be. With Daisy. I'm familiar with that area of the building, and one man won't be detected—especially if you're making some noise and talking at him out here. Let me go in." He turned to his brother-in-law. "You got some spare gear in your truck?"

"What are you thinking?"

"That I know how to find an insurgent and an IED."

In a matter of minutes, his credentials were approved and the plan was set. Harry went with Pike to his KCPD unit. They suited up in protective gear, while Pike's German shepherd, Hans, danced around inside his cage, sensing he was about to have a job to do. Donning the flak vest, gloves and helmet, Harry felt like he was slipping into a familiar uniform.

"Daisy means this much to you?" Pike asked.

"That woman saved me more than once. I owe it to her to do the same for her."

"You love her?"

Harry checked the radio unit on his vest and slipped a pair of protective goggles over his eyes, ignoring the question. He hadn't told Daisy how he felt yet, not in real words. Not out loud. It didn't feel right to say it to anybody else first.

Pike clapped him on the shoulder, forcing him to look at him. "You can't go in there if your head's not clear."

Harry pulled the extra K-9 ballistic vest from the back of Pike's truck. "Did you know you were in love with Hope before you rescued her from that jackass who kidnapped her?"

"Yes."

"Did it stop you from getting the job done?"

Pike grinned. "Hans and I will be ready to go in with SWAT as soon as you radio that you've secured the hostages. Just get them out. We'll clear the building, do a bomb sweep and neutralize the perp. Keep your com open so we know each other's twenty and don't have any surprises. You're okay to do this on your own?"

Harry went to his own pickup and opened the door, revealing Caliban in the passenger seat, eagerly sitting at attention. He slipped the vest over the dog's back and clipped it into place. "I won't be alone."

DAISY WOKE TO a hundred fireworks shooting off inside her head. Where was she? What had happened to her?

She mentally shook off the confusion and opened her eyes. She was surrounded by a sea of gray. And as she focused in on her outstretched arm, she saw spots of red on her new coat. Was that blood?

Wait. Blood?

The nightmare came flooding back. Albert. Bomb. *Mine.*

She pushed herself up to a sitting position. She was in the storage room, surrounded by windowless walls and stacked-up chairs.

"I've been waiting for you to come back to me."

Her groan was half headache, half heartache. She'd suspected a lot of people of stalking her over the last couple of weeks, but not this one. "Eddie?"

"Merry Christmas, my love."

He was sitting in a chair near her feet, holding two walkie-talkies in his lap, one which she suspected he'd stolen from her desk. He cradled a cell phone in his hands. Her cell phone. She raised her gaze above the blue school jacket and loosely knotted tie and saw a smear of pink lipstick across his mouth. Her color. She touched her fingers to her own mouth and cringed at the thought of him kissing her while she'd been unconscious—at the thought of him kissing her, period.

The bomb with the different colored liquids and ticking timer sat on the floor beside her. Instinctively, she scooted away from the deadly thing.

14:25 and counting. And Eddie sat between her and the metal door he'd pulled shut behind them. Had he found another way to lock it? She was surrounded by solid walls and a room full of potential shrapnel. This bomb wasn't about bringing down the school or hurting anyone else. This was all about her. Daisy thought she might be sick. It had always been about destroying her.

She flinched when she felt his hand on her hair. "Why don't you say Merry Christmas to me? I've seen your room and your house. I know how you love the holidays. You're the only gift I want. I love you."

Ignoring the swimming focus of her vision, she stood. "We need to get out of here."

"We're exactly where we need to be. Together." His tone was so patient, so sweet, so creepy.

"How long was I out?"

"A few minutes. Long enough for me to make sure we won't be bothered in these final, precious moments."

"Final?"

He stood and came toward her. "It's the only way we can be together."

She backed away from his outstretched hand until she ran into a rack of chairs. Everything around her rattled, giving her an idea. A heavy metal chair could be as effective as a baseball bat if she could get her hands on one. The knot on her head and the wound on Albert's scalp told her Eddie had probably already thought of that.

Albert. "Eddie, there's a student on the other side of that wall. You don't want to hurt him."

"I've done my calculations. Albert finally served a meaningful purpose." Bait to lure her down here was hardly something to brag about. "He and Bernie were wastes of time and space in your life."

"Bernie? You hurt him, too?"

Eddie touched the front of his coat. "Once I borrowed his jacket again, I didn't need him anymore."

"It was you the night of the fire."

"I was afraid your soldier boy saw me."

"He did. But he couldn't identify you. We suspected Coach Riley. His jacket…" she inhaled a sniff of the stale air around her "…*that* jacket smelled like smoke."

"Do you honestly think that blockhead knows anything other than sports?" Eddie snickered as he rested his hand on the rack beside her head and leaned in. "I've borrowed his hat and coat a couple of times since his wife kicked him out and he's been keeping an extra set of clothes at school. It's a smart way to divert suspicion off me, don't you think?"

Yeah, Eddie was smart. Crazy. But smart. She eyed the tubes of chemicals on the floor behind him. "Now you've built a bomb. Is there more than one?"

He grabbed her chin and forced her gaze back to his. "We just need the one."

She nearly gagged at the taste of his mouth sliding over hers. Although she suspected she needed to stay calm and try to talk her way out of this, she couldn't squash down her fight-or-flight response. She shoved him away, slipped to one side, grabbing a chair off the rack. Several more chairs crashed to the floor, forcing him another step back, giving her a chance to swing the chair in her hands. The blow caught him in the shoulder, knocking him to his knees.

Daisy scrambled toward the door. But the very chairs that had created a barrier between them now became a blockade she had to push aside and climb over. Before she could touch the metal latch, Eddie's arms closed around her from behind, lifting her off her feet before he slammed her into the wall beside the door. She screamed at the pain of her head knocking into another hard object. Her glasses got knocked sideways. But she pushed back. "Let go of me!"

Eddie threw his whole body against hers, crushing her against the wall. He spat against her ear. "You held me the night I told you about Jenny—how she left me."

"Your fiancée died." It was hard to talk with her face mashed against the wall.

But Eddie wasn't listening. "I was there for you after that Brock fiasco. I was at your father's funeral, holding your hand. We have a connection you can't deny."

"We were friends."

"I love you."

"I don't love you."

"Liar!" He whipped her around, roughly clasping his face between her hands. She obliquely wondered what had happened to the cell phone and if losing track of it meant the bomb was going to go off any sooner. But she had a more immediate problem with the hands sliding down around her throat and the crazed anger in Eddie's eyes. "You confided in me. It was only a matter of time before you turned to me for something more. I encouraged Angelo's little crush on you because I knew it would bother you and you'd come looking for a man. For me. But then Soldier Boy came to town."

"Ed…die," she gasped.

His hands tightened around her throat. She didn't think he was strangling her on purpose, but he was so angry. He was beyond listening to reason. He was impervious to the scratch of her fingernails on his hands, begging him to free her. "Suddenly he's doing everything for you I'm supposed to. I was outside your house last night. I saw you go up to his room. You slept with him, didn't you?" She didn't answer. She couldn't. Incensed, he threw her away from him. "I knew it. You're a traitor. But I forgive you."

For once, she relished the cold, hard concrete because it meant she was free. For the moment. Daisy coughed her bruised airways clear and scooted away from Eddie's advance. "How did I betray you? I've always loved you as a friend."

"But you're *in* love with him, aren't you?"

"Yes." Even if no one else ever heard it, she was going to state the truth. "I love Harry Lockhart."

"I've shown you real love."

Her fingers brushed against the bomb and she screeched and rolled away. "Do you think I want a man to treat me like all those pictures? They scared me to death."

"They're love scenes."

"That isn't love. That's…a sickness." The pile of fallen chairs blocked her escape.

The anger left his tone, but the crazy remained. "That's how I think about you—about us—every night. I've loved you from that first night we were together."

"Drinking coffee," she reminded him, scrabbling to get to her feet. "Having a conversation. We have never been *together.*"

"Stop fighting me on this. We are meant to be together. Always." He glanced away to look at the numbers ticking away on the bomb. "In another eleven minutes, we will be."

She had eleven minutes left to live? She'd fought off Brock and his knife, how did she fight a bomb? "How does the bomb work? When it reaches zero, it'll explode?"

"A small charge will blow out the stopper between the tubes. Then the chemicals will mix. Very volatile." He pulled her phone from the pocket of the jacket. "Or I can dial the number and detonate it sooner. Would you like that? It will be quick and painless, I promise."

"You've blown people up before?"

He smiled. "Such a wonderful sense of humor."

"I don't feel like laughing. Please, Eddie. Let me go. Let me get you some help."

"You're not leaving me."

Daisy dreamed she heard scratching outside the door. Fate coming to get her this time, she supposed. "What if I promise to come back? After you shut off the bomb and I know everyone is safe, you and I will sit down and talk."

"Liar! You'll go back to him." He reached for her again. "You're mine!"

The door behind Eddie slid open with a mighty shove. "Caliban, *Fass*!"

Attack.

A blur of black and tan charged into the room and lunged at Eddie's outstretched hand. Caliban clamped down on Eddie's forearm and knocked him to the floor. His fist hit the concrete and the cell phone skittered out of his grip. Eddie screamed. "No!"

Barely a step behind the attacking dog, Harry filled up the doorway, following the aim of the gun he held between his hands. "Down on the ground! Hands where I can see them!"

There was no time to feel relief or love or even fear of the one-man attack force looming over Eddie and taking charge of the room.

"Get the phone!" Her cell skittered away beneath a rack of chairs as Eddie and the dog struggled. She dove for the floor and stuck her arm beneath the rack, groping for the phone. "Don't let him push any numbers!"

"Damn it, Daisy. Stay back!"

"He can set off the bomb if he calls the number."

Eddie shrieked at the fangs sinking into his forearm and shaking him. "She's mine. You can't have her. She loves me."

Her fingers closed around the phone. "I've got it."

"Get behind me!" Harry ordered, moving between her and the dog and man wrestling and growling and screaming on the floor. "I'm going to call off the dog and you stay down. Understand? Do you understand?"

"Yes. Call him off."

"Caliban, *Hier*!"

The three-legged dog released Eddie and trotted back to Harry's side. Bloodied and dazed, Eddie reached into his pocket and pulled out his own cell phone. "She's mine!"

Harry knocked that phone to the concrete, crushed it beneath his boot. He smashed the butt of his gun across Eddie's face and knocked him out.

His big chest heaved with deep breaths as he grabbed her arm and pulled her close. His eyes were focused squarely on the bomb. "Are you hurt?"

"Not much."

"Stay behind me. I want my armor between us and that explosive in case it goes off early. We're backing out of this room." Daisy willingly latched on to the back of his vest and moved away from Eddie and the bomb. Part of her wanted to ask Harry why he was here. How had he known she needed him? How had he found her? Was he okay? Was this whole scene triggering the worst of his nightmares again? But she didn't ask any of those questions. The aim of his gun at the man on the floor never wavered. "Caliban!" As the dog loped out into the hallway with them, Harry turned his mouth to the radio on the front of his vest. "This is Lockhart. Hostages are secure. Move in! Move in!"

"Albert!" Daisy hurried over to the young man who was sitting on the bottom step and hugged him in her arms. "Are you all right? I was so worried."

Harry was still talking into his radio, giving information. She heard an invasion of footfalls in the lobby above her, and suddenly two men in full battle gear were charging down the stairs. Another man and woman with rifles and SWAT armor came down the stairs at the opposite end of the hallway, converging on Harry's position.

"You've got just under eight minutes." Only when the four uniformed officers entered the storage room did Harry move. He holstered his gun and cupped her elbow, urging her onto her feet. "We gotta go, honey. Clock's ticking." He pulled Albert to his feet and bent to lift the young man over his shoulders in a fireman's carry. "Up the stairs and out the front door. Don't stop moving 'til I tell you."

She nodded and climbed the stairs, with Harry and Caliban following close on her heels. When they reached the lobby, she saw another officer helping Coach Riley out the door. There was blood matted in Bernie's hair. Apparently, Eddie had knocked him out, too. He'd probably been faking the radio conversation with Bernie that she'd overheard. "Is he okay?"

She felt Harry's hand at the small of her back. "Keep movin', honey. There's still a bomb and we aren't safe. Take a right."

As soon as she hit the cold air outside the door, another officer ran forward to guide her through a line of armed responders and emergency vehicles toward the group of ambulances that were waiting in the parking lot. Even carrying Albert on his shoulders, Harry stayed close enough that she could feel him blocking the winter wind at her back.

A few minutes later, she was sitting in the back of an ambulance again while an EMT checked her vitals and crushed up an ice pack for her to hold against the knot on her head. She gasped when the back doors opened. Harry. Before she could say anything, he patted the floor of the ambulance. *"Hopp!"*

Her startled frown turned into a delighted smile when Caliban jumped up into the ambulance.

"Sir, you can't—"

"Come here, good boy." Daisy dropped the ice pack and welcomed her three-legged dog onto the gurney beside her, scratching all around his ears and kissing the top of his head as he rested his graying muzzle on her thigh. "I'm so glad you were there for Mama today. What a good, good boy." Because of this dog, she was alive. She tilted her aching head up to Harry. Because of this man, she was alive. "Is it over?"

His gray eyes reflected the bright morning light. "All except for the cleanup. The bomb was easy to defuse. A matter of disconnecting wires." His battle-scarred face was lined with concern as he studied her. "A hazmat unit is going in now to deal with the chemicals. KCPD has taken Bosch into custody."

Tears stung the corners of her eyes. She hadn't cried once when Eddie had touched her, hurt her, threatened her life. But she was about to bawl just looking at the man she loved so much.

"Give us a minute, will you?" Harry asked.

The EMT nodded and climbed out of the ambulance as Harry climbed in.

Harry picked up the fallen ice pack and sat on the other side of Caliban, reaching over the dog to hold the pack in place at the crown of her head. "Are you really in one piece?"

"Nothing a hot shower won't cure." She slipped her hand over Caliban's back to grasp Harry's thigh. "Thank you. Eddie was…" She couldn't fathom how skewed that man's brain must be to think that he loved her and that killing her was his idea of the two of them being committed to each other. A hot tear spilled over and trailed down her cheek. "I really attract the crazies, don't I?"

Harry wiped the tear away with the pad of his thumb. "I'm not going to be one of them."

A tiny knife of guilt stabbed her in the heart. She reached up to cup the side of his jaw. "I didn't mean you."

"But you're worried that me suiting up and coming after you may have triggered another episode. It didn't."

"Are you really okay?"

He shrugged and her hand dropped away. "Okay enough."

"What does that mean?" She turned to face him. "Harry, you have to know that I have feelings for you. As relieved as I was to see you coming through that door, I would never want to do anything to set back your recovery."

"You didn't do a damn thing. Bosch and no one else is responsible for what happened to you and Albert and Coach Riley today."

"Albert!" She pushed Caliban's head off her leg and tried to stand. "I need to find out if he's okay."

Harry caught her as she tripped over his feet, and pulled her down onto his lap. "He's fine. A concussion and some stitches. He and Coach Riley are in another ambulance, getting treatment. Angelo is with him and their grandmother is on her way. Right now, the only person you have to save is you."

"But if I can help…"

Harry feathered his fingers into her hair and straightened her bent glasses. "Damn it, woman, if you won't think about yourself, then think about me. I just saved your life. And I didn't crack up doing it. You're safe. It's over. And I love you." His stiff, handsome mouth crooked into a smile. "Don't you want to hug me?"

Daisy threw her arms around his neck as he pulled her to his chest. His hands fisted in the back of her coat and his nose nestled into the hair at her temple. She held on tight with all the love in her heart and wept happy tears.

Epilogue

After the last of the guests had left the party and the dogs had curled up on the couch, Harry reached beneath the Christmas tree and pulled out the present he'd wrapped for Daisy. The narrow, rectangular shape told her it couldn't be anything other than his journal. "I want you to know exactly who this is from."

Tears stung her eyes as he pulled her into his lap on the recliner. "Are you sure you want me to read this?"

"I wouldn't share it with anybody else." His arms settled around her waist and she detected a faint trembling in them. "I do a lot better telling you what I feel when I write it down." He took the ribbon and paper from her and tossed them aside. His chest expanded with a deep, steadying breath, and she knew that Harry was the bravest man she'd ever known. "Start at the end."

She pressed a kiss to his mouth, thanking him for entrusting her with this gift before turning her attention to the spiral notebook, thumbing through the pages until she reached the last entry.

Dear Daisy,
    I never thought I could be anything but a marine. Nothing useful, anyway. The Corps gave me purpose and a home when I desperately needed those things. I love my job more than anything I've ever done. If

they'll still have me—if I pass the psych tests—I want to go on being a marine until I'm ready to retire in another two years.

These ten days I've spent with you, though, got me thinking about other things. I came to you with the idea that the Daisy from your letters could save me—that you were this magic angel who could reach inside my head, erase the nightmares and make me whole again. Turns out you weren't anything like that angel. You're bold and brave. You touch and you talk. You weren't as much of a lady as I thought you'd be, and you frustrated the hell out of me more than once. There wasn't any mystical glow about you. But you were are real. You're heart and color and acceptance and hope and life and love. I'm a better man for knowing you and being a part of your crazy life. I'm healthier. Happier. I'm home when I'm with you. You weren't the woman I imagined, but you turned out to be exactly the woman I needed.

I've got some ideas now on what I could do when I leave the Corps, whether it's in a month or two years. Training dogs. Working as a cop or search and rescue with the fire department. Maybe you can even help me get through college so I can be a teacher or social worker who works with kids like Albert and 'Lo.

One thing I'm certain of, now and forever, is that I love you. If you can put up with a marine who's gone on and off for a couple of years, or with a washed-up master sergeant who isn't sure what he's going to do with the rest of his life, I want to marry you. I hope I can get my act together well enough that you would consider saying yes.

Love,
Harry

Daisy's heart swelled up and spilled over in a sob of hot, flowing tears. She threw her arms around his neck and hugged him tight.

His hands fisted in the back of her sweater, holding on to her just as tightly. "Is there anything I can write that won't make you cry?"

"A grocery list?"

He laughed, and she scrambled off his lap and ran to the kitchen, pulling a red pen from her purse. Harry followed her, winding his arms around her waist and resting his chin on her shoulder while she scrawled a message at the end of the letter. "You're going English teacher on me now? Checking my grammar?"

She signed the short missive and held it up to show it to him. "Here's my letter to you."

Dear Harry,
I love you. With all my heart. I know we can get through anything together.
When you ask, my answer is YES!
Love,
Daisy

* * * * *

"You've got to prove it, Zane."

"Prove that I want you?" His hands gripped Caroline's hips and pulled her down harder against him. "I don't think there can be any doubt of that."

"Prove that you really think I'm strong. That you're not afraid I'll break at the least little thing."

"I know you won't."

"That you can still get lost in me. That we can get lost in each other."

Zane's hand reached up and tangled in her hair, bringing Caroline's lips down hard against his. Caroline moaned. *Yes*. Yes, this was what she wanted…

PROTECTOR'S
INSTINCT

BY
JANIE CROUCH

First Published in Great Britain 2017
By Mills & Boon, an imprint of HarperCollins*Publishers*
1 London Bridge Street, London, SE1 9GF

© 2017 Janie Crouch

ISBN: 978-0-263-92939-3

46-1217

Janie Crouch has loved to read romance her whole life. The award-winning author cut her teeth on Mills & Boon Romance novels as a preteen, then moved on to a passion for romantic suspense as an adult. Janie lives with her husband and four children overseas. She enjoys traveling, long-distance running, movie watching, knitting and adventure/obstacle racing. You can find out more about her at www.janiecrouch.com.

This book is dedicated to Girl Tyler. It's wondrous to have a friend who can walk with me through this craziness known as—duh, duh, duh—writer's life. Thanks for all the talks, encouragement, TMI shares and getting messages to me from editors when I'm out of the country. And ALL CAPS. And All the Words. Boldly go, babe.

Chapter One

You're a liar. And everyone is going to know.

Caroline Gill glanced at the text on the phone, then promptly shut it down and put it away. She had ignored similar texts for the last four days, hoping they would stop. Someone obviously had the wrong number.

Caroline may be a lot of things, but a liar wasn't one of them. Life was too short to live surrounded by lies.

She'd learned that the hard way eighteen months ago.

She made a mental note to call the phone company or look into how to block texts on her phone after her shift tonight.

Because she definitely didn't have time to do it right now. She had a real crisis to deal with. As the ambulance pulled to a stop, Caroline jumped out of the passenger side and surveyed the utter chaos around her.

As she looked around the wreckage, she took a deep breath, trying to ascertain what she needed to do first. The thick morning fog that had blown in from the coast of Corpus Christi made everything more difficult to deal with—especially a deadly crash.

As a paramedic she dealt with accidents and injured people on a daily basis. Thankfully she didn't experience a situation as bad as this often: at least seven cars in a deadly pileup.

She turned back to her partner, who was just getting out of the ambulance. "Kimmie, radio Dispatch. We need help. Mass casualty. Let them know."

Kimmie did so immediately as Caroline further studied the situation before her. The fog had been a big factor in what caused this multicar pileup on State Highway 358. But a bigger factor looked to be like some idiot who had been driving the wrong way down the crowded street.

"Help me."

Caroline heard the weak voice coming from a truck a few yards away, just one of many. Some were sobbing, some begging for help, some basically screaming. Absolute chaos in a situation where no one could see more than two or three feet in front of them.

Caroline blocked out the voices—she had to, despite their volume or the words or sounds they made. She had learned a long time ago as a paramedic that the loudest people weren't always the ones who needed the most help.

Caroline pulled on gloves as Kimmie came running around from the driver's seat of the ambulance they'd arrived in together. "Dispatch is sending who they can. There's multiple calls because of this fog."

Caroline pulled out her triage kit, including the tags of four different colors inside. "We're going to have to tag everyone until help gets here. Thirty-second evaluations, okay? Green for minor injuries. Yellow for non-life-threatening. Red for life-threatening. And black..."

Caroline faded out. They both knew what black meant. Dead or so near to dead the victim couldn't be helped now.

Kimmie looked a little overwhelmed. Caroline's partner was relatively new and this was probably her first mass casualty situation. "Kimmie, you can do this. You've done it in training. Don't spend more than thirty seconds with each person and make sure the tag is the first thing seen when more help arrives."

They split up and began the always difficult job of choosing who would be treated first when more help arrived. Everyone was hurt. Everyone was scared. Everyone wanted to be the first ones treated. But they couldn't all be.

Caroline sprinted to the first victim, who unfortunately didn't take long to be evaluated. He was lying on the pavement covered in blood. He obviously hadn't been wearing his seat belt and the force of the impact had thrown him through the windshield. Caroline quickly searched for a pulse, felt none, so removed her hands before trying once more, hoping she was wrong. A lot of blood loss didn't always equate to death.

But in this case it did. "Damn it," she muttered under her breath before pulling out a black tag and placing it near the man's head. This would discourage other first responders from stopping for him until the other more critical cases could be taken care of.

She ran to the man screaming at the top of his lungs next. His car was the one facing the wrong direction. She braced herself for what she would find because of the sheer volume of the man's yells. But instead of finding some gaping wound or bones protruding in a hideous injury, she found a man, probably in his late twenties, holding his hand where it looked like his pinkie was dislocated.

"Thank God," he said as soon as she got close enough. "What took you soo-long?"

If the words slurring together didn't give her enough of a clue of his drunken state, the stench of alcohol that immediately accosted her senses did.

"Sir, are you injured besides your finger?"

"My finger is *broken*, not injured." He held it up as

proof. "And the window of my car is smashed and the door won't open. I need you to fix that right away."

What did he think this was, AAA? Caroline didn't have time for this jackass who—coupled with the fog—had probably been the cause of this entire situation.

"Sir, I need to know if you have any more injuries. There will be someone here soon who can help you get the door open."

The man just narrowed his eyes and let out a string of obscenities. "Don't you leave me here, you bitch."

Caroline could hear the cries of other people, including at least one child. She vaguely wondered if she smashed her elbow in this guy's face if it would look like something that just happened in the wreck. But she forced herself not to.

She handed him a yellow card. "Sir, give this to the next EMT or firefighter who comes your way, okay?"

The man immediately scoffed and threw it on the ground. "Don't you dare leave me. All these people were driving on the wrong side of the road." He grabbed her arm through the window. "I'll have your job if you leave me."

She grabbed his other, uninjured, pinkie, bending it back, knowing the pressure would cause him to release her arm. It was one of the self-defense moves she'd learned in the multiple classes she'd taken over the last year and a half.

No man would use his strength against her and make her a victim ever again.

"Unless you want me to break your other pinkie," she said to the drunk guy, "I suggest you let me go. Besides, you're going to be too busy sitting in jail to have my job."

The man released her and went back to yelling his obscenities at the top of his lungs. Caroline picked up the yellow tag and removed the adhesive cover on the back, sticking it to the outside of the car. Hopefully the guy wouldn't mess with it. She quickly moved on to the next car.

"Please help me." A mother was sobbing in the driver's seat, blood dripping from her face. A young girl and a baby sat in the back seat. The little girl was crying also.

"Ma'am, I'm here. It's okay," Caroline said, taking in the situation. The woman was pinned inside her vehicle where the front end had been crushed when it had been rear-ended into a safety railing. Her legs were trapped.

"My kids." The mom was hysterical, unable to see or help her children in the back. "Why is Nicole crying? Are they hurt? Is the baby okay?"

Caroline used her flashlight to shine into the car as she talked to the woman. "Hey, what's your name?" she asked the mom as she pulled on the door handle, but it wouldn't budge. The woman's legs were definitely pinned. The firefighters would have to get her out of here.

"Jackie."

Caroline couldn't tell what state Jackie's legs would be in, but for right now she was a yellow card. Needed help, but wasn't life-threatening. But the woman was still sobbing.

"Jackie, I'm going to check the kids now. But I need you to stop crying, okay? And hold this." She gave the woman the yellow tag. "This lets the firefighters know what to do."

She could see Jackie try to get herself under control. "My kids. Please, my kids."

Caroline touched her on the shoulder through the window that had been broken. "I'm checking right now."

She moved to the back door and opened it. A little girl in the back, about three years old, was sobbing, obviously terrified.

"Jackie, what's your daughter's name?"

"Nicole."

"Hey, Nicole," Caroline crooned. "You doing okay, sweetie?" The fog floating around the car and her mother's cries were frightening the girl. Caroline touched her gently on the cheek and she settled a little bit.

"I want Mama," the little girl said, hiccuping through her tears.

"I know you do. It will be just a few minutes, okay? Does anything hurt, sweetheart?" The girl seemed to be fine, but it was difficult to tell.

"No. I want Mama."

"I'm here, sweetie." Jackie was pulling herself together now that she could talk to her daughter. Nicole calmed down more as her mother did. "Is David okay?"

"Can you hold this for me, hon?" Caroline handed little Nicole a green tag. Someone else would check her out more thoroughly, but for right now, the girl didn't seem to need more medical attention. "Nicole seems fine, Jackie. I'm going to check on baby David now."

Baby David hadn't made a sound the whole time. Caroline's heart caught in her chest as she ran around the car to his side.

The baby, not older than six months, lay silently in his rear-facing car seat as Caroline pried open the door. As she reached over to check the baby's pulse, she could hear Jackie's ragged, terrified breathing.

She couldn't see any blood or noticeable injuries, but he didn't move at all at her touch. Caroline sent up a silent prayer that the child was alive. With babies, everything was tricky, since they were unable to communicate.

She found his pulse at the exact moment little David opened his eyes. He studied Caroline intently before taking his thumb and jamming it in his mouth, sucking on it.

"He's okay, Jackie. He's sucking his thumb." She reached over David and squeezed Jackie's shoulder. "I can't say for certain that he is injury free, but he's alive and he's alert." Caroline laid a yellow tag on baby David. He probably could be green-tagged, but with a baby she'd rather be safe than sorry. Someone would still need to check him more thoroughly.

"Jackie, you saved your kids' lives by having them properly restrained in their car seats. You did great. I have to check on others, so I need you to keep it together. Help will be back again soon."

Caroline didn't wait to hear any response. She rushed to the next victim. By the time other sirens approached a few minutes later, she had evaluated many victims.

Two were dead. At least two with severe injuries. A half dozen more with minor injuries that would require attention.

And a drunken jackass, still yelling, with a dislocated pinkie.

That first dead guy she'd come across had a couple of children's dolls in the back seat of his car. Somebody's dad was never coming home again. Yet a drunk driver who'd never even known he was driving the wrong way down a highway was going to be just fine.

Sometimes the world just wasn't fair. Caroline knew that much better than most by what had happened to her nearly two years ago.

This just reaffirmed it.

It was going to be a long, hard day.

TWELVE HOURS LATER, shift finished, having showered and changed at the hospital, Caroline made it home.

Except, it wasn't exactly home, was it?

It was the fourth place she'd lived in eighteen months, the place she'd moved into six weeks ago, but it wasn't *home*.

How could you call a place home when every time

someone knocked on your front door it sent you into a panic?

Caroline stood in her driveway, looking up at her town house's entrance, duffel bag swung over her shoulder, unable to go any farther. It had been the longest, professionally worst day she'd had in a long time. Her body was exhausted from the physical exertion of moving patients, administering CPR and going to one call after another today because of the fog. Her emotions were exhausted as the death toll had risen each hour.

By all means, she should go inside her house, fall into bed and be asleep before her head hit the pillow. Despite the deaths that couldn't be avoided, Caroline and the other paramedics had done good work. Had helped make sure the death count hadn't risen any further than it had. She should rest now. She deserved it.

But she couldn't seem to force her legs to move any closer to her empty house.

She knew she could call one of the officers over from the Corpus Christi Police Department to come walk through her town house for her. They would understand, and someone would come immediately.

Although not the person she really wanted—really *needed*—to be here. He wasn't part of the police force any longer. Zane Wales had hung up his white hat—literally and figuratively—the day they'd found Caroline raped and nearly beaten to death in her own home. The last victim of a serial rapist.

Caroline looked at her town house again, still unable to force herself to walk any closer.

What would Dr. Parker say? Caroline had been uncomfortable talking to a psychiatrist here in Corpus Christi, so her friend Sherry had convinced her to speak—just once—to the Omega Sector psychiatrist over the phone.

That "just once" had then turned into talking to Dr. Parker every couple of weeks.

If Caroline called Grace Parker right now—and she had no doubt Grace would take the call—would Grace tell Caroline there was nothing to fear? To just put one foot in front of the other?

No, she would tell Caroline that only Caroline could determine what would be the best thing to do. That pushing herself too far did more damage than it did good.

Her phone buzzed in her hand and she looked down to read the text.

How do you look in the mirror knowing your lies?

She rolled her eyes. Another one? This was getting out of hand. Caroline wasn't big on smartphones in general, so she didn't do a lot with hers. But she had to see if there was a way to block these texts.

The text was almost enough to distract her from her fear of entering the house. She took a step forward, then stopped, wiping her hand across her face.

She couldn't go in right now.

The thought frustrated her, but she let it go. It was okay. She would go to the Silver Eagle, a bar in town, and relax for a little while. A lot of the law enforcement and EMT gang hung out there. She could have a drink or a bite to eat or just chat. Get someone to show her how to block the annoying texts. When she was done, maybe she'd be more ready to face the big scary front door.

Once the decision was made, she didn't second-guess her choice, just jogged back to her truck, throwing her duffel in the passenger seat beside her. The ride to the bar didn't take long and she knew she'd made the right decision when she pulled into the lot.

Kimmie's little VW Beetle was parked here and almost every spot was full. Caroline would chat and unwind for an hour or two. She would face her town house when she was ready.

It had been a bad day. This would hopefully make it better.

She grabbed her purse, got out of the truck and made her way inside. The familiar smell of beer and fried food assailed her, as did the country music pouring at a perfect volume from the speakers. She smiled at Kimmie, who waved for Caroline to come join the people at her table.

Maybe being here wouldn't make her fears back at the town house just disappear, but nothing could make this day worse.

She glanced over at the bar as she walked toward Kimmie and almost stumbled as she found her gaze trapped by the brown eyes of Zane Wales. Compelling her, drawing her in, as always. She forced herself to look away from him.

Her day definitely just got worse.

Chapter Two

Zane Wales didn't come into the Silver Eagle very often. A lot of law enforcement guys hung out there, and generally Zane didn't need a reminder of what he no longer did for a living.

But today had been a long, weird day and Zane had found himself here an hour ago, rather than going straight back to his house on the outskirts of Corpus Christi. Just for a beer, a bite to eat. Hoping maybe none of the detective force would even be here.

They were *all* here.

If he could back out without any of them seeing him, he would've. But Captain Harris, along with Wade Ammons and Raymond Stone, both detectives Zane had worked with when he'd been on the force, waved him over to the bar where they sat as soon as they saw him.

Zane liked all three of the men—he really did. He chatted with them for a while before Wade and Raymond saw some ladies who interested them and said their goodbyes.

"How's the private aircraft charter business treating you?" Captain Harris asked as he took a sip of his beer.

Zane chewed a bite of the burger he'd ordered. "Today was different than most. A little crazy."

"How so?"

"Fog was causing problems up and down the interstate,

so I got called for an emergency organ donation delivery. A heart. Flew it into Houston."

The entire flight had been tense—a very real deadline looming in front of them. Zane hadn't been sure if the deadline was because of the patient waiting for the heart or if the heart itself was only viable for so long. The two-person organ donation team flying with him hadn't said. They'd just told him the deadline.

Zane had gotten them there. Not much time to spare, but enough. He hoped the surgery had been successful.

"Yeah, fog was hell around here for us too this morning. Multicar pileup with a drunk driver. Half dozen other accidents that took up all our resources. Hell, even Wade and Raymond were out helping today."

That would've meant Caroline had a hard day. Not that he could do anything about that. Moreover, not that she would *want* him to do anything about that.

"Must have been a mess if you had to pull in Wade and Raymond."

"Sounds like your day was equally exciting. Heart transplant. Important stuff. I'll bet you miss that on a daily basis when you're carting around cargo or rich people from place to place."

"Don't start, Tim." Zane already knew what was coming. A conversation they'd had more than once in the seventeen months and six days since Zane had quit the department.

"Son, I've known you since you were in elementary school. I had no hesitation at all about hiring you straight out of college or promoting you to detective, even after the trouble you got into in your younger years."

Evidently the man wouldn't be deterred. Zane raised his beer slightly in salute. "I know. And I appreciate it. High school was tough after Dad died."

"You can't tell me that running your air charter business means as much to you as chasing down criminals did."

Captain Harris was right; Zane couldn't say that with any sort of honesty. He enjoyed his business, loved to fly, loved working for himself, but it didn't challenge him the way working for the force had. Didn't challenge him nearly as much mentally or physically.

But Zane had lost his edge. Lost what had made him a good cop the day Caroline was attacked.

"I don't have it anymore, Tim. Don't have what it takes."

Captain Harris scoffed. "Don't have what, exactly? You're still in just as good a shape. I know you have a permit for that concealed Glock you're carrying."

Zane didn't ask how the older man knew that. But he was right. Zane had never stopped carrying the gun, even after he'd quit the force. He just now had a different permit for it.

"I'll bet you have just as much practice on it and have aim just as precise as you did when you worked for me."

Zane shrugged one shoulder as he took a sip of his beer. "Just because I can hit what I'm aiming for doesn't mean I'm good as a law enforcement officer, Cap."

"Just because someone you care about got hurt doesn't mean you're not one," the captain shot back.

Caroline had been so much more than *hurt*.

"The rapist was right under my nose the whole time." Zane pushed his plate away, no longer interested in his last bites of food. "I shook the man's hand multiple times."

"Dr. Trumpold fooled us all," the captain reminded him. "Including that Omega Sector agent who came here to help us."

Zane just shrugged. "Jon Hatton did everything he could." But in this case, being part of an elite law enforcement agency like Omega hadn't been enough, either.

"And," the captain continued, "if I recall correctly, if you hadn't followed your instincts and gone after Hatton and Sherry Mitchell, Trumpold would've killed them both. That it was *your* bullet that put a stop to him."

Yes, Zane had stopped Trumpold. And hadn't lost a bit of sleep when he'd died in prison a year ago.

But that still didn't change one simple fact: Caroline Gill had opened the door to a rapist because she'd thought the knock on her door was Zane. Because Zane was supposed to be with her that night.

But he'd changed his mind at the last minute, wanting for once to have the upper hand in their tumultuous relationship. Stayed away as part of the head games the two of them played with each other all the time.

He would regret that decision for the rest of his life.

"If it had happened to someone else, you wouldn't blame them, Zane," Captain Harris continued. "Why are you holding yourself to a different standard?"

"It's not about standards. It's about my instincts. I can't trust mine anymore. And I won't put anybody else at risk."

"Zane, you need to—"

Harris stopped talking as the door to the bar opened and they both—engrained law enforcement instincts kicking in—looked toward it.

Caroline.

Zane hadn't seen her in a few months. They'd run into each other at a restaurant, a totally awkward exchange where they'd both been on dates, and their dates had both known Zane and Caroline used to be together. They'd said uncomfortable hellos and then spent the rest of the night trying not to notice each other.

Now Zane stared at her from where he sat, as always almost physically incapable of *not* looking at her. Taking in her long brown hair, pulled back in a braid like it so often was. The curve of her trim body filling out the jeans and fitted sweater she wore. His body responded, as it always had, wholly aware of her anytime she was around, in a completely carnal way.

What sort of pervert did that make him? Looking at Caroline—a rape survivor—with blatant sexuality all but coursing through him?

Just reinforced his decision to get out of law enforcement altogether. His instincts weren't to be trusted.

He knew the exact second she saw him, the slight hesitation in her step, but her gaze didn't falter. She didn't smile at him, but then again, he didn't expect her to.

Of course, he had to admit, even before the attack she hadn't always smiled at him. That was how their relationship had been: fire or ice. Never anything in between.

A friend called out to Caroline and she broke eye contact with him and headed in the caller's direction. Zane felt oddly bereft without the connection with Caroline.

He should've never come here in the first place.

He was about to ask for and pay the bill when Wade and Raymond came back over to sit with him and Captain Harris again. Raymond ordered them all another round before Zane could stop him.

"What happened to your lady friends?" Captain Harris asked.

"Married," Wade and Raymond both said at the same time, crestfallen.

"I might go talk to Kimmie." Raymond took a sip of the beer the bartender handed him.

Wade rolled his eyes. "Hasn't she shut you down enough times already?"

"Yeah, but she looks happier now. Especially since Caroline's here." Both men looked over at Zane as if they'd said something wrong.

"I wasn't going to hit on Caroline, man," Raymond was quick to announce.

He damn well better not.

Of course, Zane had no say over who Caroline dated. Although she better not go out with a horndog like Raymond Stone.

Zane shrugged. "Caroline can go out with whoever she wants." He forced his jaw not to lock up as he said it and carefully kept his fists unclenched. "Does she come in here a lot?"

Damn it. Zane wished he could cut off his own tongue. Why was he asking about her? But no one seemed to make anything of his interest.

"Not as much as we would like," Wade said. "I know Kimmie, her partner, invites her all the time."

"Kimmie's her partner? How long?"

"Awhile now," Captain Harris answered this time. "I talked it over with the hospital staff and we thought Kimmie would be a good professional fit for Caroline."

"What sort of professional fit?" Maybe Kimmie had some sort of specialized training Caroline didn't have. But she looked awfully young for that to be the case.

Harris fidgeted just a little in his seat before looking away.

"What?" Zane asked. "Did Caroline need help? This Kimmie have training or something Caroline doesn't?"

Captain Harris shook his head. "No. Kimmie was pretty much brand-new. Anything she's learned outside schooling, Caroline has taught her."

That didn't surprise Zane. Caroline was stellar at her job as a paramedic. Could spot potential problems or injuries others would miss. Kept her head in a crisis. Had a way about her that kept people calm.

"So what was it about Kimmie that was a good fit for Caroline?"

Wade and Raymond glanced over at the captain, who was looking away. Then it hit Zane.

"Oh, Kimmie's a *woman*. That's why she was a good fit for Caroline. I guess nobody could blame her for asking for a female partner."

Now all three men refused to look at Zane.

Not all his detective skills had left him. "But she didn't ask for a female partner, did she? You just assigned her one."

Captain Harris pointed toward where Caroline and Kimmie sat, obviously easy and friendly with each other. "I've known Caro since she was born. Her parents are some of my best friends. So I did what I thought was right for her. She and Kimmie are a good team. It wasn't the wrong choice."

But it hadn't been *Caroline's* choice. And he would bet she hadn't liked it, no matter how chummy she and her new partner looked now. If Zane had been there, he would definitely have spoken up, at least told Captain Harris to talk to Caroline about it.

But he hadn't been there, had he? Zane grimaced.

"I'm glad they get along," he muttered.

He saw Caroline glance over at them before quickly looking away and taking a casual sip of the beer the waitress had brought. She was just as aware of him as he was of her, although he doubted her awareness of him stemmed from attraction. Disgust at best, possibly even hatred.

So they both ignored each other, which everyone in the entire bar seemed completely aware of.

"I'm glad Caroline is finally going on a vacation," Wade said, trying to break some of the obvious tension. "She deserves it."

That was good news. "Where is she going?" Corpus Christi was a beach town and she'd always loved it. Did she still after what had happened? She used to live near the beach but had moved after the attack. Nobody in their right mind blamed her after someone had broken through her front door and viciously attacked her. Zane didn't know if she still even liked the beach at all.

Wade looked like he didn't want to answer. "How hard a question is it, Wade?" he asked the younger man, smiling. "A cruise? Tropical island? The mountains?"

Oh, hell, maybe she was going with another man. Maybe that was what Wade didn't want to answer.

"Who is she going with?" Zane could feel his jaw clench but couldn't seem to stop it.

He knew he had absolutely no right to be upset if she was going with another man somewhere. It was good—healthy—for Caroline to have other relationships. Someone important enough for her to move on with, to go on vacation with.

That was why he'd stayed out of her life for so long, right? So she would have a chance to move on, to put the past—including him and his part in her nightmare—behind her?

But damned if his hands didn't clench into fists as he waited for Wade's answer. As he prepared himself to hear the news that she really had moved on. That he had officially missed his chance.

"Just say it, Wade."

"She's not going with anybody, Zane. That's her whole deal. She said she wants time to be alone. Get away from the frantic pace for a week."

Zane refused to acknowledge the relief that poured through him at the knowledge Caroline hadn't found a man she was comfortable enough to vacation with.

He turned to Wade, rolling his eyes. "Why are you jerking my chain? I don't blame her for wanting peace and quiet. I guess that means she's not going to visit her family in Dallas. It's never peaceful around them."

Wade shrugged. "Nah, she's going hiking at Big Bend. She'll get plenty of quiet there."

Zane set the glass of beer that was halfway to his mouth back down on the bar. "She's going hiking in Big Bend Ranch State Park?" One of the largest parks in Texas, covering over three hundred square miles. Breathtaking views, multiple types of terrain. A hiker's dream.

Wade nodded. "Yeah."

"Alone?"

"Yeah, but she's been planning it for months. She's got a GPS that will let the park rangers know where she is at all times and has a course all planned out. She's super excited about it."

Wade continued to talk about how prepared Caroline was, how thrilled, but Zane tuned him out. He stood up. "Excuse me."

He turned and strode toward Caroline's table with definite purpose. There was no way in hell she was going on a weeklong camping trip by herself. Obviously none of her colleagues or friends were willing to tell her how stupid an idea this was.

Zane had no such problem.

Chapter Three

Her body was aware of Zane. She'd been conscious of him the entire time they'd been here, ignoring each other while totally mindful of each other's every move. They'd always been like that. Whether they'd been about to kill each other or fall into each other's arms, they'd always been *attuned* to one another.

She was attuned to him now. Aware of how damn virile and sexy he was. Not working for the Corpus Christi Police Department hadn't turned him soft or dimmed the edge of danger that had always surrounded him.

It drew her, just like it always had.

Damn him. Because the only thing that matched her passion for Zane Wales was her fury toward him. She'd like him to come over so she could slap him across his perfectly chiseled cheek.

And as if he could hear her and was going to call her bluff, he stood up and began walking toward her table.

"Holy cow, who is that?" Kimmie asked. "The guy that was talking to Captain Harris."

Caroline didn't say anything. But Kimmie's friend Bridget, sitting across from them in the booth, spun her head to the side so she could get a look at the eye candy.

"Ohhh." Bridget's eyes flew to Caroline. "That's Zane Wales. He's Caroline's."

Kimmie's face swung around to look at Caroline, shock evident in the wide circles of her eyes. "What?"

Caroline shook her head, her own eyes rolling at Bridget's remark. "He's not *mine*."

"Are you sure about that?" Kimmie looked back at Zane. "He sure is looking at you like he's coming for you."

"We used to date back in the day. It's been over for a long time." Zane had made sure of that.

Although she had to admit, it did look like he was coming directly to their table. But it most certainly would not be to talk to her. He'd gone out of his way to avoid her for the past eighteen months.

But five seconds later he stood right in front of their table, looking ridiculously sexy in his jeans and dark blue, long-sleeved collared shirt with sleeves he'd rolled up halfway to the elbow. November in Corpus Christi wasn't cold enough for a jacket.

He wasn't wearing his hat—that damned white cowboy hat he'd worn all the time. He was a Texan through and through and wearing it had been as natural to him as breathing.

He'd taken it off when he'd quit the force and she hadn't seen him in it since. Not that she'd seen him much at all.

He didn't need the hat. He wasn't hiding anything but thick, gorgeous hair underneath it. But Caroline missed him in it. Missed what its presence had stood for.

"Hey, Zane," Bridget purred. Caroline resisted the urge to slap her. Barely.

"Hey, ladies."

Caroline didn't know why Zane was at their table, but on the off chance it was to ask Bridget or Kimmie out, she couldn't stick around and watch.

"Excuse me." Caroline started to stand. "I've got to get going, you guys."

"Actually, I'm here to talk to you, if you don't mind," Zane said. He was looking directly at her now, closer than he'd been in nearly two years. She slid back into her seat, unable to draw her eyes away from his.

"Um, Bridget and I have to use the restroom anyway," Kimmie said, standing and grabbing the other woman's arm before she could protest.

Zane nodded at them as they left, then slid into the booth across from Caroline.

"Hi."

Of all the things she'd been expecting tonight, Zane coming over to chat with her hadn't been one of the possibilities. He'd withdrawn from her so completely over the past months that a conversation hadn't even been on her radar.

"What are you doing here?"

As far as greetings, it wasn't concise or friendly, but hell, nothing about Zane made her feel concise or friendly.

"I had some errands to run in town and thought I would grab a bite to eat."

He deliberately wasn't answering the question he knew she was asking. "Yeah, it looked like you were pretty close to done when I arrived."

He nodded and eased himself a little farther back in the booth, raising one arm up along the edge and knocking his knuckles gently along the column behind him. Damn the man and his comfortably sexy pose.

And damn sexy wrists exposed by his rolled-up sleeves. How could she have such a reaction from *wrists*, for heaven's sake?

"I wanted to talk to you," he finally said.

Her eyes flew to his face at that, in time for her to see his gaze slide over to his fingers that were still tapping against the column.

So whatever it was he wanted to say, he wasn't exactly comfortable with it.

"Spill it, Wales. Just say what you came to say." She honestly had no idea what it was. Her heart fluttered slightly in her chest that maybe he wanted to apologize for being so distant. For pulling away from her when she'd needed him. For keeping himself away.

Not that she'd forgive him and just let it go. Too much time and pain had occurred. But at least it would be a start.

His arm came down from the back of the booth and he leaned forward, placing his weight on both elbows. She couldn't break her gaze from his brown eyes even if she wanted to.

"Caro…"

Now she almost closed her eyes. How long had it been since she'd heard him call her by her pet name? The name he'd called her when they were alone. The name he'd called her when they were making love.

Unbidden, she felt herself leaning closer, desperate for his next words. It didn't have to be an apology; she knew the attack had cost him almost as much as it had cost her, although in a different way. Just some sort of acknowledgment that something had to change.

He cleared his throat, then continued. "You can't go on that hiking trip. Alone? That's absolutely stupid."

It took her a second to process his words. To realize what she'd hoped to hear from him wasn't anywhere near what was coming out of his mouth.

The pain reeled through her and stole her breath. Zane wasn't here to tell her they should be together; he was here to tell her she was stupid. She wrapped her arms around her middle, almost afraid she would fly apart if she didn't.

She looked away from him now, not even able to look

him in the eye. She was an idiot. Why would she think anything had changed?

"Did you hear me, Caroline? I really don't think this solo hiking trip is a good idea."

Did she hear him?

Did she hear him?

Fury crashed over her like a tidal wave, obviating the pain. It was all she could do to stay in her seat.

"Do I hear you, Zane?"

He had the good grace to look alarmed at her quiet, even tone. At least he still knew her well enough to know when she was about to blow a gasket.

"Caro…"

"Oh, no, you don't. Don't you dare call me that." The anger felt good, washed away the slicing pain of being wrong about him again. "You don't get to call me anything with any affection ever again."

Her words hurt him, she could tell, before he shut down all trace of emotion on his features. Good. She was glad she had hurt him. Glad she still could.

"Fine," he said. "I don't have to call you any friendly name to tell you that going hiking by yourself in the middle of the wilderness is just plain stupid."

Caroline looked over at the waitress who was walking by. "I need the check, please."

"I need mine too," Zane muttered.

The woman looked back and forth between them, a little concerned, before nodding. "Sure. I'll be right back."

"Where I choose to take my vacation is none of your concern, Zane."

"It is when no one is willing to tell you how risky and stupid it is."

Her eyes narrowed. "Really? How much do you know about my plans, exactly?"

"I know you're going hiking alone in Big Bend. That's enough."

Caroline clenched her fists by her legs and forced herself to breathe in through her mouth and out through her nose. She would not get in a screaming match with Zane Wales in the middle of a bar.

Unable to look at him without giving him the full force of her opinion—loudly—she surveyed the bar. Just about everyone was watching them, waiting for the fireworks. It wouldn't be the first time they'd provided a colorful show. But it had been a long time.

"You don't know anything about my plans, Wales. You don't know anything about my life. Remember?"

"You say that like me getting out of your life wasn't the best thing for you."

She just stared at him. "Seriously?"

"And regardless, this plan of yours—" he said the phrase with such derision her eyes narrowed and she felt her temper rising to a boiling point "—is ridiculous. You can't do it."

Oh. No. He. Didn't.

The waitress brought them both their checks and Caroline counted it one of her greatest accomplishments that she didn't say anything at all. She just got out a twenty-dollar bill, threw it down on the table and stood, not caring that she was tipping the waitress almost as much as the bill itself.

She felt every eye on her as she turned and walked out the door. She didn't care and definitely wasn't afraid to go back to her house now. She was too damn pissed.

She made it to her truck before she heard him.

"You can't seriously be going on this trip."

She didn't turn around. "You know what, Zane? You don't know anything about it."

"I know it's dangerous."

Now that they didn't have an audience, she didn't even try to keep her volume in check. "No, you're making a snap judgment that it's dangerous because you don't know all the facts."

"Then tell me all the facts."

Now she turned around. "I'm not stupid. And believe me, I have no desire to put myself at risk. I have taken precautions to make myself as safe as possible."

What was more, she needed this. Had talked extensively to Grace Parker about this time by herself. The psychiatrist had agreed that, with the right precautions for her personal safety, it was a good idea.

She would've told Zane all of this already if he'd been around. If he'd been a part of her life. But he hadn't been. So by damn, he did not get to have a say in her decisions.

"You know what? Just forget it." She spun back toward her truck.

"Hey, I'm not done talking to you."

"I don't give a damn if you're done with me or not. Have you thought of that? Maybe I'm done with *you* this time."

He strode directly to her. "What do you mean, this time?"

His nearness didn't bother her. Zane's nearness had never bothered her. This entire shouting match—so much like old times—was so freeing in a lot of ways.

"You bailed on me eighteen months ago, Zane. You don't get to have a say in anything I do anymore."

His volume rose with hers. "I didn't *bail* on you. I knew me being around you would be a constant reminder of the worst day of your entire life. So I tried to do the noble thing and get out of your way."

"Noble?" She all but spat the word, poking him in the

chest. "You were too much of a coward to fight for us, so you ran."

"This discussion is not about the last year and a half. This discussion is about your asinine plan to go hiking for a week by yourself."

"Why do you think you get to have a say in what I do, Zane?"

She got right up in his face and shouted the words.

God, it felt so good to yell. To have someone yell back. To not have someone treat her with kid gloves like she was going to break any minute.

"You don't, Zane," she continued, poking him in the chest with her finger again as she said it.

His eyes flared as he wrapped his hand around her finger against his chest.

And then, before either of them realized what was happening, he yanked her to him and kissed her.

Caroline had been kissed since the rape. She'd even had sex with a couple guys since. But they hadn't been Zane. Hadn't been who, deep inside, she truly wanted.

And it sure as hell hadn't been a kiss like this.

Zane's lips were like coming home. His arms banded around her waist and hers slid up his chest and around his neck.

That hair. Thick and brown. She thought of how many times she'd flicked off his hat and ran her fingers all the way through it as he kissed her. Exactly like she was doing now.

He devoured her mouth and she couldn't get enough of it, pulling him closer with fists full of his hair, moaning as his fingers bit into her hips in his urgency to get her closer.

He backed her up until she was against her truck, then grabbed her by the hips and hoisted her up to the engine's hood. Now she could wrap both her arms and her legs around him.

Passion simmered through her blood as his lips nipped down her jaw to her neck. Not gentle, not timid. Just Zane. Fierce and passionate, the way lovemaking had always been for them. She moaned as one of his hands came up and fisted into her hair, holding her so he had better access to what he wanted.

Her.

And she couldn't get enough of it.

Dimly she was aware that they were still in the parking lot of the Silver Eagle. That any minute her colleagues, law enforcement officers who generally tended to frown on sex in public places, were going to make their way out.

This needed to be taken back to her place. Or his. Or a hotel room.

Stat.

"Zane, we've got to stop."

She sighed at another one of his nipping kisses, at the feel of him pulling her closer. She'd missed this so much.

But damn it, she didn't want to get arrested.

"Zane, stop."

She gripped some of his hair and gave it a tug.

She could tell the exact moment he came back to his senses. His hands dropped from her hair and he all but jumped back from her body.

But it wasn't until she saw his face that she understood. He was ashen. Distraught.

"Zane—" She reached for him, but he moved farther back.

"Oh, my God. Caroline, I'm so sorry. I don't know what came over me, I—"

She jumped down from the hood of her truck, desperate to wipe the distressed look off his face. Zane hadn't done anything wrong. He'd done everything right and she wanted more.

But at that moment Wade yelled from the open door of the bar. "Hey, Captain sent me out here to make sure the two of you hadn't killed each other."

Caroline rolled her eyes and turned toward Wade, waving her arm at him over the hood of her truck. "We're fine. Leave us alone and you guys mind your own business."

Wade's chuckle rang out in the still night air as he went back inside.

"So I wasn't saying, 'No, let's stop. I don't want to do this.' I was saying, 'Let's move this party someplace a little more...'" She turned back to Zane, her biggest smile in place.

But Zane was gone. She heard his truck start on the other side of the parking lot before his tires squealed as he sped onto the street.

Chapter Four

Zane woke from the nightmare, heart pounding, sweat covering his entire body despite the cool air coming through the screened windows of his bedroom.

He'd dreamed about the night Caroline had been attacked by Paul Trumpold a year and a half ago. It had been a while since he'd dreamed about it. Although it was no surprise that he'd had it again after what had happened in the parking lot of the Silver Eagle two nights ago.

He probably would've had the dream last night if he'd slept a wink.

The dream—really more of a memory—always started the same way: Zane sitting at his desk at the CCPD headquarters, even though it was late at night, doing some work, avoiding doing what he really wanted to do, which was accept Caroline's invitation to go over to her house when he got off work. He hadn't wanted to give her the upper hand in their relationship. Wanted to keep her a little off balance like she so often kept him. Wanted to let her know, for once, what it felt like to wonder what would happen next. She did it to him without even thinking. He wanted her to know—wanted *himself* to know—that he could do it to her.

It all seemed so ridiculous now.

The uniformed cop—a young kid, Zane couldn't even remember his name—who'd wanted to give Zane a heads-up before he got the official call had run up to Zane's desk, knowing Zane was lead detective in the case. The cop had been out of breath when he told Zane the serial rapist had struck again.

Zane always remembered that moment in his dream and in his life. Because that had been the last time he'd ever been okay. The last time his world had been whole.

He'd been pissed that the rapist had struck again before they could catch him, but his world had still had a foundation.

He could never stop the next moment in his dream any more than he could in real life: when the cop gave him the address of the rapist's latest victim.

Caroline's address.

He'd written down the first two numbers as the cop had said it out loud before he'd realized where it was, then had dropped everything and run as fast as he could to his car, driving way past the limitations of safety to get to Caroline's house.

Praying the entire time that there had been some mistake. That the address was wrong. That the kid cop, in all his excitement to be helpful, had gotten the numbers wrong or something.

The numbers hadn't been wrong.

The ambulance at Caroline's house had thrown him. He'd seen an ambulance there before, one Caroline had driven. Hell, she'd even driven an ambulance to his house to meet him for a quickie once.

But she hadn't driven this one. This time the ambulance had been *for* her.

The dream sometimes changed from there. He always had to cross her yard to get to the door of her house. Sometimes as he ran across the yard in his dream the ground swallowed him like quicksand, slowing him from reaching the door. Sometimes there were thousands of people all over the yard and he couldn't get through no matter how hard he tried.

Sometimes he ran as fast as he could, but the door kept getting farther and farther away.

But no matter what happened, the rapist—Dr. Trumpold—always just stood there laughing at Zane. And when Zane would finally fight his way to the door, the man would turn and whisper, "You know why she opened the door for me? Because she thought it was you knocking. Thanks for the help." Then he would disappear.

And in his place would be Caroline. Lying on the floor of her own foyer, beaten until she was unconscious. Clothes ripped off her small body. Being treated by her own EMT colleagues, handling her with care even though she was long past feeling any pain at that point.

Zane had just stared, watching his entire world lying broken at his feet. He hadn't been able to move, hadn't been able to say a thing, even if there had been something that could've been said or done.

In real life Zane had ridden in the ambulance with Caroline, had stayed by her side in the hospital until she'd finally woken up forty-eight hours later and helped them catch the rapist.

But in his dream he was always stuck there in the doorway of her house, looking down at Caroline's broken, battered body. Knowing she would never be okay again, that *they* would never be okay again.

And in the worst of the nightmares she would open her eyes from where she lay on the floor—although he knew that would've been impossible, since the blows from the rapist had caused both her eyes to be swollen completely shut—and echo her rapist's earlier comment, in an oddly conversational voice.

Where were you, Zane? I thought it was you knocking at the door.

And he would never have an answer.

He got out of bed now, knowing he wouldn't get any more sleep. Hell, he'd be lucky if he got any sleep any night this week after what had happened in the parking lot of the Silver Eagle.

He'd flown at least one flight each of the last fifteen days straight, so he should be glad he had nothing scheduled for today, but now he wished he could get back up in the air. After the nightmare, today wasn't a good day to be grounded. Zane wanted to be up in his Cessna.

Flying had been the only thing that had come even a little close to filling the hole in his life since he left the department. Like Captain Harris suggested, flying wasn't enough to completely eliminate the void, but it at least did something.

Zane wished he had another organ donor trip. That had been exciting. The deadline, the pressure, knowing someone was counting on you to get the job done.

That had been what his life had been like every day when he'd been a detective on the force.

Life when he'd had Caroline in it.

That wasn't any easier to think about than not being on the force any longer. Especially after what had happened in the Silver Eagle parking lot.

What in heaven's name had come over him? How could he have possibly treated Caroline like that?

They'd been fighting just like old times. Yelling at each other.

Then she'd poked him in the chest with that tiny finger of hers, just like she had so many times in the past. And in the past it had almost always ended with them on top of each other.

He had moved out of muscle memory more than anything else. Covered her finger with his hand like he had so many times before, moving in for a kiss.

Basic instinct, a primal need for Caroline, had taken over from there. He'd been so caught up in the kiss, knew she had been too. Had felt her hands in his hair, felt her legs pull him closer when he'd set her up on the hood of her truck. It had been so long; they'd been desperate for each other.

But then she'd told him to stop and his first instinct, the only one he'd been able to hear at all, had been to keep kissing her. Keep kissing that throat. That neck. Those lips.

Then when she should've slapped him, she'd simply tugged at his hair and told him to stop again.

And finally reason had returned.

He scrubbed a hand over his face now, despair tugging at him. He'd been holding her in place, unwilling to let her go.

Caroline, a rape victim.

He had to give her credit; she hadn't seemed panicked. She hadn't cried or punched him or run screaming back into the Silver Eagle. When he'd jumped back, she'd started to say something to him.

He could think of a number of things she'd had a right to say to him. And none of them were pretty. So when Wade had yelled whatever he had to say—Zane totally hadn't been listening—he'd gotten away from Caroline.

Because once again, as had been true for the past eighteen months, the greatest thing Zane could do for Caroline was to keep away from her. He'd made as quick an exit as he could manage.

She'd be in the middle of Big Bend State Park now, on her hike. He still didn't like it. But she'd been right in one argument: what say did he have in her life?

None. Which was the best possible thing for her.

But the thought of her hiking alone still stuck in his craw. Maybe if he had kept his temper, used reason to discuss it with Caroline, he could've changed her mind.

But who was he kidding? *Reason* had never had anything to do with their relationship. Passion, fighting, yelling, heat. All those had. But never reason.

She'd driven him crazy from the moment they'd met in high school when her family relocated from Dallas. In both the best and worst of ways.

God, how he'd missed her the last year and a half. Missed the woman who had always stood toe-to-toe with him and refused to back down.

But now all he could picture was her broken body lying in the hospital bed eighteen months ago. Crying when she didn't know he could see her.

She'd never be able to go toe-to-toe with anyone again.

Not that Zane hadn't been willing to change everything about their relationship to fit her needs. Over those first few months, he'd tried. Went out of his way to be gentle, easy, light with Caroline. It had been weird, so different than what had always transpired between them. But for Caroline he'd been willing to do it. To do anything.

But it had all just seemed to make her upset. Sad, even.

Every time he'd let her win an argument, every time she'd poked him in the chest with that little finger and he'd just pulled her in for a hug, it had just made her more sad.

Finally, Zane realized that being around him at all made her sad. So he'd given her the only thing he'd had left to give: his absence. He'd quit the department, moved to the outskirts of town, made it so they never ran into each other.

And it had absolutely gutted him. His entire life became empty.

But for his Caro he'd been willing to pay that price.

And after his behavior two nights ago, obviously he needed to continue keeping himself away from her. The thought that he could've hurt her, scared her, brought back memories of her attack ripped a hole in him.

He started the day doing paperwork—owning your own charter flight company was perhaps the only business in the world that created more paperwork than law enforcement—but soon found he needed the release of some sort of physical activity. He decided yard work was in order. If his mother came by and saw the bushes and grass looking the way they did now, he would never hear the end of it.

And at least the hard, physical work of cutting and trimming allowed him to force the thoughts of kissing a stunning brunette—and how very good it had been before turning so bad—to the back of his mind.

He was going to have to see her in a couple of weeks from now for Jon Hatton and Sherry Mitchell's wedding in Colorado, since Caroline was one of Sherry's best friends and in the wedding. But Zane would be damn sure to keep his distance.

He'd kept his distance for nearly two years. He'd keep on doing it now.

When his phone rang, Zane wiped the sweat from his head before removing his glove and grabbing the device. Speak of the devil; it was Jon Hatton.

Zane hit the receive button. "Hey, Jon, I was just thinking about you."

There was a short pause. "Well, I hope you weren't in the shower, because that would be weird."

Zane laughed. "No, just tackling some yard work that has been a particular pain in the ass."

Zane had met the Omega Sector agent here in Corpus Christi when the local police had needed help with the serial rapist case. He and Jon had solved the case, but too late for Caroline.

Jon had tried multiple times to get Zane back into law enforcement since Zane had quit, even talking to him about working for Omega Sector, but Zane hadn't budged. Although he had helped Jon with a couple of cases that had brought the man back to Texas.

"If you're calling to get me to help you pick out china patterns, I'm afraid I'm going to have to decline."

"As scary as that thought is, no, I'm not calling with anything about the wedding. We've got a problem, Zane."

Zane knew the other man well enough to know that if Jon was calling him with "a problem" it was something serious.

"What's going on?"

"Can you get to your email right now?" Jon asked.

"Let me go inside." Zane grabbed the nearest dish towel from the kitchen and wiped as much sweat and dirt off his face and arms as he could before heading into his office.

"All right, I'm at my computer."

"I'm sending a picture of a Damien Freihof."

"I've never heard of him."

"He went to jail five years ago because he was about to blow up a bank full of people in Phoenix."

"Okay." Zane had no idea what this had to do with him.

"He escaped last year. Nearly killed Brandon Han and his fiancée, Andrea."

Zane knew Brandon; the man had helped figure out who the rapist was. But he didn't know about this Freihof guy or that he almost killed Brandon.

"That time—" it would've been right after Caroline's rape "—it's pretty fuzzy for me, Jon."

"Sure, man, I understand and don't expect you to know any of this."

"Okay."

"Freihof went to ground after he attacked Brandon and Andrea. He was injured in his own explosion. He resurfaced last week."

Zane still had no idea what this had to do with him. "Okay."

"I just sent you a picture of him."

Zane opened his email. "Okay, I got it." He studied the mug shot of Damien Freihof from five years ago. "I don't recognize him at all."

"I'm sending you another picture."

The second picture was a totally different man, roughly the same height and build but different jaw, eyes, hair.

"Okay, who's that?"

"That is also Damien Freihof."

"Damn." Zane whistled through his teeth. "He's good."

"Yeah, he is." Jon's tone held grudging respect. "Good enough to beat all our facial scanning software and to avoid the statewide warrant for his arrest."

"Do you think he's moved on to Texas?" If he had, it wasn't like Zane could do anything about it.

"Two days ago, Freihof masterminded a pretty elaborate plan. A bomb that killed one of our junior agents and put another agent in a coma. Looks like Freihof wants to make Omega Sector pay for putting him in prison. Plus, he nearly killed a mother and her toddler daughter in the process."

Zane's expletive wasn't pretty. "Sounds like this bastard doesn't care about collateral damage."

"Exactly. He wants as much collateral damage as possible. We've already been given that message. He's coming after people with ties to Omega. He's trying to hurt civilians we care about in order to split Omega's focus. I'm sending you one more picture."

The picture Zane received was of some sort of wall with a staggering amount of information on it: newspaper clippings, photos, drawings, police reports, Google search printouts, fingerprints.

"What the hell is that?" Zane couldn't make any sense of it at all.

"That's the wall of clues Freihof left for us. A very complicated puzzle that points out Freihof's next intended victims."

"How the hell were you able to make any sense of it?"

"It took us a long time, believe me." Jon paused for a second. "It looks like you and Caroline are on his intended victims' list, Zane."

"What?"

"There were very specific clues referring to you by name on the wall of clues. We think he might be coming after you soon, if he's not there already."

Zane's expletive this time was even uglier. "Caroline's off on her own."

"What?"

"She's on some damfool hiking trip in Big Bend State Park. Alone. Do you think this Freihof character might be aware of this?"

"Honestly, Jon, the man is a genius. I wouldn't put anything past him."

"Thanks for the heads-up, Jon. I've got to go. I'll keep you posted." Zane disconnected the call and was running for his bedroom, grabbing his go-bag. He would call Captain Harris on the way to the airport and get him to contact the park rangers at Big Bend and find out Caroline's exact GPS location.

He would file his flight plan and be in the air in less than an hour. He'd be with Caroline in under two. A madman genius had gotten to her once. There was no way in hell he was letting another.

So much for keeping his distance.

Chapter Five

Over the last few months, Caroline had been learning to trust her instincts again. Her instincts had told her a few months ago that this trip to Big Bend would be a healing one for her.

Now, nearing the end of day two, all alone with no one around for miles, she could honestly say she was damn happy she had followed her instincts.

She hadn't done it recklessly or without proper thought. She had planned. She'd considered. And finally, she'd just decided to take the chance.

Sort of like how she'd learned to do everything else in her life. She knew that bad things could still happen; people intent on harming others would always be around. Caroline did her best to prepare herself never to be a victim again, including multiple self-defense classes and hours of strengthening her body in the gym. She'd trained her mind to be more aware of what was going on around her so things didn't catch her off guard.

But ultimately after all the preparations, she had to choose to just do it. To just do that thing that was a little bit risky.

To trust that she could handle it.

It wasn't easy. And ironically, if Zane hadn't come along at the Silver Eagle a couple of nights ago and told her she shouldn't do it, Caroline might have chickened out. But that had been the final push she needed.

"So suck it, Zane Wales!" she yelled at the top of her voice, since no one could hear her anyway.

She loved being out here in the open. Loved that there was a one hundred percent guarantee that no one would knock on her door—the one sound that threw her into a panic every time she heard it.

Why? Because there were no doors out here. Caroline grinned.

The door-knocking thing was something she and Dr. Parker had been working through. Grace warned her that it may always be a trigger, and if so, Caroline would have to learn to live with it.

She was proud of the progress she'd made. Proud of how far she'd come. Proud of her certainty that no man, no matter how big or strong, would ever be able to get the drop on her again. She may not win a fight, but she knew she wouldn't be the only person hurt at the end of it.

She just wished she could convince everyone else of that. Of her growth. She wished she could get people to treat her the way they had before the attack.

As much as she liked Kimmie as her partner, Caroline would've had no problem working with a man day after day. But Chief Harris—one of her parents' best friends and someone she'd known her whole life—hadn't asked her. He'd had clout with the Emergency Medical Service director and had just done what he thought was best.

Her parents and brother still couldn't talk about what happened to her. They had wanted to hire a full-time bodyguard for her. When she'd brought up fairly basic questions—with what money? Why would she need a bodyguard when her rapist had died in prison?—they hadn't had a good answer. So no bodyguard. But they still didn't treat her the way they had before the attack. Everything they said to her or did around her now was always tinted with some sort of combination of protectiveness, worry and pity, depending on the activity.

She hadn't told them about this trip at all. It just would've put them over the edge. She'd sworn Captain Harris—Uncle Tim—to secrecy too.

But she missed Zane most of all. She missed her friend, her lover, the person she spent hours arguing with about every topic under the sun. Of all the things she'd lost in the attack, the one she regretted the most was Zane.

Like everyone else, he hadn't known how to deal with what had been done to her. Hadn't known how to treat her. It had been even worse for Zane because he'd been the lead detective on the case and hadn't realized who the rapist was.

But hell, Caroline had worked with Dr. Trumpold for months and hadn't known it was him. They'd all been duped.

She'd needed gentleness for the first few months as her body had healed from the attack. But then she'd needed her life to get back to normal. Nobody seemed to understand that. Zane definitely hadn't understood it.

Their relationship had always been so tumultuous, almost emotionally violent. It was just how both of them were wired: live hard, fight hard, love hard. But when Caroline had been ready to get back to the fighting and the yelling and, yes, the lovemaking, Zane had already programmed himself to be something else. Something she didn't recognize. Didn't want.

And he'd quit the force. She'd been unable to fathom that. When she'd gone to his house, ready to fight him about it—honestly looking forward to the screaming match and whatever would come after it—he'd refused to engage. At all.

He'd offered iced tea and told her they should maybe talk later when they were both calm.

She could fully admit that she hadn't handled the situation well. That she'd told him she didn't want to be around him like that. That she didn't even recognize him. Didn't *want* to recognize him. To stay away from her until he could figure out who they were.

She didn't think he'd take it to mean she didn't want to ever be around him at all. But that had been the last time they'd been close to each other. Until a couple of days ago at the Silver Eagle.

She'd been such a fool thinking he'd seen the light, first when he came to talk to her and then when he'd kissed her. Zane Wales wasn't ever going to see the light when it came to her. So she wasn't going to pine for him any longer.

Instead, she was going to celebrate being out here by herself. Celebrate the development of another coping strategy. Celebrate being alive.

Trumpold had been escalating, and based on what Sherry and Jon had told her, he'd definitely planned to move on to killing.

Caroline knew, deep in her bones, she was lucky to be alive. That Trumpold hadn't been able to decide whether to kill her or not.

She was alive. She looked around at the stark landscape of the Big Bend. She loved it here. Loved the open, loved the vast skies, loved being alone in the late-afternoon sun.

She turned, annoyed at the sound of a plane flying relatively low overhead. A small plane, probably a flyby for tourists. Caroline just went back to gathering what she needed to build a small fire tonight for coffee and to warm up some of the food she'd hiked in with her. She also needed to check in with the park rangers. She did that every eight to twelve hours out of courtesy for her colleagues back in Corpus Christi. They'd get the report too and not worry.

She was tempted to tell them all to just bug off and leave her alone, but she couldn't. These were people who loved her. She wished they wouldn't smother her with that love, but she couldn't fault them for it.

The plane came back by again and Caroline rolled her eyes. Big Bend was beautiful, but there wasn't enough to see for a double flyby. Then she realized the plane was landing not even half a mile from where she was camped.

Caroline grabbed her radio. She believed strongly in her independence, but she believed more strongly in not being stupid.

"Ranger station, this is Caroline Gill." She gave them her GPS coordinates. "I've just heard a plane land about a half mile south of me. Small aircraft."

"Yeah, we received a call from a Captain Timothy Harris in Corpus Christi."

"Captain Harris, yeah, I know him. Is there some sort of emergency?" She couldn't think of any reason Captain Harris would be on his way or have someone on their way if it wasn't an emergency.

"No, no emergency. He was clear about that. He was letting us know that a detective from his precinct was coming in via small aircraft. He said you wouldn't mind. Or that you probably would, but you'd get over it."

Damn it, Captain Harris was sending a babysitter. She wondered if her parents had gotten word of this trip. She wouldn't put it past them to browbeat Uncle Tim into sending someone to watch over her.

Well, whoever it was, she was sending them right back home.

She continued organizing her little camp, refusing to let

anything get in the way of the peace she had found over the past two days. One of the things she'd worked very hard on with Dr. Parker was accepting what she had control over and what she didn't. Certain circumstances she had no regulation over. But how she responded to them was up to her.

She left her little camp and made her way the few hundred yards to the jagged edge of one of the cliffs Big Bend was known for with a stunning view of the Rio Grande river. She could feel her babysitter's eyes on her as he or she got off the plane and walked toward her, but she didn't pay any attention. Instead, she continued to stare out at the river as the sun began to dip in the sky.

Finally, she knew she couldn't avoid it any longer and turned back around.

And found Zane standing about twenty yards behind her. She froze.

"What are you doing here?" she stammered. Captain Harris had sent Zane to babysit her?

And what's more, Zane had actually agreed?

"I didn't mean to startle you. The ranger station was supposed to let you know I was coming." He took a few steps toward her.

"They did. I mean, they said Harris had called and told them someone was coming out here and to let me know. But I didn't know it would be you. What are you doing here?" she couldn't help but ask again.

"Right now? Enjoying the beautiful view."

Caroline turned back out toward the river. "Yeah, amazing, isn't it? The sun has set on the river this way for thousands and thousands of years. Makes you feel part of something much bigger than yourself."

Zane didn't say anything, simply absorbed. They stood in silence watching the sun drop farther, casting a purple

hue throughout the entire area. Caroline just took it in with
him. She had to admit, there was no one else in the world
she'd rather share this moment with than Zane. She closed
her eyes and felt the warmth of the setting sun on her face.

When she opened them again, she found him studying her.

"What?"

"Nothing. You look good. Peaceful, capable. Being here,
at this place, obviously agrees with you. I was wrong to
tell you not to come."

"You got that straight. I still don't know why you're
here."

"I needed to make sure you were all right."

He stuffed his hands in his jeans pockets just like he always did when he wasn't telling the full truth. She'd never
told him she knew that tell because she'd never wanted to
give up the upper hand.

"You know I've been checking in with the rangers every
few hours. You could've just asked them. I'm sure some of
the CCPD have, including Captain Harris."

He shrugged. "I needed to see it with my own eyes."

He still wasn't telling her everything, but she trusted
him enough to know that if there was some true emergency
he would've already hustled her off to the plane and gotten her out of here.

A thought struck her. "My parents didn't call you and
make you come, did they?"

He chuckled. "No. I just wanted to see you for myself."

Her eyes narrowed. "You flew a long way just to look
at me, Wales. You might want to consider taking a picture.
It would be a lot cheaper."

"A picture of you, here, in this light couldn't possibly
do this moment justice."

Damn it if the man didn't still know how to make her insides go gooey.

"Are you here to try to get me to leave?"

Zane looked around, taking in the vastness surrounding them. "No. I don't think there's any place else you ought to be than here right now. Like I said, it obviously agrees with you."

She shook her head and began walking back toward her little camp. She still didn't know exactly why Zane had come. He would tell her when he was ready. And honestly, as long as he wasn't here to try to make her leave her hike early, she didn't care. She didn't mind having him around. She'd never minded having him around.

"I can take care of myself, you know," she said without turning back to him.

"I'm beginning to see that more clearly," she heard him mutter.

Good. He should've seen it long before now.

Chapter Six

Zane didn't want to tell her his true purpose for coming.

He could admit he had been so wrong when he'd told
her she shouldn't do this trip. He'd been arrogant and judg-
mental. She'd been right to get angry at him.

God, she looked so beautiful out here. At ease. Strong.
Capable. With a Glock G22 in a holster at her hip.

Damn, if that wasn't just the sexiest thing ever. Like
she'd been transported through time from the Wild West.
A rancher's wife, ready to do whatever was needed to make
her way securely through this wilderness.

"You know how to use that Glock you're carrying?"

She didn't even turn around. "Don't try to piss me off
on purpose, Wales. You know I wouldn't be wearing it if
I didn't know how to use it. I told you I wasn't coming out
here unprepared."

Zane had no doubt what she said was the truth. If some
sort of animal—four legged or otherwise—threatened her,
she would be prepared to protect herself.

Of course, she wasn't exactly prepared for a terrorist,
one of Omega Sector's Ten Most Wanted, who might have
set his sights on her. How did anyone prepare for that?

She looked so relaxed and peaceful he didn't want to tell
her about Damien Freihof. Just because their names had
come up on some psychopath's wall of clues didn't mean

an attack was imminent. Zane would eventually have to tell her about the conversation with Jon Hatton, but not right now. Not when there obviously wasn't any danger out here.

Not when Caroline looked so peaceful.

He hadn't been lying when he'd said he just wanted to see her, to be with her. Hell, he'd wanted that for the last year and a half.

They talked about the weather, and how her hike had been so far. But at her small camp area she finally turned to him. "Okay, you obviously don't want to tell me the reason why you're here. And I'm assuming if someone was hurt at home, or if I was needed, we wouldn't be sitting around here chitchatting like a couple of old ladies."

Zane laughed out loud. Lord, how he'd missed her sharp tongue. "Nope, nothing like that."

"It's not Jon and Sherry, is it? Nothing's happened with the wedding?"

He stiffened at the mention of Jon's name, afraid she'd ask for more specifics about him. "No, the wedding crazy is still in full gear as far as I know."

"Good. Because I'm rocking the bridesmaid dress Sherry picked out. She let us each choose our own style as long as it was the teal color she wanted. I got a halter style."

He had no idea what halter style meant but was glad to see her so excited about it. "Wedding is still a go, so your dress is safe."

She studied him for a long while.

"Well, it's getting dark, Zane. Have you seen whatever you need to see—that I'm alive and not throwing myself off the cliff, I presume—and you're leaving? Or are you going to stay?"

"Can I stay?" He did his best not to think too much about the question and what it meant for either of them. Right now he just wanted to be with her.

She shifted her weight onto one hip and stirred her fire with a stick. "It's a big park, Zane. I don't think I can stop you from camping here. Although I do think you're supposed to have a permit."

"You know what I mean."

"Do you have your go-bag?"

"Yep, plus a sleeping bag and MREs in the plane."

"Did you grab them for this trip or do you always have them in there?"

He knew she was still trying to ascertain exactly why he was here. "They're always in the plane. Although the go-bag is fresh."

"Meals Ready to Eat aren't very tasty."

Zane shrugged. "Some of them aren't too bad. And they're better than going hungry."

She smiled. "That's true. Maybe if you're lucky, I'll give you some of my food. Real stuff."

They hiked to his plane and got out his belongings. He showed her around the small prop plane.

"Do you like it? I never knew that flying was more than just a hobby for you before you started your business."

They had gone up a few times together over the years. Zane's grandfather had taught him how to fly in high school, and he'd gotten his pilot's license not long after he'd gotten his driver's license. Of course, Caroline's parents had categorically refused to let their only daughter up in a plane with a teenage pilot while she was in high school.

When she'd turned eighteen, she'd stopped asking their permission.

"I remember how your dad lit into me after that one time for taking you up." Zane got what he needed out and handed his sleeping bag to her. "You didn't tell me that you hadn't asked."

"I was eighteen, I didn't need their consent."

"Yeah, well, evidently your dad didn't know that."

That had been one of the last times Zane had flown with her, although not because of her father's threats to kill him. They'd both gone away to separate colleges, dating other people, but never seriously. When they'd both come back to Corpus Christi, things had gotten much more serious between them.

But that wasn't what he wanted to be thinking about right now.

"Anyway, my granddad left me the plane three years ago. And Jacob Scott was retiring from his air charter business, so I just took over. Worked out for everyone."

They started back toward the camp.

"Yeah, I'm glad that worked out," she murmured.

Her tone was sad, but he didn't push it. He didn't want to fight with her. Didn't want to do anything that would spoil this time and place with her.

DAWN THE NEXT morning broke just as gorgeous over the Rio Grande as sunset had left it the night before. And despite sleeping outside with no pillow, Zane woke feeling better than he had in a long time.

Eighteen months, nine days to be exact. The day Caroline had been attacked.

They'd spent the entire evening joking and fighting and arguing ridiculous points with one another about every topic from the Texas Rangers to the Rangers hockey team. Even when they were yelling the mood was easy between them. An underscore of happiness derived just from being with each other.

She didn't seem upset about how he'd treated her at the Silver Eagle. And, if it didn't upset her, then he knew he just needed to let it go.

He still hadn't told her about Jon Hatton's call. Honestly, there hadn't been any need to. Zane didn't want to ruin her trip for no reason.

But neither was he going to leave her here alone.

"So what's your plan, Wales?" Caroline asked as they shared breakfast consisting of oatmeal and dried fruit and some coffee she'd made over the fire. "You flew a long way just to camp out under the stars. I'm pretty sure we have those back in Corpus Christi."

Zane would've flown twice as far, hell, *more*, to have gotten the hours he'd had with Caroline. Hours where his presence didn't bother her. Where she was comfortable, confident.

"How would you feel about me paring down my gear and coming with you for a couple of days?"

Her eyes narrowed as if she was trying to figure him out. If she pushed now, he would have to tell her the truth about Damien Freihof. He'd have to tell her soon anyway.

"You got water in your plane?"

"Yeah. And a purifying bottle. It doesn't work quickly, but it will get out anything that will make you sick." It was standard equipment in his plane's emergency kit as well as some protein bars and the MREs.

Not to mention the Glock and extra ammunition he'd brought. The weapon was always nearby.

Of course, as he'd noticed yesterday, Caroline wasn't without her own weaponry.

"Okay, we might have to hunt a little small game to supplement our food if you decide to hang out more than a couple days, but I'm good if you are. Let's get camp packed up and ready to go."

And that was it. Just like old times, Caroline and her no-nonsense manner.

She broke camp as he went back to the Cessna and reloaded his go-bag. He took a moment to check in with Jon Hatton while he was away from her.

"Everything okay with Caroline?" Jon asked by way of greeting.

"Yes, no problems. It looks like your Freihof guy either doesn't know she's out here or has decided not to make a play. But I'll still be keeping my eyes peeled."

"Last time he used someone else to do a lot of his dirty work, Zane. So just be careful."

He finished his conversation with Jon, then hustled back to Caroline, who was ready to go.

She turned to him, everything already packed up. "What were you doing back there, writing poetry? Let's get a move on, Wales."

Her tone was annoyed, but he saw her smile as she turned away.

"No, I was fixing my hair if you must know. Beauty like this doesn't come without a price." He heard her guffaw as they began their hike. The only trace of the camp was the small ring of ashes from their fire. In wilderness camping you carried all your supplies in and all your trash out.

Big Bend advertised itself as "the other side of nowhere." Over three hundred square miles of all sorts of terrain: rolling hills, cliffs and valleys, desert sections as well as green hills. A hiker's dream if you wanted a variety of terrain and a chance to be alone. Especially now in November. No families camping or large groups led in on horseback.

Caroline had obviously planned out where she would be going. She had a map she glanced at every so often, a compass she brought out more to make sure they were on track. She was prepared, gutsy and strong. Just like she'd always been except...

The image of her rape, of seeing her lying unconscious

on the floor, swamped him. Stole his ability to breathe, to do anything but flounder in remembered panic. In the knowledge of how scared and hurt she had to have been.

She chose that moment to look over at him.

"You okay there, cowboy?"

He tried to shake it off, to make a joke. But he couldn't. He couldn't say anything. He just stopped and stared at her.

Somehow she understood.

"Zane, we're here. We're both here and we're both good."

He just nodded.

"I need you to be in the *now* with me, okay?" she continued. "The *then* costs too much. Takes too much. Be with me—with who I am—*now*."

She reached up and touched his cheek. He stared at her for a long moment before turning his lips to the side and kissing her palm. They both nodded.

She didn't want to stay in the past. He sure as hell couldn't blame her for that. She didn't want him to keep her there, either.

He realized he'd been doing that for a year and a half. Keeping her inside the box of the attack.

She turned and began walking again.

Obviously she refused to stay in the box any longer. He needed to stop trying to fit her there.

They walked the next few hours chatting easily, at least mentally. Physically, the pace they set as they hit higher ground made talking more breathy.

Midafternoon, Caroline stopped abruptly.

"Everything all right?" he asked.

"Yeah." She nodded. "Just get out your water and let's take a drink."

They'd just stopped for water less than twenty minutes ago. Zane didn't mind stopping, but this seemed odd. Caroline took a swig from her canteen, then walked around so she was standing on the opposite side of Zane.

"Caro, what's going on?"

"I think you better tell me why you're really here."

"Why do you ask that?"

"Because for the last hour there's been someone following us. And I just caught the reflection of the sun off a riflescope again. Whoever it is is getting closer."

"Damn it. You're sure it's not just some other hikers also out here?"

She shook her head. "That's what I thought at first. I'm not sure that the person means us any harm, but someone is definitely following us. Hikers aren't out here for company. Plus, we're on a route I created, not one on any of the normal trail maps. The chances of anyone picking the exact same route I did is pretty slim."

Zane grimaced. Caroline was right. This didn't sound good.

"If you weren't here, I'd double back, sneak behind them and see what was going on."

"Do you think it's just someone in trouble?" Even as Zane said the words, he knew it wasn't true.

"If they fired that rifle in the air, I'd be back to them in no time offering assistance. Whoever it is isn't in trouble. They're gaining in speed."

Zane saw a patch of light shine onto Caroline's shoulder before it quickly moved away. She didn't look at it, although she had to have seen it.

"Was that their scope again?"

She took a sip of water again, looking at him casually, not giving any hint as to the seriousness of the conversation. "Yep. Not someone very familiar with it if I had my guess. I would imagine they're looking at my face right now. Trying to figure out why we stopped."

"Are you in range for them to shoot?" Zane casually stepped to the side so the rifle would be trained at his back, not at Caroline.

"No. If they don't even know they're giving off a glare, I don't think they would try a long-range shot. Right now they're just keeping us in their sights for whatever reason."

"Good."

"So you want to tell me why you're really here so we can formulate a plan and figure out what we need to do?"

Zane hadn't wanted to tell her. Hell, twenty-four hours ago he would've worried that maybe she wasn't strong enough to handle it. He'd been damn wrong about that.

"Jon called me yesterday. He was worried about us."

"Us? Why?"

"Looks like some guy pretty high on the public enemy list has decided to make you and me targets."

Chapter Seven

Caroline appreciated the matter-of-fact way Zane gave her the news. Didn't pull any punches, didn't sugarcoat due to any misconceptions of what might be too much for her *delicate* feelings. He treated her the way he did before the attack.

The news was a little scary, she could admit. Some guy who had already killed or injured multiple Omega Sector agents now seemed to be targeting people who had an attachment in some way to Omega.

And she and Zane specifically. Not awesome.

"So does Jon think this Freihof guy is here now at Big Bend? Is that our rifle friend back there?"

"It seems as though Freihof's MO is to get other people to do his dirty work for him. So it may not be Freihof himself."

Not being here himself wouldn't make them any less dead if the rifle guy started shooting at them. "So what's our plan?"

"First we radio in to the park rangers. See if they know anything about anyone else out here. Maybe it's just someone like you who'd planned to be here the whole time."

She shrugged. "Okay. And the truth is, if the person wanted to shoot us outright, he could've done it before now. We weren't moving fast enough to escape someone."

Zane nodded and looked casually over his shoulder in the direction where she'd seen the rifle glint. "Let's try to put a little distance between us and whoever that is, okay?"

As they restarted walking, Caroline set a pace that was fast but not fast enough to look like they were deliberately trying to get away. Zane contacted the park rangers and they found out no one had filed a hiking plan in this direction but Caroline.

It didn't mean definite bad news, but it wasn't good news, either.

"Damn it, I'm going to have to cut my trip short, aren't I?" She'd been looking forward to this for so long.

"How about when we get this Damien Freihof thing settled, you and I will come back out here for a long weekend?"

Caroline almost stopped midstep at his words. Definitely not what she'd been expecting him to say. She still wasn't sure if he was inviting himself along because he wanted to look out for her or because he wanted to be with her.

But at least he was willing to be in her presence and not treat her like she was about to break. That was all she'd ever wanted from Zane.

She glanced over at his six-two frame, dark brown hair and muscular build. Okay, maybe it wasn't *all* she'd ever wanted. But it was a start.

"I don't know, Wales. What about all the hair product you'd need for a whole weekend? Think you have a backpack that sturdy?" She looked over her shoulder at him.

He grinned and winked at her. "Maybe I'll wear my hat."

Caroline's stomach did the craziest little somersault as much from his smile as his words. She would give anything to see that old cream-colored Stetson back on his head. Even if it didn't mean he was going back to work for the police department. It would just mean he hadn't given up on himself. On life. On there being good in the world.

Whatever it had meant when he'd stopped wearing it.

She smiled back. "Then it's a hiking date."

Less than an hour later, both of them knew they were being hunted. "Whoever it is is gaining," Zane said to her.

"Yeah, I noticed. But I've got a plan formulating. How do you feel about rappelling?"

He gave her a sidelong glance. "I've done it a couple of times, why?"

"There's a cliff edge coming up that has some rappelling ropes and gear already in place. I wasn't planning on using it this trip because it's dangerous alone, but it would get us back down to the river, where we can circle back around to your plane."

Zane glanced back over his shoulder again. "You think we should just give up all appearances of not knowing someone's following us and just make a run for it?"

"Yep. It's our best bet against someone who has a rifle compared to our sidearms. No way we're going to get the same range. We don't want to take a chance on getting into a firefight."

"Smart."

She shrugged. "You know we might be making a mountain out of a molehill. The difference between binoculars and a riflescope is impossible to tell from a sun reflection."

Zane glanced over his shoulder. "You could be right. But to be honest, I'm not willing to take that chance. Not when the person has been steadily gaining on us despite this pace."

"Yeah, my gut says we need to bail. Fast. And if there's one thing I've learned, it's to listen to my gut." It had been one of the first things she and Dr. Parker had worked on: learning to trust her instincts again.

"I agree."

"I say we ditch the packs and run. We can ask the park rangers to come out for them later. Given the psychotic killer possibly targeting us and all, they probably won't mind a trip out here to observe."

He was already stealthily unbuckling his backpack. "They'll probably only laugh at us a little bit."

"Let's hope it's nothing and we can all chuckle. The cliff is about a quarter mile from here. Are you ready to go on my signal?"

He nodded. "Yep, call it and we ditch the packs and run."

They were still walking, but now both of them had moved their hands to the buckles of their backpacks, after Zane grabbed a couple things as casually as he could from the outer side pocket of his. Caroline could feel eyes on them. She unhooked the small strap across her shoulder and moved her hands to the larger one at her waist.

"Now!" she said through gritted teeth. She pulled at the latch at her waist and the pack fell heavily to the ground. Zane's did the same. They both sprinted toward the cliff wall.

Not five seconds later a bullet bit into the ground behind them. Not close enough to be life-threatening, but definitely enough to prove the other visitor definitely wasn't just some lost hiker.

Zane cursed as two more shots hit the ground behind them, ricocheting off the ground. Caroline didn't know if the shooter was just a bad shot or what; she was just glad he wasn't cutting off their route to the cliff edge. As a matter of fact, the shooter was almost guiding them that way.

Because the guy hadn't studied Big Bend like Caroline had. Didn't know there was rappelling equipment at this particular cliff. He thought he was trapping them, but he wasn't.

She and Zane dived behind a large boulder at the edge of the ravine, giving them some cover. No more shots rang out.

He tucked his head to the side and grimaced. "Park rangers are definitely not going to laugh at us."

"Let's just hope we make it back to them."

The rappelling harnesses lay inside a box next to the boulder. They didn't waste any time getting them onto their bodies and clipping the carabiners onto the rope. Zane snatched his shirt off and ripped it into four pieces.

"We need gloves, but this will have to do. We'll burn our hands otherwise."

Caroline took the material, grateful he'd thought of it. She wouldn't have until she'd been over the cliff.

"Do you think he's heading toward us?" she asked as she wrapped the material of the shirt around her hands and refused to gape at how ridiculously sexy Zane looked in just his jeans with no shirt on.

"I think he thinks he has us trapped, so he's probably not hurrying. And might even think we'll be laying down some cover fire. But I don't think we should waste any time."

"He probably doesn't know about the rappelling."

"Let's hope not."

They kept as low as possible as they had to leave the cover of the boulder in order to clip into the rappelling rope. Caroline expected a few more shots but heard nothing.

"It's been a while since I've done this," she admitted as she clipped in and looked over the side of the ledge. Forty yards was a long way to fall.

"Yeah, me too. But it's better than being shot at."

As if the shooter could hear their conversation, a shot rang out near the boulder where they'd just been.

"Take it slow and steady," he told her. "Ready?"

They both got to the edge, then pushed backward, leaping straight back from the top, letting rope go slack as they both slid down about eight or nine feet, then stopped themselves with their hands as they caught their weight against the cliff wall with their feet.

"Good," he told her. "First leap is the hardest. Let's keep moving."

He didn't have to tell her twice. Caroline was well aware of how precarious their situation was if the rifle guy figured out they were no longer behind that boulder and were making a getaway. They would be sitting ducks if he came to shoot at them while they were rappelling down the side of the cliff.

They moved as quickly as their lack of real gear would allow. Caroline was thankful again for the pieces of shirt wrapped around her hands.

Halfway down she began to really believe they were going to make it. She wished she could be doing this under different circumstances because it would be a lot of fun.

She looked over to see Zane grinning like an idiot and knew he felt the same way as she did.

He reached over to high-five her.

Which saved her life as her rope came unattached to its place at the top of the cliff. She immediately began to tumble backward, falling with nothing to catch her and yards to go before the bottom of the ravine.

Zane grabbed for her with his free hand, his quick reflexes allowing him to catch her wrist. Caroline immediately wrapped her fingers around his wrist in a vise and swung her other hand up to latch on to him too.

There was no smile on his face now as he used all his strength to hold on to her.

"I'm okay," she said, and he nodded. She could see sweat breaking out all over his forehead at the exertion of holding both of them.

Suddenly Zane's line jerked also.

Zane said nothing, just pulled her up so they were torso to torso and she could wrap her arms around his shoulders and legs around his waist. He began sliding them both rapidly toward the ground. There was no way he could leap out to get slack on the rope without slamming her against the cliff, so he had to use sheer muscle to get them down.

A few seconds later his rope jerked again, dropping them both five feet.

"Your rope can't hold us both."

"It'll hold," he said through gritted teeth, continuing to work them down. Caroline just tried to keep herself still to not make his job any harder.

The rope sustained them until they were less than ten feet off the ground. Then it gave way with a gentle hiss just as hers had. With nothing now to hold them at all, they both fell backward, landing hard on the ground.

Caroline lay for long seconds just trying to get air back into her lungs, unable to move.

Finally, she looked over at Zane. He was alive, conscious.

"Okay?" he wheezed.

She nodded.

He stood and helped her to her feet, both of them still struggling to take in air. As he wrapped his arm around her shoulders, he began moving them to the east.

"We've got to get back to my plane, but we're going to have to circle around backward to do it. The rifle guy has the higher ground. It won't take him long to figure out we're down here, and once he does, he's definitely going to try to pick us off."

They kept as close to the cliff wall as they could, trying not to give the shooter a target. Without the packs they could move much more lightly and quickly. The hike that had taken them four hours took just half that going back with the punishing pace they set for themselves.

They both had their water canteens, and Zane had grabbed a protein bar before ditching his pack, which they shared without stopping. They never let up the pace even when no shots were fired. Caroline still couldn't shake the feeling that they were being watched.

But that didn't make sense. If this Damien Freihof—or whoever he was working with—was still after them, he would've been shooting. Even if he wasn't good enough to kill them at that distance, he could've still kept them pinned down.

But even though Caroline didn't see any more reflections off riflescopes, she couldn't shake the feeling that danger was only a step behind them.

Zane must have felt it too, because he never once suggested they slow down or that they might have shaken the shooter.

The sun was beginning to set as they got to the plane. They approached it together, both of them with their weapons drawn.

No one was there. No evidence the door had been tampered with or of any problems. Zane did a more thorough check, making sure there weren't any leaks or noticeable trouble before jogging back to her.

"Let's get out of here," he said to her, opening the hatch door so she could climb through. He followed immediately behind her, grabbing a shirt from a small backpack he had in the cockpit. "I know it sounds crazy, but I feel like we're about to be ambushed at any moment."

Caroline shook her head, still looking through the window. "No, it's not crazy. Even though no one has been shooting at us, I feel the same way."

They buckled themselves into the harness-type seat belts and slipped on the communication headphones as Zane started the engines. He eased the plane to the farthest end of the open area where he'd landed. Caroline held on to the seat belt straps where they crossed over her chest as he eased the throttle back and sent the plane speeding down the field. Moments later they were airborne.

As they climbed into the air, she relaxed. She had no doubts whatsoever about Zane's ability as a pilot.

"Okay, I have to admit I was expecting bullets to be flying at us or something," Zane said into the headphones.

"Yeah, me too."

"I've got to call in to the nearest air traffic control. Declare an emergency flight plan. There's going to be a crap ton of paperwork to fill out with this, but—"

A deafening roar and loud popping sound came from the engine to their left before it stuttered to silence.

"What just happened?"

"Engine flameout," Zane said, both hands wrapped in a death grip on the steering column, struggling to keep the plane steady. "We can still fly with one engine, but it's not optimal. I'll need to inform ATC so we can declare it and get back on the ground as soon as possib—"

His words were drowned out by another roar, this time from the right engine. Caroline could see the glare of the flames out of the corner of her eye for a minute before it went out.

Now they were flying with no power in either engine, the silence in the cockpit giving new meaning to *deafening*.

Zane struggled to control the Cessna at all now. "Get the radio and call out a Mayday." He nodded toward the GPS unit between them. "Give them our closest coordinates."

Caroline grabbed the radio and turned it to the frequency she'd used for the ranger station. No one was manning it, since it wasn't her check-in time, but she kept repeating the Mayday and coordinates just in case.

She could see Zane looking around for anywhere they could possibly land. Big Bend wasn't set up for planes and most of the ground wasn't flat, especially in the direction they'd been heading before the engines blew.

"What do we do?" Caroline asked. It was much easier to hear her now with no engine noise.

"We need to find a place to put her down. Fast. Any open area. No big rocks or trees."

That wasn't going to be easy.

"I think that dried-up riverbank is our best option. It's probably our only option." Zane motioned to the left with his head and maneuvered the plane, almost by sheer willpower, toward it.

"C'mon, baby," he muttered as the plane shuddered slightly, resisting his ease toward the opening in the earth in front of them.

An eerie shadow joined the already eerie enough quiet as the plane dipped lower and cliff walls surrounded them on either side.

"Caro, we're going to be coming down fast and hard. Make sure your harness is on as tightly as possible." Zane did the same to his own.

Caroline did all she could do, which basically was not scream at the top of her lungs and distract Zane, as the ground kept moving rapidly toward them. He needed every bit of concentration he could get.

"You can do this, Zane."

She didn't know if he heard her as the Cessna hit roughly along a higher section of the creek bed, then bounced hard against the ground. The force flung Caroline back against the seat as the plane flew back up, then came down roughly again. The impact was bone-jarring, but at least they were still alive.

Zane slowed the plane as much as he could and then turned the yoke sharply so they began to slide to the side. Working against their own speed snapped them around hard, collapsing one side of the plane as the landing gear gave out, slowing them down. She didn't know if it would be enough to stop them from slamming into the ravine wall.

Zane took his hands off the yoke; there wasn't anything he could do to steer now. The weight of the plane teetered forward as they continued their rapid approach toward the wall.

He reached out his hand to grab hers. "Hang on, we're going to flip," he said. Caroline grasped his hand, doubtful they'd live through the next thirty seconds.

The plane flipped, ripping their hands apart as they slammed into the ravine wall.

Then there was only blackness.

Chapter Eight

Zane's eyes opened and it took him a minute to get his bearings. He was hanging in the seat sideways, the harness holding him in. The entire cockpit tilted at a precarious angle. But he was alive.

His attention immediately focused on Caroline. Her much smaller body may not have withstood the impact so well. He couldn't see her from where he was trapped against the seat. Now that the plane had flipped, Caroline was above and a little bit behind him. And the plane was rapidly filling with smoke.

"Caro?" Nothing. "Caroline? Talk to me."

He pushed himself up from the seat so he could get a glimpse of her. She hung limp against the harness holding her, her arms and her hair just fell forward, lifeless.

Zane forced panic out of his system as he reached down to unhook his safety harness. After a tug-of-war of brute force, Zane won. He slipped his arms from the belts, ignoring the pain, grateful he could move at all.

"Wake up, Caroline. Can you hear me?" She still hadn't moved or said anything.

He worked his way up to Caroline's seat, where she lay motionless against the belts. He didn't see any blood or any obvious injuries but knew they could be internal.

He was reaching for her pulse when she moaned and

moved slightly. Zane felt relief wash through him. She wasn't dead.

But smoke was definitely filling the cockpit at an alarming rate. He needed to get them out of the plane immediately.

"Caro? Baby, can you hear me? We're alive, but we've got to get out of here."

He tried pulling at the release mechanism of her harness, but it was jammed. Breathing was getting more difficult.

Zane grabbed his army knife from his jeans pocket. Bracing his legs against the small side window, which was now on the ground, he used his strength to lift Caroline's unconscious form, then sawed through the canvas of the harness belts.

It wasn't an easy process. Even as light as she was, holding her dead weight up so he could cut the straps without cutting her took all his strength. The smoke was really becoming an issue. It was coming from the back of the plane, but once it hit the engines, this thing would be a fireball.

He felt one of Caroline's arms brace herself on his shoulder, holding part of her weight. He looked up from where he was cutting the straps to see her green eyes peering down at him.

"Hey."

"We're alive," she whispered.

"Yes. But it's just a matter of time before the fire makes its way to the engines. We've got to get out of here."

"You're bleeding." Her voice was tight.

He looked over at his arm where he'd been cut. "I'll be fine. Push yourself up as far as you can."

"I can only do it with one arm, I'm pretty sure the impact knocked my other shoulder out of joint."

Zane muttered a curse. "Okay, just hang in there."

She grimaced at his poor choice of words.

Cutting the side where she could hoist herself became much easier with her assistance. He had to brace his arm against her chest and push to get the other side. He could tell by her labored breathing that his actions were hurting her. When the last of the belts finally gave way, she fell heavily on him. He caught her as gently as he could.

"You okay?" She nodded and he put her gingerly on her feet and helped her gain her balance as he began to climb over the pilot seats. Both of them were coughing now.

"Let's get out of here," Zane wheezed. He grabbed his small backpack—it didn't have much in it in the way of usefulness, but it was better than nothing.

He pulled himself up and through the flimsy cockpit door that had broken away and into the main cabin, reaching back to help Caroline. They could both see flames now.

"I'm fine," she told him. "You get the outer door open. I'll get myself out of here."

Zane nodded and proceeded to put all his effort into opening the door that would lead them outside. It was caught against the ravine wall and didn't want to budge. When using his back and shoulders didn't do much, Zane leaned his weight against one of the passenger seats and used the muscles in his legs to try to force open the door. Caroline made her way out of the cockpit and added her strength to the effort.

Damn it, they couldn't survive the crash just to die here from smoke inhalation.

Their eyes stung and lungs burned, but finally the crushed door gave way on the hinge side and slid open enough for them to fit through. Zane steadied her as much as he could as they half ran, half stumbled away from the burning plane.

He knew the moment his livelihood blew up. The force

literally swept them off their feet and threw them forward onto the ground. He heard Caroline cry out as her injured shoulder hit the ground hard. Zane wrapped his arm up over her head as pieces of the plane became projectiles all over the ravine.

The quiet after the explosion was unnerving. Both of them lay on the ground trying to catch their breath for a long while. Finally, Zane flipped himself over and sat up, gently helping Caroline to do the same.

She reached over and touched her injured shoulder, wincing. "Definitely out of the socket. It's going to need to be put back in."

That didn't sound good in any way. "Like you running into a wall and knocking it into place?"

She rolled her eyes. "You've seen *Lethal Weapon* too many times. No, the acromioclavicular joint can be eased back into place with much less violence."

He noticed she didn't say with much less pain.

"You're going to have to do it, Zane."

"Hang on a second, I'm not the medical professional. You are." Plus, the thought of hurting her made him almost physically ill.

"I can't do it. It takes two hands to slip the joint back in properly."

She was already looking pale, and he could tell every time she gave a residual cough from the smoke it was causing her more pain.

"I don't want to hurt you."

She took a step toward him. "Once you do it, it will hurt a lot less, believe me. And there's no way I'm going to be able to climb out of here with a dislocated shoulder. Plus, the longer we wait, the more swollen and aggravated it will get. It's an anterior dislocation, so that's good."

He didn't know what that meant, but didn't see anything good about it.

"I'm going to lie on the ground so there's no weight on this shoulder." He helped her get down on the ground as she explained what he needed to do. Which way to pull her arm and which way to twist once he did. He knelt down next to her injured arm.

She reached up with her good arm and pulled his face down so their foreheads were touching. "Thank you," she whispered. "Remember, slow and easy, no quick, jerky movements."

He shifted slightly and kissed her forehead. It was time to get this done so both of them could stop hurting. "Ready? One, two, three."

Zane did exactly as she'd instructed, wishing to God roles were reversed so he could take the pain instead of her. He heard a broken sob come out of her mouth at the very last moment before the joint slipped back into place.

He wiped her hair off her brow as her breath shuddered out. But he could tell immediately by the way all the muscles in her body relaxed that she was in much less pain now.

"Thank goodness," she murmured.

"Does it still hurt?"

"Not nearly as much as it did thirty seconds ago."

They both sat there, just catching their breath.

"How about you? Are you okay? I know you have that cut on your arm."

He looked down at it. "It's already stopped bleeding."

Zane did a physical inventory of the rest of his body. Everything seemed to be moving, even now that adrenaline wasn't fueling all his thoughts and actions. No sharp or overwhelming pains, but a ton of little ones.

"You doing okay?" he asked her.

She grimaced and didn't open her eyes. "My entire

body hurts, but I don't think I have any life-threatening wounds."

"That's basically how I feel."

Now she opened her eyes. "But considering we just crashed into a ravine, I think we're in pretty good shape."

"Damn straight."

They both sat up although neither of them were very interested in doing more. "How exactly did that happen anyway? I'm going to assume that us being shot at and then both engines of your plane blowing out on the same day are not a coincidence."

Zane shook his head. "There's no way in hell it's a coincidence. If one engine had blown, I might have called it suspiciously bad luck. Both engines? That's sabotage."

They both stared off at the wreckage in silence for long minutes. "I know you didn't have time to do a full walkthrough before we took off, but did you see anything suspicious?"

"No." Zane stretched his shoulders, trying to work out some of the stiffness. "I looked for obvious problems—leaking fluid that would signify cut lines—but didn't see anything. But if someone knew about planes, there are easy ways—like putting sugar in the gas tank, which clogs the fuel lines as it dissolves—to bring a plane down."

"Now we know why our shooter didn't take any more shots at us. He wanted us to make it back to the plane."

Zane nodded. "And now we know we're likely dealing with more than one person. Someone with the rifle and someone who sabotaged the plane. And I don't think it was coincidence that our rifle friend decided to wait until we were at the rappelling equipment before taking his first shots."

Caroline grimaced. "He was leading us there."

"Yep. And then that equipment just happened to be

faulty? I don't think so." Zane shrugged and stood. "We've had two attempts on our lives today and neither of them have been by rifle shot. All the shots did was lead us where they wanted us to go. Someone wanted us dead but wanted it to look like an accident."

He reached down a hand to help Caroline up also, careful of the arm that was still sore. "What happens now?" she asked.

"That Mayday you got off to the ranger station will give them a rough idea of where we are."

"Yeah. I've studied the topography maps of Big Bend for weeks, and unfortunately, we are pretty far from any of the ranger stations."

"And none of them have a helicopter or rescue plane just sitting around, I'm sure. Even if they go to the coordinates you gave them in the Mayday, we're still twenty-five miles away from that. It's going to take them a while to find us, even once they have the right equipment to do so."

She tucked a strand of hair behind her ear the way she'd always done when she was thinking. "We don't have any supplies and a storm set is supposed to move in tonight. It's part of the reason I studied the maps so extensively. I wanted to be able to change course as needed based on weather. Where we were before wouldn't have been in the line of the storms, but here…"

"Then let's get out of this ravine in case the storm does come our way. Climbing out of here when it's dry is going to be hard enough." He looked up and around them.

They were in a much more remote and rugged section of the park. No rappelling equipment would be found around here. They would have to take it very slowly and carefully up the steep walls of the ravine. It wouldn't exactly be rock climbing, but it would be close.

Plus, they were overstimulated, hungry and tired. This wasn't going to be fun.

"You ready to do this?" Zane asked as they found the least steep section of the ravine. It was still thirty feet, but at least not at a ninety-degree angle.

Caroline nodded.

"You go up ahead of me." Zane wished he could go first, to help find good footing, but still be under her in case she fell. He couldn't be in two places at once. "Just take it slow. Stop and rest whenever you need to."

He looked up and over at the sky. Zane didn't tell her that time was of the essence—it was getting dark and a storm would be coming in soon. Caroline already knew.

Too slow and they'd be halfway up the ravine and caught in the dark and a dangerous storm. Too fast and one or both of them might fall and seriously injure themselves.

She took her first steps toward the wall, walking at first, then hoisting herself as it became more vertical. They talked through different hand and foot holds, especially as they made it ten, then fifteen feet up the ravine.

A fall now could prove just as deadly as the crash had been. But Caroline never wavered. It was one of the things he'd always admired about her: her ability to focus, set her mind to a task and complete it. It made her one hell of a paramedic.

Not to mention her body had a toned strength to it now that she hadn't had before. She'd always been slender, too skinny in his opinion, but not anymore. A couple of years ago she would've had a difficult time making it up this cliff, even despite her slight size.

But now she had a strength, in both her arms and legs. Even with the injured shoulder, he could tell by the way she was able to stretch, hoist herself up. To use both her arms and legs to lift her body weight. He'd noticed her strength earlier when the repelling gear had given way. Without her grasp on him, keeping herself supported, he wouldn't have been able to get them both down safely.

He could see her lithe muscles moving under her pants and long-sleeve shirt and had to force the thought of what her body would look like now—no clothes at all—out of his head. Now wasn't the time to be doing anything but focusing completely on the task at hand. Not that fantasizing about Caroline was ever appropriate.

About ten feet from the top of the ravine they came to a large crevasse in the rock. An opening big enough for them both. It gave them a chance to rest and sit down.

And realize that the storm was approaching faster than either of them had thought. The temperature had dropped ten degrees since they'd started their climb.

"I think we better stay in here and ride out this storm," Zane said. "Even if we make it up to the top, there's not much shelter up there at all. At least here we'll have a better chance of staying dry."

They needed supplies. Water-resistant material, warmer clothes, sleeping bags. But all those items were still in the packs they'd dropped when they ran. All they had was what Zane had taken out of his hiking pack and left in the small backpack in the plane. In other words, stuff that hadn't been good enough to make first string.

He took the backpack off his shoulders and brought it around to unzip it. He had a second pair of jeans, an extra pair of socks, a sweatshirt and a half-full water bottle. But best of all, a rain poncho.

"Don't guess you have a satellite phone in there?" she asked as he set the items out.

"I wish. Nothing particularly great."

"But added warmth and element protection. So better than nothing."

They decided that Zane would put on the extra pair of jeans under his current hiking pants. It wouldn't be comfortable, but at least it would be an added layer. Caroline slid on his socks which came up to well over her knees and put on the sweatshirt. Her smaller frame would need the warmth more than his would.

She pulled the hood of the sweatshirt up over her head. "At least it's not yellow," she murmured.

Zane had forgotten about that. Caroline's attacker had worn a yellow hoodie. In her pain from the attack, and the way the man had blitzed her, hitting her before she could truly react, she had mistaken a yellow hoodie for blond hair. It had caused the police to arrest the wrong man at first—someone with long, bright blond hair.

Zane wasn't sure exactly what to say. "Are you okay?"

Caroline nodded. "Yeah, believe me, if it will keep me warm, I don't give a damn what color the hoodie is."

"Good. Because that storm is looking uglier every minute." They both looked out at the dark clouds rolling in.

They split the water in the water bottle between the two of them, then Zane set it on the outside of the ledge, where it would catch some rain. He braced it with some of the little rocks around.

Then they slid back as far as they could, about two feet from the outer edge. They lay down nearly on top of one another and cocooned themselves as much as possible in the rain poncho.

And waited for the storm to hit.

Chapter Nine

Hours later, rain pouring all around them in the inky blackness of the night, Caroline lay in Zane's arms.

Somewhere she'd never thought she'd be again.

She wanted to enjoy it, she really did. But huge waves of agony kept pouring over her. Every way she shifted to try to get comfortable on the wet, hard ground of the crevasse just made some other pain worse.

It was everything she could do not to cry. And Caroline was not a crier.

"What if I lie on my back and you ease onto my side. Will that help any?" Zane asked.

"That's just going to cause you to get more wet and cold."

"I'm feeling a little too hot anyway, so why don't we try it?"

She tried to give a small laugh, but it just came out as a puff of air. There was no way Zane was feeling too hot. The weather had dipped another fifteen degrees since nightfall and even in the partial shelter of their overhang they were both still getting wet.

But Zane still moved onto his back, careful to keep the poncho around both their heads and torsos to keep them as dry as possible. Caroline was able to shift some of her weight onto his chest and almost moaned out loud at how good it felt to be more comfortable.

When Zane's arm reached around her and forced her head down on his chest, taking even more of her weight, she couldn't stop the moan.

"That's right. Never let it be said that I don't know how to show the ladies a good time."

Now Caroline did chuckle. He sounded as physically miserable as she felt. "If this is a date, you've definitely got the excitement factor down pat. I'm waiting for a lion to jump up here and attack us, just to finish this day off."

"That's not scheduled for another hour, so you can relax." He shifted a little so more of her weight rested against him. "Are you doing all right? I know your shoulder has to hurt."

"I'd give a lot of money for some ibuprofen right now," she admitted, but didn't want to complain anymore. "How about you?"

"Not comfortable, but considering what we went through? Very grateful we're both alive. I'm sorry your hiking trip was ruined."

"I'm even more sorry that you were right and it ended up being dangerous." She made a sour face.

Zane laughed and pulled her closer. "If it helps, I don't consider myself to be right. I think having one of federal law enforcement's most wanted criminals personally targeting you counts as extenuating circumstances. Otherwise I think your trip would've been perfectly safe."

"Definitely added some factors I didn't plan for. And by the way, thank you. If you hadn't come out here, I would've been dead a couple times over."

"I wouldn't be too sure of that. I think it's possible that Freihof and his partners followed me. Or that I at least tipped them off as to where you were. It's interesting that you didn't have any trouble at all until after I got here."

"Maybe."

"I can promise you that we're going to catch this guy once we make it back to civilization."

Caroline wondered if Zane knew how much like law enforcement he sounded. Not that she doubted him.

"I believe you. Although it sounds like you might have to get Captain Harris to reinstate you, super cop." She snuggled a little closer. "You always make me feel safe, Zane."

She probably shouldn't admit such a thing; it would make him uncomfortable given how he'd kept himself away from her for so long. It must be the exhaustion or pain getting to her. But it was still the truth.

She couldn't see his face but heard the derision in his laugh. "You're kidding, right?"

"About Harris reinstating you? He would be beside himself with ex—"

"No. About feeling safe with me. Don't joke about that, Caroline. It's not funny."

She shifted her head up slightly, wishing she could see him in the darkness. She might as well tell him the truth; it wasn't like he could be around her any less than he'd been the last year and a half.

"I've always felt safest around you."

"Maybe before you were attacked."

She shrugged painfully. "The attack changed how I saw and thought about pretty much everything. Changed my very DNA, I think, sometimes. But around you is where I have always felt safest."

She could feel tension flood his body. "God damn it, Caroline, you were raped and nearly beaten to death because of me."

Tension flooded her. "What are you talking about? I was attacked because Trumpold was a psychopath."

"Trumpold overheard our conversation, Caro. He knew

you had invited me over that night. Knew you would expect *me* to be knocking on your door when I got off my shift. But I decided not to go."

His voice dropped lower.

"We'd been arguing about something that day. For the life of me I can't remember what it was. You were winning, as usual, so I thought I would get the upper hand by not showing up that night."

"Zane, don't—"

His voice rose much louder than needed to be heard over the storm. "You cannot tell me that you didn't open your door to that sicko because you thought it was me knocking."

She heard the agony in his words and would give anything to be able to tell him that. If only to give him the peace of mind he obviously so desperately searched for. But she couldn't. No matter what she and Zane were or weren't to each other, no matter how tumultuous their relationship, they'd always been honest.

"Yes, I opened the door because I thought it was you," she said softly.

She felt his arm drop from her completely. Felt him almost deflate. Wither.

"How can you say that you feel safe around me after that?" he finally asked. "The night you needed me most I was too busy plotting how to get the upper hand in our relationship."

They lay there for long minutes, silence surrounding them as completely as the storm.

Caroline thought Zane had distanced himself after the attack because he couldn't stomach what had happened to her. That he thought she was too delicate to go back to what their relationship had always been: passionate and sometimes almost violent in its intensity. And maybe that was still true. But she realized now that guilt was the bigger part of what had driven him away all these months.

"Zane, it was Dr. Trumpold. He blitzed his way through the door as soon as it was cracked open. He hit me immediately in the face, and I never saw it was actually him."

"I know." The words were ripped out of Zane's chest. "And you cracked the door in the first place because you thought it was me."

"Maybe." She had to make him understand. To help Zane realize why it had never occurred to her to even partially blame him for what had happened. "Zane, I *knew* Dr. Trumpold. Worked with him almost every day. Yes, I opened the door thinking it was you. *But I would've opened the door to him anyway.*" She spaced out each word to make sure he understood.

It hurt to say them, to even think about that man. She hated that a knock on her door still caused her to blanch and that her first instinct everywhere she went now was to look for danger.

Zane didn't say anything and she didn't really expect him to. He had to process this at his own rate. She didn't blame him; she never had. But she couldn't force him to accept that. They lay there in silence, but eventually Zane's arms found their way back around her, moving in gentle circles on her waist.

"We were fighting that day over which was better, A&M or Austin," she finally said. "I'd insulted your precious Longhorns." She knew that because as she'd come out of the coma, before she'd remembered anything about her attack or felt any of the pain, she'd thought of another point in her argument in the superiority of the Aggies over the Longhorns.

They'd never finished that argument.

She heard Zane curse softly. "I should've known it was about a stupid football team."

"If it hadn't been that, it would've been one of the other hundred topics you and I bickered about on a daily basis. We fought, we made up. We were rough. It's just how we always operated, Zane. It's what worked for us."

Right up until it didn't. Until he stopped fighting. She felt him nod from where she still lay against his chest.

"Our relationship was always so volatile," he whispered softly.

Yes, their passion for each other had been almost violent in its intensity sometimes. She'd loved that they hadn't always made it to the bedroom because they couldn't wait to get at each other. "I remember. Believe me. I remember."

"You say that like it's a good thing."

"Who cares if it was good or bad? It was *us*. And whether people understood it or not, we were good together. Even during our loudest screaming matches."

"But then everything changed." The sadness was pronounced in his tone.

"It didn't have to."

"You told me to stay away from you." He shifted slightly under her. "Not that I blamed you for that. Still don't."

She sighed. "I didn't tell you to stay away from me. I told you to stop treating me like I was some sort of delicate doll."

"God, Caro, I watched your broken body lying on the ground. I sat by your hospital bed for two days while you were in a coma. And I was the lead detective on the case, so I've seen all the photos of everything else."

She sat up, wanting to be close to him but needing a little distance. At least the rain was starting to back down some.

He continued as if she hadn't moved. "Nobody would've

blamed you for never wanting to be around another man ever again. Much less be with me. Not only was it partially my fault…"

She wasn't having any of that. "No. It wasn't."

"But our relationship always bordered on rough anyway. How in the world could I think you would ever want that?"

"So you tried to make it into something it wasn't."

"I wanted to be what you needed." He scrubbed a hand across his face.

"What I needed was someone who didn't treat me like I was never going to be anything but a recovering rape victim! I thought that person was you. It was everything I held on to in the hospital and all through my physical therapy."

"Caro—"

All the feelings and frustrations were flooding out of her now, her own violent storm. She couldn't stop it if she wanted to. "I waited and waited, but you never showed up, Zane. Someone who looked like you did. He held my hand and talked to me. But it was just a pale copy of the original. I needed *you*. I needed *us*. So you're right, when you couldn't provide that, I didn't want you around. I wanted you to treat me like I was *me*."

Zane sat up with her, pulled her closer. She didn't resist. "Caroline."

"But when I told you to go, I never meant for you to stay away forever. I just wanted time to heal. For both of us to heal. Because you needed to just as much as I did."

"You're right. I did." He nodded, still holding her against him.

"But you didn't heal, Zane. You quit the job you loved, the one you were so good at, where you made a difference, and you never came back. You just vanished. You left me too."

"I thought being away from you was the best thing I

could do. That you wanted me away. It was the only gift I had left to give."

She wanted to cry. For the past that couldn't be changed. "That was never what I wanted."

He pulled her tighter to his chest, laying them both back down. "I see that now. I didn't handle the situation very well. I know that. My only excuse is that I thought I was doing what you wanted—keeping away from you."

"Maybe we both didn't handle the situation very well." She sighed.

"You had enough to deal with, just getting through every day."

"I would've rather had you there with me."

"I'm here with you now."

She could hear his heartbeat under her cheek. He was with her now. Maybe that was enough.

"You can't treat me like I'm fragile, Zane. Everyone else still does. Like I'm going to crack at any moment. I'm not. I'm strong. That's part of the reason I was hiking out here. To prove I was okay."

"Everyone knows you're strong."

"Do *you*? Do you really, Zane?"

"Yes. I've always known it. But what I saw you do today? Hold it together as the plane was coming down? Direct me with how to get your shoulder back in joint, then climb up a ravine wall? I don't think any sane person could doubt you're strong."

She wanted him to prove it. Prove that he believed it.

Not with words. She knew he could say the words. Knew he even believed the words.

She needed him to show her—to show *both* of them— right now that she wasn't breakable.

The pain in her shoulder didn't matter, the aches and bruises they both had weren't relevant. Caroline wanted to feel alive on the inside. Wanted to feel alive, feel strong and womanly, the way only Zane had ever made her feel.

The storm had slipped by. All they had left was night. Tomorrow the rescue would come.

Tomorrow they'd be going back to real life.

But first she would enjoy Zane the way she had in the past. Before they'd let someone take much more from them than they ever should have given up.

She shrugged the poncho from over her shoulders and threw it to the side. Then she slid up from where she was lying on her side against him so she was straddling his hips. The narrow spacing of the crevasse didn't give her room to sit straight up, so she was forced to hover over him, her breasts pressed against his chest.

"Whatcha doing?" he murmured, his face only inches from hers.

"You've got to prove it."

"Prove that I want you?" His hands gripped her hips and pulled her down harder against him. "I don't think there can be any doubt of that."

"Prove that you really think I'm strong. That you're not afraid I'll break at the least little thing."

"I know you won't."

"Prove it, Zane. Prove that you can still get lost in me. That we can get lost in each other."

His hand reached up and tangled in her hair, bringing her lips down hard against his. His tongue thrust into her mouth and she moaned. Yes. Yes, this was what she wanted.

His teeth nipped at her lips and his arms wrapped more tightly around her.

Their harsh breaths filled the alcove when he broke away after long minutes.

"You want this? Us?" he whispered, pulling her hips more tightly against his.

"Yes. Hard. Now, Zane."

"Fine. But we do it my way."

She cocked an eyebrow. "Your way? Have things changed so much that your way and my way are no longer the same?"

He pulled her down for a punishing kiss. One that bruised her lips.

One that eased something inside her. Revived places in her that had lain dead for too long. She moaned into the kiss and his groan soon joined hers.

"You still have the smartest mouth, that's for sure," he said against her lips. "Here's my deal. I won't hold back. And believe me, Caro, that won't be a problem."

"Good. That's what I want too."

"But…"

She didn't want to hear the but. She covered her lips with his to shut him up. And it worked. For a couple of minutes.

But then his hand wrapped more fully in her hair and pulled her back so he could talk.

"But," he began again as if she hadn't stopped him before. "You're injured from what happened today. So if something starts to hurt too badly, you tell me immediately, okay?"

That she could handle. "Yes."

His fingers eased from where his fist had gripped the roots at her skull. His other hand moved up from her hip and soon both hands were cupping her face, dwarfing her cheeks.

"And if anything else starts to bother you, darkness starts to creep in, anything gets too overwhelming, you have to tell me."

"I thought that you believed I was strong enough to handle it."

"I do. But part of that strength is being willing to speak up if it's too much. You want me to let go? Fine. You're not fragile and I'm not going to treat you like you are. But I have to know, hell, Caro, *you* have to know that at any point a single phrase can stop this."

"Like a safe word?"

"I don't care what you call it, but we've both got to know you've got the means to stop this at any time necessary."

He was right. It was what they should've done years ago. What they should've worked through together from the beginning, but they'd been too stubborn and stupid.

Of course, they'd been that way before the attack too.

"Airplane," she said.

"What?"

"Airplane. That's what I'll say if I'm getting too overwhelmed."

He laughed. "Perfect. At least it's not 'Zane is a jackass.'"

She reached down and kissed him again. "I say that too often for it to be a safe phrase."

"You promise you'll use *airplane* if you need it."

"I promise. You promise not to treat me like I'm going to break."

He kissed her again and her breath whooshed out as he wrapped his arms around her tightly and spun them both so that she was pinned underneath him.

"I promise," he said against her lips. "Tonight we both burn."

Chapter Ten

Waking up with Caroline in his arms was something Zane had given up on ever happening again.

Happening in an alcove in the wilderness twenty-five feet off the ground after their plane had crashed and someone had been shooting at them didn't make it more believable.

The sun was coming up, the worst of the storm had passed and at least rain wasn't pelting them any longer, although Zane knew the low clouds would slow the rescue effort.

Caroline's small body rested, sprawled almost completely on top of his. The low temperatures had demanded they get all their clothes back on before sleeping, but having her this close was almost like skin to skin.

Somewhere in the midst of their lovemaking he'd understood what she'd been trying to tell him. What she wanted from him. From them.

She hadn't wanted him to hold back. But she hadn't been talking just about physically.

Lovemaking between them had always been raw and passionate—rarely ever soft and sweet—and last night hadn't been an exception, as visceral as always. But that wasn't necessarily what Caroline had meant when she'd asked him not to hold back.

She'd wanted him not to hold back *mentally*. Not to let the past take any more away from them than it already had. To not look at her and wonder if she was okay, if something was scaring her, was hurting her, was bringing back memories of the attack.

She wanted him—*them*—to be like it was before those were ever questions in his mind.

She wanted him to want her. Zane wanting Caroline.

And he had.

God, how he had.

And he'd trusted her to tell him if things got to be too much. To use her safe word, airplane. It hadn't been easy to trust her. At first he'd been studying her, pausing, moving with deliberate care to make sure everything was okay with her.

But then he realized that was exactly what she'd been talking about. That was exactly what she *didn't* want.

So he'd let go. Trusted her. Trusted her strength.

Trusted that she would tell him if something didn't work for her. But evidently everything worked for both of them, because once he'd let go, he'd *really* let go and Caroline had been right there with him.

He pulled her closer onto his chest, wincing for her when she moaned slightly in pain even in her sleep. Their escapades last night definitely had not helped all their minor injuries. But neither of them had complained at the time.

He would let Caroline sleep as long as she could, then get the bottle that had collected the water from the storm. It wouldn't be much, but it would be enough.

As soon as the rain cleared, they'd need to make it the rest of the way up the ravine and try to light some sort of signal fire. It would be the most assistance they could offer the rescue plane that would come after them. And Zane knew they would as soon as the storm cleared. Which thankfully wouldn't be too much longer. They had limited food, limited water and no shelter besides this crevasse.

Holding his arms steady around Caroline, staring up at the rock just a couple feet over his head, Zane knew he had to accept that his means of livelihood now lay as charred pieces of metal in the bottom of the ravine. Until he worked out the insurance paperwork and issues, he was without a job.

Which was fine, since he planned for his new full-time job to be protecting Caroline until this Damien Freihof guy was caught. It had nothing to do with not trusting her to take care of herself. Zane would be damned if he would leave her to face this alone.

He held her for the next couple of hours, dozing himself. When he woke again, the rain had completely stopped.

As much as he didn't want to, it was time to get moving.

"Hey, sleepyhead." He rubbed a hand gently up and down her back. "It's time to get up."

He could tell the exact moment she woke up. Her entire body tensed. Zane wasn't sure what it meant: if she was scared, hurt, embarrassed. All?

He slid his hands off her so she wouldn't feel like anything was trapping her in any way.

"Zane?" she asked hoarsely as she pushed away from his chest, then gasped, he was sure, at the pain it caused her shoulder.

He kept his tone even. "Just me, sweetheart. Hanging out with you here in our little alcove."

He felt her relax as she remembered, although not nearly as relaxed as when she'd slept. "That's right. I remember."

He chuckled. "I hope so. If not, I wasn't doing my job right."

She snuggled a little closer to him like he'd hoped. "I

think you did it just fine. But man, I need a toothbrush." Her stomach growled. "And something to eat."

"I have a packet of crackers in my backpack and hopefully the water bottle got filled in the rain. But no toothbrush, sorry."

"Then you definitely won't want to kiss me."

He reached down and tilted her head up until they were face-to-face. "Believe me, I want to kiss you. No matter what the circumstances, I always want to kiss you." And he did, not giving her a chance to get embarrassed and pull away.

He wanted it to go further. Could tell they both wanted it to go further. But he eased back after a few minutes. They couldn't take a chance on missing the rescue plane when it came by.

"We need to get up to the top," he said as he helped her sit up. "That last part is the steepest, and with your shoulder, it's going to take longer."

He crawled over and got the water bottle, glad to see it was full. They both drank from it, then Zane got the cracker packet out of the backpack. Sharing three peanut butter crackers apiece wasn't going to satisfy hunger very long.

"Do you think they'll find us today?" she asked between bites of cracker.

"Yes. We need to build a fire if we can. Something really smoky will be easier for a pilot to spot than just two people."

"That's good." She nodded. "Because with as wet as the wood is going to be, a smoky fire is going to be the only thing we can get."

They finished their meager meal and began the slow progress of making it up the last ten feet of the ravine wall.

Caroline's arm had stiffened while she slept and the swelling from joint trauma had left her hardly able to move it.

To get her up, Zane stood right behind her, supporting her body with his as she hoisted herself up with one arm.

He could tell she was worried and uncomfortable as they made their way up. He didn't blame her. She had to lean all her weight back on him as she moved her one workable arm from one holding point to another. If he lost his grip, they would both fall to almost certain death.

"You're doing great, you know that?"

"Whatever." Her tone was short. He had no doubt if he could see her face she'd be rolling her eyes. Caroline didn't like feeling weak.

But he couldn't see her face because he was behind her, with his body pulled flush against hers. He used that as a method of distracting her, nuzzling his face into her neck.

"I'm in no hurry to get up the wall if it means I can be this close to you."

He felt her ease just slightly.

"You're lucky I have to keep my grip on the rocks or you might be in trouble," he continued. "Do you remember that shower in Houston?"

She'd had a weekend class she was taking to further her paramedic training. Zane had surprised her by meeting her at the hotel and upgrading the room to a special suite. The shower had a rock facade for one of the walls. And Zane had wasted no time getting Caroline's body pressed up against it, not unlike how he had her pressed against the cliff now.

"Yeah, but there I wasn't about to cause us both to fall to our death because I couldn't get my stupid arm to work properly."

"Trust me, darlin', I'm not going to let either of us fall."

She relaxed back against him more and then climbed

the last few feet up to the top. He could tell the effort had taken quite a bit out of her. She needed painkillers, something to reduce the swelling, a full meal and a hot shower.

Zane prayed they had a capable pilot in whoever was working the rescue attempt. These low-lying clouds would make everything more complicated. If the pilot wasn't good at his job, finding them would take a lot longer.

Starting a fire took a long time, since all the wood was wet. Once they did get it started—using every skill Zane had learned as an Eagle Scout and had him swearing he would trade his firstborn child for a set of matches—Caroline was right; it smoked like hell.

But it would be a signal. No one could doubt it was a man-made fire.

Which was good because Caroline's pallor concerned him more with each passing hour. He knew she felt bad when she didn't argue with him about resting rather than helping him gather more firewood. She just nodded.

So when they heard a low-flying plane a couple hours later, Zane's relief was profound. He immediately began fanning the fire with his backpack. Caroline jumped up and waved her good arm. As the plane passed over them, its wings tilted back and forth like a drunk stumbling down the sidewalk. It then flew out of sight.

"Oh no," Caroline cried. "Did they miss us?"

"No, the pilot saw us. That's what the tilting of the wings signified. His best way to signal us."

"But he just left."

"As we found out the hard way yesterday, there's no real place to land around here. Too many trees, and the ravine didn't prove very fruitful as a runway. The pilot will radio in our location. Someone will be here as soon as they can."

Zane was right. A few hours later a park ranger vehicle showed up at their location, complete with food, water and a first aid kit.

After twice the normal dosage of ibuprofen and a relatively full belly, Caroline fell asleep in the back seat of the vehicle as they headed to the ranger station.

"We appreciate the effort you guys put in to finding us," Zane told the park ranger, whose name was Ron Nixon, as they neared the ranger station. They'd kept quiet much of the way to allow Caroline to sleep.

"We're just glad you're both all right. Captain Harris from the Corpus Christi police station had put in a special request to us to keep an eye on Ms. Gill."

"You mean like having her check in with you every few hours?"

Ranger Nixon gave a guilty grimace. "Actually, he asked us to drive out to see her every day. Just make sure she was okay. Told us what had happened to her."

Zane shook his head. Now he understood even more Caroline's insistence on him not holding back, on treating her as if he trusted her to be able to handle the situation put before her.

Because evidently, based on Captain Harris's actions, people were still trying to smother her.

But none of that was Ranger Nixon's fault, so there wasn't any point getting upset with him. He was just doing what had been asked of him. Captain Harris shouldn't have been so quick to share Caroline's personal story. She'd be mortified if she knew.

She just wanted to leave the past behind her. But evidently it was the people she cared about the most who wouldn't let her do that. Zane had been one of those people until last night.

He turned to Nixon. "I think she would've been fine under normal circumstances. No need for anyone to look out for her. This was a case of someone specifically chasing us."

"We're just glad you were able to land the plane. When we got your Mayday, we knew there was trouble based on the location."

"I think *landing* may be too polite of a word for what we did."

Nixon shrugged. "Anything you walk away from is a landing, right?"

Zane smiled. "I'm thankful you could find us this morning. I'm surprised you had a plane out as soon as you did. I thought you might have to bring one in as well as a pilot."

Ranger Nixon pulled the vehicle down the drive to the ranger station. "Normally, we would. But this morning a plane and a couple of pilots showed up on our little landing strip here. Evidently news about your Mayday had gotten around."

"Let me guess. To Captain Harris?" The Corpus Christi PD didn't have an airplane, but Zane wouldn't put it past the man to beg, borrow or steal one to come look for him and Caroline.

"No, not Harris. Much bigger than that."

Nixon didn't need to say any more; the people walking out the door of the ranger station said everything Zane needed to know. Jon Hatton and Lillian Muir from Omega Sector. They'd been the ones who had delivered the plane. One of them had been piloting it, which explained how he and Caroline were found so quickly. There wasn't anyone better in all the country when it came to search and rescue.

As Nixon pulled to a stop, Zane got out of the SUV. He went to shake Jon's hand as the man walked up, but Jon pulled him in for a quick, hard hug instead.

"I'm glad you're okay, brother," Jon murmured. "You and Caroline both."

Hard to believe this was a man Zane had fought with so hard when they'd first met nearly two years ago.

"Me too. She's conked out in the back. Had a dislocated shoulder I had to slip back into joint. That helped, but she was still in a lot of pain."

"Ouch," Lillian murmured.

Zane smiled at the petite woman, a member of the Omega SWAT team. She was damn tough. Zane wouldn't doubt she'd had a dislocated limb at some point in her past. "Thanks for coming, Lil."

"Glad to get away from all the wedding craziness happening at Omega. Steve Drackett got hitched last month. Now this one—" she nudged Jon "—and Sherry. Then Brandon Han and Andrea Gordon are scheduled for February. It's like there's something in the water."

Zane smiled. "By all means, let's get to some more fun stuff, then. Like catching the psychopath who's trying to kill us."

Chapter Eleven

Damien Freihof couldn't have orchestrated this situation any better if he had planned the whole thing himself.

Oh, wait, he *had* planned the whole thing himself, and yep, it had worked exactly how he'd envisioned it.

Damien read again the report given to him from the secretive Mr. Fawkes, a mole inside Omega Sector working with Damien to take the organization down. Damien still didn't know the man's real name, but as long as he kept providing valuable information, he could remain as taciturn as he wanted.

Profiler Jon Hatton and SWAT team member Lillian Muir had rushed down to Texas from Omega Sector headquarters in Colorado to help when they'd heard trouble had found Zane Wales and Caroline Gill. To offer their assistance in any and every way possible, including the use of the search and rescue airplane.

Evidently a Mayday report had come from Zane Wales's plane to the ranger station. The ranger station had notified the Corpus Christi Police Department, who had notified Omega Sector, who in turn, inadvertently of course, had notified Damien.

Damien didn't much care if Zane Wales and Caroline Gill were dead already or not. If they weren't yet, they would be soon. Besides, they were just a means to an end.

Making Omega Sector pay. Making the members of Omega Sector understand the agony of losing people they love. Damien had already taken the life of one Omega agent, but his plan wasn't to kill off agents one by one.

He wanted to kill the people they *cared* about. Snatch them away. Gut Omega from the inside.

Just like they'd done to him when they'd killed his Natalie. Omega thought the battle had started with him when Damien had gone after SWAT member Ashton Fitzgerald and his lover, Summer Worrall. But it had really started seven years ago with Damien's wife's death in an Omega raid on his home.

Natalie had been his most prized possession. She'd made him the envy of all his friends when she'd married him. He could still picture her beautiful face, her long blond hair, her beautiful blue eyes. The classic American beauty. And she'd been *his*. Only his.

Until Omega took her life.

And now they would pay. One loved one at a time. And then when they knew the agony of love lost, Damien and the mole, Mr. Fawkes, would destroy Omega for good. Mr. Fawkes had his own political agenda, but Damien didn't care much about that.

A text came to Damien's burner phone. He knew it had to be one of two parties. Either Mr. Fawkes or the Trumpolds, the people who wanted to kill Zane and Caroline.

Mr. Fawkes.

Wales and Gill are still alive after the plane crash. Jon Hatton and Lillian Muir are going with them from Big Bend to CC.

Of course Jon Hatton would go with his friends to Corpus Christi, even with his own wedding coming up next week. After all, Zane and Caroline meant so much to Jon. They meant a lot to many people at Omega Sector.

That was why this entire plan would work. If Omega didn't care, killing the couple in Texas wouldn't make any difference.

Now he had another call to make. To Nicholas Trumpold. Brother of the late Paul Trumpold, the man who had attacked and raped Caroline Gill.

Damien had spent considerable time over the last few weeks convincing Nicholas and his sister, Lisette, that their beloved brother had been framed. That Caroline Gill had lied about the attack and Zane Wales, as an officer of the Corpus Christi PD at the time, had helped frame Paul.

That the police department had been so desperate to make the public think they had put the serial rapist terrorizing the city behind bars they'd looked the other way at evidence that would've exonerated their brother.

None of that was true, of course. Paul Trumpold had been a psychopath intent on hurting women. The hospital photos of the women he'd attacked told a story of sick violence and desire for their humiliation. Trumpold, about to be caught and arrested, had then attacked Jon Hatton and his fiancée, Sherry Mitchell, and nearly killed them both.

But Paul Trumpold's siblings, who had idolized their big brother, had been easily convinced of their brother's innocence.

They'd just wanted to believe it so badly. That he couldn't possibly be the monster he'd been made out to be. Paul had died early in prison and hadn't been around to tell them anything.

The falsified documents Damien had created, making it look as if Caroline and Zane had both lied about the entire situation, had just sealed the deal. From there it hadn't taken long for Damien to convince the Trumpold siblings to get revenge on their brother's behalf.

Of course, they had no idea that them taking revenge would also suit Damien's purpose—it would tear at a piece of Omega.

Omega knew Damien was behind the attacks on their loved ones. Heaven knew, he'd left them enough clues, a whole wall's worth. They even knew about Damien's ability to change his appearance. To make himself look like someone completely different every time he stepped outside. That was what had kept him ahead of law enforcement, and all their facial recognition software, for the past year, since he'd escaped from prison.

Sometimes he went out with no disguises on whatsoever just to mess with them. It was fun to hear about them scurrying around trying to find him like ants.

But now he had a business call to make. He dialed Nicholas Trumpold's number to give them the news that Zane and Caroline were still alive.

"Hello, Damien."

"Where are you, Nicholas?"

"We're outside of Big Bend, if that's what you're worried about. After we sabotaged Wales's plane and led them back to it, we didn't stick around."

"I'm sorry to inform you that Mr. Wales and Ms. Gill made it out of the crash alive." Damien wondered how the other man would take the news.

Silence for a long moment. "Good."

"Good?" That wasn't what Damien had been expecting to hear.

"Lisette and I discussed it. That we had been rash in our decision to kill Wales and Gill and make it look like an accident."

It sounded like the Trumpolds were having second

thoughts. Damien had very little patience for people who deviated from the plan.

Especially when those people were expendable in the overall strategy like the Trumpolds. But Damien kept his patience. "Nicholas—"

"What I mean by that is that if Zane Wales and Caroline Gill had died in either the rappelling accident or the plane crash we set up for them, then the world wouldn't know the truth about our brother. Wouldn't know they lied."

Damien's eyebrow rose. Interesting. "That's true."

"So it's good that they made it out alive. Lisette and I have a new plan."

"And what is that?"

"We're going to get them to confess. To state publicly what they did and clear Paul's name."

There was no way in hell that was ever going to happen, but Damien kept that knowledge to himself. "They've kept it a secret for over eighteen months now. I don't think they're just going to confess."

"Lisette and I have already talked about that. We'll force them to confess."

"Sounds painful." Damien smiled.

"I'm sure it will be."

Evidently Paul hadn't been the only psychopath in the Trumpold family. Sounded like Nicholas was pretty excited about the thought of torturing Zane and Caroline. To get them to confess to something that was completely untrue.

Damien grinned. It was unfortunate for the Texan couple. But it worked just perfectly for him.

FORTY-EIGHT HOURS after Zane's plane had crashed, they made it back to Corpus Christi. Caroline had barely had time to say hello to Jon and Lillian at the ranger station before she was immediately whisked off to the local hospital just outside of Big Bend. An X-ray and MRI had shown that she had no breaks or fractures and that Zane had done a pretty damn good job getting her joint back into the socket.

The doctor gave her a prescription-level painkiller and sent her on her way, calling her very lucky.

Caroline already knew that. Not just because they'd survived the crash, but because of what had happened afterward between her and Zane.

Their lovemaking had been downright fantastic. Not just the physical aspect of it, although that had been awesome too, but the fact that for the first time since the attack Caroline had just felt *normal*.

Maybe not actually normal, since they'd been in an overhang on the middle of a cliff surrounded by a storm after surviving a plane crash. But normal as in Caroline and Zane.

Not rape survivor Caroline. Just *Caroline*.

And it had felt amazing.

In all possible ways.

She knew it didn't solve all the problems, particularly the fact that they had someone trying to kill them. But damned if Caroline didn't feel better than she had in months.

Zane had made love to her like he used to. Like he wasn't afraid she would break or run screaming. She peeked over at him from where she sat in the passenger's seat now, his strong arms gripping the steering wheel, easing them through Corpus Christi traffic. They'd just come from the police station.

"Captain Harris looked pretty giddy to have you back." She couldn't help but tease him. They'd dropped Jon and Lillian at the department so Jon could brief Harris and the other officers about what was going on. Harris, once he'd heard about Zane's plane, had told him the only logical thing—given the circumstances—was for Zane to be reinstated as law enforcement.

Kill two birds with one stone: Zane needed temporary employment, and Corpus Christi needed one of their best detectives back on the job.

Zane grimaced. "I thought he might actually break out into a jig when I said I would come back temporarily."

"He never filled your detective position, you know. Hemmed and hawed about budget cuts, but we all knew he was hoping you would return."

She saw his fingers tighten on the steering wheel. "I don't think Harris or anybody else should put too much faith in me. Not only am I rusty, I wasn't at the top of my game when I left."

Caroline studied him. She'd lost so much in the attack, but Zane had lost a lot too. The difference had been that her wounds were visible and she'd therefore gotten all the help and support she'd needed.

Had Zane gotten any help or support? Would he even have accepted it if anyone offered? Knowing him, probably not.

"Airplane," she said to him.

"What?" He glanced at her before looking back at the road. "Wait. Is there a reason why you're using your safe word? Are you okay?"

"No, I'm fine. But you need a safe word. Have you ever thought of that?"

"What?"

"Okay, maybe not a safe word. But you know how I had to almost force you into treating me normally in the ravine? When we—" She floundered, unable to get the words out, suddenly feeling a little embarrassed.

He glanced at her again, eyebrow raised. "Had incredibly awesome sex?" He reached out and grabbed her hand, entwining their fingers.

She flushed but grinned. "Yes. That. It wasn't until I demanded you treat me normally that you did it."

"Okay, I still don't understand what this has to do with me needing a safe word."

"You don't need a safe word. But you do need to force yourself to start treating *you* normally."

He glanced at her with one eyebrow raised. "I'm pretty sure I don't know what you're talking about."

But he did. She knew he did. "I'm pretty sure you do. Enough, Zane. Just like you had to stop treating me like I was broken, you have to stop treating yourself that way."

He let go of her hand, making it look like he needed both of his on the wheel, but she knew him well enough to know that he didn't like to think she might be right.

"You have to admit what you lost in the attack, Zane."

"I lost you."

"You lost more than that. You lost your faith in yourself. Your confidence as a law enforcement officer. Things were taken from *you* in my attack too."

Zane scoffed. "Oh, boo-hoo. Compared to what you lost, who gives a rat's ass what I lost."

"It's not a damn competition, Zane. Nobody gets a trophy for losing the most." Her voice was rising. His was too.

But she didn't mind fighting with him. It was just more proof that he wasn't holding back.

"I know that." He slid his fingers through his hair in a frustrated gesture. "But I also know that what I lost was nothing compared to what you did."

"And I had people lining up down the block to help me. To talk to me. Do you know that Grace Parker, the top psychiatrist at Omega Sector, has been counseling me?"

"No." He glanced at her again. "I assumed you had

someone you talked to, but I didn't know it was someone with Omega."

"She's the best there is. I love her."

"I'm glad you have someone. That's important in a situation like this."

"Exactly." She paused for just a minute. "Who do you have, Zane? Who have you talked to?"

He didn't answer, just stared out the windshield.

"This was too big to tackle on our own. For either of us," she said quietly. "Even now."

"Well, I'm fine. People have different ways of coping. You talked to a shrink. I—"

"Ran away from a job you loved and moved to the outskirts of town so you would never have to run into me or any of your colleagues unless you wanted to." Now it was her turn to raise an eyebrow at him.

"Just leave it alone, Caroline. I did what I thought I had to do."

Knowing what he thought, how he blamed himself for her attack, Caroline understood that. But it was time for a change.

"Do you still feel like it's what you have to do? Even after what happened between us at Big Bend?"

"I feel like right now we need to focus on keeping Damien Freihof and whoever he's working with from carrying out their plans to kill us. The rest can wait."

"You're avoiding, Zane."

"I'm working on keeping us safe."

Caroline had meant to tell him where her new town house was, the one she'd moved into just a couple of months ago. But she realized Zane already knew.

"You know where I live." Her tone was accusatory.

"Yes."

"I only moved there six weeks ago."

He shrugged. "I knew when you moved. I've always known. I knew when you moved to the place before that. And the other. I knew when you moved out of your parents' house. Although I wasn't surprised at that."

"I couldn't live there anymore. None of us ever wanted to set foot there again. They sold it."

"I don't blame you. Don't blame them."

"Then the other places… I just had a hard time. Tried living with a roommate, and that didn't work. Moved on my own. Tried a second-floor apartment. Just trying different things to see what worked for me."

"And this new place?"

"I've come to discover it's not really the place that makes that much of a difference. It's my frame of mind. Sometimes I have no problem for days or even weeks. But then sometimes…" Caroline shrugged. "The other night when we saw each other at the Silver Eagle, I was there because I couldn't force myself to go into my town house alone."

"I'm sorry."

"I have good days and I have bad days. That would be true for you too if you came back to law enforcement, you know. You would have some bad days. But some would be good."

"Give it a rest, Caro. I'm already temporarily reinstated."

"Maybe I miss your white hat."

"You hated that hat. Knocked it off my head every chance you got."

Only so she could run her fingers through his hair, but she didn't have to tell him that. "Well, now I miss it."

He pulled up to her town house. "I'm not leaving you here, by the way."

"I can take care of myself."

"That's great. You can take care of yourself with me at your side. Keys."

She rolled her eyes. "Whatever. I just want to get into some different clothes. We can fight about this later."

She tossed him the keys and he opened the truck door before turning back to her. "Wait here. Just in case."

He drew his gun from his belt holster and moved into the town house. Just a couple minutes later he came back out.

"Okay, looks like we're clear."

Entering her town house was quite a bit easier with Zane by her side, she had to admit. But even then she felt compelled to do her normal safety routine as soon as she walked in.

She looked at him. "Um, airplane."

He immediately stepped closer, face concerned. "What's going on? How can I help?"

She wanted to kiss him for knowing the perfect thing to say without even thinking about it. She knew he took her seriously without wanting to fix it himself.

"I have a process. Something I do every time I come home. I need to do that now, if it's okay."

He looked relieved. "Sure."

"It's a little weird."

"Does it involve you getting naked and dancing in the middle of the living room?"

She smiled. "No, sorry."

"Damn it. Whatever, then. Do your boring little weird thing."

Caroline began walking around the living room, running her fingers along the bottom of each of the window-sills where they met the apron—the little ledge sticking out. By the time she got to the third one she knew Zane had to wonder what exactly she was doing, but he waited patiently.

After she'd checked all the windows she walked to the back door and crouched down. She looked toward the bottom of the door and froze at what she saw. "Zane?"

"Yeah?" He was to her in a second. "What's going on?"

"Someone has been in my town house."

Chapter Twelve

Zane immediately had his sidearm out again. He'd already checked her small place pretty thoroughly.

"There's no one in here now, that's for sure. How do you know someone has been in here?"

She showed him a piece of clear tape she'd put at the bottom of her back door. Immediately he realized how it worked. The tape was unnoticeable when the door was closed, covering both the door and frame. But if the door opened, the tape came unstuck from the door frame.

Very simple but very effective. It was what she had been checking for at each of her windows also.

"I always have this on the back door and windows." She grimaced. "It's one of the coping mechanisms Dr. Parker and I came up with."

He put his gun away. "To know if someone has been in the house?"

"About eight months after the attack I started waking up at night terrified someone was in the house with me. That was the second time I moved into a place that had as few windows as possible." She shrugged. "The tape was a simple method that allowed me to know for sure, to convince my terrorized mind at three o'clock in the morning that no one could possibly be inside."

He reached over and yanked her into his arms, thankful when she didn't stiffen or pull away, as emotion nearly overwhelmed him. Her words broke his heart and yet made him so damn proud of her at the same time.

"I think it's brilliant if you ask me."

He felt her good shoulder shrug slightly. "At first I considered myself a coward. I could understand and condone moving out of my parents' beach house, where the attack happened. But moving to the second place, with less windows, just seemed cowardly."

"But it wasn't."

"No. It took me a while to figure that out. Recovery is not a straight line. It's sometimes one step forward and half a mile back. Setbacks are part of the process."

Zane realized *he* should have been part of her process too. Maybe he could've helped her through some of this if he'd chosen to really listen to her needs rather than give her what *he* thought she needed.

Maybe the tape still would've been necessary. But maybe knowing he was there would've been enough.

"Hey, in the now, Wales."

"What?"

"Whatever it is that has you all stiff? Let it go. We can't change the past. We can only change what we choose to do today."

She was right. And today, right now, involved the fact that someone had been inside her town house. He reluctantly let her go.

"I assume you didn't ask anyone to water plants or bring in your mail while you were gone?"

"No. No plants. And I had asked the post office to hold my mail."

"It could be innocent. Smoke detector malfunctioned and the landlord came in. Something like that."

But after someone had tried to kill them multiple times,

neither of them actually believed that was the case. And since he hadn't planned on leaving her alone anyway, he might as well take her with him instead.

"Let's get what you need. Try to touch as little as possible. I'll send the CSI team in here to see if we can get any prints. Since the perp didn't think you'd know he was in here at all, maybe he didn't wear gloves."

"I hadn't thought of that. I have a landline if you want to call it in." They'd both lost their phones at Big Bend.

"Really? Most people don't anymore. Just use their cell phones."

She shrugged. "Another coping mechanism. Knowing I would always have two different ways of calling for help if needed."

"Smart again."

"One of the first things Dr. Parker and I discussed was that I didn't need to apologize for how I chose to survive. I wasn't doing drugs. Wasn't drinking obsessively or breaking any laws. So anything I did to help cope wasn't anything to be ashamed of."

He kissed her forehead. "Damn straight."

He helped her gather a couple of changes of clothes and toiletries.

"Where are we going?"

"We'll go to my place. But first things first, we've got to get both our phones replaced."

They left Caroline's town house and took care of the tedious job of getting new phones. By that time Caroline was looking pretty tired and Zane was feeling it too. They needed a good night's sleep to face what was ahead.

Not to mention he very much looked forward to having Caroline in an actual bed.

But when they arrived at Zane's house, he didn't need

a broken piece of tape on the door to know someone had been in his place.

Someone had completely trashed it.

Once he got the door open and saw the damage, he immediately drew his weapon. "Caro, go wait outside."

"What? What is it?"

"Someone's been in here."

"I'll call Captain Harris."

"Call Jon and Lillian too."

Zane's house on the outskirts of town wasn't much. Two bedrooms, one bath. He'd basically rented it because of its proximity to the airfield he spent so much time at with his business. And because he hadn't been able to force himself to live at the house he'd bought.

Whatever care the intruders had taken at Caroline's house to make sure they would go unnoticed, they'd done the opposite here. Furniture was overturned, dishes broken, contents of drawers strewn everywhere.

Someone had been pissed off when they did this.

"Jon and Lillian are on their way. ETA about ten minutes. Captain Harris said he would have the crime lab techs come over here as soon as they're done with my town house."

"Okay."

"Is it all right for me to come in or should I stay outside?"

In most cases Zane would have people wait outside. Less chance of contaminating possible evidence. But he didn't want Caroline out there exposed in case the person who did this wasn't done with their little temper tantrum.

"Do you mind coming in but just staying by the door?" They'd still be able to see and hear each other.

"Sure."

He heard Caroline's low whistle when she saw the state

of his house. "Unless your housekeeping skills took a sharp turn for the worse after we broke up, someone was really angry in here."

Zane nodded. "Generally speaking, destruction of this magnitude would suggest that the perp knows me personally. Has a personally directed anger toward me."

"You and the contents of your fridge." She pointed toward the kitchen, where everything that had been in his refrigerator now lay all over the floor.

"Sometimes someone can be searching for something and when they can't find it they go into a rage. But this is extreme even for that."

"And what would someone have been looking for in your house?"

"I have no idea. And especially Damien Freihof. I didn't even know who he was until Jon told me about him."

"Me neither. And I can't figure out what he has to do with us."

"Only that we have ties to Omega. That seems to be it." Zane looked through his bedroom and the bathroom—same sort of destruction, no discernible pattern—before coming back out to the kitchen.

"Did the same person who broke into my house do this to yours?" Caroline asked from where she still stood just inside the door.

"Probably."

"Why were they so destructive here but not at my place?"

He stood in the middle of the room, turning so he could see everything, trying to look at it from a detached, professional opinion.

"Either they escalated in anger, maybe starting with something at your place, then ending it here. Or..." He trailed off, not liking where his thoughts were heading.

"What?"

"Or they've been after me from the beginning and I led them straight to you at Big Bend."

"I thought Jon said both our names were found in whatever clues Damien Freihof left for Omega."

"Yes, but you can't deny that there's definitely an anger here that wasn't present at your house."

"But maybe they came here first."

Zane had to admit that could be true. There were too many unknown variables. But one thing would give him some information: the food.

He walked into the kitchen and bent down to where the half gallon of milk had been thrown onto the ground and spilled.

He smelled it.

"I'm SWAT and don't really do much detective work, but I'm going to go with my gut on this one and say that's milk," Lillian said from the door.

Zane got back up from the ground. "Hey, guys."

"Wow, they really did a number on this place," Jon said, pulling on a pair of gloves.

"Yeah. Forensics team is on their way over," Zane told him. Lillian stayed near Caroline at the door. "The milk has no smell."

"None? Not the least bit of souring?"

"No. As a matter of fact, it's still a little cool."

Both men now had their hands near their sidearms. It was warm enough in Zane's house that milk that had been out for a day or two would've at least been room temperature. Not cool.

This had happened recently. Whoever had broken into Zane's house had done it in the last few hours.

Jon crouched down next to Zane to touch the milk himself.

"Whoever it was could've been here waiting to ambush

you or figured you would both be here," Jon said in a volume that wouldn't carry to the door.

Zane glanced over to where Lillian and Caroline were talking to each other. "Yeah, if we hadn't had to replace our phones, we would've been here hours ago. I've got to take Caroline somewhere safe."

"Hotel?"

"No. I have someplace else in mind." A place he'd never planned to tell Caroline about. But it would be much more comfortable than a hotel. "It will be better, since we don't know how long it will take to catch Freihof and his goons."

"About that." Jon grimaced.

"What?"

"We had a confirmed sighting of Freihof in Colorado Springs at the same time your trouble was happening in Big Bend. I mean obvious. Freihof is pretty brilliant when it comes to disguises and he definitely wanted to make sure we knew it was him and we knew he was in Colorado."

"So whoever tried to kill us wasn't him."

Jon shrugged. "He wasn't physically present in Texas is all I'm saying. The last person who came after someone at Omega wasn't actually Freihof—it was someone he had convinced needed to take revenge."

Jon explained about SWAT member Ashton Fitzgerald and how he'd been hunted down by Curtis Harper, the son of a man who'd been killed in an Omega SWAT raid years ago. Freihof had told Harper he would help the man get his revenge.

Harper had nearly died in the process, since Freihof hadn't mentioned that he would blow up Harper along with any nearby Omega agents.

"Lillian is here, if needed, as a sort of protection duty for Caroline. I thought Caroline might be more comfortable with a woman," Jon continued. "If you weren't around."

And there it was again. The good intentions Caroline spoke about. People—even her best friend's fiancé—wanting to protect her, but it made her feel weak, breakable.

But on the other hand, Zane knew what Lillian could do. Could kill a man with her tiny bare hands and not break a sweat. As far as protection detail went, very few could beat Lillian Muir, man or woman. And right now, no matter why Lillian was the one chosen, they needed all the help they could get.

"So if Freihof didn't do it, then he's either hired someone to come after us or has found someone from my past. I've arrested a lot of people. Quite a few who would be pretty pissed off. A couple who it wouldn't take much to talk into coming after me."

Both men stood. "And honestly, brother, it wouldn't take very much observation to realize that the best way to get to you, to cause you pain, is through that lady over there." Jon pointed at Caroline.

"I've got to keep her safe, Jon. I can't stand the thought of anything happening to her. Not again."

"I know. You get her someplace safe, away from her house or here. And until we know more, telling as few people as possible where that place is might be a good idea. Lillian and I will wait for the crime scene team here."

Zane nodded. "Thanks, Jon. I'll be in touch tomorrow."

Jon slapped him gently on the shoulder as Zane turned toward Caroline.

He would keep her safe no matter what. Knew where it was that he would take her. Even if it meant giving up the secret he never meant to share with anyone. Especially her.

Chapter Thirteen

"Zane, where are we going?"

They'd been driving around in his truck for nearly an hour now. Every time she thought she knew where they were headed, Zane would make a sudden turn, leading them to another part of town.

Not that Caroline minded riding around in his truck like old times, but Zane was becoming more tense as they drove.

"I don't think either my house or yours is safe. As a matter of fact, Jon and I both feel whoever broke in did it after the attempt on our lives at Big Bend, not before. Maybe even earlier today."

Suddenly the danger seemed even closer and she understood why Zane was driving them around. He was making sure no one was following them. That would also explain his tension.

"So a hotel? Somewhere to hang out?" They needed rest. She needed rest. She needed to feel Zane's arms around her again.

She realized they were headed toward the beach, maybe a hotel nearby. She hadn't been there in a long time. She sighed. Yet another thing she'd allowed to be taken from her in the attack. But it would be different with Zane with her.

Zane's presence always made everything different.

Zane didn't answer her question, and she didn't push. He obviously had a plan and she trusted him. It wasn't long before they pulled up to a house a couple blocks from the oceanfront, and only a couple of neighborhoods over from where her parents' house used to be.

There weren't any hotels in this area of the beach. Just houses.

"Where are we going? There aren't any hotels here."

"We're not staying at a hotel."

She looked around, unable to decide if this area should make her uncomfortable or not. It wasn't anything at the beach that had hurt her. The man who had caused her such pain was dead.

"A safe house? Something of the department's?"

She didn't think they would have an oceanfront safe house, but crazier things had happened.

"No, it's not the department's. But it is safe."

They pulled into the drive of a small house, about a block and a half from the actual waterfront. Like many of the houses so close to the ocean, there was no full bottom floor. It was built on glorified stilts to keep the water from doing much damage during hurricane season. The entire living area started on the second floor. This allowed Zane to pull his truck all the way under the house to park.

They both got out and Zane grabbed their duffel bags from the cab behind his seat. He led her up the stairs and pulled out a key on his normal key ring and unlocked the door, holding it open for her, and walking in behind her.

She looked around, taking in the open floor plan with the cozy living room—complete with couch and love seat—opening up into the kitchen. From first glance there looked to be three bedrooms, two on one end of the living room, a master bedroom on the other side.

Zane wasn't looking around at all, obviously familiar with the house and its layout.

"What is this, a rental? A friend's place?"

He set the bags down. "No. Actually, I own it."

She spun to stare at him. "You own a house at the beach." She couldn't help but laugh. "You hate the beach. I used to have to drag you here whenever I wanted to go. What, did you buy it as an investment property or something?"

"Something like that."

"I guess it's hard to rent it out during the winter."

Zane just shrugged, walking over to get a bottle of water out of the refrigerator. Except, why would he know there was water in the fridge? He shouldn't be that familiar with what was on the inside of the rental property.

There was something Zane wasn't telling her.

"Does anyone know we're here?"

"I gave Jon and Lillian the address, but not anybody from the department. Why?"

She walked over and opened the refrigerator. It didn't have a lot of stuff in it, but neither was it empty. "I just wondered if you had someone come stock the house for us."

"No, I wanted to keep our whereabouts as tightly guarded as possible."

She turned around to face him, crossing her arms over her chest. "You don't rent this place out, or at least you haven't for a while."

Zane took a chug of his water. "No. You're right. I don't rent it out."

"Do you live here too?" Caroline couldn't figure out what piece of the puzzle she was missing. "Two houses or something?"

"No. I've slept here occasionally when I haven't wanted

to drive all the way back out to my house. But, no, I don't live here."

"So let me see if I understand. You own a pretty nice beach cottage. It would make a great place to live, but you don't live here. It would also make a great rental property, but you don't rent it out."

"Just leave it alone, Caroline."

She shook her head. "Why? What is there to leave alone? It's weird, Zane. And not very financially smart."

"Yeah, I'm well aware of the fact that a mortgage and a separate rent payment every month, even though my place near the airfield is pretty negligible in terms of rent, is not the best plan."

This was ridiculous. "Then why the hell are you doing it? Move here."

"I can't. Like you said, I don't like the beach."

She rolled her eyes. "Then sell or rent this place, for heaven's sake."

"I can't do that, either."

"Why the hell not?" Her volume was going up, but she couldn't help it.

His fist slammed down against the kitchen island. "I bought this place for you, okay? For us."

"What?" She reared back a step.

The anger in his voice had disappeared. "I closed on this house two weeks before you were attacked. I had planned on asking you to move into it with me. But then…"

But then everything changed.

She took a step closer, but it felt like a chasm separated them rather than one small kitchen. "You never told me. Even after."

"There was never a good time. First you were in recovery. Then you wanted nothing to do with the beach. Then…" He trailed off, turning away and walking over to the massive doors that led out to the deck. He opened them and glanced back at her over his shoulder. "Then you wanted nothing to do with me."

Caroline watched as he walked outside, bracing his forearms on the rail of the deck, looking out at the view of the ocean the house afforded.

She looked at the house with new eyes. He'd bought this for *them*.

It was perfect, she realized. Would've been just what she would've wanted to start a life together with Zane.

She wanted to yell, to scream out her pain. To find that she'd lost even more than she'd ever known was almost too much to bear.

She'd already lost so much. They both had.

She looked at Zane standing out on the deck, staring at the sea. Standing on the deck he'd known she would love. Hell, she already did and she hadn't stepped foot out there yet.

Could she walk out there to Zane right now, on the deck that should've been theirs, and try to make everything right? To make their relationship what it was?

No, she couldn't. Too much time had passed. For both of them. Things were too different. Their relationship could never be what it once was.

But that didn't mean it had to be nothing.

She'd spent a lot of time with Dr. Parker in those first few months just trying to get things back to standard, to ordinary. Except Caroline had no idea what ordinary was. She and Dr. Parker had worked long and hard on establishing a new baseline of normal. Of accepting that things would never go back to the way they were, but that didn't mean you were never okay again.

She and Zane had to establish a new baseline of normal. Starting right now.

She began walking toward him just as he turned to look at her. They were in sync, the way they'd always been. She stepped out onto the deck and he reached his hand out toward her. Neither of them said anything, just held on to one another's hand.

Finally, Zane pulled Caroline against his chest as he leaned back on the railing. She wrapped her arms around his trim waist, hooking her thumbs into the back belt loops of his jeans. The beat of his heart under her ear reassured her of her safety much more than the waist holster she'd felt briefly as she'd slipped her arms around him.

She wished she could just stay against him forever.

But her phone chirped obnoxiously from her pocket.

"Text?" he asked.

"Yes," she murmured, her mouth half against his shirt. "Just ignore it."

"It might be Jon or the precinct." He slipped his fingers into her pocket to pull it out. "Or, God forbid, your parents."

Caroline smiled, letting him read the text. Her parents hadn't ever really liked Zane. Or at least hadn't liked how volatile their relationship was. But they would have no idea he was around, so she doubted it would be anything about Zane.

But she felt him stiffen beneath her. "What the hell, Caroline?"

"What?"

He spun the phone around so she could read the message.

You're a liar and you deserve everything you've got coming to you. Don't think you've escaped.

Caroline grabbed the phone. "Oh yeah. I forgot about these stupid texts. I keep meaning to ask someone how to block this number."

"How long have you been getting them?"

"I don't know." She pulled away, the peace she'd known just a few moments before, gone. "A week? Why are you getting all angry? It's just a wrong number."

"A wrong number? Someone is trying to kill you, Caroline. You should've told me about this. They've got to be connected."

"I didn't think about it, okay? And then I didn't have my phone, so I didn't get any messages."

She looked up at him, ready to blast into him again, but realized there was something else. "What? What aren't you telling me?"

He reached into his pocket and held out his phone so she could see the message that had just arrived for him.

What you hid will come to light. Soon the whole world will know.

She grabbed the phone out of his hand. "What? Is this your first message?"

"No. Like you, they've been coming for a week."

"Zane—"

He took her hand and led her inside. "Yeah, I know. This means we're both being targeted. We've got to get these phones to the station, see what info the tech department can get from them."

"Do you think it's someone local?"

"I don't know. But I plan to find out."

Chapter Fourteen

"Okay, I know this is a hard question, but I need honesty from both you guys," Jon said to them as they sat around the table in the Corpus Christi PD conference room.

They'd brought the phones back last night and left them for tech—happy to get the overtime—to sort through. Zane had let Jon and Lillian know about the texts but then had explained they were going back home.

Home. Zane didn't let himself think too much about that. For nearly two years he hadn't let himself think about the beach cottage and what it represented and how he hadn't been able to let it go. A shrink would have a field day with that one. Maybe that was why he'd never gone to talk to anyone about his feelings.

But taking Caroline home with him, despite the danger, had just felt right. And getting her into a bed with him and making love, slowly, softly—such a different pace for them—had definitely felt right.

But now the time for tenderness was over. It was time to do whatever was necessary to find who was targeting them and make sure Caroline was safe again.

"Despite what the texts imply, Jon, I don't think either Caroline or I have anything to hide."

Jon leaned back in his chair. "I don't doubt that. But I thought we should start with the opening. If either of you took up shoplifting or ran over your neighbor's cat and buried it in your yard, now is the time to come clean with that."

It was good to have Jon here with them. It eased some of the pressure. He knew them, they didn't have to go through the awkward stages of building up trust. Jon wanted to protect Caroline and stop whoever was behind this almost as much as Zane did. After all, Caroline was the best friend of Jon's bride-to-be. The wedding was scheduled for this weekend.

"All right," Caroline said. "I'll admit, the first bridesmaid dress your fiancée picked out? I threatened to kill her if she went with that one. Pretty sure I said it publicly."

Jon chuckled. "The powder blue one?"

Caroline rolled her eyes. "For an artist, she had some pretty big missteps there for a while. Fortunately, she finally picked a great one and I didn't have to kill her."

Jon smiled. "But seriously. Zane, any corners you cut as you got your business started? Caroline, any accidents where maybe you covered a bad call by telling a lie?"

Zane could see both he and Caroline becoming defensive. Nobody liked to have their integrity questioned.

Jon held out a hand. "Listen, you guys are like family to me. And I would personally vouch for both of you without question. But if you've got something you need to get off your chest, now is the time."

"I've got nothing, Jon." Caroline sat up taller in her seat as she said it. "There was a drunk who was threatening to get me fired a few days ago at an accident scene, since I wouldn't stay and look at his dislocated pinkie when I had a bunch of other people around me with serious injuries. But that's the only incident I can recall in the recent past. Since the attack, I've basically just spent most of my time surviving and coming to grips with reality."

Jon nodded, then turned to Zane. "You? I remember

you had quite the hot temper when we worked together nearly two years ago."

Zane shrugged. "Still do. But I've kept to myself. Hell, I can't even remember having a real conversation with anyone outside my friends on the force for the past six months."

"Okay." Jon put both hands down on the desk. Obviously, he believed them and wasn't going to belabor the point. "Then let's talk about what the tech folks found out about the texts to your phones."

Jon pulled out papers and handed Zane and Caroline both copies. "Here's a list of all the texts that both of you received and the day and time they were sent."

"They were all sent close to the same time to both of us," Caroline pointed out.

"Yes." Jon nodded. "And they all came from the same phone. Not listed as registered to anyone, unfortunately."

Zane looked at the list of messages. There had been fourteen sent over the last eight days. Each one called Caroline a liar in some way and accused Zane of hiding something.

"So is this a dead end?" he asked Jon.

"We've got Omega looking into it. They've got more sophisticated technology to pull data from the phones. Maybe they can get something Corpus Christi couldn't."

"Okay." Zane sat back in his chair. "Did the CSI crew find anything at my house? Fingerprints?"

He appreciated that Jon had been keeping an eye on this so that Zane and Caroline could get a night of much-needed rest.

"Nothing usable. I stayed with them to see if I could figure out any patterns. See what the perp's overall plan was. But it honestly just looked like a fit of rage to me."

One of the CSI personnel came rushing into the room.

"Detective Wales, Agent Hatton, we have something you need to see in the lab."

Zane grabbed Caroline's hand and they rushed with Jon down the hall to the lab. They were met by Susan McGuinness, head of the CCPD crime lab.

"Zane, good to have you back here. We've missed you."

"Thanks, Susan. What's going on? Did you find something at my house?"

"No, actually, we found something at Caroline's house."

"Mine?" Caroline asked. "There wasn't any damage at my house."

"If it wasn't for Caroline's trick with a piece of tape, we wouldn't have known anyone was in there at all."

Susan nodded. "No doubt that's what the person who broke in wanted."

"Tell me you found a fingerprint, Susan."

"Would that be enough to get you to agree to return to the force full-time?" the older woman asked.

Zane could feel Caroline's smile and her eyes on him. He just shrugged. "Maybe."

"Well, unfortunately, it's not a fingerprint we found. But it is something much more interesting."

"What?" He, Jon and Caroline all asked at the same time.

"Transmitting devices. Hidden in two of Caroline's lamps."

Of all the things Jon was expecting to hear, this didn't even make the list. "Are you serious?"

"It wasn't us who found them, actually. It was that other Omega Sector agent. The lady," Susan said.

Jon looked closer at the bugs. "Lillian Muir. She's actually SWAT, not an investigator."

"Well, she was the one who found the bugs after we'd already left."

Jon nodded. "She and I agreed to split up. This morning we wanted to make sure no one was returning to the scene of the crime looking for either of you. She probably went inside to check."

"When she found something unusual, she went out and called us," Susan continued. "Smart on her part. We were able to figure out they were transmitting devices and that they were still actively transmitting."

Zane turned to Caroline and Jon. "That was probably why they trashed my house. To keep us focused over there instead of at your house, Caro. I never even thought to look for transmitting devices."

She shrugged. "I wouldn't have, either."

Jon turned back to the crime lab director. "Can we get any information from the devices? Anything specific about them?"

Lillian walked through the door. "You guys hear about the bugs at Caroline's house?"

"Susan was just telling us," Zane responded. "We're trying to figure out if there's anything usable in the bugs."

Susan looked over at Lillian. "We don't know."

"When will you know?" Zane asked.

"Well." Lillian smiled. "The lab doesn't know anything about the devices because I talked them into leaving them functional at Caroline's town house."

Caroline's eyes flew to Zane's, distress clear, but Zane already knew what Lillian was thinking. "So we can set a trap," he said.

"Yep." Lilian nodded. "I was very careful not to report finding the bugs while I was inside the house, and I made sure none of the nerds—" she turned to Susan "—no offense, said anything while we were inside."

"None taken," Susan responded. "It's a solid plan."

"So the perp doesn't know we know," Zane said, reaching for Caroline's hand. "This could be the break we need."

Caroline still didn't look convinced. "So we, what, go back to my house and give who is listening false information?"

Zane nodded. "Sort of. We can tell them whatever we want. They've got no reason not to believe it."

"We'll fabricate a situation where you guys are away from the department," Jon said. "Dinner or a walk or something."

"I don't want to take a chance with Caroline."

"Zane—"

He cupped her cheek with his hand. "It has nothing to do with not trusting you or thinking you can't handle yourself. I swear to you I would say this about any civilian. You don't have the training to be used as bait. It's too dangerous."

"Caroline, Zane's right," Lillian said. "It's a much better plan to let me wear a wavy brown wig and pose as you. We're roughly the same build. Until someone got right up on us, they wouldn't know it wasn't you."

Jon smiled kindly. "And once the perp is close enough to know the difference, we'll have officers waiting to arrest him."

"How do we know the guy won't just shoot? He was shooting at us at Big Bend," Caroline pointed out.

Zane could see her point. "He was trying to make our deaths look like an accident. Shooting us won't give him that."

"But he could decide to take his chances," Lillian pointed out. "We'll have to give a situation where you're vulnerable, but long-range shooting isn't an option."

Zane nodded. There were a lot of options. They just needed to figure out the best one. He didn't mind putting himself in danger if it meant catching the person intent on hurting Caroline.

"I don't like you setting yourself up," Caroline looked up at him with her big green eyes. "The same way you don't want me to do it, I don't want you to, either."

He smiled gently. "If I'm law enforcement, it's what I do."

She kissed the palm of his hand cupping her cheek. "Law enforcement or not, you watch your back."

"I won't have to. I've got the best doing that for me."

THEY DIDN'T WASTE any time putting their plan into action, knowing every moment they didn't make a move gave the killer more time to scheme.

So a few hours later Caroline found herself and Zane back at her town house, playing out a script they'd already formulated at the station.

"I just need a break, Zane," Caroline said as they walked in the front door. "This was supposed to be my vacation."

"It's not my fault someone is trying to kill you," Zane said, playing his part. "It's just not safe for you to go anywhere alone right now."

"I spent the entire day at the police station. I don't like the station. You know that. It brings back bad memories." Those words didn't require much acting. She still felt uncomfortable around the police station. "It makes me feel like a victim. Powerless."

Zane's eyes flew to hers. He knew she was speaking the truth now, having gone slightly off script.

"You might always feel that way," he said softly. "It might never be a place you're totally comfortable with."

She shrugged. "I have to admit, it's easier when you're there."

He walked over and wrapped his arms around her. "But I know you can handle it either way."

She needed to get them off her personal feelings and back on script.

"I know what I want to do!" This was it. The part of the plan Zane and Jon thought whoever was after them would go for. All Caroline had to do was sell it to whoever was listening.

Zane chuckled. "Wow, haven't seen you this excited for a while. What do you want to do?"

"There's that new shop, Taste Unlimited, downtown. It sells all sorts of foods made for picnics, but also wines and desserts."

"Sounds great to me."

"Let's go there and I'll pick out the food and you pick out the wine and dessert. It'll be a crazy hodgepodge and perfect for a picnic. We can even have the picnic in the station if you want to, since I'm sure going to the beach or a park is off-limits for a while."

"I just want to keep you safe."

His statement was part of the script, but she also knew it was true.

"But I guess a little shopping before locking us away at the station isn't a problem. And it sounds like we might come up with some crazy combinations."

Caroline reached over and kissed him. "That will make it even better."

Zane looked at his watch as if he was considering the time. "Okay, let's shower and I want you to take a little nap first. We'll leave for your Taste Unlimited place and their vast offerings in, say, three hours? Then we have to go to the station so I can get some work done."

He phrased it as though he wanted to make sure that was okay with her. As though they hadn't carefully discussed how much time to give whoever was listening so he could have a chance to investigate the store, see if it would be a great place to try to grab Caroline or Zane and formulate a plan.

There were already officers at the store waiting. Watching for anyone who might come in looking to scope out the place. Especially aware of what Damien Freihof looked like.

Caroline and Zane had laid the bait. Now it was time to see what they would catch in their trap.

Chapter Fifteen

A little more than three hours later, Zane was pulling into a spot in Taste Unlimited's parking lot. Lillian sat in the passenger seat next to him. Her normal dark hair was covered by a brown wig and she wore a pair of large sunglasses.

Not much could be done about her darker skin—Lillian's heritage was Latina, as opposed to Caroline's light skin and freckles. Lillian wore a long-sleeve shirt and a maxi skirt that covered most of her legs, but that was as much as could be done.

If anybody got a close look at Lillian, they would know she wasn't Caroline. But hopefully it would be enough. And thankfully Caroline currently waited at a safe house a few miles away. A protection detail with her. Knowing she was safe was the only thing that allowed Zane to be able to focus on this mission.

"Ready?" Zane asked Lillian.

"Yep. Let's get this son of a bitch."

Zane smiled. Nobody messed with Lillian who didn't live to regret it.

"So far we haven't seen anything unusual," Jon's voice said inside Zane's ear. He was in a van with a painter's logo, parked just outside the front door of the shop. Inside were detectives Wade Ammons and Raymond Stone, one working the register, the other the sandwich counter. The owners of Taste Unlimited had been fully cooperative, a fact for which Zane was truly grateful.

"Okay, Jon. We're going in."

"Roger that."

Another undercover officer would enter the store after Zane and Lillian and together they'd all be looking for anyone who seemed suspicious or overly interested in either Zane or Lillian's Caroline.

"All right, let's do this," Zane said to Lillian. She also could hear Jon through her earpiece.

Zane jumped out of the truck and hustled around it to open the door in a grand romantic gesture. Knowing the guy might be watching them even right now, Zane immediately tucked Lillian into his shoulder. She did her part, burying her head into his chest, wrapping both her arms around his waist.

To anyone else it would just look like a loving couple on their way to pick up food for a picnic with just a tad too much PDA. He hoped.

Zane glanced around without trying to give the appearance he was doing so. There was only so much he could do without giving himself away. He had to trust the people on the team. They were good at their jobs and had a much more natural vantage point, able to watch without being noticed.

He'd worked with Wade and Raymond for years in the department. Jon was also top at his job. Zane knew he could trust them all.

Once inside the store, he and Lillian split up.

"Pick us out something good," Lillian said to him, playing her part. She was keeping her sunglasses on even though they were inside. It would look unusual, but better than giving someone a clear picture of her face.

They were inside the store for about five minutes when Jon reported.

"Okay, we've got an SUV with tinted windows pulling up on the east side of the parking lot. Near the back exit. Single male, midforties, about to enter through the front door."

"Roger that," Zane murmured as everyone else did the same.

Zane positioned himself in a row where he could see the front entrance while appearing to be studying a label on a bottle of wine. He saw the man enter.

Nothing about the man's actions could be considered casual. He looked down one aisle, then another. He didn't do anything overtly suspicious, but neither did he look like the other customers. If they weren't looking for someone who had nefarious intentions, no one would probably take much notice of the man at all.

But expecting a killer? This man fit the bill.

He glanced over at Zane, then looked away quickly. Zane pretended to study the wine bottle as he watched the man pick up a jar of olives and do the same.

"Lillian, get in position by the back door. Let's see if we can tempt him into making a move." Jon's voice came over everyone's earpiece. "I'm running this guy through facial recognition, but unless we get super lucky, we're not going to get a response in time for it to be helpful."

The man set the olives on the shelf and began walking.

"He's coming your way, Lil," Zane whispered.

"Roger."

Zane moved through the aisle, wanting to be near in case something went down.

"You've got another couple coming in through the front," Jon said seconds before the door opened and the electronic chime gave its short whistle.

Counting the one pair who had already been inside the store, the man and the new couple, they had a total of five potential suspects.

Jon said what Zane was thinking. "Remember, we might not be dealing with a lone suspect. So don't discount these couples."

Zane heard Wade talk to one duo as they selected products. Lillian still had her back to the man to keep her face hidden. The man was slowly working his way up toward her.

"Lil, he's about seven feet behind you," Zane said, wanting to give her as much of an advantage as possible. From where he stood, he could see her nod her head just the slightest bit.

The new couple who came in knew exactly what they wanted. Grabbed a meat and cheese platter and a bottle of wine and were soon paying Wade at the register.

The suspicious man still hadn't made any moves, but neither were his actions normal. He was staring at different items up and down the aisles, as if he had no idea what he wanted.

Or he wasn't in here to buy anything at all. Maybe just like the team, he was scoping things out, checking to see if anything was fishy before he made his move.

Zane eased himself back just as Jon made the same call. "Everybody, the main suspect might be scoping, so don't do anything suspicious or draw attention to yourself. We've got a group of three women coming in the door, early twenties. And another single man, African American, midthirties."

Having more people in the store both helped and hurt. It made Zane and the crew less conspicuous, but it also gave them more people to have to watch. Even the group of women couldn't be ruled out.

"Roger," Raymond whispered into the comm unit before turning to the new customers and offering his assistance. Zane looked at the man he still found most suspicious. He seemed to be easing his way toward Lillian.

"He's about five feet from you now, Lil," he said softly. "Why don't you go check out that counter near the back door? I'm going to hang out near the front door in case he decides he wants to take me instead."

They were counting on the fact that the man would probably use a concealed sidearm to try to get either Zane or Lillian, or both, to leave with him. But in case he had other plans and decided shooting within the store was acceptable, the team all had their own weapons ready. Not to mention SWAT outside, who could be called in on a moment's notice.

Lillian moved toward the back door and Zane followed, still holding the bottle of wine he'd been studying but with his left hand so he'd be easily able to draw his gun from the holster with his right.

When the guy shifted his weight back and forth on his feet—deciding if this was worth it?—then moved toward Lillian, Zane was sure they had their guy.

"I think he's about to make a move," Zane said into his comm device. "Get ready to lock it down, Jon."

"Roger."

Zane could see Lillian, looking so much like Caroline with the brown wig, tense just slightly, not enough to be noticeable to a bystander but enough for Zane to be sure she was ready.

"Zane," Jon said. "We've got another single male entering the store. Parked where I would if I was the perp. Backed his car in for an easier getaway."

Damn it, Zane didn't want to split his focus between the guy almost on Lillian and the new one. He couldn't talk easily into his comm unit without the first guy hearing him.

"Zane," Wade said when he got a visual on the man entering the store, "This guy was at the store earlier. Came in, bought a sandwich and left. Big guy. Caucasian. Midtwenties."

That changed things. Someone who had scoped out the store earlier and then parked in a way that made an escape easier?

Suddenly they had two equally potential perps.

"I'm sending in another undercover officer, Joanna Cordell," Jon said. "Zane, you stay with Lillian and the first guy, and Joanna will be on the second."

Joanna had been on the force for a long time. She was in her fifties but was a good officer. Not to mention no one would pay much attention to her. She just looked like a friendly motherly type.

Zane turned and took a couple steps back so he couldn't be heard. "Remember, we need them to make a move before we take them down. We can't arrest anyone for being creepy."

"Roger that," Jon said. "She'll be coming through the door in fifteen seconds. Raymond, you work with her on the new guy. Wade, you get ready to go whichever way is needed."

"Roger." Both men's muffled responses came through.

Zane turned his attention back to Lillian and the agitated guy. He was still moving closer to her and seemed to be more nervous. He picked up one more bottle, then put it down, before walking right over to Lillian.

"Excuse me, miss?" Zane's hand was at his weapon before the guy even tapped her on the shoulder. But Zane kept his cool. Asking someone a question wasn't a crime.

"Contact," he murmured into his mic for the team to hear.

"Yes?" Lillian responded, keeping her face slightly averted from the guy. Depending on how familiar he was with how Caroline looked, this would play out for only a minute at best before he realized it wasn't really her.

"Do you know anything about capers?"

Capers?

To Lillian's credit, she kept her wits about her. "You mean, like the stuff that goes in Greek salads?"

The guy looked visibly relieved. "Yes. Exactly. My wife is seven months pregnant and she sent me out demanding capers. And hell if I know what capers are. I thought they might be olives."

This could still be a ploy, but if so, it wasn't a very strategic one. The guy was leading Lillian away from the back entrance, where it would've been so easy to just grab her arm and pull her out, and back toward the middle of the store. Where the damn olives were.

"I'm pretty sure this first guy isn't our perp," Zane said into his comm unit. "I think he's just freaking out because his wife is pregnant and is craving specialty food. But I'll keep watching."

"Joanna is moving in toward guy number two," Wade murmured. "We probably need to get Lillian close to the back entrance again if we're eliminating guy number one as a suspect."

"Let's have someone tail guy one when he leaves, just in case he got spooked." Seeing if the guy really did have a pregnant wife and asking him some general questions about Taste Unlimited wouldn't be hard.

"Roger that," Jon said from out in the van.

Zane turned to the side so no one could tell he was speaking. "Wade, can you move over to help the pregnancy guy out? That will free Lillian to move back toward the exit to see if we get a rise out of suspect two."

Over the comm unit Zane could hear Wade ask Lillian and the pregnancy guy if they needed any help. The guy told Wade about the capers and Lillian eased away, wishing him luck. Wade did his best to figure out what the hell capers were and where they were located.

"The second guy is staring at Lillian," Jon said. Zane couldn't see them from the aisle he was located in. "Be sure to keep your face averted toward the east wall, Lil. He's studying you pretty hard."

"Roger," Lillian said. She moved from the olive section, away from Wade and the pregnancy guy, back to where she'd been perched before, right by the exit. She studied the trail mix and different bags of nuts and seeds there. Carefully picking up one container after another and reading the back.

Zane worked himself closer so he could have visual contact with Lillian and the guy.

He was definitely studying her.

He took a few steps down the aisle toward her, but then the three twentysomething gals came around the corner. They were laughing and joking and asked his opinion about something.

As soon as he had the attention of three attractive women, the man obviously forgot about Lillian altogether. Zane watched discreetly for a few more minutes to make sure this wasn't part of a ploy.

It wasn't. The guy was here because either he liked the sandwich he'd gotten earlier or he figured out a lot of attractive women hung out at Taste Unlimited. Or both.

"You see this, Jon?" Zane asked.

"Yeah. Doesn't look like he's our perp, either. Just out trolling for women. I'll still have someone follow him, just in case."

They stayed at the shop another thirty minutes, watching as a number of people came in and out, but none of them approached either Lillian or Zane. When they'd been there over an hour total, Zane finally decided to call it.

"This is a bust, you guys. Whoever was listening isn't coming. Perp either decided it wasn't worth the risk or somehow spotted us and left."

"I agree," Jon said. "But in case you're still being watched, you and Lillian buy some stuff and head back out to your vehicle. The bugs might still be useful. We'll try again soon."

It just meant another night where Caroline wasn't safe. Another day where they couldn't get on with their lives. Couldn't be together just as a normal couple.

He wanted to give her that—give them *both* that—so badly he could taste it.

They got a bottle of wine and threw in a few food items, paid Wade at the register and walked out the front door.

"Sorry, Zane," Lillian murmured. "Maybe I didn't look enough like Caroline to draw the perp in."

Zane shrugged. That might be true, but there wasn't anything they could do about that. "Maybe. But if so, it wasn't due to lack of effort on your part."

"Like Jon said, we'll try again. Just because it didn't work this time, doesn't mean it won't work at all."

"Yeah. We've just got to come up with another location that is secure but also—"

Jon's voice interrupted their conversation. "Zane, we've got a problem."

"What?"

"I just received an SOS from the safe house. Caroline's in trouble."

Zane and Lillian both dropped their groceries and sprinted for the truck.

Chapter Sixteen

Caroline didn't like being out of the action, but she understood the need for it. She wasn't a trained law enforcement officer. Yes, she'd done some significant self-defense training since the attack, but that didn't mean she knew enough for undercover work. She was nowhere as good as Zane and Lillian and Jon.

They were capable. More than capable. Skillful. But still it was hard being protected here inside the safe house knowing they were out there facing possible danger.

It had all been very cloak-and-dagger. She and Zane had napped at Caroline's town house—although neither of them had really slept—then gotten up and ready for their date, talking about normal stuff.

Zane had been crisp and collected, helping lead Caroline into conversations that seemed mundane, normal. Helping her forget there was someone trying to kill them listening on the other end of those transmitting devices.

He rescued her every time she started to flounder, panicked that she might say something wrong. Once when she'd been getting too flustered, he'd backed her up against the refrigerator and kissed her senseless.

That had made her forget her own name, much less that they were on some supersecret mission.

When it was time to leave, having given the bad guys

plenty of time to scope out Taste Unlimited and figure out how to make their move, Zane mentioned he needed to go to the bank before their date. He and Caroline had walked into the bank together.

A few minutes later, Zane and Lillian, wearing the same outfit as Caroline, had walked out and gotten into Zane's truck.

Caroline had been escorted out of the bank by a plain-clothes officer named Gareth Quinn about fifteen minutes later and taken to a safe house, which was actually just a couple miles from the Taste Unlimited store. He'd explained how he understood why she wouldn't want him staying in the house with her and would stay out in the car.

Captain Harris's—her adoptive uncle Tim's—doing, no doubt. She loved the man and had known him since birth, but he couldn't seem to let her attack go. Did he really think that Caroline was so fragile that she wouldn't even want to be around a male police officer for a couple hours? So the captain had ordered Quinn to wait outside.

That was the problem with family, wasn't it? Even adopted family, like Tim. They loved you, but they never allowed you to change. Caroline was always going to be the victim to them. To her uncle especially, since he worked in law enforcement and saw the worst of humanity. Which sucked, since he was also the captain of police and worked very closely with her bosses.

Zane and Lillian would've been at the shop for almost an hour now. She hoped no news was good news. That not hearing from them meant they had caught whoever was behind all this and were in the process of throwing the book at him. Or them. Whatever.

She knew Zane would call as soon as he had something concrete to tell her. This safe house wouldn't be her home for more than a few hours. She and Zane had considered taking her to his place at the beach but decided the fewer people who knew about that, the better. But she would've rather been there.

A knock on the door froze Caroline's blood. Damn it, would that happen for the rest of her life? Would her mind always automatically go back to the day of the attack whenever she heard a knock? It was one of the things she hadn't been able to get any control over. No matter what, when she heard a knock on the door, her entire body clenched in panic.

She walked to the door, trying to get her fear under control. She was in a safe house with an officer outside. Nobody but law enforcement knew where she was.

But when she opened the door just the slightest bit, a man came crashing through.

Just like what had happened the day she was attacked.

If she thought panic assailed her just at the knock, it was nothing compared to the sheer terror that sucked her under now. Every self-defense move she'd learned, every means of protecting herself, vanished from her mind.

The man pushed her to the ground and Caroline cried out. Scurrying back, getting away from him, was all she could think to do.

She couldn't scurry away fast enough. The man walked over to her and gripped her by her hair. Caroline cried out.

"It's time for you to come with me."

He began pulling and she began to struggle, kicking out toward him, which he just easily sidestepped.

Her terrified mind waited for the blows to come. The blows that would break her bones, deliver pain she hadn't thought was possible, like it had before. Somewhere in the back of her mind she knew this wasn't Paul Trumpold. He'd been younger, stronger. Had delighted in her pain.

This man was not as fit, was older. Didn't seem intent on delivering physical blows.

But when she looked up into the doorway, she swore she saw Trumpold. His dark hair and good looks that had fooled everyone, hiding a monster. Caroline wretched, vomiting up the entire contents of her stomach.

She struggled to remember a self-defense move, to force herself to do more than just squirm and kick at the man. She sobbed in frustration as he pulled her toward the door, grabbing at his hand to relieve the pressure in her scalp.

"If you don't come with me, I'll be forced to kill you here."

The man sounded like he almost regretted that fact, but Caroline knew she couldn't let him take her from the safe house. She knew firsthand the sort of pain the human body could endure before death. She didn't want to die here, but she couldn't let him take her from this house.

But then he was gone, his hold of her scalp ripped free as he went flying past her deeper into the room.

It took her a moment to realize there was a tangle of two bodies. And the other one was Zane.

Lillian stood in the doorway, gun raised. "Are you okay, Caroline?" she asked, her eyes surveying the room rather than looking at her.

"Y-yes. I'm okay."

Zane was fighting with the other man, if you could call it much of a fight. Zane was younger, stronger and obviously enraged.

Lillian stepped in, gun still raised to chest level. She scoped out the rest of the room.

"Did the guy come in alone?" she asked, ignoring the punches being thrown by Zane and the intruder.

"I... I don't know." Caroline barely got the words out. "I thought I saw a second man standing at the door, but I'm not sure." She also thought the man was Paul Trumpold, but he was dead. Caroline knew she couldn't trust her own mind.

Lillian quickly made her way into the one bedroom of the safe house, the bathroom and the kitchen.

"We're clear here," she said into some sort of communication unit.

Jon came running through the door, looked at Caroline huddled up against the wall and Zane and the other man still rolling on the ground throwing punches at each other.

"Zane, enough," Jon said. "We need to question him, not put him in the hospital."

Caroline watched Zane pull himself together and get off the man, who lay moaning on the floor. Both Lillian and Jon had their weapons trained on him. He wasn't going anywhere.

"Cuff him," Zane told Jon, then walked over to Caroline.

She wanted to go to him, to meet him halfway, but couldn't seem to get herself off the wall.

He held his arms out in front of him, the way someone would do if they were proving they meant no harm or sudden movement. She knew then that she must look as frightened and horrified as she felt.

"Zane," she whispered his name and fell into him. He caught her and lowered them both to the ground, his arms wrapped securely around her.

"Are you hurt?" he asked. "Do we need to get you medical attention?"

"No," she whispered. "He didn't hurt me."

For the longest time they said nothing else, just held each other. She could hear Jon read the guy his rights before they cuffed him. Multiple officers came in and out of the safe house, including Gareth Quinn, who evidently had been knocked unconscious in the car on the street but then came to and called in reinforcements.

Zane just sat against the wall holding Caroline the whole time.

"Let's get you home," Zane finally said.

"Don't you need to go question that guy or something?"

"It will wait. They'll get all his info, but they won't start questioning him without me."

Caroline just tucked herself into his arm. She didn't want to look around. Didn't want everyone to know that they'd been right to be so protective of her. That when literal push came to shove, Caroline had frozen.

That she was as weak as everyone thought.

She'd sworn she'd never be a victim again. Had gone through hundreds of hours of therapy and physical training to keep from being a victim again, but when the crisis moment had come, she'd just folded and begun to cry.

Caroline wanted to cry now. Huddled against the door of Zane's truck, staring blankly out the window, she wanted to bawl her eyes out. She'd been fighting so hard for her independence, swearing she could handle herself, that she was so strong.

One knock on a door and two minutes of a man pushing through had shown her otherwise. She was never going to be okay again.

"Caro," Zane whispered, not trying to touch her. "Are you sure you're not hurt? Don't hide it if you are. Tell me."

"No, he didn't hurt me. Didn't hit me at all. Was just pulling me out the door by my hair. You're more hurt than I am." She didn't look away from the window as she said it.

They rode in silence until Zane eventually pulled up to his beach house. They went up the stairs, Zane unlocking the door, then checking to make sure the house was secure. Caroline didn't wait outside for him to finish this time. She entered, then crossed all the way to the living room to the outside deck. She crossed to the railing, staring out at her beloved ocean. From this direction she couldn't see the sun that was beginning to set but knew it was by the purple hues being cast over everything.

"Caro." She heard Zane from the doorway. "Tell me what's wrong. It's more than just the guy breaking in, isn't it?"

She could hear him come a little closer.

"Although, that's upsetting enough for anyone. To think you're safe, that the danger is elsewhere, but it's not. That's scary. And not just to you, to anyone."

He fell into silence when she didn't say anything. How could she make Zane understand? He'd always been so strong, so capable. Never plagued by doubt or frozen into inaction.

Not like her.

It was a crippling thing to realize all the progress you thought you'd made—you'd worked and scraped and clawed for—was just a figment of your imagination.

"He knocked on the door." The words were out of her mouth before she could stop them.

Zane didn't push, just came and stood by her at the railing.

"Trumpold knocked. The day he attacked me, he knocked on my door." Caroline knew this was a sore spot for Zane. That he blamed himself for not being the one who had knocked on her door that day. But he didn't draw the conversation to him or his guilt. She appreciated it. Appreciated the strength in his silence.

"So when this guy knocked, I panicked. I should mention that I always panic when someone knocks on my door. God forbid you be the poor package delivery guy in my neighborhood. He must think I live on the verge of a nervous breakdown." She tried to laugh, but it didn't sound the least bit amused even to her own ears.

"It's an understandable trigger, Caro. You know that, right?" he said softly.

"Oh, God, yes, I understand that. I have spent more time in therapy talking about knocks on doors than anything else. It's ridiculous." She tapped her knuckles against the railing. "Even knowing it's me, watching my own knuckles hit the wood, I still get slightly nauseous at the sound."

Zane nodded, not saying anything. She couldn't blame him. What could you say to that?

"But I thought it was probably that officer, Gareth Quinn. And I knew I was being a complete coward. So I opened the door."

She took a deep breath.

"It was only opened a crack when he pushed his way through, slamming the door open."

"Just like Trumpold," Zane finished for her.

"Yes." Caroline could barely get the syllable out.

Zane put his hand over hers on the railing. "I'm so sorry."

She pulled her hand out from under his. "But that's not it, not really. If that is what had happened and the dude had scared the life out of me and you'd gotten there just in time to save the day, I'd be fine with that."

"I don't understand. I thought he didn't hurt you."

"He didn't, Zane. He was planning on dragging me out of the safe house, told me he was going to kill me, but you got there in time."

"That's good, right?" He obviously couldn't understand the distress tainting her tone.

"I froze."

He didn't ask what she meant. He'd been in law enforcement too long not to understand.

"I've spent so much time studying self-defense since the attack. Months of classes. Hundreds of hours. But when he forced his way in, it was like I forgot it all."

"Caro—"

She shook her head. "I can see it all playing in my head like it's a movie. And I want to scream at that girl on the ground, 'What's the matter with you? You know how to break his hold. Hell, you know how to break both his arms. Do it!'"

Her hands clenched into fists. "I just laid there on the ground, crying, Zane. I even vomited. That guy wasn't as fit as Trumpold, wasn't as strong, hadn't stunned me the way Trumpold had with his first two punches. But I just laid there, blubbering. I don't know what would've happened if you hadn't gotten there when you did."

"Caroline, it happens. People freeze up. Even in law enforcement it happens."

His matter-of-fact tone, devoid of anything that could be considered condescending or pitying, helped her in ways he couldn't possibly know.

"I hate myself. I hate myself for being so weak. A victim." She turned away from the view of the ocean and leaned her back against the railing. "Again."

Zane came to stand right in front of her, his hands on her shoulders. "There's nothing about you that's weak, Caro. And you're no victim. You were stunned. A situation you couldn't possibly have expected caught you off guard. It happens."

She didn't want to look at him, but he caught her chin with his thumb and finger and forced her to look up. Forced her to look into those rich brown eyes, where she didn't see anything close to pity or concern. Didn't even see love.

She saw respect, and it meant more to her than all the other emotions could've meant combined.

"We got there when we did, and thank goodness," Zane continued. "Because those punches I got in on that guy, I needed them, and they're probably the only ones I'll legally get."

She couldn't help but smile a little at that.

"But I have no doubt you would've bounced back, Caro. That training you've done, it would've filtered its way back into your mind, into your muscles. You wouldn't have let yourself be taken by that guy. I would bet every cent I have in this life and the next one that you would've taken him down in the next few minutes."

Caroline leaned into his chest. "I just wish I had a replay button. That I could go back and do it again. Make it different."

He wrapped his arms around her like he planned to never let her go. "Believe me, I've wished for one of those too. But we can only move forward. All I know is that you have the inner strength to withstand damn near anything."

Chapter Seventeen

Zane didn't go back into the station that night. Caroline and her needs were more important to him than questioning the perp they'd caught right away. Plus, Zane probably needed a little more cooling-down time anyway.

He'd probably lose his newly reinstated status pretty quickly if he started punching on a suspect in custody.

He had let Jon and Captain Harris know he wasn't coming in until this morning and both had agreed it was the best thing to do. The suspect—Jon informed Zane that the guy's name was Donald Brodey, a name that sounded vaguely familiar to him—would wait.

But now Zane was ready. Wanted some answers. Lillian was hanging out with Caroline so Zane could be at the station getting them. He didn't want to take any chances until they knew exactly what was going on. After what happened yesterday, Caroline wasn't as resistant to having Lillian around, which broke his heart.

Caroline's reaction to the break-in at the safe house wasn't unheard of and certainly wasn't anything that should cause her shame. He'd gotten through to her the best he could about that, but he knew she regretted how she'd reacted. But any law enforcement officer knew full well that practicing, drills, sparring were all well and good, but that in the heat of the moment, training didn't always translate to perfect real-world responses.

He wished Caroline could have another chance to fight down the guy breaking through the door, but he damn well hoped it would never happen again. Zane would help her find other ways of making sure she didn't freeze up again that didn't involve her being in actual danger.

Zane found Jon back at the little corner desk beside the copying machine, where the department had so rudely put him when he'd come here initially working the serial rapist case. Nobody in the Corpus Christi PD had wanted an outsider coming in to help with the case. They'd thought Jon would be a hotshot know-it-all.

He'd been neither.

"You know we'll get you a regular desk, Jon. You don't have to be all Harry-Potter-living-under-the-stairs anymore."

Jon smiled. "This desk holds some pretty fond memories for me. Led me to my soon-to-be wife, you know."

Zane smiled too. Couldn't argue with that. Sometimes bad circumstances were what ended up pointing you in the right direction.

"So does the name Donald Brodey seem familiar to you?" Jon got up and handed a file to Zane.

"Vaguely."

"That's because you arrested him eight years ago. Felony breaking and entering coupled with burglary."

Zane opened the file. "Yes. Now I remember. It was one of my first cases as a detective." He studied the mug shot of Brodey from nearly eight years ago. He'd been in his late thirties then, which put him in his midforties now.

"Looks like a pretty cut-and-dried case. His prints were at the scene. He'd already done a couple of years for misdemeanor B and E charges."

Zane's eyes narrowed. "But he always said he didn't commit this particular crime. I remember that."

"Did you believe him?" Jon asked.

Zane shrugged. "Not really. But I have to admit, I might have been more interested in proving my worth to the department than I was interested in listening to some repeat offender argue about his innocence."

"Looks like he served six years. He's been out for about a year and a half."

"Honestly, I haven't thought about Brodey since he went to prison. I definitely wouldn't have pegged him for trying to kill me. For a damned B and E conviction." Zane closed the file.

"Well, he wanted to talk to you."

"Then let's give the man what he wants."

They cleared it with the captain and had Brodey brought to an interview room from holding. The man was definitely bruised from their tussle yesterday, but then again, so was Zane.

"Detective Wales." Brodey smirked as Zane and Jon entered.

"Brodey." Zane took the seat directly across from him. Jon took the one at the corner of the metal table. Jon read the man his rights.

"Not going to call for your lawyer, Brodey?"

The older man sat back in his chair. "Nope. Ain't got nothing to say that a lawyer will change."

"I suppose you're innocent of this just like you were innocent all those years ago?"

Brodey's eyes narrowed. "I was innocent of that B and E and you know it."

Zane shook his head. "Is that why you've been sending me all those texts? My 'secret' that would come to light."

"Yeah. You can't hide your secrets forever, Wales." He crossed his arms over his chest.

"And Caroline Gill? What does she have to do with my secrets?"

"Everybody knows the best way to get to you is through Caroline Gill. That's why I was trying to take her yesterday. I knew if I could get her, it wouldn't be any problem to get you to surrender."

"And what were you going to do once I surrendered?"

"You were going to pay for them permanently, Wales. For the lies you told. For the years I lost."

Zane glanced over at Jon, who looked as surprised as he did. For someone who'd always claimed his innocence about a crime eight years ago, Brodey had just confessed to a much bigger one.

"What are you doing, Brodey? Why are you telling me this? You know it's just going to get you sent back to prison."

"Maybe it's worth it. Maybe seeing you pay for your sins is worth the risk of going back to prison."

"You've been out of jail for eighteen months. Why did you decide to just come after me now?"

"Somebody made me see the light. A fellow I think you guys know. Name is Freihof. Damien Freihof."

Brodey had their attention now.

"Freihof put you up to this? To trying to kill both me and Caroline?"

Brodey smiled. "Yep. Helped me to understand that you needed to pay for what you'd done. That I lost years of my life thanks to you."

"But what about Caroline? She never did anything to you, Donald. Why take out some sort of misguided revenge on her?"

Brodey looked down for just a minute and shifted in

his chair. Then he looked back up at Zane. "Did you know I had three kids when you put me in jail, Wales? They needed their daddy and they lost him. Because of you. Sometimes innocent people get hurt. Your girlfriend was like my children."

"How did you know where Caroline would be yesterday?"

"I planted bugs in her house so I could listen to what you said."

"We found those. But we never said anything about where Caroline would be staying." Zane knew full well they wouldn't have given that information away in their conversation, knowing someone was listening.

"Yeah, but you didn't find the device I put in your truck. I could hear all your conversations there too. I knew you were using that other lady as bait to try to draw me out."

Zane grimaced. They hadn't even thought about a transmitting device in their vehicles. But they should have.

"So I followed you to the bank yesterday," Brodey continued. "Then followed her from there instead of you."

It was a smart plan and had almost worked. If Brodey had moved a little quicker. If he'd knocked Gareth Quinn a little harder on the head so the other man didn't wake up so quickly and report the problem, Brodey would've gotten away with it.

Zane and Jon spent the next few hours questioning Brodey, trying to get as much information as they could about Damien Freihof. Brodey wouldn't admit to anything that happened in Big Bend but gave fairly consistent answers to questions about yesterday's attack.

Two days ago he'd broken into Caroline's town house and planted the transmitting devices. He'd then immediately gone over to Zane's house and trashed it. They'd missed catching him by only thirty minutes.

Brodey knew his best bet was to get Caroline alone. To kidnap her and draw Zane out. Realizing the info Zane and Caroline were providing in her town house was a trap, Brodey decided to use their own plan against them.

And Damien Freihof was at the heart of it all. Encouraging Brodey. They'd never met, but Freihof had spent the last two weeks by phone and video messaging convincing Brodey of the justice of taking Zane down. Brodey had agreed.

By midafternoon, Zane had done all the questioning he could. Brodey had written down his confession. His intent. Brodey would be going back to jail, probably for the rest of his life.

Zane and Jon filed the paperwork they needed, then went to Zane's house to break the good news to Caroline and Lillian.

It wasn't often in a law enforcement officer's career where the bad just up and admitted to a crime, even signing a confession. Sure as hell made the case easier.

They explained everything while Caroline cooked a simple spaghetti dinner with salad.

"So it looks like Brodey will be going away for a long time," Zane finished.

"Omega Sector still has to catch Freihof, but Brodey's failure to kill you at least slows his plans considerably. It will take a lot of time and effort to convince someone else to take on the job of trying to kill you," Jon said.

"Is that what you think this Freihof guy will do? Just keep trying to find people to convince to hurt us?" Caroline asked.

Jon shook his head. "Honestly, no. I think this is a game for Freihof, with rules. Rules that he establishes, but rules nonetheless. I think for each target he has one puppet—for lack of a better word—that he's created and molded."

"With Fitzy, that was Curtis Harper," Lillian said.

Jon nodded. "Exactly. Freihof convinced Harper to kill SWAT member Ashton Fitzgerald. When that didn't work, I think that part of the game was over. Freihof doesn't seem to be going after the same people more than once."

Zane looked over at Caroline, loving the relief that was evident on her face. He reached over and grabbed her hand.

"Until we arrest Freihof, none of us are completely safe, but probably the part of the game involving the two of you is over for him."

"Thank goodness," Caroline murmured under her breath. "I mean, I know that's probably wrong of me to say, since if he's finished with us, it means he's just moving on to someone else."

"Nothing wrong with being thankful that you're out of a madman's scope," Lillian said around a bite of pasta. "And we're going to do our damnedest to make sure Freihof doesn't have the time or means to target someone else."

Caroline smiled. The first real smile he'd seen from her since they were hiking in Big Bend, before all of this started. Zane squeezed her hand. "I'm going to have to take you out so you can finish your Big Bend hike."

"Maybe in a few months. I'm itching to get back to work right now. Back to some sort of normal."

Zane didn't blame her. Caroline needed the parts of her life she had control over. Her job as a paramedic was a big aspect of that. "I'm sure the hospital won't mind having you back a couple days early from vacation."

"Speaking of, I've got to go back to all that wedding nonsense at Omega. It's out of control." Lillian sighed dramatically.

Jon smiled. "Excuse you, I happen to be a big part of that 'wedding nonsense.'"

"I know. You're almost as bad as Sherry."

"Be sure to tell Sherry I can't wait to see her," Caroline said. "Just a few more days."

"I will. It will be nice to have a drama-free weekend for a change."

Chapter Eighteen

The first sight of a broken ankle at a bike accident the next day had Caroline feeling great. That probably made her a little weird, but she didn't care. She was back at work, at a job she knew she was good at. She hated that the cyclist was in so much pain but loved having something to physically do with her hands. With her brain.

How she'd reacted when Donald Brodey broke into the safe house two days ago still stung. But Zane was right: she couldn't let that paralyze her. Couldn't let that stop her forward progress or growth. He'd talked about helping her with some situational awareness exercises and training where she could be caught off guard.

She smiled as she helped brace the young man's foot in preparation to move him into the ambulance. Zane helping her improve these skills would make her more ready for anything that came her way. Any training that made her less of a victim, she was up for.

But more important, it meant that Zane wasn't planning on running back to his little pocket of Corpus Christi after this was all over, never to be seen again. She didn't know if he was going to continue to work for the police department—although everyone had to admit, he'd flowed right back in as if he'd never left—but he wasn't going to disappear again.

She wasn't exactly sure where that left them personally. Eventually they'd need to broach the subject. But right now, sleeping in his arms every night in the house he'd bought for them, the house he hadn't been able to force himself to sell or even rent to someone else? It was enough for her.

They drove the cyclist back to the hospital and Caroline and Kimmie made a beeline for the coffee shop. They'd already been going for four hours in a twelve-hour shift, and you never knew when an emergency call would come in. So you took advantage of coffee breaks while you could.

"I don't think you've stopped smiling all day," Kimmie said as they paid for their brew, preferring the specialized coffee at the shop over the muck that often waited in the free areas of the hospital.

"I'm sorry. I'll start frowning immediately."

Kimmie smacked her lightly on the arm. "You know I think it's great. Although I'm sure that guy with the broken ankle thought you were some sort of sadist—so happy about his pain."

Caroline chuckled. "Yeah, that probably wasn't sensitive."

"I'm assuming your happiness has to do with the arrest of the guy who was trying to kill you."

Caroline added sugar to her coffee. "It's definitely a relief."

Kimmie nudged her. "And don't think it escaped my notice that Zane Wales dropped you off at work this morning."

Caroline tried not to blush. "It was on his way, since he's working at the police station."

"And because you guys were making wild, passionate monkey love all last night, weren't you? Gosh, he is so gorgeous, Caroline. Sigh. I want a super hunk like that."

Out of the blue, Caroline pulled Kimmie in for a hug.

Kimmie hugged her back—as Caroline had no doubt she would—and laughed as they broke apart. "What was that for? We've been partners for nearly eighteen months and I don't think we've ever hugged."

Caroline had resented being partnered with Kimmie. She'd known Uncle Tim had done it because he'd deemed that, after the attack, Caroline needed to work with a woman. Someone nonthreatening and lighthearted. Caroline had tried to never let her resentment show to Kimmie; after all, it wasn't Kimmie's fault she was the most perky, sweet partner they could find. Tim had done what he'd thought was best for Caroline.

Ended up he'd been right. Kimmie was probably the best partner Caroline could've had for the past year and a half. Not because she wasn't a man, but because she was hardworking, enthusiastic, and wanted to learn what Caroline had been ready to teach.

Caroline smiled. And Kimmie was always perky.

"You're a great partner, Kimmie. And a good friend. I just wanted to hug you."

Kimmie hugged her again quickly. "I just wanted to get another one in before you go back to non-hugging mode." She pulled away and they walked down the hallway with their coffee.

They'd barely finished half their cups before they got the call. A warehouse fire down near the oil district. Multiple injuries, utter chaos. An all-hands call.

Caroline and Kimmie dumped their coffee and ran for the ambulance, pulling out of the hospital parking lot rapidly along with other ambulances. Fire and rescue vehicles would be joining them on-site.

As they pulled up to the location, Caroline could see it was worse than she'd thought.

She turned to Kimmie. "The fire chief will be calling

out orders. It will be pretty chaotic, so just take it one patient at a time. Don't get overwhelmed."

Caroline had worked only one other fire like this, about five years ago. She'd gotten a little panicked and didn't want the same thing to happen to Kimmie.

They jumped out of the ambulance and reported over to the fire chief, who was barking out orders. He pointed at Caroline and Kimmie.

"Office workers. Southeast corner." He pointed in the general direction. "Smoke inhalation mostly. Evaluate, get the most severely injured to the main hospital. Gill, coordinate and see who needs to go to the local medical center if the main hospital ER can't take them."

It was a big job, to coordinate what patients would go where, but Caroline appreciated the trust the fire chief was putting in her. She was one of the most seasoned paramedics out here. She wouldn't let him down.

"Let's go, people." The EMTs and paramedics—EMTs with more schooling—all followed after Caroline. She split them up into groups and soon everyone had a job to do caring for the injured.

Caroline spent the next six hours coordinating between hospitals and the EMTs, evaluating burn and smoke inhalation victims and getting them where they needed to be. This fire couldn't have happened at a worse spot for casualties. A factory with hundreds of people inside had been affected.

Things were just starting to slow down enough for Caroline to eat a protein bar, something every paramedic kept stashed for situations just like this where a meal wasn't possible. She washed it down with another bottle of water, although she'd been careful to keep herself hydrated throughout the day. She didn't want to end up as someone needing medical attention rather than giving it.

When she had a short break, she grabbed her phone to text Zane.

Massive fire in oil section. Won't be done for a while.

His response was almost immediate.

Be safe. Text me when you're done.

She looked over at the firefighters. They seemed to be getting it under control. Most of the critical victims had been seen and escorted to hospitals and medical centers in the greater Corpus Christi area.

Caroline scoped out the scene. They'd done a good job here today. Loss of life had been minimal thanks to the work of the firefighters and EMTs.

"Hey, Caroline, somebody was looking for you. An EMT," Kimmie said. Caroline had been split up from her partner for most of the day. She pointed to the far side of the building. "Around the corner there. Someone else told me, so I don't know what it's about. Sorry. Want me to go ask?"

Caroline grabbed a protein bar. "No, you stay here and eat this. Take five minutes. You've been working hard today. We all have. I'll go see what's needed."

Kimmie smiled. "Thanks. Wanna hug?"

Caroline rolled her eyes, knowing the woman was kidding. "Yeah. It can be our new thing."

She jogged over to the far side of the building. It was much quieter over there, away from the action. An EMT was crouched down near the back corner.

"Hey, is everything okay?" Caroline asked. "I heard you needed me."

The woman glanced over her shoulder at Caroline.

"Yeah, do you mind coming over here? I think you should see this."

Caroline prayed it wasn't a body, although she didn't see how it could be in such a small space.

She squatted next to the woman and looked into the hole where she stared. Caroline didn't see anything but dirt.

"What are we looking at?" she asked.

Caroline felt a prick at the back of her neck and swatted at whatever bug had bitten her. A few seconds later the woman stood. Caroline tried to stand too, but found herself dizzy.

"Whoa. I think I need to eat something besides a protein bar." She looked back at the hole again. "I'm sorry. What did you want me to see here?"

The woman didn't answer and Caroline turned to look at her again.

She was spinning.

The entire world was spinning.

This wasn't low blood sugar from not eating enough. She'd been drugged.

Caroline looked at the woman again and realized she wasn't really wearing an EMT uniform, just similar colors.

"Who are you?" Getting the words out were more difficult than they should be.

"I'm the person who's going to show the world what a liar you are, Caroline Gill. Finally show everyone what you've done and how my brother's death was your fault."

Caroline tried to stand again but couldn't. She began to crawl away, but much more slowly than she wanted. Her muscles refused to work. She held on to consciousness for as long as she could, even knowing she was fighting a losing battle against whatever drug the woman had given her.

"My brother was a doctor, so I know a little about temporary paralytic drugs," the woman said, inching her face closer to Caroline. "You should never have lied about him, Ms. Gill."

Through the fuzziness in her mind Caroline realized who the woman was. She was the sister of Paul Trumpold, the man who viciously attacked and raped Caroline.

And she thought Caroline had made up the whole story.

She clawed through the dark to try to keep hold of consciousness, knowing this woman intended to harm her, but couldn't do it. Her panic got even worse as she saw someone who looked just like Paul Trumpold standing behind her. As Caroline laid her face on the ground, the woman did the same, facing her.

"Don't worry. We'll talk soon."

The vicious hatred in the woman's eyes was the last thing Caroline saw before the darkness overtook her.

Chapter Nineteen

Zane sat back in the chair at his desk in the Corpus Christi Police Department. When he'd come back in this morning, instead of having to work in the conference room, since he had no desk assigned to him, he'd found his old desk back in place. His old chair at it and nameplate on the front.

Almost like he'd never left.

He would've thought there would've been some hard feelings, either about him returning or about him leaving in the first place. And maybe there was. But as a whole the department had banded together and welcomed him back into their midst.

Zane had to admit leaving again would be difficult. He missed detective work. Even now that they had found the person trying to hurt him and Caroline, he didn't know if he could walk away. The people he worked with here were family. They understood what the attack on Caroline had cost him and supported him—then and now—the best way they could.

Today that had been dragging his desk and chair back to where they'd once been.

But the part of him that enjoyed sitting in this chair, the part of him that had missed law enforcement work every day for the past eighteen months since he'd quit, knew that something wasn't right.

Donald Brodey's arrest. His confession. All of it. As much as Zane wanted it to be perfect and tidy, it wasn't. It just didn't sit well with him.

Something wasn't right.

Jon walked over and leaned on the corner of the desk. "Looks like they're carving out a permanent place for you here."

Zane leaned back, stretching his legs out in front of him. "Nice of them, I have to admit."

"You going to stay?"

"I think so. It's not like I have any other job around right now. They're still picking up pieces of my Cessna in Big Bend."

"Not to mention you miss police work." Jon's eyebrow rose, daring him to deny it.

Zane shrugged. "It's true. I do."

"You're good at it, Zane. Got a natural talent and a good temperament for it."

"I know."

"Plus, that incredible humbleness."

Zane chuckled, but then it faded out. "The only problem is, right now my detective spider senses are telling me there's something wrong with Donald Brodey."

Jon sat at the chair by Zane's desk. "What about him?"

Zane shrugged. He wasn't exactly sure what he meant and didn't want to bog Jon down if his fears amounted to nothing. "I know you need to go. I don't want Sherry getting mad at me because I kept the groom away for too long."

"I've got an hour before I need to leave for my plane. Plus, Sherry is capable of handling anything thrown her way. One of the things I love most about her."

Jon and Sherry were a good fit. Partners in every sense of the word.

"Do you have any wild parties coming up? In your last few days of singlehood?"

Jon shook his head. "Nah. The guys and I will probably go out for a few beers, but I'm not interested in a strip club or the 'normal' bachelor stuff."

Zane wasn't actually surprised. "Oh yeah?"

"Once you have the one you really want, all of that seems ridiculous, you know? I have no interest in seeing any other naked or partially naked woman besides Sherry."

Zane knew what he meant. He wouldn't go to a strip club now if someone dragged him. It wasn't what he wanted.

Caroline was what he wanted. Today. Tomorrow. The rest of their lives.

Jon leaned back in his chair. "So tell me what you think is going on with Brodey."

"I reviewed his case again this morning. From the original B and E."

"And?"

Zane shifted slightly. "Now, with nearly a decade more experience, I'm looking at the arrest in a different light. Brodey claimed his innocence the whole time. Said someone planted his fingerprints at the scene."

"Do you believe him?"

"I believe we caught another burglar six months later and the evidence suggested he'd been placing fingerprints that weren't his around crime scenes to make himself less of a suspect. I think it's possible that Brodey was telling the truth. That someone did put his prints on the scene."

"Brodey had already been convicted two other times, you know. So it's not like this was some innocent guy off the street who got thrown in jail."

"Actually, that's what convinced me. I went back through his other case files, cases I wasn't part of at all, to see if he claimed his innocence then. To see if that was just his MO."

"And?"

"Nope. Served his time, never claimed innocence once."

Jon shifted in his chair. "Okay. Then, that just supports his claim that he was out for revenge. That's why he came after Caroline—to get back at you."

Zane picked up a pencil on his desk and began twirling it between his fingers. "That's what I thought too. That this Damien Freihof guy had just gotten his claws into Brodey and twisted his thinking. And I have to admit, that's possible."

"But something has you questioning it."

"Brodey wasn't ever violent, Jon. All of his crimes involved breaking into houses where no one was home. The man has a family. Kids."

"You're thinking that it's a pretty big jump to go from a family man with no history of violent crime to kidnapping and attempted murder."

"Yes. Exactly. And moreover, I can see why he would still be mad at me. But Caroline? It would take a pretty hardened criminal to kill her for something I did."

"People change. Jail hardens them. Then someone like Freihof comes along and pushes them in a certain direction, even one they wouldn't normally take on their own."

"Yeah, I guess you're right."

Wade Ammons walked through the door of the detective section.

"Hey, Wales, you look pretty good sitting in your old spot. Does that mean you're going to be staying?"

"I'm thinking about it. If you guys and the captain really want me back around."

The younger man smiled. "We do, believe me. It's been hard trying to make this place look good all by myself."

Jon stood. "I've got to move if I'm going to catch my plane. Call me if you need to talk some things through. I'll also keep searching with Omega resources. Make sure we're not missing something."

Zane shook Jon's hand. "Thank you, for everything. I guess Caroline and I will be up this weekend to see you get hitched."

"See you then."

Jon headed out and Zane sat back down at his desk. "Where is everybody, Wade?"

The detectives' desks were on the second floor of the building that housed the police department. It was generally more quiet here than all the uniformed officers' desks and general processing. But it was never this quiet.

"Huge fire down in the oil district started an hour ago. Most of the station is down helping."

"Casualties?"

"Yeah, a lot. A bunch of office workers got trapped. Caroline's down there. Last report was that she was directing ambulance traffic to different hospitals."

It was a crazier day than she'd expected to go back to, but Zane knew she could handle it. She was probably glad to have such a busy day. Caroline liked to keep focused. She excelled at it.

"Let me know if you need any help with anything or if I'm needed at the oil district."

"Will do. Sounds like the worst of it has passed, though."

"I'm going to get Brodey out of holding and talk to him one more time. I feel like we're missing something."

Wade nodded. "We're gathering everything we know about the last eighteen months of Brodey's life since he made parole. As soon as the file is ready, I'll get it to you."

Interviewing Brodey again wasn't hard, since he was

still being housed in the temporary cells inside the department until his bail hearing date. But the man was much less cooperative this time. Sullen almost.

"You still have a right to an attorney, Brodey. You know that," Zane finally said when Brodey hadn't given him nearly as open answers as yesterday. "Do you want a lawyer?"

The man had already signed a confession, so it wouldn't help much. But it was still his right.

"Naw. I don't want no lawyer."

"Tell me more about Damien Freihof. How did he contact you?"

Brodey looked down at his hands. "Freihof called me on the phone. Said he'd been over my case. That he thought you were a crooked cop and that I should take my revenge on you."

"I see."

"I lost a lot of years of my life because of you."

"You already had two strikes before you even came across my radar. So it's difficult to believe that you think I'm responsible for all your woes."

Brodey just crossed his arms and leaned back in his chair, staring at the table.

Zane decided he needed to take another tack. "But okay. What if I said, looking back at the case now, I can see why you said you were innocent. That I agree with you that someone should've looked more closely into your case when we discovered someone was, in fact, planting prints of other criminals."

Brodey straightened for just a moment, looking Zane in the eye. "That's what I told you from the beginning."

"And I was wrong, Brodey, I should've listened. But I was young. Yours was one of my first solo detective cases. I wanted to make a splashy arrest maybe more than I wanted to make sure justice was served."

"You tell my wife that, okay, Wales?" It was the first time Brodey hadn't seemed dour. Seemed legitimately invested in what he was saying. "You tell her that I wasn't lying about not being the one who broke into that house."

"You're going away for attempted murder, Brodey. Why the hell will your wife care about a B and E from eight years ago?"

Brodey seemed to wilt right in front of him. "You're right, I guess. But if it ever comes up, you tell her that, okay?"

Zane tried to get more details from Brodey after that. About Freihof, about Big Bend. But the man wasn't talking.

"I signed a confession. I don't have anything more to say." And that was it. The longer Zane talked, the more silent the older man became.

Zane got a text from Caroline telling him she would be running late and texted her back. He spent some more time with Brodey trying to get him to spill any more details, but the man obviously was done talking.

Finally, Zane had him sent back to his cell. He left the interview room with no more information than when he'd started, besides an odd statement about letting Brodey's wife know he was innocent of a crime that in the greater scheme of things didn't really matter.

As promised, Wade had left a file on Zane's desk about Brodey's whereabouts and activities since he'd been released from prison. He'd been out for eighteen months, unemployed. He and his wife were separated, but not divorced. She'd stayed with him even when he'd been incarcerated. They had three teenage children.

Their financial situation was pretty grim, Zane had to admit. The wife and kids were living in a two-bedroom apartment, and they had missed multiple rent payments. Zane didn't doubt they'd be evicted soon.

There was only one picture of the family. The youngest, Brodey's son, seemed to be using some sort of braces in order to walk. Zane grimaced. Medical bills for an illness or disability could cause even further financial hardship.

He turned the page and everything made more sense for him.

Two months ago, Donald Brodey had been diagnosed with cancer and had less than six months left to live.

No wonder Brodey had wanted him to pass along the message to his wife. The way things were going, with his confession, he would probably never see her again. At least would never see her as a free man.

Maybe Jon was right; maybe finding out he was dying had changed Brodey. Instead of wanting to right any wrongs before he died, he wanted to exact his revenge on Zane. Freihof just happened to contact him at the right time.

Zane leaned back in his chair, the one in which he'd done his best detective work over the years. There was a big piece of the puzzle he still wasn't seeing. He knew that with every fiber of his being.

He just hoped he'd figure it out before disaster struck.

Chapter Twenty

Caroline woke up slowly, feeling like she'd had way too much to drink the night before. But she couldn't remember any drinking.

And why was she sitting if she was waking up the morning after with a huge hangover? Shouldn't she be lying in bed?

She finally pried her eyes open, then immediately closed them again when dizziness and nausea assailed her. She couldn't help the groan that fell from her lips. She tried to raise her hand to her head to help relieve some of the pressure but found she couldn't move her arms.

Then it all came back to her. Not drinking. Drugged. By the sister of the man who had tried to destroy her life.

"Yeah, that chloral hydrate is a bitch, isn't it?" Caroline couldn't tell exactly where the woman's voice was coming from. She was evidently walking around the chair Caroline was bound to. Not helping the dizziness. "Quick to knock someone out, but a little more difficult to recover from."

Caroline felt a sting in her scalp as the woman grabbed her hair and yanked her head back. "But that queasiness? Trust me, that's the best you're going to feel all day. It's just going to get worse from here."

"Who are you?" Caroline pushed the words past the

dryness of her throat, her voice sounding strange even to her own ears.

"That's right, we haven't formally met, have we? I'm Lisette Trumpold."

"Paul Trumpold's sister."

The woman snatched Caroline's head back by the hair again. "Don't even say his name." The woman's voice was rising in both pitch and volume. She slung Caroline's head forward. "You ruined his life with your lies. You don't deserve to say his name."

Now it was more than just the drugs that made Caroline want to vomit. After living through the vicious attack by Paul Trumpold, to hear someone defend him—even a family member—made her want to hurl her guts out.

"I never lied about your brother and what that sick bastard did."

The world spun wildly out of control as the back of Lisette's hand connected with her cheek. If she hadn't been tied to the chair, she would've flown out of it.

"Liar!" Lisette screamed right in Caroline's face, spittle flying everywhere. "I've seen the truth, the real medical reports, not the ones you and your boyfriend fabricated and gave to the police."

Caroline tasted blood in her mouth from where her teeth had scraped the inside of her cheek. She tried to gather her thoughts, figure out exactly what this crazy woman was talking about.

Caroline breathed deeply, trying to take in as many details as possible. Lisette hadn't killed her outright at the fire scene, so evidently she wanted Caroline alive for some reason. That was good. Gave her time to figure out some way of escape.

And she was talking about different medical reports? Caroline had no idea what the hell that meant. Her medical records had definitely been a part of the case against Paul Trumpold, but there had been only one set.

She needed to figure out exactly what Lisette wanted. Then she could better formulate a plan.

"Recognize where we are yet?" Lisette asked.

Caroline forced herself to open her eyes despite the dizziness and nausea it caused. She breathed in and out through her nose, lifting her head and looking around. She knew immediately where she was.

She was in the house where she'd lived when Trumpold attacked her. On the floor right under the chair that she was tied to right now, he had beaten her into a coma and raped her.

Caroline could feel the onslaught of panic. Looking at the door just a few feet in front of her, she could easily envision the day she'd opened it just a crack and he'd forced his way through. Could feel the pain—a thousand times worse than the slap Lisette had just given her—as his fist connected with her jaw, shattering her cheekbone.

She heard herself whimper, struggling through the effects of the drug to know what was now and what was then. She closed her eyes again, trying to hold on to her sanity.

It was Zane's face in her mind, his voice in her subconscious, that got her through.

All I know is that you have the inner strength to withstand damn near anything.

The words he had said to her after Donald Brodey attacked her at the safe house. She held on to them like a lifeline.

Inner strength. Inner strength. Withstand damn near anything.

Caroline opened her eyes, no longer picturing Trumpold pushing his way through the door.

Paul Trumpold was dead. He could never hurt her again.

His psycho sister, on the other hand, was alive and circling Caroline like some sort of predator. Caroline fought hysteria, knowing she had to work the problem in front of her, just like she did every day as a paramedic.

"You brought me to the house where I used to live," Caroline said as evenly as she could, studying Lisette.

"Yes." Lisette actually looked pretty excited that Caroline recognized it. "I rented it from the new owners."

Caroline resisted the urge to point out how sick that was.

"Are you working with Donald Brodey?"

Lisette began pacing back and forth. "To a degree. He had his usefulness."

That didn't make any sense to Caroline, and it ultimately didn't matter, since he wasn't here to help Lisette, so Caroline decided to try a different tack. The most direct one. "What do you want, Lisette?"

"I want you to pay for what you've done. I want you to tell the truth."

That sounded like what Zane had told her Donald Brodey had said. But Brodey wasn't connected to the Trumpolds in any way that they knew of.

"And what truth is that exactly?"

"I want you to admit to the world that you lied about my brother. About what you said he did to you. I know you lied."

She could see the other woman getting worked up just thinking about it. "Lisette, why do you think I lied? What reason would I have to lie about something like that?"

Lisette stopped her pacing and stared at Caroline. "He said you would say that. That you would say you had no reason to lie."

"Who said that? Brodey?"

Lisette didn't even listen to Caroline, just kept on talking. "But he showed me the reports. He showed me how you and Zane Wales got together and faked the whole thing."

Caroline shook her head. She didn't want to make Lisette angry, because God knew the woman was already unstable enough, but she honestly had no idea what she was talking about.

"Lisette, I think there was some mistake. Maybe you got the wrong medical reports by accident or something. Mine were very clear about what happened to me."

Lisette stormed over to a nearby table and brought a file back, opening it and holding it in front of Caroline's face.

"This is the medical report that went to the police department."

Caroline didn't need to look at it for long to recognize it. That was very definitely her battered face in the picture. Very definitely pictures of bruises and welts covering half her body. She didn't even try to read the trauma that had been done by the rape itself.

"Yes, that's my medical report." Caroline kept her voice as even as she could, swallowing the tremors.

Lisette flew back to the table and picked up another medical report, holding it in front of her again. "But this is the actual medical report after your so-called attack, isn't it?"

Caroline studied the file, unsure at first of what she was looking at. It was definitely her, but with much less trauma.

Then she remembered.

"Lisette, this is also a medical report for me. But it wasn't after my rape. This was from two months before. I was accosted by a man during one of my calls as a paramedic. He was robbing a convenience store and pushed me over trying to flee from police. My medical report was going to be used as part of his prosecution."

Lisette just stood there, smiling.

"What?" Caroline finally asked.

"That's exactly what he said you'd say. He was right about everything. You don't have any remorse at all, do you?"

"Look, those medical reports are two separate incidents."

"Not according to the dates," Lisette spat.

"What?"

"The dates are the same."

"Then it was a mistake. A typo. Or someone deliberately changed them to try to trick you."

"Or you and Zane Wales turned in a completely false medical report in order to get my brother arrested. You weren't nearly as hurt as you pretended to be."

Caroline tried to reason with her. "Lisette, I know you don't want to hear this about your brother. I'm sure you loved him."

Caroline had a brother and loved him. Of course, he would never attack a woman and beat her until she went into a coma. But she had to stay focused on reaching Lisette and making her understand.

"Brodey or someone else is feeding you lies, Lisette. Someone is trying to trick you into believing that Zane and I did something we didn't do. We had no reason to frame your brother."

"Donald Brodey has nothing to do with this!" Lisette screamed.

And suddenly it all became so clear to Caroline. No, not Brodey.

Damien Freihof.

He was the one who had manipulated Lisette like this. Or had taken what the woman so desperately wanted to hear and given her reason to believe it.

"Damien Freihof has been lying to you." Lisette's eyes

flew to Caroline's at the mention of his name, confirming Caroline's suspicions. "He's using you."

"Freihof has done nothing but show me the truth. You are the one who has been telling lies. But I'm going to make sure the world knows the truth."

"And how are you going to do that?"

"You're going to admit what really happened while I record it."

Caroline wanted to point out that even if she retracted her entire account of what Paul Trumpold did to her, it wouldn't change anything. Trumpold had attacked Jon Hatton and Sherry Mitchell. Had admitted to raping Caroline and six other women. He had stabbed Jon and Sherry both and been about to kill them when Zane arrived and shot him.

In the overall process, Caroline's version of the story didn't even matter. Paul Trumpold would've gone to jail with or without her medical record or testimony.

Although she'd been glad to give both to help make sure Trumpold went to prison for as long as possible.

But bringing this to Lisette's attention would probably just cause her to kill Caroline.

"I don't think changing my statement alone would do anything to clear your brother's name." Not that Caroline would do it anyway. There was no way in hell she would amend, modify or otherwise revise even one single line of the truth about what happened to her.

She looked Lisette straight in the eye. "And I won't change it anyway. If you hurt me, people will be able to tell I was only doing it under duress."

"We'll see about whether you won't change your lies when I start cutting off Zane Wales's fingers." Lisette laughed as Caroline blanched. Caroline had no doubt she meant it. "That's why I want you to call him and tell him to meet you here."

Caroline shook her head. "You might have wanted to ask me to do that before you told me you were going to cut off his fingers."

Lisette reached into the pocket of Caroline's paramedic jacket. "I sort of thought you might say that. So I guess I'll just text him with your phone."

She spoke as she typed. "I need you to come to my old house ASAP. Something important to show you. Can't talk now."

Caroline watched as Lisette sent the text, then cringed when the phone buzzed in response a few seconds later.

"What is it?" Caroline asked. Lisette read the text from Zane out loud.

"We won't answer him." Lisette smiled at Caroline. "How about that? It'll make it seem all so intriguing."

A few minutes later Caroline's phone rang. No doubt Zane calling when she didn't respond to his text. Lisette just held it until it went to voice mail. It rang again a few seconds later, and Lisette just threw it on the table.

"A missed text and two calls?" Lisette smiled. "A mysterious request to meet him at the scene of the crime? I think it's fair to say our white-hatted hero is on the way."

Lisette walked over to the table and began taking out an assortment of knives and guns. "I'll just get everything ready for when he arrives. I bet he'll knock on the door just like you said my brother did. But this time he'll get the surprise of his life."

Chapter Twenty-One

When Zane got another text from Caroline a few hours after the first telling him about the fire, it was because he figured she'd finally finished her shift, a twelve-hour one that had turned into closer to fourteen hours. He hadn't minded staying to do some more work. Trying to figure out what was missing with Brodey and glancing at some other cases. Detectives rarely got to work one case at a time.

But when he looked down at his buzzing phone for the text he thought would be a request to come get her, he did a double take.

I need you to come to my old house ASAP. Something important to show you. Can't talk now.

Zane couldn't think of any reason Caroline would set foot into that house again. Especially without at least talking to him about it first. He texted back.

What is it?

No response. He waited a few minutes in case she was busy with something, but when she didn't answer at all, he called.

Straight to voice mail.

Called again. Same thing.

Zane didn't panic. It had been a long day for both of them. The fire in the oil district wasn't terribly far from the beach section. Maybe she hadn't wanted to come all the way out here to the station just to drive all the way back to the house for whatever she wanted him to see. He began walking to his truck.

Caroline didn't have her truck, so she couldn't have driven herself over there. Someone had to have taken her, so that might explain why she wasn't answering her phone—she was talking to someone else.

But his gut told him that Caroline wouldn't enter that house again casually. Wouldn't just drive by and go inside for no reason. She was strong enough to handle a visit there, but she wouldn't go without planning.

Zane picked up his pace. Something wasn't right here.

"Wade," he called to the other man as he passed him. He gave him Caroline's previous address. "I need you to look up that address and see who owns it now. Any info. It's where Caroline lived when she was attacked."

"Got it."

"I need it fast, Wade. She just texted me from there."

"She in trouble?"

"Nothing to indicate it. But she wouldn't just go back there without a reason."

"I'll call you with the info."

Zane ran out of the station and to his car. The more time that passed without hearing from Caroline, the more worried he became. She should've at least seen he'd called or texted and responded by now. Given all that was going on, the danger they'd faced, she wouldn't just leave him without any communication.

He was just pulling out of the parking garage when his phone rang. He switched his phone to the hands-free speaker so he could continue to drive without looking at the number.

"Caroline?"

"No, man, it's Jon. Were you expecting a call from her?"

Zane explained what was going on and where he was headed.

Jon cursed under his breath. "I put in a request for Donald Brodey's financial records before I got on the plane. I just got to the Omega office and the report was ready."

This couldn't be good, not if Jon was calling so fast. "What?"

"Last week Brodey had a sizable deposit put into his bank account."

"How sizable?"

"Half a million dollars."

Zane whistled through his teeth. For a man who was about to go back to prison, that would help his family out quite a bit.

"Well, I discovered Brodey is terminally ill. Only a couple months left to live. So Freihof must have paid him to come after Caroline and me. Which makes more sense to me than him wanting revenge enough to want to kill us."

"That's just it, Zane. I tracked down the money. It didn't come from Freihof."

"Are you sure? I can't imagine he'd just use his real name on an account."

"Someone did use their real name, but it wasn't Freihof who paid Brodey."

"Who was it?"

"A Lisette Trumpold. Younger sister to Paul Trumpold."

Zane stomped on the gas, no longer caring about breaking any speed limits. "Damn it, Jon. Caroline texted me from the house where Trumpold attacked her."

"I think Lisette paid Brodey to take the fall for her

handiwork in Big Bend. She knew once we had someone in custody—someone who admitted to the crimes—your guard would be down."

"That's why Brodey didn't really have a lot of details today when I went to talk to him. I thought he was just regretting signing the confession. But really it was because he didn't have details to tell."

"And because he didn't want to lose his payoff," Jon finished for him. "I'll call Captain Harris and have him send uniforms to the address."

"Tell him to keep them quiet. If this is a hostage situation, I don't want Lisette to panic. I'm only five minutes out."

Another call beeped in. "I've got to go, Jon."

"Be safe, brother."

The call disconnected and Zane connected to the other one, praying it would be her. "Caroline?"

"No, sorry, man, it's Wade."

"Did you find out anything?"

"The house is owned by a Jack and Marty Smith. They rent it out. Current rental for the month of November is…"

"Lisette Trumpold."

"Yeah, do you know her?"

Zane gritted his teeth, wishing he could make the miles fly by faster. "She's the sister of Paul Trumpold, the man who attacked Caroline."

Wade let out a string of obscenities. Zane couldn't agree more.

"Jon Hatton is calling the captain even as we speak to get squad cars out here. They can't come in blazing, Wade."

"I'll make sure they don't."

"I'm not waiting for backup. I'm going in."

"Be careful."

Zane parked his car two houses down from where he needed to be. If Lisette had Caroline, which at this point he couldn't doubt was the case, he sure as hell wasn't going to just go knocking on the front door. Then Lisette could just kill them both.

Not to mention a knock on that door would scare Caroline. He never planned to knock on any door around her for the rest of their lives.

If Lisette had been sending those texts about Caroline being a liar and Zane keeping secrets, then Freihof had obviously gotten his hooks into her. Convinced her somehow that her brother was innocent and he and Caroline were at fault.

As utterly untrue as that was, it at least made sense.

But Lisette had made a tactical error in bringing Caroline here to this house. Caroline had lived here for years before the attack, and Zane had spent so much time here that it was like he had lived here too. He knew which windows creaked and which deck beams would hold his weight as he climbed up.

Weapon drawn, Zane made his way to the bathroom window on the side of the house. He and Caroline had joked and called that window a pervert's delight. If a Peeping Tom got lucky, he could catch someone in the bathroom, if not, he'd still have a view of almost the entire bottom floor.

He saw Caroline tied to a wooden chair in the middle of the hallway. The pressure in his chest eased. She was alive. That was the most important thing.

And he was damn well going to make sure she stayed that way.

He wasn't sure if Lisette was working alone or not, and he could bet she was armed to the teeth, so he couldn't just barge in. He prayed the squad cars would follow instructions and not come in lights and sirens blazing.

He slipped up the back outer stairs to the far bedroom. It had a door that led out to the deck and was his best chance of getting into the house unnoticed.

It still wasn't going to be easy.

He put his gun back in its holster as he arrived at the door. He let out a sigh of relief when he realized the new owners hadn't been willing to spring for a new, more fortified one. Applying the right pressure at an angle, he was able to slip his credit card in between the handle and the frame and popped open the door.

Caroline had once locked herself out and had shown him the trick. He'd told her how ridiculous she was not to get that door fixed. If she could get in the door like that, then a burglar could too. She'd laughed, saying it was so much more likely that she would forget her keys than it was for someone to break into her house.

He'd always meant to get that door fixed, even if just to piss her off. Thank God he hadn't had the chance and the new owners hadn't, either.

The door creaked slightly as he opened it and he immediately paused, wincing. But he could hear Caroline downstairs, talking to Lisette pretty loudly. He didn't know if she was doing it to help him, but either way it would cover the noise he was making trying to get to her.

He eased the door closed behind him, not wanting to take a chance on the wind blowing something over if he left it open.

"If your boyfriend doesn't get here soon, maybe I'll just start with your fingers."

"Maybe he's not coming. Maybe he has other things to do with his time besides run over here just because he got a cryptic text from me."

"He'll be here. I have no doubt about it. I've seen the way he looks at you. I saw you kissing in the parking lot of the Silver Eagle last week. That's when I realized what Damien told me had to be the truth."

"Just because Zane and I have a physical relationship?"

"Damien told me that you guys had kept apart for all these months to throw off suspicion about your lies. He told me that once you thought it was safe, you'd get back together. He was so right. Damien was right about everything."

"Damien Freihof is a pathological liar and genius using you to get back at a law enforcement group called Omega Sector. You're his pawn, Lisette. You don't have to be."

Zane grimaced as he heard Lisette strike Caroline. "Don't try to talk to me like you know me. You cost my brother his life. I loved him and you cost him everything."

Zane eased down the hall while Lisette paced back and forth in a frenzy. Then she went over to a table and pulled out a gun and pointed it right at Caroline's head.

Ice flowed through Zane's veins. He could jump from where he stood at the banister, but Lisette would definitely have time to shoot Caroline before he landed.

Caroline cleared her throat. "All right, Lisette, you want your confession from me? I'll give it to you. Set up the camera."

Zane could finally breathe again when Lisette removed the gun and walked over to set up her camera. Caroline was keeping her head, biding more time. Zane eased down a couple of stairs, staying in the shadows. The next time Lisette came close to Caroline, he would be able to pounce and catch her.

"Start from the beginning," the other woman said. "And if you tell the truth, maybe I'll kill your boyfriend quickly and you won't have to watch him suffer."

Caroline looked into the video camera Lisette had set up on a tripod a few feet in front of her. "My name is Caroline Gill. I am here to set the record straight about Dr. Paul Trumpold and my claim that he attacked me."

Zane could tell getting the words out were difficult for Caroline. She was doing her best just to keep it together.

"I need some water, Lisette. I can't get through this whole thing with my throat this dry. I was working at a fire all day today."

"Fine." Lisette did something to the camera, then stormed into the kitchen. When Zane heard the sink faucet come on, he stuck his hand over the banister.

"Caro," he whispered.

She looked up, eyes wide. He put his finger over his lips. "Anybody else here?" he asked as quietly as he could.

"No, just her." He could tell she wanted to say more, but there wasn't time.

"I'll jump her when she gives you the water."

He'd barely moved back into the shadows before Lisette came out of the kitchen. "You know, it's good that we stopped. It reminded me you can't be tied up when you give your confession. Then everyone is just going to think you were coerced."

Zane cursed under his breath as she picked up a knife and the gun again. She held the gun to Caroline's head once more as she cut the binds on her wrist. Zane couldn't risk the jump. She cut the rope on the other wrist before handing Caroline the water.

"Now, let's try this again. Take two." Lisette laughed wildly, like some demented film director.

They needed to get Lisette to come back over to the stairs but without the gun. Zane didn't know how to get her to do that without risking Caroline's life.

Caroline started talking again.

"My name is Caroline Gill. I'm here to set the record straight about my claim that Dr. Paul Trumpold attacked me."

Lisette's eyes narrowed as she paused the camera again. "I will come over there and cut you if you don't give me the truth."

"Okay, Lisette, the truth. You deserve that."

"Damn straight I do."

"Here's the truth." Caroline paused and took a deep breath. "I was standing right about here when someone knocked on my door. Do you know that hearing someone knock on a door still has the power to make me cower on the inside? Because right after I opened the door, your brother burst in, his fist striking my face before I could even react."

"Tell the truth, you bitch!" Lisette screeched.

"I am telling the truth. He hit me so hard that the bones in my cheek shattered. I fell to the floor, ironically, right here. Right here under my feet was where your brother attacked and raped me, Lisette."

Lisette stormed at Caroline, knife in hand. But a knife wasn't a gun and Zane was faster. He leaped over the banister, placing himself between Caroline and the madwoman rushing toward her. Lisette obviously wasn't expecting that. She brought the gun in her other hand up, but it was too late. With one quick uppercut Zane had the woman laid out on the floor.

He quickly took both weapons from her. She was already regaining consciousness and moaning as Zane handcuffed her hands behind her back.

"He hit me just like that, Lisette, but your brother didn't stop with just one punch," Caroline said hoarsely.

Then she sat down on the ground, on the floor where so much pain and humiliation had happened to her, and cried.

Chapter Twenty-Two

It was a beautiful day for a wedding.

Caroline had known Sherry Mitchell since they were both in college. They'd remained close through the years. Standing up here as part of the bridal party was an honor. She was delighted to be a part of her friend's special day.

A couple of weeks ago Caroline might have been nervous about standing in front of a hundred people. In a dress. In heels. None of those were things she was comfortable with. But given everything that had happened over the last two weeks, standing here didn't seem like such a terrorizing event after all.

Besides, she knew she looked good in the dress, especially if the way Zane couldn't take his eyes off her was anything to go by.

Maybe she'd have to start wearing dresses more often. Her paramedic uniform involved blue cargo pants and a blue button-down shirt. When she wasn't in that, she tended to be in jeans and a T-shirt.

No one would ever accuse Caroline of being too girlie.

But Zane hadn't taken his eyes off her from where he sat in the second row since the moment she'd walked down the aisle in front of Sherry a few minutes ago. He was still staring. And damn if she didn't like that hungry look in his eyes.

It was definitely enough to make a girl wear a dress more often.

Jon and Sherry had decided on a small wedding in a simple church just outside of Colorado Springs. Even being small there were nearly a hundred people here, many of them Omega Sector agents who worked with Jon and Sherry. They were more than just colleagues; it was easy to tell. They were family.

The wedding official was starting the charge to the bride and groom when Caroline caught sight of the videographer making his way straight up the middle aisle. The photographer had taken a much more conservative post in the back of the church.

Caroline tried to ignore the videographer, with the camera stuck to his face, but the guy seemed to be coming straight toward her, not caring at all about the service.

When she got married, she didn't want any disruptions like this guy. She would make sure that the videographer and photographer both knew she and Zane wouldn't tolerate a disruption like this.

Caroline's eyes flew to Zane's. Had she just made wedding plans with him in her mind? She ought to wait until he actually asked her.

The videographer looked like he was going to come all the way up onto the platform with the minister. Caroline just rolled her eyes as he did exactly that. But instead of having his camera pointed at the bride and groom, it was pointed at her. And then he dropped it from the front of his face.

Caroline felt terror shoot through her.

It was Paul Trumpold. And he was coming toward her, gun now in hand.

She forced herself not to let the panic take her under.

She needed her wits about her. No, this wasn't Paul Trumpold. He was dead.

But it was the man who had been in the doorway at the safe house and who she saw before the drugs had knocked her unconscious at the oil fire.

"That's right," he said. "I'm Nicholas. Paul and Lisette's brother."

How many violently crazy people could one family have?

She heard gasps and movements as Nicholas pulled her down in front of him, using her as a shield as he pointed his gun toward her head.

"You lied about my sister and my brother. He's dead and she's in jail because of you."

His voice, so similar to the one she heard in her nightmares, brought waves of terror. But this time she refused to give in.

She'd frozen the last time a man had grabbed her. Forgotten all her training and panicked. She wouldn't let that happen again.

Nicholas obviously wasn't expecting any fight out of Caroline. She certainly hadn't given one as he'd watched Brodey try to take her from the safe house.

This idiot probably didn't know that he'd walked into a church full of highly trained special agents. Caroline didn't know if any of them were carrying weapons, but she knew Zane was. He'd balked about having to get a special permit for his ankle holster for the plane ride here yesterday. But he wasn't planning on going anywhere without a weapon after what had happened recently.

All she had to do was give Zane a chance and not let this guy drag her out of the building.

Caroline met eyes with Zane, who gave her the slightest nod. He knew what she was planning, in sync with her the way they always had been. He trusted her to be able to do it.

Without warning she let all her weight go limp in Trumpold's grasp around her throat. When he shifted his stance to get a better hold on her, she made her move. She threw her heeled shoe back as hard as she could, gouging him in the shin, causing him to loosen his hold. She spun in his loosened grip, bringing her elbow around to clock him in the jaw.

When his head snapped around at her strike, she continued her momentum, swinging her arms around in a double fist, knocking the gun out of his hand and straight toward Zane. Then Caroline dropped to the ground, out of the way.

She hadn't been there the day Zane shot Paul Trumpold, saving Jon's and Sherry's lives and ending Trumpold's reign of terror over so many women.

But she was here this time when he put a bullet in Trumpold's chest before he could get his gun up and pointed at her. She was sure it was just as impressive.

That was *her* man. And she loved him.

In the aftermath of the situation, it was easy to tell who was an Omega Sector agent and who wasn't.

Everybody from Omega came forward to make sure Nicholas Trumpold was secure. Everybody who wasn't an agent made a mad rush to an exit to get away from a possibly dangerous situation.

Knowing Trumpold was taken care of, Zane moved quickly to Caroline, his face worried. His hands were gentle, ready to pull away if she seemed overwhelmed by what had happened.

"Caro, are you okay?"

Was she okay? Was he kidding? She knew she was grinning like an idiot but couldn't find it in her to care.

She had not been another damn victim.

"Did you see that move? Would've been a hell of a lot easier if I hadn't been in this dress."

The worry slid out of his eyes and he pulled Caroline against his chest. "It was pretty impressive. Trumpold definitely didn't expect it."

"But you did. You knew I could do it."

He kissed her forehead. "Of course you could do it. You just had to believe in yourself."

He wrapped his arms tighter around her as a couple of agents handcuffed Trumpold.

"I guess he's not dead."

Steve Drackett, head of the Critical Response Division of Omega, shook his head. "No. He'll soon be joining his sister in prison. Charged with attempted murder and ruining a perfectly good wedding day."

They all looked up at the bride and groom. Sherry looked white as a ghost and Jon was holding her tightly.

"I'm so sorry, Sherry." Caroline left Zane's arms and walked toward her friend. "He ruined your wedding."

"No, that's not it," Sherry said, looking at Caroline, then over at Steve and the other Omega agents. "I saw Damien Freihof. He was in the back corner of the church." She pointed in the direction. "He gave me a wave, then left in the middle of the panic."

Zane could hear the muttered curses of the agents around him, toned down because they were in a church.

"How did he know about this wedding?" Steve asked. "How did either of them know about this?"

The wedding hadn't been a secret, but it hadn't been made public in any way, either. Omega had too many enemies for that, Freihof being number one of them.

"We've got a mole, Steve," Jon said. "We can't deny that anymore. Damien is working with someone inside Omega Sector."

THE WEDDING WAS moved to the Omega Sector chow hall. It was the only place big enough to hold all one hundred guests.

And after what had happened, nobody minded having to go through a metal detector to get to the ceremony.

Jon and Sherry were determined that their wedding would go on. Today. Exactly one year to the day from when Jon had proposed. Damien Freihof would not stop them from getting married on the day they had planned.

Zane had to admit it was the most unique wedding he'd seen, but that didn't make it any less beautiful. Maybe it was because the bride and groom were so obviously in love with each other.

The caterers had transported the food over from the original reception site, and the musicians had just packed up their instruments and brought them over. The cafeteria opened into a small terrace, so people flowed both inside and out.

After the ceremony Zane planted an arm around Caroline and didn't plan to let her go from his side for the rest of the night.

Hell, he didn't know if he was going to let her go from his side for the rest of forever.

"That was some pretty impressive teamwork you two showed at the church today," Steve Drackett said as they mulled around talking to people and eating the finger food.

"Thank you," Caroline said. "Although, we didn't plan it, believe me. I'm just glad I didn't freeze up."

"Well, if you two decide you're ready to get out of Corpus Christi, be sure to come see me about openings here at Omega. We could always use people who stay cool under pressure." Steve turned to Caroline. "And we could use a good medic for our SWAT team."

Zane loved Caroline's smile, and if she had expressed an interest in Steve's offer, Zane would've followed her lead.

"Sorry, afraid we're Texas folk, through and through. I don't think we could ever truly leave," Caroline said.

"I certainly respect that. But let me know if you change your mind."

A beautiful lady with a dark-haired baby in her arms came up to Steve. "No shoptalk at the wedding. I could tell from across the room you were talking business."

Steve reached down and kissed her and took the baby from her arms. "Busted." He smiled at Caroline and Zane as he led his wife back to the action.

Caroline turned to him, worry in her eyes. "I shouldn't have spoken for you, Zane. I'm sorry. Omega Sector might be a dream come true for you."

He wrapped his arms around her and pulled her closer. "No, I don't want to leave Texas. Especially not now just as I'm getting re-situated in the police department. Tim Harris would have my ass if I quit now, even for Omega Sector."

"You're really going to go back to the department full-time?"

"Yeah. It's where I belong. We both know that."

Her smile beamed. "Stay right here. I brought something with me and I think it's just about time."

"What is it?"

"I'll get it and show you."

"Maybe I don't want to let you go."

"I'm just going across the room." She rolled her eyes.

He pulled her up tight against him. "Maybe I'm not just talking about here. Maybe I'm talking about forever."

She reached up and put both her hands on his cheeks. "I can't promise you forever, Zane. Not yet. There's something missing."

He fought to tamp down the disappointment that swamped

him at her words. She needed more time, he had to understand that. After what she'd been through, who could blame her for needing more time?

It was hard, but he let her go. He watched as she scurried across the room to a gift bag she'd brought and left by one of the doors. She'd had it on the plane and even had it at the church earlier. He'd assumed it was a gift for Jon and Sherry, but now she was bringing it back to him.

She held the string of the bag with one hand as she stopped directly in front of him. She reached into it and pulled out his white cowboy hat.

Zane didn't know what to say. She must have grabbed it from his house, although he hadn't seen her do it. Before he could think of anything, she slipped it onto his head.

"Now," she whispered, dropping the bag and smiling up at him.

"Now what?" he said, unable to stop the smile spreading all over his face. He pulled her to him, knowing he would never be able to let her go again.

"Now you're ready to rejoin the force, and you and I are ready for our forever."

* * * * *

Look for the next book in Janie Crouch's
OMEGA SECTOR: UNDER SIEGE
series next year.

And don't miss the previous title in the
OMEGA SECTOR: UNDER SIEGE *series:*

DADDY DEFENDER

Available now from Mills & Boon Intrigue!

Sheriff Flint Cahill can and will endure elements far worse than the coming winter storm to hunt down Maggie Thompson and her abductor.

Read on for a sneak preview of
COWBOY'S LEGACY,
A CAHILL RANCH NOVEL *from*
New York Times *bestselling author*
B.J. Daniels!

SHE WAS IN so fast that she didn't have a chance to scream. The icy cold water stole her breath away. Her eyes flew open as she hit. Because of the way she fell, she had no sense of up or down for a few moments.

Panicked, she flailed in the water until a light flickered above her. She tried to swim toward it, but something was holding her down. The harder she fought, the more it seemed to push her deeper and deeper, the light fading.

Her lungs burned. She had to breathe. The dim light wavered above her through the rippling water. She clawed at it as her breath gave out. She could see the surface just inches above her. Air! She needed oxygen. Now!

The rippling water distorted the face that suddenly appeared above her. The mouth twisted in a grotesque smile. She screamed, only to have her throat fill with the putrid dark water. She choked, sucking in even more water. She was drowning, and the person who'd done this to her was watching her die and smiling.

Maggie Thompson shot upright in bed, gasping for air and swinging her arms frantically toward the faint light coming through the window. Panic had her perspiration-soaked nightgown sticking to her skin. Trembling, she clutched the bedcovers as she gasped for breath.

The nightmare had been so real this time that she

thought she was going to drown before she could come out of it. Her chest ached, her throat feeling raw as tears burned her eyes. It had been too real. She couldn't shake the feeling that she'd almost died this time. Next time…

She snapped on the bedside lamp to chase away the dark shadows hunkered in the corners of the room. If only Flint had been here instead of on an all-night stakeout. She needed Sheriff Flint Cahill's strong arms around her. Not that he stayed most nights. They hadn't been intimate that long.

Often, he had to work or was called out in the middle of the night. He'd asked her to move in with him months ago, but she'd declined. He'd asked her after one of his ex-wife's nasty tricks. Maggie hadn't wanted to make a decision like that based on Flint's ex.

While his ex hadn't done anything in months to keep them apart, Maggie couldn't rest easy. Flint was hoping Celeste had grown tired of her tricks. Maggie wasn't that naive. Celeste Duma was one of those women who played on every man's weakness to get what she wanted—and she wanted not just the rich, powerful man she'd left Flint for. She wanted to keep her ex on the string, as well.

Maggie's breathing slowed a little. She pulled the covers up to her chin, still shivering, but she didn't turn off the light. Sleep was out of the question for a while. She told herself that she wasn't going to let Celeste scare her. She wasn't going to give the woman the satisfaction.

Unfortunately, it was just bravado. Flint's ex was obsessed with him. Obsessed with keeping them apart. And since the woman had nothing else to do…

As the images of the nightmare faded, she reminded herself that the dream made no sense. It never had. She was a good swimmer. Loved water. Had never nearly drowned. Nor had anyone ever tried to drown her.

Shuddering, she thought of the face she'd seen through the rippling water. Not Celeste's. More like a Halloween mask. A distorted smiling face, neither male nor female. Just the memory sent her heart racing again.

What bothered her most was that dream kept reoccurring. After the first time, she'd mentioned it to her friend Belle Delaney.

"A drowning dream?" Belle had asked with the arch of her eyebrow. "Do you feel that in waking life you're being 'sucked into' something you'd rather not be a part of?"

Maggie had groaned inwardly. Belle had never kept it a secret that she thought Maggie was making a mistake when it came to Flint. Too much baggage, she always said of the sheriff. His "baggage" came in the shape of his spoiled, probably psychopathic, petite, green-eyed, blonde ex.

"I have my own skeletons." Maggie had laughed, although she'd never shared her past—even with Belle—before moving to Gilt Edge, Montana, and opening her beauty shop, Just Hair. She feared it was her own baggage that scared her the most.

"If you're holding anything back," Belle had said, eyeing her closely, "you need to let it out. Men hate surprises after they tie the knot."

"Guess I don't have to worry about that because Flint hasn't said anything about marriage." But she knew Belle was right. She'd even come close to telling him several times about her past. Something had always stopped her. The truth was, she feared if he found out her reasons for coming to Gilt Edge he wouldn't want her anymore.

"The dream isn't about Flint," she'd argued that day with Belle, but she couldn't shake the feeling that it was a warning.

"Well, from what I know about dreams," Belle had said, "if in the dream you survive the drowning, it means that a waking relationship will ultimately survive the turmoil. At least, that is one interpretation. But I'd say the nightmare definitely indicates that you are going into unknown waters and something is making you leery of where you're headed." She'd cocked an eyebrow at her. "If you have the dream again, I'd suggest that you ask yourself what it is you're so afraid of."

"I'm sure it's just about his ex, Celeste," she'd lied. Or was she afraid that she wasn't good enough for Flint—just as his ex had warned her. Just as she feared in her heart.

THE WIND LAY over the tall dried grass and kicked up dust as Sheriff Flint Cahill stood on the hillside. He shoved his Stetson down on his head of thick dark hair, squinting in the distance at the clouds to the west. Sure as the devil, it was going to snow before the day was out.

In the distance, he could see a large star made out of red and green lights on the side of a barn, a reminder that Christmas was coming. Flint thought he might even get a tree this year, go up in the mountains and cut it himself. He hadn't had a tree at Christmas in years. Not since…

At the sound of a pickup horn, he turned, shielding his eyes from the low winter sun. He could smell snow in the air, feel it deep in his bones. This storm was going to dump a good foot on them, according to the latest news. They were going to have a white Christmas.

Most years he wasn't ready for the holiday season any more than he was ready for a snow that wouldn't melt until spring. But this year was different. He felt energized. This was the year his life would change. He thought of the small velvet box in his jacket pocket. He'd been carrying it around for months. Just the thought of it made him smile to himself. He was in love and he was finally going to do something about it.

The pickup rumbled to a stop a few yards from him. He took a deep breath of the mountain air and, telling himself he was ready for whatever Mother Nature wanted to throw at him, he headed for the truck.

"Are you all right?" his sister asked as he slid into the passenger seat. In the cab out of the wind, it was nice and warm. He rubbed his bare hands together, wishing he hadn't forgotten his gloves earlier. But when he'd headed out, he'd had too much on his mind. He still did.

Lillie looked out at the dull brown of the landscape and the chain-link fence that surrounded the missile silo. "What were you doing out here?"

He chuckled. "Looking for aliens. What else?" This was the spot that their father swore aliens hadn't just landed on one night back in 1967. Nope, according to Ely Cahill, the aliens had abducted him, taken him aboard their spaceship and done experiments on him. Not that anyone believed it in the county. Everyone just assumed that Ely had a screw loose. Or two.

It didn't help that their father spent most of the year up in the mountains as a recluse trapping and panning for gold.

"Aliens. Funny," Lillie said, making a face at him.

He smiled over at her. "Actually, I was on an all-night stakeout. The cattle rustlers didn't show up." He shrugged.

She glanced around. "Where's your patrol SUV?"

"Axle deep in a muddy creek back toward Grass Range. I'll have to get it pulled out. After I called you, I started walking and I ended up here. Wish I'd grabbed my gloves, though."

"You're scaring me," she said, studying him openly. "You're starting to act like Dad."

He laughed at that, wondering how far from the truth it was. "At least I didn't see any aliens near the missile silo."

She groaned. Being the butt of jokes in the county because of their father got old for all of them.

Flint glanced at the fenced-in area. There was nothing visible behind the chain link but tumbleweeds. He turned back to her. "I didn't pull you away from anything important, I hope? Since you were close by, I thought you wouldn't mind giving me a ride. I've had enough walking for one day. Or thinking, for that matter."

She shook her head. "What's going on, Flint?"

He looked out at the country that ran to the mountains. Cahill Ranch. His grandfather had started it, his father had worked it and now two of his brothers ran the cattle part of it to keep the place going while he and his sister, Lillie, and brother Darby had taken other paths. Not to mention their oldest brother, Tucker, who'd struck out at seventeen and hadn't been seen or heard from since.

Flint had been scared after his marriage and divorce. But Maggie was nothing like Celeste, who was small, blonde, green-eyed and crazy. Maggie was tall with big brown eyes and long auburn hair. His heart beat faster at the thought of her smile, at her laugh.

"I'm going to ask Maggie to marry me," Flint said and nodded as if reassuring himself.

When Lillie didn't reply, he glanced over at her. It wasn't like her not to have something to say. "Well?"

"What has taken you so long?"

He sighed. "Well, you know after Celeste…"

"Say no more," his sister said, raising a hand to stop him. "Anyone would be gun-shy after being married to her."

"I'm hoping she won't be a problem."

Lillie laughed. "Short of killing your ex-wife, she is always going to be a problem. You just have to decide if you're going to let her run your life. Or if you're going to live it—in spite of her."

So easy for her to say. He smiled, though. "You're right. Anyway, Maggie and I have been dating for a while now and there haven't been any…incidents in months."

Lillie shook her head. "You know Celeste was the one who vandalized Maggie's beauty shop—just as you know she started that fire at Maggie's house."

"Too bad there wasn't any proof so I could have arrested her. But since there wasn't and no one was hurt and it was months ago…"

"I'd love to see Celeste behind bars, though I think prison is too good for her. I can understand why you would be worried about what she will do next. She's psychopathic."

He feared that that maybe was close to the case. "Do you want to see the ring?" He knew she did, so he fished it out of his pocket. He'd been carrying it around for quite a while now. Getting up his courage? He knew what was holding him back. Celeste. He couldn't be sure how she would take it—or what she might do. His ex-wife seemed determined that he and Maggie shouldn't be together, even though she was apparently happily married to local wealthy businessman Wayne Duma.

Handing his sister the small black velvet box, he waited as she slowly opened it.

A small gasp escaped her lips. "It's beautiful. *Really* beautiful." She shot him a look. "I thought sheriffs didn't make much money?"

"I've been saving for a long while now. Unlike my sister, I live pretty simply."

She laughed. "Simply? Prisoners have more in their cells than you do. You aren't thinking of living in that small house of yours after you're married, are you?"

"For a while. It's not that bad. Not all of us have huge new houses like you and Trask."

"We need the room for all the kids we're going to have," she said. "But it is wonderful, isn't it? Trask is determined that I have everything I ever wanted." Her gaze softened as the newlywed thought of her husband.

"I keep thinking of your wedding." There'd been a double wedding, with both Lillie and her twin, Darby, getting married to the loves of their lives only months ago. "It's great to see you and Trask so happy. And Darby and Mariah… I don't think Darby is ever going to come off that cloud he's on."

Lillie smiled. "I'm so happy for him. And I'm happy for you. You know I really like Maggie. So do it. Don't worry about Celeste. Once you're married, there's nothing she can do."

He told himself she was right, and yet in the back of his mind, he feared that his ex-wife would do something to ruin it—just as she had done to some of his dates with Maggie.

"I don't understand Celeste," Lillie was saying as she shifted into Drive and started toward the small Western town of Gilt Edge. "She's the one who dumped you for Wayne Duma. So what is her problem?"

"I'm worried that she is having second thoughts about her marriage to Duma. Or maybe she's bored and has nothing better to do than concern herself with my life. Maybe she just doesn't want me to be happy."

"Or she is just plain malicious," Lillie said. "If she isn't happy, she doesn't want you to be, either."

A shaft of sunlight came through the cab window, warming him against the chill that came with even talking about Celeste. He leaned back, content as Lillie drove.

He was going to ask Maggie to marry him. He was

going to do it this weekend. He'd already made a dinner reservation at the local steak house. He had the ring in his pocket. Now it was just a matter of popping the question and hoping she said yes. If she did… Well, then, this was going to be the best Christmas ever, he thought and smiled.

* * * * *

COWBOY'S LEGACY, available wherever Mills and Boon Books and ebooks are sold.

www.millsandboon.co.uk

WE'RE HAVING A MAKEOVER...

We'll still be bringing you the very best in romance from authors you love…all with a fabulous new look!

Look out for our stylish new logo, too

MILLS & BOON

COMING JANUARY 2018

MILLS & BOON®

INTRIGUE
Romantic Suspense

A SEDUCTIVE COMBINATION OF DANGER AND DESIRE

A sneak peek at next month's titles...

In stores from 14th December 2017:

- **Gunfire on the Ranch** – Delores Fossen *and*
  Safe at Hawk's Landing – Rita Herron
- **Ranger Protector** – Angi Morgan *and*
  Whispering Springs – Amanda Stevens
- **Soldier's Promise** – Cindi Myers *and*
  Forgotten Pieces – Tyler Anne Snell

Romantic Suspense

- **Colton Baby Rescue** – Marie Ferrarella
- **In the Bodyguard's Arms** – Lisa Childs

Just can't wait?
Buy our books online before they hit the shops!
www.millsandboon.co.uk

Also available as eBooks.